The Château by the River

Chloé Duval

Translated from the French by
Domitille Vimal du Monteil

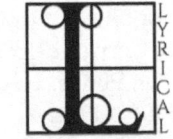

LYRICAL PRESS
Kensington Publishing Corp.
www.kensingtonbooks.com

LYRICAL PRESS BOOKS are published by

Kensington Publishing Corp.
119 West 40th Street
New York, NY 10018

A sa Rencontre by Chloe Duval © Bragelonne 2017
Translated from French by Domitille Vimal du Monteil © Bragelonne 2018

All Kensington titles, imprints, and distributed lines are available at special quantity discounts for bulk purchases for sales promotion, premiums, fund-raising, educational, or institutional use.

Special book excerpts or customized printings can also be created to fit specific needs. For details, write or phone the office of the Kensington Sales Manager: Kensington Publishing Corp., 119 West 40th Street, New York, NY 10018. Attn. Sales Department. Phone: 1-800-221-2647.

Lyrical Press and Lyrical Press logo Reg. US Pat. & TM Off.

First Electronic Edition: December 2018
eISBN-13: 978-1-5161-0090-3
eISBN-10: 1-5161-0090-5

First Print Edition: December 2018
ISBN-13: 978-1-5161-0091-0
ISBN-10: 1-5161-0091-3

Printed in the United States of America

A faded photograph will lead one young woman to a ruined French castle where she will discover the truth of her own identity . . . and the enduring mystery of love.

Traveling to France on business, Alexandra Dawson has decided to seize the opportunity to explore a mysterious piece of her own heritage—a half-burnt picture of a woman who looks eerily like her, taken more than a hundred years ago in a local castle. In the charming rural village of Chandeniers, she discovers something else too—the gruff, ruggedly good-looking heir of the crumbled château.

Éric Lagnel is completely uninterested in Alex's queries, until he realizes that she may have stumbled on a way to save the building. Their unlikely partnership is a surprise. But as Alex slowly unravels the secrets of her great-great-grandmother's photograph—and the true history of the château—she begins to understand that no one is ever prepared for the ways love can heal old wounds and open the hardest hearts.

Books by Chloe Duval

STOLEN TIME
THE CHÂTEAU BY THE RIVER

To my grandmother, who loved beautiful stories
And to my mother, who is just the same

Acknowledgments

Some stories are so easy to write they just flow from mind to screen. Some are harder, more demanding, a storm that ravages everything on its way and leaves you wrung out and slightly dazed, wondering whether you will ever be able to resume a normal life. *The Château by the River* is part of the latter category. And I would never have made it out alive—physically and emotionally—without the amazing help and support of the people around me. They are the ones I want to thank.

My Prince Charming—without his help, I wouldn't have been able to leave aside the everyday chores of life in order to immerse myself in the writing of this novel. His sharp eye was invaluable in tracking down the typos that managed to slip into the manuscript despite my best efforts.

Carine, Céline, Marine, Caroline and Stéphanie—the first recipients of my despair-filled messages. They never stopped telling me I could do it, that I would finish it and that running away to a desert island to hope the world would forget about me was not a viable strategy.

Suzanne and Jo Ann—their unwavering support and their daily reminders to stay cool kept me sane.

Pousson and Poilet—the girls' nights out to remind me there was a world out there, outside my castle, were salutary.

My French editor, Anne-Laure. She trusted me, gave me extension after extension after extension on my deadline, and without her, this novel would not be *anything* like it is today.

Last but not least—Tara, my wonderful American editor, who trusted me with this book and gave me the opportunity to write it as I had in mind.

As always, a huge thank-you to you, dear readers, for your kind words and for trusting me enough to pour some of your hard-earned money into this book. Without you, this book would never have made it so far, and neither would I.

Author's Note

Dear Reader,

First of all, I'd like to thank you all, from the bottom of my heart, for picking up this novel. I put all my heart and all my soul into it and I hope you'll love my characters as much as I do. I've lived with them for so long that to this day yet, almost a year after writing the words "The End," I still have trouble remembering that they are not living people who I can visit anytime I want to. I hope they will feel as real to you as they do to me.

But before you dive into their story, please let me tell you about the real fairy tale behind *The Château by the River*.

A few years ago, as I was surfing idly on the internet, I found an article from a French online newspaper, telling the story of a very old and very beautiful castle in ruins, lost to the wilderness of nature after a huge fire destroyed it in the 1930s: le château de la Mothe-Chandeniers, situated in the small town of Les Trois-Moutiers, in the Loire valley. Because the fire had rendered it uninhabitable, the castle had quickly been abandoned by its owners. Without any maintenance, each year that passed after that fateful day, the castle deteriorated a bit more, until it became a real danger to the life of anyone who approached it. For the last few years, the current owner had tried everything he could think of to save the castle from total destruction, but to no avail. When the article was written, tired of fighting without any results, he had decided to have the castle dismantled.

When I read the article, my heart broke, and for a few days, I could think of little else than this castle. I wanted to do something, anything, because the castle lover in me couldn't bear the thought of such a magnificent building, so old, which had lived through most the events that forged France, being destroyed. But I didn't have the first idea of how to be useful. So I did the only thing I could think of: I wrote a book about it. For the necessities of my story, as I was a romance novelist and not a historian, I changed the name of the castle, and a few details of its history, so that I could do what I wanted with it. That's how Gabrielle and Thomas, and Alex and Éric were born.

It took me around a year and a half to write *The Château by the River*. And by the time I was finished and it was published in France, the real castle had made the headlines: after a very successful crowdfunding operation, the castle had been bought by a few thousand contributors, from all around the world, with the intent of stopping its destruction.

The doomed castle, "my" doomed castle, had been saved.

As you can imagine, dear reader, I was really, really happy to see that unexpected turn of events! The next few years will tell how this fairy tale will unfold. But for now, let's dive together into Alexandra's and Gabrielle's story, and the castle that linked them through time.

Happy reading!

Chloé Duval

Prologue
Thomas

La Rochelle

February 1900

Thomas leaned on the rail of the *Étoile du Nord*[1] and stared at the horizon, waiting.

He waited for the bell signaling the ship's departure, waited for the coast to fade and disappear beyond the waves, waited for the pain to subside and for the gaping hole in his chest to close over.

Time heals all wounds, they said. He would forget.

But he knew all too well it was a lie. He would never forget her.

In the distance, the first glimpses of daylight were beginning to chase the dark away. The deck was bustling, awash with a diffuse unrest from which an occasional order or question could be heard. The seagulls' hungry cries rang out overhead as they fought over a bread crust or an old piece of vegetable, viciously pecking at each other.

In spite of the freezing cold, the docks were crowded with fishmongers, sailors, and traders come to oversee the delivery of their various goods. A few latecomers ran up, dragging heavy luggage behind them. And at the very end of the dock, swaddled in several layers of clothes to keep out the cold and biting wind, the passengers' loved ones waved as they exchanged a last goodbye, a final smile, a lingering gaze with those they would not see again for a very long time—if they ever did.

---

1   Northern Star.

Thomas stepped back, retreating to the bow of the ship, away from the commotion and tearstained smiles. *How ironic life could be,* he thought bitterly. Six months ago, he had nothing to look forward to other than a dull life and endless days to fill as best he could—and he was content. What one does not have, one cannot lose.

He had found out in the most brutal manner that he was entirely wrong. There is always something that can be lost.

Or someone.

Fleeting images crossed his mind, and he closed his eyes, jaw clenching painfully as his heart broke again.

The sailors on the dock were casting off, and the railing began to hum softly under his fingertips; the tugboats stood by, ready to tow the ship out to sea so it could begin its long journey toward America, where he could start over again and leave his past behind.

Everything was ready and had been for a long time. He had crossed the sea several times, met with investors, partners, chosen warehouses and workshops.

He'd had it all planned out.

And everything had changed.

She'd waltzed into his life one day with her sweet smile and dreamy gaze and upended all of his carefully prepared plans, illuminating every aspect of his life.

For a few wonderful weeks, he had felt himself change under her influence, becoming happier, lighter. Life—*his* life—had begun to hold meaning.

He'd found himself thinking of the future. Hoping. Dreaming.

But dreams were fickle, deceitful things. When they lasted too long, you started to believe in them. And when they fell apart, when the bubble burst and reality came rushing back in, the fall was a hard one. And the higher you climbed, the harder you fell.

He had hurtled down the whole damn mountain.

He'd found the strength to stand back up, somehow, keep his head high and move forward even though he was only an empty shell, a shadow of his former self. A shadow of the man he'd been with her.

But a shadow could be a positive thing. It was a close friend, almost comforting. He'd been lost in the shadow once before. He was familiar with it. He almost relished the return.

He knew it would in time swallow the pain that ran through every inch of his being. He would grow numb again, distant.

He wouldn't fall for the same trick again. Angels couldn't love monsters.

The ship slowly drew away from the dock. At last, Thomas was leaving. For good.

There would be no going back this time. Not ever. He was leaving the country that had brought him only pain and shattered illusions, never to return.

He kept his gaze on the horizon, refusing to acknowledge the sharp knife piercing through his heart, or the urge to jump ashore and run to her to beg on bended knee for her to explain. To love him.

It was too late anyway.

Chapter 1
Alexandra

Chandeniers-sur-Vienne

Present day

"In fifty meters, turn left. You have arrived at your destination."

The low, masculine voice purring with a delicious Scottish accent was coming from the GPS on my phone.

Don't judge me. We all have our guilty pleasures. I'd downloaded the app six months ago and ever since then, I sometimes—read: every day—turn on the GPS to drive home, just to hear its husky, sexy accent.

Even if all it did was tell me to merge and keep right.

Jamie's fault, Your Honor. Everything is James Alexander Malcolm MacKenzie Fraser's fault.

I looked around for the crossroads Fake-Jamie had just signaled and switched on my turn signal to swerve onto an adorable paved street. A few seconds later, I drew level with the aptly named *L'Auberge du bout de la rue*,[2] which was indeed at the end of the street. I had booked a room there for the next few days.

I smiled to myself as I got out of the rental and spun on the spot, taking in the scenery, the ambience, the sounds, the smells.

This was it. This was what France meant to me. Charmingly old-fashioned cities with cobbled streets and centuries-old stone buildings. In this place, everything breathed history. No matter where you went, where you looked, you could almost feel the presence of the people who had lived

---

2   The Inn at the End of the Street.

there a hundred, two hundred, a thousand years earlier. And the town of Chandeniers, at the very heart of the Loire valley and the surrounding vineyards, was the perfect embodiment of my idea of a historical French city, from the little stone bridge to the old water mill and the many book stands lining the banks of the Vienne River. After several weeks' hard work, I was more than ready to kick back and enjoy playing tourist.

I sighed blissfully and swung the car door shut. Like most of the houses on the street that ran parallel to the river, the inn was built with white stone and had blue shutters. Its name gleamed in wrought iron letters over the door.

"If I could afford it, I would buy a vacation home here in a heartbeat!" I muttered to myself as I climbed the steps. "This place is amazing!"

I reached for the heavy doorknocker to signal my arrival when the door abruptly swung open and I came face-to-face—or rather, face to shoulder—with what seemed to be a Tom Hiddleston doppelganger with a little boy clinging to his hand.

"See you tomorrow?" He dedicated a smile—one I could objectively say was devastating—to someone inside the house.

"See you tomorrow!" a female voice confirmed.

He turned around and almost ran straight into me.

"Sorry."

"Don't worry about it."

He stepped to his right just as I stepped left. We repeated the maneuver for a few seconds before we came to a stop, laughing.

Yup, that smile definitely qualifies as devastating.

"Shall I go right and you left?" he suggested.

"My left or yours?"

"Mine, or else we could be here all night. While it *is* the intended purpose for an inn, it kind of defeats the point if you stay on the threshold."

I held back another laugh and stepped right, he shifted the other way and at last we could resume the courses of our normal lives.

"Good day to you."

"You too."

"Come on, Quentin, let's go."

"Yes, Papa."

I watched them walk away then turned back to the door, which was still hanging open. A woman in her thirties stood there. There was a distinctive pout on her impish, bright-eyed face as she tracked the man for a few moments, before she shook her head slightly and turned to me.

"Hi, what can I do for you?"

"Hi. I'm Alexandra Dawson; I phoned this morning to confirm my booking."

"Ah! I was waiting for you! Please come in." She moved back to let me through. "I'm Marine Clément, the owner. Welcome to the *Auberge du bout de la rue!*"

"Thank you, Ms. Clément."

"Please! Call me Marine. Ms. Clément is my mother!" She laughed. "I don't think I'm quite old enough to go by Ms.!"

"I will, if you call me Alexandra," I replied brightly. "I couldn't agree more, to be honest." I leaned closer to add in a mock whisper: "Ever since I got here, everyone's been calling me Ms. Dawson; it feels like I aged twenty years in a month. I feel like I should check for wrinkles every morning!"

"Don't worry, there isn't one in sight!"

"Phew! What a relief!"

We moved inside as we joked together and she proceeded to charm me utterly. The inside was just as lovely as the outside. The furniture was rustic but modern, in shades of faded pink, beige and plain wood. Potted plants and flowers in every nook and cranny completed the inn's old-fashioned charm. It was cozy, warm, comfortable. In a word, perfect.

"Wow. I love what you've done with the place," I told her.

"Thank you! I'm glad you like it. You're from the US, right?"

"Is it that obvious?" I joked. "And here I thought my accent was perfect."

"Oh, it's fairly good. But you can't hide it completely. Where are you from?"

"California, the Napa Valley more precisely. Ever heard of it?"

"Wine country, right?"

"Exactly!"

"Well, you must feel right at home here. Wine is kind of our local product."

"I'm one hundred percent in my element. Actually, I even work for a wine company."

"So you're here on business?"

"Yes and no. I was on a business trip with my supervisor, but she went back yesterday and I stayed to take a vacation."

"You're going to think I'm biased, but you couldn't have chosen a better place. We're at the heart of the Loire valley, there are castles all around, a wine road to die for, and just between the two of us, Chandeniers is the most beautiful city in the world."

"Nice speech."

"One hundred percent unbiased too." Marine laughed and added, "Shall I show you to your room?"

"Lead the way."

I followed her up the stairs and down a narrow corridor to a smallish, absolutely adorable room tastefully decorated in shades of blue and off-white. The bed—a four-poster—had thin, transparent blue curtains, the same tone as the walls and the window curtains, hanging from the canopy, and an antique bedside table with a pretty reading lamp. A small desk and chest of drawers, obviously antiques as well, sat in a corner. Perched on the edge of the windowsill, a lavender bouquet gave off a sweet and enticing aroma. The pictures on the walls represented the town of Chandeniers, adding the final, perfect touch to the room.

"The bathroom is through there," Marine indicated as I entered. "There are some extra blankets and towels in the cupboard. If you need anything just let me know. I hope you'll be comfortable."

"I'm sure I will be." I couldn't contain my enthusiasm. "This is amazing! Everything in this house is amazing."

"Thank you. I got everything from bargain hunting and yard sales and renovated all the furniture in the inn myself."

"Everything? That must have taken ages!"

"It did, but I enjoy it so I don't mind. I'm working my way slowly through the furniture, replacing what came with the house with my own projects. It's my hobby, but I don't have as much time to devote to it in the summer."

"Well, kudos to you. You not only have exquisite taste, you also have a knack for making all this old stuff look new again."

"Thank you! I love anything that has to do with the past."

"Oh? Are you something of a historian?"

"Not really, but I do know quite a bit of history, especially if it's local. I've done some research on the town's past."

Interesting. Duly noted.

"Oh, and before I forget, here's the Wi-Fi code for the inn, and your key." She handed me a small card and a keyring.

"Thank you. This is perfect."

"Do you need anything else?"

"I don't think so."

"I'll let you settle in. Oh, and I have some hibiscus mint juice in the fridge. Would you like a glass?"

"How nice. Yes. Thanks a lot!"

"Do you want me to bring it up here, or should I serve it in the garden out back? It's lovely under the trees."

"Garden, no hesitation."

"Then come and join me when you're ready."

"I'll be right down."

When Marine had left, I fished my phone out of my handbag and snapped a few pictures of the room that I immediately forwarded to my best friend, Bea. The poor thing was no doubt even now working in her air-conditioned bank office in Santa Rosa.

Her reply came almost immediately.

> *I hate you.*

I laughed and sent back:

> *Love you too.*

> > *Way nicer than the places you've been staying in*
> > *for work so far.*

> *Totes. I'm in love.*

> > *When are you starting your investigation?*

> *Soon as I'm settled in and have finished my*
> *hibiscus juice.*

> > *Luxury at its finest!*

> *Embracing the holiday feeling!*

> > *I want updates. Every minute.*

> *Done.*

> > *My supervisor's here. Meeting in five. See you*
> > *later, Ms. Family Girl.*

Later, alligator. Good luck with the meeting. Call
you as soon as I've done recon.

I then fired off another message to my fiancé to tell him more or less the same thing, but with a lot more "<3." I finished with:

Call you soon? I know you're busy but I miss you!
<3 Luv ya.

I put the phone away. Given the time, I was ready to bet Spencer was in a meeting and wouldn't be able to reply for a while. But a beeping sound almost immediately proved me wrong. Against all expectations, my lawyer boyfriend had written back.

Hello you!! Got to go to a meeting but promise,
I'll try to call as soon as I'm out. Miss you too.
<3 Be careful and keep me posted. Luv ya more.

I read it several times, happy at the thought we'd be able to speak at last. Between the time difference—a horrible thing, I cursed whoever had invented it—my work and his, over the last few weeks our communication had come down to brief texts sent between meetings, lunches and business interviews. I had reached the point where I'd called his answering machine a couple of times in the middle of the night or early in the morning just to hear the sound of his voice. I make no apologies. I missed my fiancé, and sometimes when life doesn't deliver, you have to resort to desperate measures. So I made do with his answering machine and waited for things to get better.

I'd been waiting for things to get better for quite some time now.

Spencer was about to become the youngest partner of the prestigious Wilson, Murdoch and Finch legal office. He'd been working for two years now on a huge case—something to do with corruption inside a pharmaceutical company that had cost several dozen people their lives—that required all of his attention and time. So it wasn't unusual for me to spend my evenings alone while he locked himself in the office or met with colleagues.

I wasn't happy with our situation. To pretend otherwise would be a lie. Solitary evenings were long and weekends even longer. But it was the price to pay to be with him, and I had known it when I had signed up for a relationship with him. Spencer was a top-notch lawyer, and he never backed down on anything. I'd never seen him sacrifice his work for his private life. The stakes were too high, and they were worth neglecting our time together for a while. When the trial was over, I'd have him all to myself again, and I'd be able to show him just how proud I was of him.

In the meantime, I had to be patient.

I clicked on the answer bar and typed a new message, my fingers flying over the digital keyboard.

> *Be careful too. And don't forget to eat. Wouldn't want you to lose those perfect muscles of yours.*

> *I always knew you only liked me for my looks.*

> *Of course! Why else would I marry you? ^^ Go and save the world. It needs you. Xoxo*

I smiled as I closed the messaging app and put my phone down. I sat on the bed and grabbed my handbag—or rather, the suitcase, masquerading as a handbag—and extracted the folder containing the reason for my presence here. An old, yellowing photograph, the edges slightly scorched, whose every detail I knew by heart.

Gabrielle Villeneuve.

My paternal great-great-great-grandmother.

Chapter 2
Gabrielle

Angers

November 1899

It is a truth universally acknowledged that what can go wrong in life... *will* go wrong. Thus, it is always whenever one has forgotten their umbrella at home that it starts raining—both quite suddenly and unexpectedly hard for November.

This is not my lucky day, Gabrielle thought glumly. *Any more trouble and this would read like a comedy of errors.*

She looked up from beneath the entrance porch where she'd taken shelter and sighed.

The entire day had been a nightmare.

She'd woken tired—hardly surprising since she had been reading well into the early hours of the morning—and she'd needed to summon her entire force of will to part with the cozy comfort of her goose-feather quilt and pillow. It had taken a truly herculean effort to rise. The ambient humidity had further made it impossible to brush and style her hair. The hairpins she usually generously littered her thick, unruly waves of hair with had chosen this as the perfect time to hide—of course they had.

The rebellion had continued with her hot chocolate deciding that it belonged on her dress rather than in her cup. Gabrielle had barely avoided a serious burn and had to return upstairs to change—and fix her hair again, as the painstakingly tied knot had come loose when she'd peeled her stained garments off. With so many mishaps, it was a miracle she'd managed to open the bookstore on time. By the time she'd flipped the sign on the door, Gabrielle had been expecting the worst to be yet to come.

But contrary to her expectations, the rest of the morning had been relatively calm—apart from a definite lack of cooperation from the ladder she had used to retrieve a book on botanicals. Only one thing had kept her from falling flat on her face with an utter lack of anything resembling grace or balance—the presence of Étienne, the store employee.

That had almost been the last straw. Gabrielle had given serious thought to going back to bed, where she would not risk a major accident every few minutes. But the prospect of seeing Sophie for lunch had proven too alluring. The brief moments she could share with her best friend were all too rare and precious for her to give up on them for so small an inconvenience. As the clock struck twelve, she'd fled the bookstore and her own bad luck as though the devil himself were on her heels.

Gabrielle noticed Sophie's excitement from the moment she sat across from her, out of breath but rather relieved to have made it in one piece without any further misadventures.

"Gabrielle, I have a marvelous idea!" Sophie exclaimed as soon as her friend sat down, even as she absentmindedly pushed the books she'd borrowed last week across the table.

"It must be truly marvelous. You look ready to skip! What is it?"

"Would you like…"—she paused for dramatic effect, then plunged ahead—"to travel with me to Paris next May to visit the great *Exposition Universelle*?"

"Just the two of us? You and me?"

"Yes! Just the two of us, like we always dreamed."

"Yes! A thousand times yes!"

For an hour, they discussed their plans, eyes bright with excitement, picturing themselves dressed in their very best dresses and hats, arm in arm, strolling down the streets of the City of Lights, that magical capital of culture, romance and adventure. Men would stop and stare as Sophie walked by—they always did. They would laugh, happy and carefree, with nothing on their minds except for the fun they would have and the opportunity to discover everything Paris had to offer.

They suggested dates, worked out how much money they'd need to save to be able to afford such an extravagant trip, planned the shoes and clothes they would need to pack. But time flew by and they promised to speak of it again as they parted ways, quietly cheerful, the morning's misadventures forgotten.

Gabrielle might have managed to forget her bad luck, but it certainly had not forgotten about her. She'd barely gone three steps before the first drops of rain hit. Less than thirty seconds later, the sprinkles had turned into a downpour, soaking the precious books she carried—not to mention her clothes—and forcing her to shelter under the nearest porch roof.

Dear Lord. She sighed. She most definitely was cursed today.

Across the street, her reflection in the grocer's shopwindow seemed to mock her. Grimacing, Gabrielle gave herself a quick once-over. With no hat to hold them back—she had left in a hurry—unruly blond locks had already begun to unravel from the bun at the back of her neck. Any longer in the rain and she'd look like a wet dog. She considered her options. Even if she ran as fast as she could with a drenched skirt that clung to her legs and a pile of books under her arm, it would take at least two or three minutes to return to the bookstore. She had two choices, then: wait here for the rain to abate, which did not seem likely in the foreseeable future, or accept that she would look like a pathetic mutt left out in the storm when she reentered the store.

Sighing, she hefted the books higher under her left arm, seized her skirt in her right hand and ran out in the rain, hoping against hope she wouldn't twist her ankle on the cobblestones.

That would really be the last straw.

A few minutes later, drenched and shivering and her books utterly soaked despite her best efforts, she pushed open the door to *Les livres d'Héloïse,*[3] sending the bell clanging merrily. She paused on the threshold and leaned on the doorframe, out of breath, gazing over what had always been her home. Immense oak shelves lined the soft beige walls she had painted with her father a few years ago, overflowing with books. Pictures painted by a local artist, all featuring books and readers, dotted the room with splotches of color, as did the vases of fresh flowers she made a point to replace regularly. Today's were vivid crimson roses she had bought at the market the day before, giving off a sweet scent that filled the store. All these elements painted a picture of comfort, of coziness and warmth, a cocoon to retreat to when the world proved too difficult to deal with. Gabrielle took pride in what her father and she had created here. And she hoped that so did her mother, from where she now dwelt.

A wave of nostalgia washed over her.

Her father had built the bookstore for her mother. Héloïse Villeneuve, née Héloïse Desmarais, a booklover if ever there was one, had dreamed all her life of living among books. "Gabrielle," she used to say, "books

---

3   Héloïse's Books.

are an inexhaustible treasure trove. Every book is a door to a new world, one where anything is possible, where anyone can dream without limits and be totally, utterly free. A book is the greatest gift one can give to another." Héloïse loved books, Maurice loved Héloïse, the decision had been easy—Gabrielle's father had opened a bookstore and named it after his wife: *Les livres d'Héloïse.*

Gabrielle had been seven when her mother had died from the consequences of a miscarriage. After her death, nothing had been the same; nothing had the same flavor or the same touch of magic. Her mother had the ability to transform their ordinary lives into a fairy tale with nothing but a smile, and Gabrielle had needed many months before she could overcome her grief and begin to enjoy life again.

Her father, though, had never quite recovered. In order to make up for Héloïse's absence, he'd smothered his daughter in love and affection, becoming father and mother, brother and sister, teacher and mentor. He'd been the one to reinstate the tradition of bedtime stories, which they had never since stopped, though these days Gabrielle was the one to read to her father.

The bookstore was the only thing they had left of Héloïse, and whatever energy Maurice did not pour into raising his daughter, he devoted to it. As the years went by and Gabrielle grew older, her role and duties at the bookstore had steadily become more important. Until one day she was in charge of the day-to-day running of the store while Maurice, who, unlike his wife and daughter, had always been more interested in books as objects rather than their contents, immersed himself in a new task: locating and buying specific books for his customers. He quickly gained a reputation as a learned bibliophile, able to find any book wherever they might be and whatever the effort involved.

Gabrielle felt a smile stretch her lips.

Maman would be proud of us, truly.

Movement from the back of the shop caught her eye. Étienne, the assistant her father had hired two years ago, was waiting on Mr. Demers, one of their oldest patrons. He looked up when the bell jingled and his gaze slid—very, *very* slowly—over Gabrielle. All of a sudden uncomfortably aware of the way her soaked dress clung to her body, she motioned for him to keep quiet, unwilling to let their customer see her in such a state. Étienne nodded slightly to indicate his understanding and turned back to Mr. Demers, though not without one last glance toward her. From where she stood, Gabrielle could not decipher his expression, but she didn't need to. For some time now, she had noticed the way he looked at her.

She did her best to ignore the blazing glances he directed her way, hoping the sudden crush he seemed to have developed would fade if she did not encourage it. So far, she hadn't had much luck and Étienne did not seem to catch her drift.

Étienne is a nice boy, she thought as she slipped through the shelves, *but he doesn't make my heart skip.*

No one had made her heart skip yet.

She had almost reached her destination—the narrow staircase at the back of the shop, leading to the apartment she shared with her father over the store—when the door flew open and Gabrielle hit…a wall.

I forgot there was a wall here, she thought as she swayed and one of her books toppled to the ground.

A noise came from the wall, and two powerful hands reached out to grab her and hold her steady.

And now the walls move and talk. Curiouser and curiouser.

Had she fallen down the rabbit hole? She was suddenly aware that said wall wore a thick black wool coat, still damp, and exuded far too much warmth for an inanimate object. Still breathless, Gabrielle let her eyes wander up the coat's arm to broad shoulders, absently noting the tie partially hidden behind a black scarf, and from there to a man's face half shadowed by the brim of a hat, where they fell prey to the steel-gray gaze.

The world fell away in an instant. The bookstore, Étienne and Mr. Demers, the great *Exposition Universelle*, her disheveled appearance, the drenched books she had to dry as soon as possible, the water streaming from her clothes and hair and puddling at her feet… Everything disappeared, leaving only the gray gaze plunging deep into her own, undecipherable, unfathomable, bewitching.

And just like that, Gabrielle's heart skipped a beat.

The moment lasted only a few seconds, a few brief heartbeats during which she felt adrift in a timeless bubble, soaring away from reality, toward a world she never wanted to leave. Then her father exited his study, papers in his hand and glasses on the end of his nose, and the bubble burst, disappearing as fast as it had appeared. With great regret, Gabrielle's feet returned to earth. It had been so nice, up there in the clouds.…

"There you are, Gabrielle!" Maurice exclaimed as he spotted her. "I was looking for you!"

His voice made the gray-eyed man turn away. Blinking as though to gather his thoughts, he stepped back, resolutely looking somewhere toward the door to the bookstore.

"Are you all right?" Maurice asked, brows furrowed. "You're soaked to the skin!"

"Don't worry, Papa," she replied, gathering from somewhere a calm she did not feel. "I just got caught in the rain as I made my way back from lunch with Sophie. I was about to go up and change when I bumped into this gentleman. My apologies." She smiled. "I hope I didn't hurt you."

"You didn't."

His voice was deep and gravelly, and he suddenly looked embarrassed.

Now she was at a more respectable distance from the stranger, Gabrielle was able to take in the rest of his appearance. He was impressively tall and well built, with jet-black hair that curled as wildly as hers did, a square, determined jaw covered in several days' stubble.... And a scar running over his left eyebrow down to his ear. Pale and jagged, it seemed old—and it looked as if he had only barely kept his eye. Despite the scar—or maybe because of it?—he exuded an old-fashioned sort of presence, reminiscent of a knight ready to lay down his life for what he believed in, an animal charisma that radiated from him and awoke feelings and emotions Gabrielle had never experienced before.

"This is precisely why I was looking for you," her father continued, unaware of her turmoil. "Let me introduce our new patron, Mr. D'Arcy. Mr. D'Arcy, this is my daughter Gabrielle."

Gabrielle froze. Had she heard right? *Darcy?*

Chapter 3
Alexandra

Chandeniers-sur-Viennes

Present day

"Mrrrraow!"

I set the photo of Gabrielle aside and leaned down to reach for the adorable black fuzzy furball creeping into the room.

"Ooooh! Hello, you!" I cooed, depositing him gently onto my lap. "Aren't you the cutest thing ever?"

I stroked his ears. The kitten purred blissfully and nestled closer to me.

"Comfy, huh? But are you sure you're allowed in here?"

The cat raised its head and meowed some more at me.

Of course I'm allowed, his eyes seemed to say. *I'm a kitten, I'm allowed everywhere. Haven't you seen* Shrek?

"You're just trying to wheedle me into letting you stay."

And it was working. I loved cats, and had two of my own, a handsome pair that went by the names D'Artagnan and Milady. I'd left them in Bea's care—Spencer was way too busy to remember to feed them.

"You can't stay here, you know." I didn't stop petting him, though. "I'm parched and there's a delicious glass of fresh hibiscus juice waiting for me downstairs. And then I've got a suitcase to unpack and research to do. My ancestors aren't going to just find themselves, you know."

You aren't going to do any of that, the green orbs seemed to say. *You're going to stay here and play with me.*

Was it just me, or was this kitten trying to use the Force on me?

"No deal. You won't catch me that easily, Mr. Kitten!" I pretended to scold him. "I do have things to do, Your Highness!"

I got to my feet, cradling him in my left hand. With my free hand, I stored the photograph in my handbag. I let the door swing shut behind me as I went in search of my hostess and the promised drink.

I found her, as anticipated, sitting in the garden reading a book whose cover I immediately recognized—the latest volume of Diana Gabaldon's Outlander saga.

I'd read and reread each book in the series at least four times. It had been good fodder for many an evening of discussions and daydreams with Bea.

Not to mention the TV show. *Aaah, that show...* My soft little heart hadn't quite gotten over it yet, I had to admit.

I skipped the few steps down from the porch and joined her. Marine looked up as the gravel crunched under my feet, and she smiled.

"I found a stowaway in my room." I pointed to the kitten I was carrying. "I think he likes me!"

"Berlioz!" Marine exclaimed. She set her book aside and reached for him, lifting him out of my hands. "I'm sorry! He belongs to my daughter, Océane. She's with her father right now, so I'm the one left with this little kitty to take care of. He's not allowed in that part of the house, but you know cats. There's no stopping them when they've decided on something."

"I do know, but don't worry. I don't mind, I love cats."

"I'll make sure he doesn't wander into your room."

"Really, don't bother. I'm glad to have the company."

"That's sweet of you, but I'm sure you'd prefer to have the bed to yourself at night. Please, sit down. Drink?" she offered, waving at the pitcher full of clear pink juice. Two glasses and a mouthwatering assortment of biscuits sat next to it.

"Yes, thank you."

"Do you want a biscuit? I bake them myself. Peanut butter and chocolate chip."

"You know how to speak to women!" I bit into one. "They're delicious."

Marine laughed and poured a glass of hibiscus juice. I sipped at it and sighed blissfully. It was so refreshing I barely stopped myself from draining all of it in one go.

I took another biscuit and pointed to her book with a sly glance.

"So. Jamie, huh?"

Marine grinned.

"Jamie indeed."

"They don't make them like that anymore, unfortunately."

"Such a shame. I'd give up a lot of modern amenities for a Jamie in my life."

"I don't know. I kind of like the small creature comforts. You know, running water, heating, medicine.... Keeping my teeth past the age of thirty..."

"Ah, what a cruel choice. Then what say we bring Jamie back to the future."

"The perfect solution."

"All right. Next step—find some standing stones and cross our fingers. Brittany is almost as good as Scotland, and it's not that far from here. I have a friend there, so we could visit her. I'm sure Flavie knows a good place to time-travel to catch ourselves a Jamie."

"Done!" I giggled. "Let me pack a toothbrush and I'll be right behind you!"

* * * *

Later, after a serious talk the like of which only two passionate booklovers can have, Marine asked why I'd come to this part of France.

"I hope you don't mind me asking, but American tourists are kind of rare here."

"Oh, it's no secret. I'm not here just to play tourist. I'm doing some genealogy research."

Her eyebrows rose.

"You have ancestors from around here?"

"It seems so." Marine leaned forward, apparently intrigued. "After my great-grandmother died, three years ago, I found a photograph among her belongings. It features a woman who looks a lot like me, and on the back you can read, just barely, 'Gabrielle Villeneuve, Chandeniers, 1899.'"

Marine grimaced slightly, apologetic.

"I'm sorry, that doesn't ring any bells."

"Don't apologize. I wasn't expecting you to recognize the name. According to my grandmother, she was her French great-grandmother. She remembers her mother saying that some of our ancestors came from France to the States a long time ago, but she didn't know anything more. So I did some digging. Finding Chandeniers was easy enough, but Gabrielle was harder to track. I wrote to your town council to find out if they had any information, but they said they couldn't help me unless I knew the year of her birth, which I didn't, of course. So I decided to start from the bottom and I traced out my family tree. And it was kind of fun."

"I can understand that," Marine agreed. "I also did some research on the history of the region and I learned some fairly outlandish stories about people who lived here a few centuries ago. Enough to write another *Game of Thrones!*" She laughed. "Did you find Gabrielle in the end?"

"I did."

I gave her a victorious smile as I related how I'd tracked down Héloïse, Gabrielle's daughter, after many research-filled evenings and weekends.

I'd been leafing through a seemingly endless register when a name had caught my attention. 'Héloïse D'Arcy, married name Forsythe, born New York, 1902, from Gabrielle Villeneuve, married name D'Arcy, and from Thomas D'Arcy,' and deceased slightly after WWII. That was how I had discovered, upon reading the whole record, that my ancestor was in fact from Angers, and her husband had been the one who was born and had lived in Chandeniers.

"A few days after I found Héloïse's birth certificate, the wine company I work for announced it wanted to open a branch in France and create a French vintage. Which meant they had to send a team to find a site. The chance was too good to pass up, so I moved heaven and earth to get appointed as interpreter, arguing that I'm fluent in French. And here I am!"

"Amazing. Have you been to Angers yet?"

"No, I intend to go this week. Since the picture mentions Chandeniers, curiosity led me here first. Actually, I think it was taken in the castle of Chandeniers."

"The castle? You mean your ancestors lived there?"

Surprise bled through Marine's voice.

"I think so. Or at least they worked there. Let me show you the picture; you can tell me what you think."

I ran upstairs to fetch the picture and was back before you could say "ballroom." "She's gorgeous!" Marine exclaimed, staring at the photograph. "You're right, you do look a lot like her."

"Right? And look here, on the other side."

She flipped the picture and deciphered the writing that I now knew by heart. I'd read and reread it hundreds of time over the last few months.

'…brielle Villeneuve
…rté-Chandeniers, 1899.'

"According to my research, this is the only place that matches. It has to be here."

"You must be right. How extraordinary! A truly amazing coincidence."

The phone rang, cutting Marine off.

"Sorry. I'll be right back." She rose from her seat.

"Don't worry about it."

I watched her disappear into the house. As I waited for her to return, I examined the picture again. I traced the jagged edges with the tip of my finger, followed the shape of Gabrielle's face, by now as familiar as my own. It was a black-and-white photograph, a three-quarter view of her sitting on a love seat, an open book in hand. She seemed to be in a library—or so the shelves loaded with books seemed to suggest. She looked beyond the photographer, apparently at someone. Her clear gaze was slightly dreamy, and a half smile stretched her lips. Her face was soft with love and happiness. I sighed, wondering for the millionth time what her story was. I sincerely hoped my time in Chandeniers and Angers would help me uncover something more about this ancestor I resembled so strongly.

Marine popped her head around the glass door, startling me out of my daydream.

"Sorry, this is going to take a while."

"Oh, no problem, I was about to go out anyway. We can talk later, when you have more time."

"Perfect. One last thing—the name of your ancestor is D'Arcy, right?" I nodded. "Hmm. I'll see what I can find out. I have to go, let me know when you get back!"

She vanished inside the inn.

I drained the last of my juice, nibbled on a biscuit and, picture in hand, made for my car to retrieve and unpack my suitcase.

Next stop, Ferté-Chandeniers castle.

Chapter 4
Gabrielle

Angers

November 1899

In the end, the mysterious stranger from the bookstore turned out not to be a dark, modern reincarnation of Jane Austen's iconic hero, despite what Gabrielle's vivid imagination would have her believe. Mr. D'Arcy—with an apostrophe—was a French businessman who had emigrated to England many years ago and now found himself—for reasons he declined to disclose—the executor of the late baron Victor Leroy de Saint-Armand. The baron, recently deceased, had owned a castle near Angers filled with various works of art and an immense library that held several thousand books, including a few parchments dating back to the Middle Ages and old maps of the world. The prestigious Society of Bibliophiles had recommended Gabrielle's father to Mr. D'Arcy for a comprehensive inventory in order to sell off the books as soon as possible. Maurice Villeneuve had immediately accepted, of course, and Mr. D'Arcy had soon left the shop with all the details arranged, leaving in his wake an equally bright-eyed father and daughter—though not *quite* for the same reasons.

A few days later, Maurice departed for the castle of Ferté-Chandeniers, suitcase in hand, promising to write frequently to keep his daughter updated on his progress.

* * * *

In her father's absence, Gabrielle took over the bookstore, assisted by Étienne. True to his word, Maurice sent regular letters detailing his long but fulfilling days, the rare and precious books he handled. He carried out the inventory and little else, but he still found time to talk with the other inhabitants of the castle during mealtimes. As letters piled up, their names kept recurring: Hélène, Guillaume, Agnès, Céleste. And Mr. D'Arcy, whom Maurice seemed to have grown very fond of. Every time his name appeared on the paper, Gabrielle's heart leapt in her chest. In spite of all her efforts, she could not chase her encounter with the mysterious, troubling man from her mind. On several occasions, she found herself thinking of him, dreaming of his eyes on hers, of the sound of his voice.

But Gabrielle did not *truly* expect to see him again, even though she secretly wished it a little more every day. Hence her surprise when two weeks after her father's departure, upon returning from delivering a book to one of their patrons, she found the object of her thoughts in her office. "Mr. D'Arcy!" she exclaimed, surprised.

Their eyes met, and she felt her cheeks heat up as her fantasies clashed with reality. Her heart started beating in earnest, so loudly that for a moment she feared he might hear it.

"I did not expect to see you here." She moved closer to him, hoping to conceal her turmoil. "What...?"

She cut herself short when she caught sight of his somber demeanor. All thoughts vanished as fear washed over her.

"What happened?" She didn't bother with manners. "Did something happen to my father?"

Distress lit up Mr. D'Arcy's face as he nodded.

"I'm afraid he's taken seriously ill."

He stepped toward her.

"I think he needs you."

* * * *

An hour later, they were on board a train for Chandeniers.

Snow fell heavily outside, draping the entire world in a cocoon that stretched across the horizon. Hands clenched tightly together in her lap, Gabrielle stared sightlessly out the window.

She had always loved snow. The slow twirl of snowflakes in the sky, as though all the stars had suddenly begun to dance. The caress of the snow on her cheeks, the cool taste of snowflakes melting on the tip of her tongue. And the calm, serene silence that seemed to cover the entire world after a storm, muffling sound and swallowing color. It was a sight she never tired of. But today, even the billowing gusts of snow that buffeted the train could not capture her attention. One thought only ran through her mind, making her throat tighten and her insides burn.

Please don't let it be serious.

She wished she could already be at her father's side and care for him as he so often had, from the time she was a child. She hoped it wasn't too late, that her father would have the strength to recover. She did not know what she would do if the worst were to happen.

A shiver ran through her, and a hand, strong yet gentle, draped a heavy wool coat over her shoulders. It was only then that she realized that she was positively chilled to the bone, her fingers stiff and numb in spite of the thick woolen gloves she was wearing.

"Thank you," she murmured, nestling deeper into the comforting heat his body had left behind.

"Everything will be fine," Mr. D'Arcy assured her softly, wrapping his hands around hers. "Everything will be fine."

Perhaps it was the feeling of his hands on hers, his thumb rubbing gentle circles into her skin as though it were the most natural thing in the world. Perhaps it was the quiet, reassuring rumble of his voice, a cocoon that soothed and blanketed her away from the world. Perhaps it was simply his presence at her side. Whatever the reason, the instant his hands touched hers, Gabrielle did not feel alone anymore.

She felt calmer.

As though a part of her anxiety had lifted.

She looked up, meeting her traveling companion's gaze. His silver-gray eyes held a mix of sincere concern and deep compassion, as if he knew from painful experience exactly what she felt. Through her haze of worry and fear, she could not help but feel moved by his actions. This man barely knew her, did not owe her anything, and yet he had come all this way for her. To fetch her and bring her to her father's side.

Many in a similar situation would probably have settled for a telegram, or, in a surge of generosity, dispatched a servant. After all, from what she had gathered from her father's letters, Mr. D'Arcy had much more pressing matters to attend to than to accompany her back and forth across the country and hold her hand.

"Thank you," she said, keeping her eyes on his.

He did not reply, but a brief gleam lit up his gaze and he nodded slightly.

For an instant, they stayed there, eyes fixed upon one another, her hands in his. Against all expectations, she almost wished time could pause.

* * * *

Somewhere along the road, the train was detained in a station, probably because of the snow. Mr. D'Arcy muttered something Gabrielle did not catch and left for a few moments. He returned shortly after and handed her a steaming cup.

"Drink this. You'll feel better," he told her.

Gabrielle did not ask where it came from. She wrapped her cold hands around it.

"Thank you."

She sipped the scalding drink appreciatively. She noted the tang of the alcohol he had doctored it with. The welcome bite seared down her throat.

"Do you feel better?" he inquired in a low voice, reclaiming his seat across from her.

"I do, thank you," she replied automatically, before busying herself by gulping down more of the drink.

Her words had been perfunctory rather than sincere, but she quickly realized that they were in fact true. The combination of warm drink and alcohol seemed to soothe her frayed nerves. Once she had finished the cup her concern remained, a persistent, sly beast, but her hands had ceased shaking.

"We're almost there," Mr. D'Arcy assured her as he retrieved the empty cup and handed it over to the train conductor passing by their compartment before sitting back down.

Gabrielle nodded weakly, summoning a tremulous smile.

"Your father is in good hands," he went on. "My housekeeper, Hélène, has taken over his care."

"Thank you."

Please don't let it be serious.

* * * *

An hour later they reached the town of Saumur. Wordlessly, Mr. D'Arcy hauled Gabrielle's suitcase from the luggage rack—he had not allowed her to carry it since they had left the bookstore—and led her to the front of the station, where a young man awaited their arrival, leaning on a small two-horse carriage. He was tall and broad shouldered, though not as imposing as Mr. D'Arcy, Gabrielle noted reflexively. In the evening half-light, his light brown hair appeared to be black. He seemed lost in thought until a third horse hidden behind the carriage neighed as they approached.

Catching sight of Mr. D'Arcy, he straightened.

"I brought Tornade too," he announced as soon as they had reached him. "I thought perhaps you and Mademoiselle Villeneuve would prefer to reach the castle faster."

"Thank you, Guillaume." Mr. D'Arcy turned to Gabrielle. "Would you rather take the carriage or ride back with me on Tornade? You'd be dry in the carriage, but on horseback we can cut across the fields and make better time. Do you know how to ride?"

She shook her head.

"But I'd still rather go with you," she insisted. "If you don't mind and it's not too heavy a load for the horse to carry."

"Of course not. Guillaume will take your suitcase to the castle with the carriage and you'll ride in front of me. It might be a little bumpy, but we ought to reach the castle within half an hour."

She accepted with a nod.

Guillaume took her suitcase from Mr. D'Arcy and handed him Tornade's reins. With his characteristic near silence, her companion helped her climb onto the horse, lifting her in a single motion, as though she weighed no more than a feather. He swung into the saddle behind her and looked back to Guillaume.

"Is there a blanket in the carriage?"

There was, and the young man drew a heavy wool throw from a small chest under the driver's seat. Mr. D'Arcy accepted it and wound it around Gabrielle's shoulders. He then directed a few words she did not catch at Guillaume and wrapped one arm around her waist, drawing her closer to him. He gripped the reins tight in his right hand and spurred the horse into a gallop.

She could not help it. Despite the urgency and worry that tormented her, the closeness of their bodies, greater even than when they had met two weeks previously, troubled her. She could feel his chest against her back through the layers of her clothing. His presence surrounded her entirely. His powerful arms framed her body over the blanket, holding her close, preventing her from falling with every jolt of the horse's gait, reawakening fleeting images of the dreams that had plagued her nights ever since their first meeting.

Chapter 5
Alexandra

Castle of Ferté-Chandeniers

Present day

The castle was only a few minutes' drive away. I parked on the side of the road and walked up to a metal gate opening onto a large winding gravel alley that disappeared behind a cluster of trees. I looked for a way to announce my presence but found none. No intercom or anything like one.

"Mr. Lagnel?" I called. My preliminary research at home had helped me uncover the owner's name.

Unsurprisingly, there was no reply.

I hesitated for a few seconds longer. Curiosity lured me forward, and I trudged up the alley, calling as I went. And it was then, as I emerged from behind the cluster of trees, that the castle suddenly appeared in its majestic splendor.

Wow!... If I ever win the lottery, I'm buying a castle like this one.

Enthralled, I walked toward the huge stone building. Of course, I had seen photos. I thought I had been prepared for the sight, but I did not expect the romantic, almost magical atmosphere surrounding the castle, as though it were straight out of a fairy tale.

It was a mix of Roman and Gothic architecture, an array of square towers pierced with high rectangular windows adorned with mullions four stories high. The towers mapped out a rectangular inner courtyard I could not quite see from where I was. Small round turrets capped each corner, probably ancient watchtowers. A moat surrounded the castle, making it seem as though it rose from the water.

An opening gaped in the square tower opposite me, and a wide stone bridge spanned the moat. A heavy iron gate, half of which was a closed solid steel plate, hid the inside of the castle.

I wandered a little closer as I recalled the meager amount of information I had been able to collect about this castle's history.

Built in the Middle Ages, it had been torn down during the French Revolution. Baron Henri Leroy de Saint-Armand had bought it back under Napoleonic rule and restored it in a style similar to the famed Château de Chambord. It had burned down one night in February 1900, shortly after the death of the last baron de Saint-Armand. The fire had destroyed not only the castle but also the riches it had held at the time. Valuable tapestries, jade statuettes, Oriental rugs, masterful paintings and an immense library of rare and precious books. After the incident, the castle had been abandoned for several years, for lack of means to restore it. In the end, a bank had bought it, but it had been forgotten again during the wars.

And now, a thousand years after the first stone had been laid, this jewel of French history was only a shadow of its former self, a ruin overrun by nature. Grass had grown between the cracks of the cobblestones, branches emerged from the window, as though a forest had sprouted inside the castle itself from the very stone.

Sleeping Beauty's castle, trapped in the evil fairy's curse.

How sad, I thought.

I had to find the current owner and hope he would be able and willing to help me with my research. I crossed the stone bridge and reached the iron gate, still calling for Éric Lagnel—fruitlessly.

I tested the gate, banging with my fist, but it stayed closed and nobody appeared.

I chewed my lip as I considered my options. I knew I was overstepping a little by showing up unannounced, without even knowing if Mr. Lagnel lived here. Given the state of the castle and grounds, it seemed unlikely. Bolstered by curiosity and impatience, I had wanted to try my luck straightaway, and now I came up empty-handed.

The best course of action would probably be to return to my car and try and reach Éric Lagnel. I didn't have his number, but surely someone in Chandeniers could help me if he wasn't in the phone book. Maybe Marine even knew him and could introduce me.

Yes, I decided, that was the thing to do.

Yet I stayed where I stood, not quite ready to give up so soon.

Dammit! I hate it when things don't go as planned!

I was about to retrace my steps when a surge of curiosity pushed me to indulge my inner rebel. After all, what the owner didn't know couldn't harm him...and seeing how he obviously wasn't here... I looked around to check if I really was alone and seized the iron bars, standing on tiptoe to peer inside. No luck. Unless I could somehow make my neck longer, it was impossible to see anything.

Damn.

It was then that a loud bark rang out behind me. I jumped and let go of the bars, turning around just in time to see a huge dark shape throw itself at me with all the speed and weight of a cannonball, complete with deafening bark. Before I could even understand what was happening, I found myself on my ass, my skirt riding up my thighs, way closer than I ever wanted to be to the slavering muzzle of a huge white pit bull. For a heartbeat, I thought it was going to bite me and rip my face to shreds. Panicking, I shrieked in terror—until a male voice called:

"Max! Come here!"

The monster immediately abandoned me without a backward glance, loping happily toward its master like it hadn't been inches away from tearing my heart out with its teeth a few seconds earlier. I let out a shaky breath and unsteadily found my feet. Heart throbbing in my chest and legs like jelly, I adjusted my skirt and blouse with clumsy hands, trying to gather my thoughts.

"Thank y—" I began, but the man didn't let me finish. He looked me straight in the eye and asked curtly:

"What are you doing on my property?"

His voice made me grimace.

Forget about Sleeping Beauty.

I'd stumbled upon the Beast's castle.

I decided to ignore his hostility and summoned my warmest smile, extending a hand. "Are you Mr. Lagnel? Pleased to—"

"You're an American?"

I halted, surprised.

"I am, but that's not important. I came to—"

"This is private property," he interrupted.

"I know, I—"

"You Americans are all the same. You behave as if you own the world!"

"And you, sir, are one of the rudest people I have ever had the misfortune to meet! The French have a reputation for arrogance; I see there's some truth to it," I hissed in my best French.

Without a hint of a stammer. Almost as if, unlike most people, my proficiency with foreign languages grows whenever I'm angry. And this man's tendency to interrupt whenever I spoke was seriously starting to annoy me.

He must have been surprised by my comeback, because he froze and looked me up and down. His eyes were a beautiful, clear blue, I noted in spite of myself.

He was good looking in a rough sort of way. Probably in his thirties, black hair that seemed to disbelieve the very existence of gravity, high cheekbones, straight nose, a few days' stubble on his square jaw. He wore an open red-and-black-checkered shirt over a white tee and cargo pants that had seen better days. He looked nothing like a model, but there was a palpable charisma radiating off him.

Éric Lagnel could have been irresistible—if he did away with the superior, condescending expression on his face.

"Rude, huh?" He huffed a short laugh. "Well, this rude man is ordering you off his property before he calls the cops on you and has you evicted, with or without your consent. And believe me, I won't hesitate for a second."

The blazing anger in his face told me he wasn't lying.

With one last, threatening look, he turned around and strode away, the dog at his side, its tongue lolling out. I sprang after him.

"Well if you were willing to stop listening to the sound of your own voice for even just a minute and hear what I have to say, we might be able to get somewhere!"

Holy shit, he's fast! I grumbled to myself as I had to run to keep pace with him. That's the issue when you don't even reach the five-foot mark—you have to take a lot more steps and walk a lot faster than everybody else if you don't want to get left behind.

"I'm not interested in anything you have to say," Éric Lagnel grunted.

He was really starting to try my patience. Hell, would it be that much of a chore to just let me speak long enough to explain why I was here? I wasn't a criminal, for God's sake! I hadn't broken in, the gate had been open!

I tried to catch my breath and called out desperately: "I was looking for you!"

It wasn't *quite* true, but at least it made him stop.

"Me?" His sarcasm was perceptible as he turned to face me. "You were looking for me through the bars of the castle?"

"Yes, well, no, not exactly—"

This is not the time to mess up!

"Yes or no?" His glacial demeanor didn't waver.

Okay, he'd reached the end of my tolerance. I was getting sick of being treated like this. I took a deep breath and looked him straight in the eye.

"I came to see you because I believe my ancestors lived in this castle and I wish to visit it."

There, I said it!

I'd been sure he wouldn't let me finish. But just as the last word left my mouth, I knew it hadn't been the right way to frame my request.

Éric Lagnel stared at me impassively for several seconds.

I met his gaze, but it would be a lie to say I was perfectly comfortable. My nose itched suddenly; I felt the urge to push a lock of hair behind my ear and shift my weight from one foot to the other as his eyes raked over me. His reply slammed right into me.

"No."

Chapter 6
Gabrielle

Castle of Ferté-Chandeniers

November 1899

The physician was at her father's side when the young maid who had welcomed Gabrielle led her to his chambers. Anxiety wrung her insides as she waited for his verdict, praying it would not match her fears.

After what seemed like an endless wait, the physician straightened, tugged the covers back over Maurice's chest and put away his stethoscope. Then he turned to Gabrielle, brows furrowed, and wordlessly led her away from the bed. Just then, Maurice burst into a cough, grimacing in pain. Gabrielle felt her heart clench.

"I will not lie to you, his cough concerns me," the physician began, redirecting her attention toward him.

Oh Lord, she prayed, a hand over her heart. *Calm down, Gabrielle. Breathe. Panic won't help your father.*

"What is the matter with him? Is it serious?"

"Well, his lungs are infected," the physician explained, "and his temperature is very high. He's got a dry cough, which is somewhat reassuring, but we'll have to keep an eye on it. If it starts to become loose and if there's blood in it, call for me at once. His lungs need to heal, and we have to bring his fever down quickly if we don't want his infection to turn into pneumonia. I don't need to tell you how serious that would be.... Has your father ever had a respiratory infection?"

Gabrielle shook her head.

"Not that I know of. He had influenza a few years ago but that's all. He's always been very healthy."

"That's good; it means he will be able to fight the infection. Make him drink water as often as you can to keep him hydrated; it's very important. Apply some poultices and give him this." He handed her a small of vial of amber-colored liquid. "It's ipecacuanha wine. It should help clear his airways. Small doses only, it's very powerful. A couple of fingers twice a day should do it for now."

"Understood." She grasped the vial.

"Let him sleep. It's the best way for him to recover. He needs to rest as much as he can, at least until we manage to make the fever abate."

"Very well."

"I will be back in a couple of days. Call for me immediately if he should take a turn for the worse."

Just then, the door to the room opened and suddenly the very air seemed to change. Gabrielle's heart began to beat faster, and she fancied she could feel Mr. D'Arcy's presence at her back, equal parts imposing and soothing. With a glance, the physician conveyed to his host that he was ready to depart; then he looked back to Gabrielle and laid a reassuring hand on her forearm.

"Your father will heal, Mademoiselle Villeneuve. He is strong, you have told me so yourself, and it will take more than a cough and a fever to bring him down."

Gabrielle gave him a wan smile and nodded. She knew the physician was only trying to comfort her, but the worry she could still read in his gaze concerned her.

"Thank you for coming in this weather, Doctor."

"Do not mention it. Take good care of your father, now."

"I will walk you out," Mr. D'Arcy told him.

With one last nod, the physician exited the room with the master of the castle, leaving Gabrielle alone with her father.

She pulled an immense armchair closer to the bed and settled in. She was cold and her dress was soaked, but she did not care right then. She stroked back a cowlick from her father's brow. Unruly hair was a Villeneuve trademark.

Unable to mask her concern, she whispered, "If you missed me that much, Papa, you only had to call for me and I would have come! No need to go to such lengths!"

The sound of her voice seemed to rouse him. He opened an eye and gave her a pale smile. He tried to speak, but a fit of coughing interrupted him.

"Don't say anything," she ordered. "Here's some water."

She poured him a glass and brought it to her father's lips.

"Is that better?"

He nodded very slightly.

"You shouldn't have come all this way, sweetheart," he croaked. "I'm sorry to be such a bother."

"Nonsense. I wasn't going to leave you alone."

"You're an angel. I don't know what I'd do without you." His voice was hoarse.

"Not much, probably. You know you'd be lost without me."

He smiled at her quip.

"I think the inventory is going to be…late."

"I'll take care of it, Papa, don't worry."

"What about the bookstore? Mr. Harnois's order? Did you—"

"Don't worry about it! Everything is under control. Étienne will handle everything fine. That's what you hired him for. Just focus on getting better. The physician said you needed to sleep."

"I am tired, true. I think…I think I will rest a little."

Gabrielle rearranged the covers as her father closed his eyes.

* * * *

A few minutes later, the door quietly swung open and the young maid came back in, holding a water pitcher, a basin, and a pile of clean laundry on one arm.

"Here you are, ma'am," she whispered. "I thought you might need these for Mr. Maurice."

"Thank you…I'm sorry, I'm afraid I don't know your name," Gabrielle replied apologetically.

"Agnès, ma'am."

So this was Agnès. She was exactly as Gabrielle had pictured her from her father's letters—blond and sweet with a fair, smiling face and beautiful almond-shaped green eyes. She looked like an angel.

"Thank you, Agnès. I'm Gabrielle. It's a pleasure to meet you."

"Likewise, ma'am. Your father speaks very often of you. I hope he will heal fast. We're all very worried for him."

"Thank you."

"Would you like something to eat? I can bring up a tray."

"No, thank you. I'm not really hungry."

"Very well. Please let me know if you need anything."

With one last backward smile, Agnès left the room, closing the door behind her.

Once alone, Gabrielle wet a linen and dabbed carefully at her father's brow, hoping the cool water would help lower his fever. A sharp knock at the door made her look up. She rose to open it and found herself face-to-face with a middle-aged woman, tall and willowy, carrying a tray laden with a bowl of steaming soup and some bread and cheese.

"Hello my dear, I am Hélène, the housekeeper. I've brought you some supper."

Gabrielle thanked her and moved aside to let her through. The housekeeper deposited the tray on a table a few steps away from the fireplace. She smiled benevolently at Gabrielle.

"Come have a seat and eat. You must be famished...and chilled," she added, eyeing Gabrielle's clothes. "Your dress is soaked; I'll fetch you a shawl until Guillaume returns with your luggage. He shouldn't be long now."

"Thank you very much, Hélène. I'd be very grateful."

"I'll retrieve it right away. In the meantime, some nice warm soup is exactly what you need."

She left the room and returned almost immediately with the promised shawl. Gabrielle wrapped it around herself and thanked her again.

"Come eat while it's hot, now."

"Thank you, but...I'm not hungry." Gabrielle grimaced apologetically. "I—"

"Hush now!" Hélène broke in. "Going hungry never solved anybody's problems. You won't be any use to your father if you don't take care of yourself."

She drew back the chair in front of the tray.

"Come eat." Her tone brooked no arguing.

"I assure you, I'm not hungry," Gabrielle protested. "I don't think I can stomach anything."

"Your appetite will return if you start eating. Come here," Hélène insisted.

Her tone, though firm, was kindly. Gabrielle gave in and sat at the table as the housekeeper settled across from her. As she soaked in the comforting warmth from the fireplace, Gabrielle swallowed a little soup, bread and cheese, at first unenthusiastically, then, at Hélène's prompting, she helped herself again, once, twice, three times. And before she knew it, she'd picked the tray clean.

"I think I was indeed hungry," she admitted ruefully. "You were right."

She almost expected the housekeeper to reply that she was always right, but she refrained from doing so. Instead, Hélène gave her a gentle smile.

"It's only natural. When was your last meal?"

"This morning, I think."

"That was over twelve hours ago!"

"Yes. But I had a drink on the train."

"That doesn't fill your stomach. Do you feel better?"

Gabrielle nodded. "Very much, thank you."

"You're welcome, Mademoiselle Villeneuve."

"Please, call me Gabrielle." She paused for an instant and added, "Thank you for caring for my father until I arrived. It's very kind of you."

Unbidden, tears rose to her eyes, and she blinked them back down.

"I'm sorry," Gabrielle mumbled, looking down.

To her great surprise, Hélène rose and enfolded her in her arms.

"I promise he'll get better," she said stoutly. "He's in good hands. And you're at his side. He can only improve."

The embrace bolstered Gabrielle's confidence. It had been a long time since somebody had hugged her to comfort her, and for an instant she closed her eyes and gave in to the soothing feeling of not being alone in this difficult moment.

Just then, a new fit of coughs rattled Maurice's body. Immediately, Hélène broke free and moved to give him some water, speaking in a reassuring voice. Once done, she returned to Gabrielle's side, sat down and declared, "Your father is a good man."

"He's the most wonderful man in the world," Gabrielle replied proudly.

"He's spoken of you a great deal since he got here, you know. You are his entire world."

Gabrielle's gaze strayed toward the bed.

"That's because it's just him and me. My mother died when I was seven."

"Yes, he told me so. He explained how exactly she had…passed away."

"Oh." Gabrielle couldn't mask her surprise.

To this day, her mother's death remained a sensitive topic for Maurice. He rarely spoke of her, even with Gabrielle. He must truly have felt at ease with Hélène to mention it to her.

The housekeeper got to her feet and gathered the contents of the tray.

"I have to go; duty calls." She smiled. "Mr. D'Arcy had me prepare the room next door for you. I will have Guillaume bring up your suitcase as soon as he gets here. Do you need anything else?"

"No, thank you, Hélène, you're a godsend."

"I don't know about that," she said with a laugh. "But I'll be downstairs if you need anything. And don't worry, we'll take care of our Maurice."

"Our" Maurice? Gabrielle noted.

It seemed her father had left a few things out of his letters.

Chapter 7
Alexandra

Castle of Ferté-Chandeniers

Present day

Once he'd made sure to convey his refusal in the most unpleasant way he could, Éric Lagnel turned his back on me and walked away as if I didn't exist.

I raged silently. No! I hadn't come this far to be denied even a chance to explain my goal. "Mr. Lagnel! Please wait a minute! Why don't you want to let me in? I'm not asking for much."

"It's private property. Do you always go around asking people to let you into their homes to gawk?"

"Of course not! But this is a special case."

"I don't see how."

"I told you! My ancestors lived in this castle just before it burned down. I only want to look around; I'm not going to scrawl my name on the walls or try to dig up some treasure!"

"There is no treasure in this castle; it's just a ruin. And that's a good story—nobody's ever shared that line before, I'll give you that. But you're going to need a little more to convince me to let you in."

"But it's the truth!"

"And I'm the king of France."

"Will you just hold on a second? I have proof!"

Éric Lagnel sighed wearily and riveted his sky-blue gaze on me.

"All right, let's get this over with."

I rolled my eyes and prayed for calm, then dug into my handbag and handed him the folder containing everything I had found—photos, family tree, articles pulled from the internet and notes I'd jotted down.

"A few years ago," I explained, "I found a half-burnt picture in my great-grandmother's stuff. It seems to have been taken here in the castle in 1899." I pointed it out to him as he flipped the folder open. "This woman is Gabrielle Villeneuve, my ancestor. In 1900, she married Thomas D'Arcy in New York. Thomas was born right here in Chandeniers. I can prove all that; I have the documentation. I managed to trace back my family tree to them. I even have a copy of their wedding announcement."

Éric Lagnel examined the picture as he listened. I took advantage of his silence to plunge on.

"On the back of the picture, you can see that it was taken here. It's barely legible, but you can make the words out. I did some research. There's only one place whose name ends this way. So I think the picture was taken here, in the castle. Which means my ancestors either lived or worked here at the time."

I fell silent, waiting for his reaction. Éric Lagnel stared down at the picture, turning it over in his hands, deciphering the writing on the back. I was growing impatient when he looked back up at me.

"That's an impressive amount of research. Are you a historian?"

That was not the reaction I had been hoping for.

"You don't have to be a historian to be interested in your family's history," I replied shortly.

If he wanted to be an ass, fine. But I wasn't going to let him get away with it. I could sling comebacks with the best of them.

I expected him to lash back at me, but he only sighed.

"You know, it's just a ruin." He hesitated. "Apart from the stones and vegetation, there's nothing to see. All the furniture and paintings are gone. Anything that survived the fire was moved or stolen."

It wasn't a yes, but it wasn't as strong a no as previously. I pushed my luck.

"I know. But that's not the point. I couldn't find any contemporary pictures of the castle, so this is the best I can hope for. I just want to have a look. I know I'm not going to find anything, that there's nothing left of my ancestors, but if I have the slightest chance of walking in their footsteps, finding out who they were, I'd like to seize it. I promise I'll be very respectful; I won't touch anything. But please let me in. It's very important to me."

For a long moment, Éric Lagnel hesitated, staring at me, looking for something—proof of my honesty? His examination lasted so long I thought I had failed to convince him.

"All right," he finally decided. "But I can't show you everything. Some places are too dangerous; the walls need to be reinforced." I nodded, and he sighed. "Come on, the key to the gate is at my place. The sooner we get there..."

He trailed off, but I didn't need for him to finish. Pushing down an irritated scowl, I fell into step with him, the dog padding at our heels.

"So you live here?" I asked.

"Yes. The stables were rebuilt into a house."

We trudged up a hidden path I hadn't noticed previously toward a wide stone building.

"You're renovating?" I questioned, catching sight of a workbench and construction materials laid out in front of the door.

"Yes."

So much for small talk. I followed him silently to a small door on the side of the building.

"Wait here," he ordered, opening the door.

I bit down on a "Sir, yes, sir!" The door was still open, and I peeked inside. The stable seemed to have been converted into some kind of loft, tastefully and simply furnished. I wondered whether Éric Lagnel lived here alone. It seemed fairly big for a single person. But maybe he had a wife, five children and a pack of pit bulls, after all.

Speaking of pit bulls...I had barely escaped being eaten alive a few minutes earlier, but the dog seemed to have changed its mind since. It stuck fast to my side, begging for attention.

"Well, you sure changed your spots," I whispered as I cautiously patted its head. "Your master might not like you fraternizing with the enemy, you know."

The dog didn't seem particularly fazed by its shifting allegiance and wagged its tail as I kept petting it.

After a few moments, the cantankerous owner came back, clutching a large iron key. He glared at his dog.

"Come on," he told me.

I raised my eyebrows briefly and followed. I could feel the excitement bubbling up inside me. Here I was at last. I had dreamed of this moment for so long, ever since I had discovered the picture. I was finally going to enter the castle where it had been taken, where my ancestors had lived!

In the courtyard, my heart clenched again at what I saw. Éric Lagnel hadn't exaggerated; this was a ruin. The west wing, the largest, and the south wing, which opened on the back of the castle, were completely razed to the ground. Only the east wing and part of the north wing were still somewhat upright.

"Do you know what caused the fire?" I asked, saddened by the sight.

I noticed the grass growing between the cracks in the cobblestones, and the tree branches protruding from the glassless windows.

"A loose wire in the electrical grid, apparently. The baron had electricity installed a few years previously, but it seems the setup wasn't secure enough. A faulty contact set fire to the tapestries in the gallery of portraits, just outside the library, and the fire spread to the entire wing."

"What a pity... I read that there were a lot of precious works of art in the castle."

"There were. Most of them in the west wing. All were lost in the fire."

"That's awful."

"There are worse things. Children are starving to death across the world this very instant, or dying from diseases because of polluted water."

I stared at him for an instant, disturbed. He was right, yes, but you could be affected by both, right? Lament the loss of precious cultural artworks *and* world hunger. Did regretting that these books had burned make me shallow? I didn't have long to ponder the question.

"Are you coming?" my bad-tempered guide grunted. "I thought you wanted to visit the castle?"

* * * *

For the next half hour, he led me around the east wing, which included servants' quarters, the kitchens and communal areas, then to the north wing, reserved for guests, which held the main entry and the immense marble staircase. We finished with the old dovecote that bridged the south and east wings. There was also a small chapel, miraculously well preserved, on the first floor of the south wing.

"I wondered how many weddings were celebrated here," I breathed, dazzled.

Éric Lagnel looked at me as if he severely doubted my intelligence.

"You don't celebrate weddings in chapels like these. They're only for prayer. You really think a priest could officiate in so small a place? And I don't want to burst your little bubble, but it was rare to marry for love at the time. Weddings were just another contract, a pact between two families, a transfer of property or a dowry to bail out empty coffers."

Annoyed at being treated like a little girl, I stiffened.

"So sorry for not knowing all about the religious customs of French castles. You see, there are *so* many of these in America. And do you have to be so cynical? How can you know there wasn't a single true love story in this castle in over a millennium? I'm sure *my* ancestors married for love!"

"Come back to earth, princess." He snorted. "Life isn't a fairy tale."

"Thank you *so* much for the little lesson. I have no idea how I managed so far without that pearl of wisdom," I shot back.

* * * *

The rest of the visit was rather colder. I stopped asking questions, and he contented himself with naming the rooms we went through in a neutral, tired tone of voice. I did learn what was in the two wings we couldn't enter: the vast library, the ballroom, the portrait gallery, the baron's rooms, the nursery and the living rooms.

"It's a pity it's in such a sorry state." I couldn't help but sigh once the visit was over.

We'd reached the castle gate, and I turned back for one final glance. Éric Lagnel surveyed the place.

"I know."

"Haven't there been any attempts to restore it?" I asked.

For an instant, he seemed weary to the bone.

"Do you know how much it costs to restore this kind of place?"

"A lot, I imagine."

"A fortune. And I'm not made of money."

"Have you asked for subventions from the state or local heritage societies?"

"I have."

He didn't elaborate, but I could tell from the look on his face it hadn't panned out. I sighed again.

"What are you going to do? Sell it?"

"I hope not, but I might have to."

"To whom?"

He shrugged. "I don't exactly have a lot of buyers. I might have to sell to the kind of investors that will tear it down and build a holiday camp or a theme park or some other stupidity."

A gleam of regret and pain appeared in his eyes as his words made their way through my mind.

"But that's awful!" I gasped, my accent bleeding through once again. "You have to do something! Go see a bank, write to the ministry that deals with heritage sites, speak to the press, or—"

"I'm doing what I can," he interrupted shortly. "Look, I let you in for a visit when I didn't have to, and I answered all your questions. I've been patient. But you have no right to tell me how to manage my inheritance."

Underneath his harsh words, I could feel that his anger wasn't entirely directed at me. It was rage at his powerlessness.

I stayed silent. What was his history with the castle? How had he come to own it? I knew he wouldn't answer if I asked. He would tell me it was none of my business. And he would be right.

Yet I could tell there was a heavy weight on his shoulders. And I didn't know why, but right then, deep down, I wanted to help him.

So I kept quiet and smiled at him politely.

"Thank you for the visit, Mr. Lagnel." He waved my thanks away. "Good luck with restoring it. I hope you find a way to save it."

I spun on my heel and walked across the stone bridge. My lips quirked up into a smile as I noticed the dog was still following me.

"Have a nice trip back to America!" its master called.

I looked back. He was leaning on the gate, his eyes on me.

"I'm not leaving just yet. But thanks!" I added with a parting smile.

I walked back down the path, the dog still at my side, until its owner called it back.

Chapter 8
Gabrielle

Castle of Ferté-Chandeniers

November 1899

Dawn found Gabrielle half asleep, curled up in what would soon become "her" armchair. Pale light poured into the room through the window. She'd forgotten to draw the curtains. Maybe that was what had woken her, or perhaps it was the crick in her neck.

She groaned in pain and straightened. Massaging her neck, she examined her father's face.

The night had been difficult.

Shortly after midnight, his fever had suddenly climbed, spawning nightmares that had left him exhausted and even weaker than he already was. For hours, she had listened to him moan and mumble. One name kept coming back, breaking her heart every single time—Héloïse.

Hands clenched around her father's, her throat tight and tears in her eyes, she had listened to him call for her mother again and again, praying with all her soul to anybody who might be listening to let him live.

All night, anxiety had been a tight ball in her stomach, an iron band around her chest keeping her from breathing. She felt lost and powerless. She would have given anything to soothe her father's suffering.

Dawn had broken by the time he'd slipped into a more peaceful sleep— though he still wheezed and coughed.

Gabrielle smothered a yawn and rose, stretching, and tugged on the covers of the bed, careful not to wake her father.

She moved to the window, which looked out onto the inner courtyard. Snow was falling, creating an almost enchanting atmosphere. She gazed for a while at the snow spinning and dancing with every gust of wind, trying to forget her fears—unsuccessfully.

The morning slipped by, punctuated by Hélène's comings and goings, attentive to their every need, and by the faces that would peek in to inquire about Maurice's health.

"Is he better?"

"No…"

At lunchtime, Hélène brought up a tray laden with food and sat across from Gabrielle to make sure she ate enough.

"Would you like some books?" she asked while Gabrielle ate in silence. "I think he would enjoy you reading to him."

"I know he would, but I don't want to be a bother…."

"Don't worry about it. Mr. D'Arcy himself told me to offer. I'll let him know as soon as you're done with lunch and he will bring you a few books himself."

"It's very kind of him, but he really shouldn't feel he has to."

"He insisted. He's been asking after you and your father all morning."

"Oh. Why didn't he come, then?"

"I think he didn't want to impose."

"It wouldn't be an imposition. On the contrary, I haven't had a chance to thank him yet for all he has done for us. I'm so grateful to all of you for looking after my father the way you do."

"You don't have to thank us, Gabrielle. I told you, we're all very fond of Maurice. And Mr. D'Arcy has a lot of respect for him."

Hélène's words warmed Gabrielle's heart.

When the housekeeper left, carrying the tray, Gabrielle returned to her father's bedside. Silence fell quickly, and she rose again to look out the window, retreating to the peace and quiet emanating from the snowy view. A thousand thoughts flitted through her mind. She thought of Mr. D'Arcy and his unassuming personality that masked such generosity. She was growing ever more curious to know him better, eager to discover what kind of man he was. She thought of Hélène and her boundless devotion. Her motherly behavior was a comfort, a source of warmth, and pushed back the sense of loneliness that threatened to engulf her. She thought of her mother, of the pain of her absence that her father's fevered delirium seemed to have reawakened. She missed her more acutely than ever. She needed her through this trial.

She sighed for the millionth time since she had reached the castle.

Please let him live.

Gabrielle would have known him anywhere, even without the discreet cough with which he made his presence known. Something in the air changed when he entered a room, something she was particularly attuned to. Her heart beating slightly faster, she turned around and stared in surprise at the tall pile of books in Mr. D'Arcy's arms. Smiling shyly, he was about to speak when alarm stole over his face.

"Mademoiselle Villeneuve, you're crying! What is it? Is your father...?"

He crossed the room in a few strides, depositing the books in the armchair, his eyes on hers, searching worriedly.

Confused, Gabrielle was about to reply that she wasn't crying; but when she reflexively touched her cheeks, she realized they were wet, streaked with tears she hadn't felt escape.

"Oh, no," she breathed, embarrassed. "Everything is all right. It's just... old memories."

Seeing the worry linger on Mr. D'Arcy's face, she added, "I assure you, everything is fine, Mr. D'Arcy."

She summoned her bravest and widest smile—under the circumstances—and asked, as much out of curiosity as to steer the conversation away from her:

"That's a fair number of books. Did you empty your library?"

He gazed at her a little longer, as though to make sure she really was all right, before he replied.

"Hélène told me you'd enjoy something to read. I didn't know what you'd like, so I chose a few. I hope you'll find something that suits."

"Thank you. It's very generous of you. I promise I'll take good care of them."

"I don't doubt it." He watched her skim through the pile.

She was surprised to realize that, apart from Balzac, whom she'd never managed to take to in spite of her best efforts, it only featured authors she enjoyed: Alexandre Dumas, Gustave Flaubert, Chrétien de Troyes, Paul Féval, Jules Verne, Mark Twain, Alexander Pushkin, Jane Austen and the Brontë sisters.

She smiled as she hefted a heavy volume.

"*Jane Eyre* is one of my favorite novels. I think I know it by heart." She examined the book with a professional eye.

It was a magnificent collector's edition. Bound in red leather, embossed in gold with an elaborately framed cover and hand-drawn ornamentations. She had rarely seen so fine—or so expensive. It was probably worth more than she and her father earned in one week from their bookstore.

"Why is that?" Mr. D'Arcy inquired curiously.

"I don't know exactly. I felt a connection to this book the first time I read it. Maybe because of the hero. I think he's one of the most moving characters in modern literature. Have you read it?"

"No."

"It's the story of a young, rather plain woman, with no relatives or friends, trying to find out who she is. She becomes a governess to Mr. Rochester's ward. He's a somber man, rich, rather ugly, cynical and jaded, and he has a hidden past. Jane Eyre is his light and his redemption. In a way, it's a story of two lonely people meeting, two people battered by life who have a hard time finding where they belong and who find they belong with each other."

She glanced up, met Mr. D'Arcy's fathomless gaze resting upon her and, once again, almost drifted away in his steel-gray eyes.

"I'm sorry, it's probably not very interesting to you." She looked down. "I can be a bit of a chatterbox when I'm talking about books, especially this one. Anyway, this copy is beautiful. Mine is falling apart, I've read it so many times. It...belonged to my mother."

"Keep it, then. It's yours."

Their eyes met.

"I can't," she protested. "It's much too precious."

"I insist."

"You can't give me something this valuable, just like that."

"Can't I? Why not?"

"Well... Because I... You don't know me and..."

"Keep it," he murmured. "Please."

Gabrielle gave in. What else could she do?

"Thank you, Mr. D'Arcy," she whispered, hugging the book to her chest.

He nodded slightly, then looked back at Maurice, asleep, red faced and feverish.

Once more, Gabrielle realized, Mr. D'Arcy's presence, his gaze, their conversation had almost made her forget about her concerns.

Almost.

"How is he?" Mr. D'Arcy asked.

"Not very well. I'm afraid he's worse off than yesterday."

"Should I call for the physician?"

She sighed. "I don't know. Hélène said we should wait for the treatment to operate, but..."

She broke off, looking away as her voice grew hoarse, clutching the book to her chest. Out of the corner of her eye, she saw him reach for her, pause and let his hand fall back.

"What about you?" he asked gently. "Are you all right?"

"Yes. I'm…I'm just worried."

"Trust Hélène. If someone can help him pull through, it will be her."

"I can believe that." She smiled as she thought of the housekeeper's unwavering devotion. "She is a force of nature."

"No one can resist her. Not even me."

"Really?"

He shook his head, smiling slightly.

"I tried, once. I don't remember why exactly. I thought she was going to grab me by the ear and send me into the corner, or make me write a hundred times 'I will not disobey.'"

Picturing Mr. D'Arcy's tall frame hunched up like a scolded child was just too amusing—Gabrielle couldn't contain a small huff of laughter. He smiled more widely and went on: "Are you sure you don't need anything? Please don't hesitate."

"Thank you, but you've already done so much. I don't know how to thank you."

"Anyone would have done the same."

"I don't believe so, sir."

He shrugged and started to reply, but someone knocked on the door and it swung open to reveal Hélène for a new round of treatment.

Mr. D'Arcy declared he was going to take his leave, then turned back on the threshold.

"May I return to know how your father improves?"

"Of course. As often as you like."

* * * *

Three days went by.

Three endless days during which Maurice's health went from bad to worse, his nightmares recurring every night before he slipped into unconsciousness from which he surfaced only briefly.

Seventy-two agonizing hours during which Gabrielle's world stopped at the door of the bedroom.

Four thousand three hundred and twenty trying minutes during which she barely slept, fearful the worst might happen while she slumbered.

Two hundred and fifty-nine thousand and two hundred seconds of uninterrupted panic.

The physician had returned once but been unable to do any more. "We must let the body defend itself," he had said. "We must wait."

Wait.

Gabrielle did little else.

It was as though her life was suspended, her mind overrun with worry.

During those three days, Hélène managed to be at Gabrielle's and her father's side as often as possible. Gabrielle was boundlessly grateful for her care and unending support, a ray of sunlight in a dark and stormy sky.

Mr. D'Arcy returned frequently to inquire after Maurice's health, replacing his housekeeper as Gabrielle's companion. He usually kept silent, his mere presence a discreet but strangely reassuring comfort, listening with his eyes closed as she read to her father.

* * * *

On the morning of the fourth day, Gabrielle was alone with her father, curled up in what had become "her" armchair. She was reading the adventures of three musketeers squaring off against the English, enjoying Alexandre Dumas's humor, when she suddenly realized she could no longer hear her father's breathing.

Panicked, she dropped her book and rushed to his side, and was surprised to see that he was in fact sleeping peacefully, no longer wheezing painfully. Anxiously, she laid a hand on his forehead. His cheeks were still red, but he was no longer sweating.

She could only accept the obvious—his fever seemed to have fallen.

A wave of relief washed over her. But she didn't dare rejoice yet. Not before the physician had assured her that her father was out of danger.

Running out of the room, she slammed into a wardrobe.

"Mademoiselle Villeneuve? What is the matter?" Mr. D'Arcy asked worriedly, reaching out to stop her from falling over—just as he had done a fortnight earlier.

"I'm sorry, sir, I wasn't watching where I was going. My father...I think his fever has receded. Could you—"

"I'll fetch the physician," he interrupted before she could even finish.

* * * *

The physician soon confirmed that Maurice was out of the woods and only needed rest now. The news was greeted with great joy from all the inhabitants of the castle.

Gradually, the comings and goings into Maurice's room ceased as each returned to their daily tasks. Shortly after, Gabrielle found herself alone with her sleeping father.

She closed her eyes and sighed. The weight that had rested on her shoulders for so long seemed to have vanished, and she felt so light all of a sudden....

As though out of nowhere, a sob wrenched itself from her throat, taking her by surprise. Tears began to roll down her cheeks, and her breath hitched. And suddenly, unable to restrain herself any longer, she collapsed into her armchair, crying her heart out, one fist clenched tight over her mouth to muffle her sobs.

A moment later, as she tried bravely to recover her breath and blink back her tears, she heard the door open. Footsteps drew closer, and she felt his presence in front of her.

He knelt in front of her, his hands on the armrests.

"Mademoiselle Villeneuve? Is everything all right?"

It seemed to her that he was asking this for the thousandth time since he had come for her in Angers.

"Yes. I... It's... It's fine." She hiccupped. "I..."

She began to sob again.

Wordlessly, Mr. D'Arcy gripped her hands and drew her to him. His arms closed around her, and Gabrielle, try as she might, could not help but cling to him as though her life depended on it.

Many minutes later, Gabrielle's tears finally ran dry.

Mr. D'Arcy did not release his embrace.

Gabrielle knew she should pull away, but she could not muster the strength. She was so comfortable in his arms. She was safe. A tight cocoon she did not want to leave.

Seconds passed by to the ticktock of the clock and the rhythm of their hearts beating as one. Gabrielle felt Mr. D'Arcy's arms hold her a little tighter, his cheek resting on top of her head, his breath rippling her hair.

Warmth spread through her, and in spite of herself, she sighed with pleasure.

"You should sleep," he murmured into her hair. "You must be exhausted."

"Yes," she said with a sigh, her face against his chest.

But she did not move.

Neither did he.

"I will watch over your father while you rest. I promise."

"Yes," she repeated.

But she still made no move to leave. She couldn't. Perhaps she was too tired to move; perhaps a part of her did not want to. She felt she was in a bubble that might burst if she drew away.

Her eyelids, however, grew heavier. Exhaustion was taking its toll. She could have gone to sleep right there in his arms.

"I will carry you to your bedroom," he said.

"Mmmmh."

Gabrielle felt him lift her in his arms and carry her to the next room. The room she probably hadn't spent more than thirty minutes in since she'd arrived. Mr. D'Arcy deposited her on the bed, and through the veil of sleep, she thought she felt his hand on her hair and his voice murmuring, "Sleep, Gabrielle. I will watch over you and your father."

Then she knew no more.

Chapter 9
Alexandra

Chandeniers-sur-Vienne

Present day

After leaving Mr. Sarcasm, I returned to town. I wandered aimlessly through the streets, taking note of several posters advertising celebrations the following week. Apparently, this was the anniversary of the founding of the town, some thousand years ago, and a costume ball would launch a week of festivities.

Amused, I promised myself I would find a costume and go. I reached the banks of the Vienne and spent an hour browsing through the stands of old books, barely resisting the urge to buy them all. I did fall for just one, a red leather-bound book whose cover seemed to be calling out to me. "Pick me, pick me!" the golden letters of the title seemed to cry. And because I am weak, I could not resist. Who *could* resist *Jane Eyre*, anyway? Especially when this edition featured a dedication that set my squishy little heart aflutter—*To my Jane, from her Rochester. I love you.*

And so I became the happy owner of a fifth edition of my favorite book. You can never have too many books, right?

* * * *

After this literary interlude, I resumed my walk. Charmed by the city, I paused frequently to sit on a bench, the edge of a well or a flight of stairs and sketch the picturesque sights in front of me: the vast, shimmering waterwheel, the bookstands by the river, the main street and its cobblestones and adorable little shops, their wrought iron signs swinging in the breeze, the clock tower, the church belfry....

In the early evening, I had a *croque-monsieur*, a salad and a glass of white wine at a terrace with Edward Rochester for company.

Night had fallen by the time I returned to the inn. Eager to try out the four-poster bed, I took a record shower and sprawled blissfully across the sheets. I was exhausted, both from the trip and the tiring weeks beforehand, not to mention the whole castle ordeal, and my body practically begged for a good night's sleep. Yet I could not drift off. Too many images, thoughts and emotions were jumbled inside my head.

I had at last found the birthplace of my French ancestors. I had visited the castle they had lived in, and discovered it was about to be torn down. I had met the owner, a frankly unpleasant man.

I was happy, excited, bubbling, impatient and sad all at once.

Giving up on sleep for the time being, I got up, put on some yoga pants and decided to go for some air. I left my laptop in its case but took my tablet, hoping I might be able to talk to Spencer. He *had* promised to call me as soon as he could, but I could still try my luck. I really wanted to hear his thoughts about the castle and its future—or lack of one.

After several calls failed to connect, however, I could only conclude he was still in a meeting. I gave up on him for the time being and called my best friend instead.

She answered at first ring.

"Tell me everything. Have you seen the castle? I want to know every detail!"

"Wow, you sure don't waste any time."

"Well, we already spoke a few hours ago."

"True. How are my cats? Do they miss me?"

"They're fine, they're not starving and they're not depressed, don't worry about them. Go on, tell me about the castle."

I briefed her about my meeting with the unpleasant owner of the castle, the visit and the dreary future that awaited the ruin if we couldn't find a way to save it.

"'We'?" Bea noted. "Aren't you jumping a little ahead of yourself, getting involved?"

"I meant 'he,' of course. But really... I don't know, Bea. It feels like such a shame to let it be destroyed."

"I know, sweetheart, but unless you have a couple of millions to invest or very rich relatives, I don't see how you're going to be of any help. And you're returning to California in ten days, anyway. Kind of seems like short notice to start moving mountains." She frowned. "You *are* coming back, right? I certainly hope you're not going to chain yourself to a vineyard to stay in France!"

I burst into laughter.

"Don't worry, I won't. I'm still coming home as planned. I miss you and I miss my cats. And Spencer too."

"I notice Spencer comes after me and the cats. I'm not sure he would appreciate that." She giggled.

"Probably not!" I laughed even harder.

"Speaking of Spencer, what does he think of all this?"

"I couldn't reach him; he's very busy today."

"Ah, lawyers, always overworked."

"You're telling me! The price of success, I guess."

Bea's shrug was compassionate.

"What are you going to do now?" she asked.

I sighed and looked up. A shooting star trailed overhead, and I reflexively made a wish. Then I turned back to my friend.

"About the castle? I don't know. Mr. Sarcasm clearly told me it wasn't any of my business. It's his castle, after all." I shrugged. "I'm just going to move my research elsewhere. There's nothing more to see there; it's really just ruins. I'm going to start looking for Thomas's birth certificate. Maybe I can find it here, or maybe I'll have to go and look in the department archives. In a few days, I'll go to Angers to try and find Gabrielle's. I'm hoping I come across traces of their parents too. I know I'm reaching a bit—that's starting to stretch to quite a long time ago, after all. There's a risk nothing exists anymore. But I'm hopeful I can find at least something to put me on the right track. I'll also ask the town hall about the castle. If I'm lucky, someone may be able to point me to a historian able to tell me about the people who lived there...and Marine, the innkeeper, knows a lot about the town and its history. She'll probably have things to tell me even if there's no straightforward connection with my ancestors."

Bea smiled. "Ever the optimist."

"Six weeks in France weren't enough to change me, you know."

"Thank goodness! Okay, beautiful, I have to go. It's back to work for me."

"See you later, then."

"Keep me posted, okay? I want to know everything. I want to live your French adventures vicariously."

"I promise. But you might be disappointed. I'm not the adventurous type; you know that."

Once we'd hung up, I tilted my head back, gazing up at the stars again, lost in thought. The castle was at the forefront of my mind, and Éric Lagnel's face drifted in front of my eyes. The look on his face when he had admitted he'd probably have to sell it had moved me. There had been deep regret in his eyes. Yet not once during the visit had he shown any attachment to the ruins. He'd answered all my questions dispassionately and cynically.

I knew I hadn't imagined the glint of sadness and pain that had flashed through his eyes. All right, it had quickly given way to anger, but it had been there. I was sure of it.

Which meant that whatever he might pretend, the fate of the castle was important to him. Very important.

I scowled and absentmindedly fiddled with the string on my yoga pants.

I knew there was no lack of castles in the Loire valley—or in France—but was no one really going to do anything to save this one? It was a part of history that would disappear with it. A part of my own history too, in a way.

But I had no idea where to start. And even if I did, *he* didn't want my help. He'd made that much clear. I had no way to take action. I was nobody.

Since my mind didn't seem ready to go to sleep, I picked up my tablet again and opened a new browser window. The internet was one great information source, but it was also—some might even say especially—a place you could waste *a lot* of time. You know how it is—one minute you're looking for a butter chicken recipe and suddenly it's an hour later and you're reading about rice fields in India...or watching cat videos.

Since I was no exception to the rule, I started out checking the opening hours of the Chandeniers and Angers town halls, and a few minutes later I found myself researching ongoing castle restoration projects. I was so absorbed I didn't hear Marine come up behind me.

"Can't sleep?"

I leapt out of my chair like a cat caught red pawed murdering the local goldfish.

"Oh my God, you scared me!" I gasped, a hand over my heart.

"I'm sorry, I thought you'd heard me. I wasn't exactly quiet."

"I was so caught up in my reading the world could have caught on fire without me noticing!" I joked.

"Well, that certainly happens to me often enough. Can I sit with you? I found out some information I think you're going to like." There was an excited gleam in her eyes.

"Really?" I perked up curiously, motioning for her to sit.

"Really," she confirmed, taking a seat across from me. "I went to the castle this afternoon, I wanted to check something."

"The castle of Ferté-Chandeniers?"

"Yes! The owner is actually my cousin," she explained, seeing the puzzled look on my face.

"Éric Lagnel is your cousin?"

"Yes. That's the coincidence I wanted to tell you about when we got interrupted earlier."

Well, today certainly was a day for surprises.

"I thought about your ancestor's name, D'Arcy, all day," she went on. "I was sure I'd heard it somewhere—apart from Jane Austen, of course," she quipped, "but I couldn't remember where. So I decided to look through the file my uncle, Éric's father, put together about the castle. It was his passion—or, well, my aunt's, but over time it became his too."

"Wait a minute," I interrupted, one hand raised to try and stem the flow of information, slightly dizzy. "Éric's father has a file on the castle? Where can I find him? I have a thousand questions for him!"

Marine's smile turned sad.

"He passed away six months ago. Heart attack."

Oh.

"I'm sorry," I said.

"It was difficult for all of us, especially for Éric since he'd already lost his mother...he had to come back from Africa to take care of the inheritance and the castle his father had left him."

So Mr. Sarcasm had lost both his father *and* his mother! Which might explain why he was so cynical. Life had been harsh with him. What had he been doing in Africa? And the castle had belonged to his father before him?

"Anyway," Marine went on, "from what you told me about your ancestors, I was almost sure the file was where I had seen that name. So I checked."

"And? Did you find anything?" I pressed her.

"I did," she said mysteriously.

My heart started beating wildly.

"Tell me!"

"Your ancestor was the executor for Victor Leroy de Saint-Armand, the last owner of the castle," she announced.

"He was in charge of making sure his will and testament were fulfilled."

"Exactly." She paused, letting the tension rise unbearably. "But that's not all."

"It isn't?"

"No." She smiled mischievously. "He wasn't *just* the executor, even though that was the main reason for his presence in the castle."

Excitement bubbled up inside me. I could barely sit still.

"Marine, if you keep on maintaining the suspense, I might just die from anticipation," I warned her.

She leaned toward me, a giddy glint in her eyes.

"According to the documents I found in my uncle's file, your ancestor, Thomas D'Arcy, was the son of Victor—which means he was the heir to the castle."

She paused again, bright gaze fixed on me, and declared, "Alexandra, I think you're descended from the last baron de Saint-Armand."

Chapter 10
Gabrielle

Castle of Ferté-Chandeniers

November 1899

Gabrielle awoke with a start to pitch blackness and was, for a moment, completely disoriented.

Then everything came rushing back.

The fever, the anxiety. Her father's turn for the better, her relief. And Mr. D'Arcy's arms around, carrying her, holding her close to his chest.

His hand in her hair, her name on his lips, ringing with kindness and endearment.

And her utter trust, the sensation that she was protected, soothed.

Heat rose to her cheeks, and her pulse quickened.

Oh Lord, what was he going to think of her?

She closed her eyes and sighed deeply.

She shouldn't have collapsed against him, but she had been unable to stop herself. His arms had felt so right around her. As though that was where she belonged.

Utter foolishness.

Face scarlet and pulse throbbing in her temples, Gabrielle rose to her feet and groped for the oil lamp. She was unlikely to come across anyone at this time of the night, so she simply tugged at her dress to make it somewhat presentable and slipped out of the room without a glance in the mirror. She tiptoed down the corridor and eased open the door to her father's room. To her relief, he was still peacefully asleep, his breathing calm and even.

She was about to turn back, her mind at ease, when she caught sight of Mr. D'Arcy in "her" armchair, deeply asleep.

At once, images of the previous evening flooded her mind, and she unthinkingly skirted the bed and came up to him, watching him with keen, curious eyes.

Just then, with his tie loosened, his shirt slightly askew, and his hair wilder than ever, he looked…peaceful. Relaxed.

He looked, she decided, like a child blissfully falling into sleep, knowing that he was perfectly safe from the world outside.

Smiling softly, she fetched a blanket from the foot of the bed, unfolded it and spread it over him. Her fingers lingered, hesitated for a second. She longed to smooth down the unruly cowlick…in a burst of daring, she reached out until her hand brushed against the black curls, but retreated at the last minute. She couldn't.

Shaking her head slightly, Gabrielle stepped back. Any desire to return to her room had vanished. She took the other armchair across from the bed, her hands closing automatically on the nearest book.

But her eyes never even touched the book; they were glued on her sleeping host.

The man intrigued her. What secret hid behind his gray eyes, his undecipherable looks and scar?

Gabrielle's vivid imagination did not fail her. For an instant, she pictured her father's mysterious benefactor as the captain of a ship, sailing the seas in search of bloodthirsty pirates, or as an army officer prepared to fight for king and country. In another life, she thought, in another century, he would have been a knight or a musketeer. Better still—a masked avenger, unsheathed blade shining in the pale moonlight or bow in hand, a Black Tulip or a Robin Hood, possibly Lagardère from the cloak-and-dagger novels she loved so much.

Whatever the truth, whoever he was, one thing was very clear in Gabrielle's eyes—Mr. D'Arcy was an honest, upstanding man, probably brave and heroic. In a word, the type of man novels were written about.

As though he could feel her gaze upon him, he opened his eyes, immediately meeting hers. She smiled.

"Good evening," she whispered. "Or rather, good night."

"Good evening." He sat up, the blanket falling to his feet. "How do you feel? Did you sleep well?" he inquired immediately.

His concern pleased her far more than it should have.

"Even Sleeping Beauty could not have slept better than I did!" she jested softly. She paused, then added, more seriously: "Thank you for watching over my father."

"Of course. I promised you I would."

Gabrielle nodded slowly. A peaceful quiet fell over the room, barely troubled by Maurice's calm, even breathing. Now that the anxiety and oppression that had been hanging over her ever since she arrived had vanished, Gabrielle felt invigorated, full of energy, eager to discover the castle her father had spoken of so fondly. One room in particular...

She hesitated, biting at her cheek, hands playing with the leather cover of the book in her lap, wondering whether she dared. Curiosity finally took over.

"Mr. D'Arcy? May I ask you something?"

"Naturally, Mademoiselle Villeneuve. What is it?"

"Would you...show me the library?"

He raised an eyebrow.

"Now?"

Gabrielle shrugged. "You are not asleep, neither am I.... Why not?"

He must have felt her impatience. An amused grin tugged at his lips, and he nodded. "Follow me."

* * * *

It seemed like hours to Gabrielle, but it must have been only minutes. They walked a myriad of corridors, winding staircases, galleries each more sumptuous than the last. Some were lined with magnificent marble busts while others were guarded by standing suits of armor, but all of them were hung with works from master painters, rich hangings or tapestries from the Gobelins. In every room they crossed, Mr. D'Arcy lit the electric lamps. Light pooled from the gorgeous crystal chandeliers to spill over the many treasures housed inside the castle. Impressed, slightly intimidated, Gabrielle looked around, convinced she would never manage to take everything in, absorb it, commit it to memory.

Never in her entire life had she been close to so many riches. It was simply...

"Magnificent!" she exclaimed when they entered a gigantic gallery lined with mirrors in which their reflections seemed to go on and on. A real-life fairy tale!

Mr. D'Arcy muttered something she did not catch. A truly nightmarish sight had caught her eye in the mirror opposite her. In typical fashion, her hair had come loose from her bun and now curled wildly around her face, utterly disheveled. Grimacing, she pulled back a few locks behind her ear before redirecting her gaze to her companion's reflection. She had never been very tall, but his massive body dwarfed her. As they walked side by side in silence, she lingered for a few moments on his right profile, the rugged, masculine lines of his face, almost hoping she might uncover in the corner of his mouth or the shape of his jaw the secrets masquerading behind his quiet demeanor and few words.

"This castle is immense," she remarked, trying to fill the silence, her voice echoing through the room. "Much larger than I would have believed. Please don't abandon me," she added mischievously, "I might never find my way out."

To her satisfaction, he laughed quietly.

"I promise not to abandon you here. But the castle is not that vast. It is just an impression. You will get used to it."

"Perhaps, but for now I am completely unable to tell where we are, so please don't forget me in some room, or else I would have to ask one of the ghosts haunting the castle my way. If there are any, of course…"

"I am sorry to disappoint," Mr. D'Arcy intoned, "but to my knowledge there are no ghosts here."

"What a pity! Are you sure? The castle must be very old."

"It is. It was rebuilt after the Revolution, but the foundations date back a thousand years."

"Then there must be ghosts. And secret passages. It seems obvious."

"My apologies, but there aren't any secret passages either."

"No secret passages? I must protest, sir!" Gabrielle cried, carried away by their discussion so far as to forget all restraint. "I must rebel! This is utterly unacceptable. To qualify as a castle, you must have a ballroom, wide staircases, ghosts and at least one secret passage. That is nonnegotiable!"

"I'm very sorry to say there are no secret passages or ghosts. But we do have a ballroom and staircases, as you saw. Will that be enough?"

Gabrielle sighed dramatically.

"It will have to be. Ah well…you can't have everything you want in life."

Mr. D'Arcy looked at her sideways.

"But if there were ghosts here, wouldn't you be afraid to stay?"

Gabrielle pretended to ponder the question.

"I don't think so. After all, they could be friendly ghosts." She grinned, entertained. "There would be no way to know until you met them."

"Do you think there is such a thing as friendly ghost? I find the idea difficult to grasp."

"Why not? Why shouldn't a ghost be kind and gentle if their soul was so in life? Why should they necessarily be sinister and threatening?"

"It is said that ghosts are the shades of people who have died a violent death and remain caught between worlds. I would think that it would make them…irritable and hardly inclined to kindness and generosity," Mr. D'Arcy noted drily.

"Hmmm… You're not wrong. But I would rather stand by my theory." Next to her, Mr. D'Arcy simply smiled.

"But are you sure there are no ghosts?" Gabrielle insisted. "You seem to know the history of this place; are you positive nothing tragic ever happened here? Not even during the Revolution? Should we ask a medium to know for certain?"

The amused gleam in Mr. D'Arcy's eye abruptly disappeared, followed by his smile. To Gabrielle's great surprise, he seemed to withdraw, his body tense.

She frowned and was about to ask him what troubled him so, when he turned away from her and quickened his pace, clearly indicating that their conversation was over.

Gabrielle followed suit, suddenly no longer enthused. They made their way in heavy, uncomfortable silence. Confused, she ran through the conversation mentally, trying to understand what could have triggered such an about-face. She did not understand. One instant they had been laughing, bantering lightly—it had been nonsense, but he hadn't seemed to mind—and the next he had become as cold and distraught as the love child of Heathcliff and Rochester. Had she been too aggressive? It would not be the first time someone told her so. Perhaps she had been too presumptuous as to the closeness that had occurred between them over the last few days, taking inappropriate liberties, overstepping her boundaries? After a few moments she could bear it no longer and spoke up.

"I apologize if I offended you," she murmured. "I did not want to.…"

He halted and turned toward her, stony faced.

"No, you said nothing that could cause offense. It has nothing to do with you. It is I who…" He sighed and ran a hand through his hair. "My apologies. Perhaps you would be better off on your own. I am not very good company. I will lead you to the library and leave you to your own devices."

"I don't understand. Did I say something I oughtn't?"

"No, not at all. I'm sorry. Please forget about it, will you?"

Gabrielle considered him for a moment, then nodded. They resumed walking in silence until she glanced up at him from the corner of her eye and dared a quip, her tone as light as it had been before, making a show of looking around her.

"You assured me the castle was not as vast as I imagined, but how many more galleries will we cross until we reach the library? Should we have packed some provisions?"

The corner of his lips curled up.

"Have no fear, Mademoiselle Villeneuve, we are almost there," he replied.

Relieved now that the unease had subsided, Gabrielle smiled back, and silently swore she would keep any future musings about ghosts to herself.

* * * *

There was only one more gallery left, Gabrielle soon realized—the portrait gallery.

"Are these the members of the Saint-Armand family?" she asked, peering at the frames.

"Yes. The barons and their families."

They walked up the gallery slowly, pausing to look at the portraits. At the very end of the room, Mr. D'Arcy stopped in front of the last portrait, featuring a young couple holding a baby. The man was blond, with the harmonious features of an Apollo: blue eyes, not a hair out of place, a face without a flaw. *And completely uninteresting,* Gabrielle thought. She looked at the woman.

She was beautiful, with jet-black hair and a face like an angel. She gave off an impression of infinite gentleness and kindness. She smiled, but Gabrielle could not help but think it masked an immense sadness.

"Who are they?" she asked in a low voice.

Mr. D'Arcy cleared his throat.

"Victor Leroy de Saint-Armand, the…late baron, and his wife, Adaline."

"Is she still alive?"

Somehow, Gabrielle thought she knew the answer already.

If the castle and all it held were to be sold, there probably were no heirs left.

"No, she died a long time ago," Mr. D'Arcy confirmed. "She was still young. Much too young," he added, a surprising amount of regret and bitterness in his voice.

Had he known her?

"What happened? Was she ill?"

"An accident, it was said."

'She was beautiful."

"She was."

"But she doesn't look happy."

"She wasn't."

"Oh."

Mr. D'Arcy's gaze stayed on the woman an instant longer; then he turned to Gabrielle and before she could ask any more questions, he announced: "This is it. The library is right here."

All other thoughts fled Gabrielle's mind, her eyes lighting up as she grinned widely.

"What are we waiting for?" she exclaimed, reaching for the door he pointed to.

"Wait!" He held her back. "Close your eyes."

Gabrielle's eyebrows rose.

"You want me to close my eyes?"

"Trust me, the sight will be even more impressive."

Intrigued, hopping from one foot to the other impatiently, she obeyed and waited. A door creaked open, and a warm hand wrapped around hers and led her into the next room. She took slow, faltering steps, fearful she would trip and make a fool of herself in front of her host.

After a few meters, he stopped and released her hand.

"Wait a little longer," he told her softly.

Eyes still shut, Gabrielle heard the sound of his footsteps move away, muffled by the carpet, and detected the light through her closed eyelids when he switched it on. He returned to her side and solemnly declared: "You can open your eyes now."

She obeyed.

And froze on the spot, wonderstruck.

The library was straight out of a dream.

There were dozens, hundreds, thousands of books, leather bound in red, blue, black and brown, lining immense shelves of solid oak that rose two stories high, adorned with sliding wooden ladders and narrow winding spiral staircases.

Gabrielle could barely contain her excitement. She wanted to shout in delight, clap her hands and skip everywhere like a small child on Christmas morning. Of course, she did no such thing, clamping down on her enthusiasm, trying to maintain a dignified façade. She could not, however, hold back a quiet, heartfelt "Whoa." With all the restraint she was capable of, she moved toward a large oak desk, stopped and spun on the spot, head thrown back and eyes wide open the better to take in the room.

"Do you like it?" Mr. D'Arcy asked.

"Do I like it? You mock me," she gasped, turning to face him. "This is amazing! I have never seen so many books in my entire life! I could live here for the rest of my days and never be bored for a second!"

Her reply, and the enthusiasm with which she delivered it, drew a new smile from Mr. D'Arcy.

"It's incredible," she went on. "It looks like Captain Nemo's library!"

"Captain Nemo?"

"He's a character from one of Jules Verne's novels, *Twenty Thousand Leagues under the Sea*. He is the captain of a submarine in which there is a magnificent library that holds a copy of every single book ever published throughout the world."

"I'm not sure there is a copy of every single book ever published here," Mr. D'Arcy remarked.

"Maybe not, but that doesn't make it any less impressive!"

She wheeled around again, breathing deeply, taking in every detail of the library with all of her senses. Her eyes fell on her father's tools, spread out over the large desk, and she felt a tug on her heartstrings when she suddenly realized that this extraordinary collection was fated to disappear.

"Did the baron have no heir, for you to have to sell such a unique collection?" she asked, suddenly no longer giddy. "What happened to the child in the portrait? Did he die too?"

"No, he… He still lives."

"Why doesn't he come take possession of the castle, then, so the treasures it holds do not have to be sold off to the highest bidder?"

"For several reasons. The first is that Victor de Saint-Armand was an avid collector and had a love for…shall we say, beautiful things, but he was not so talented when it came to managing his finances. He squandered his fortune and his bride's dowry on an increasing number of statues and paintings, so no one but he could claim to own these works of art. In the end, he died and left behind only debts, and selling the castle is the only way they can be settled."

"Oh." She was surprised at the bitterness in his voice. "And…what are the other reasons?"

"Well, the…baron's son did not want the inheritance."

"He did not want it?" Gabrielle repeated, surprised. "I don't understand. How could anyone not want such an estate? I'm sorry," she hurried to add, "I am being very indiscreet. Please don't feel you have to answer my questions."

Mr. D'Arcy kept silent for a few seconds.

"It's...a complicated story," he finally said. "Truth be told, he had been estranged from his father for many years. He even thought he had been disowned and disinherited."

"Oh," Gabrielle said again. "I understand. That must have been a hard thing to undergo."

He shrugged.

"He survived. People can survive anything."

"That is true. I survived my mother's death. It took some time, but you can become used to anything, even the void of absence."

For a time, silence fell as Gabrielle wandered up the shelves, hands trailing over the spines of the books, eyes roving. There were all kinds of books. Medicine, literature, biology, ornithology... Classical works in Greek and Latin. Modern authors such as Émile Zola and Victor Hugo. Some books were recent, other far more ancient. She explored further, feeling Mr. D'Arcy's gaze upon her back with every step. She could see him hesitate out of the corner of her eye.

"How old were you when you lost your mother?" he inquired at last.

"I was seven," she replied without pausing in her wanderings.

"I was nine."

"Oh." She turned back to him. "I am sincerely sorry."

"It was a long time ago. As you said, you can become used to anything."

"But you never really forget, do you? You simply learn to live with the emptiness inside."

"Yes."

"Do you miss her?" she asked.

"Every day."

"So do I. What was she like?"

"Beautiful. Extremely beautiful. A ray of sunshine. Kind and generous. Always smiling."

"She must have been a wonderful person."

"She was."

He seemed to hesitate again, gestured toward her, opened his mouth and closed it again. Then he breathed out deeply.

"Do you remember the woman in the portrait? Outside the library?"

She nodded.

"That was her. My mother."

It took Gabrielle a few instants to understand what he had just said.

"You mean...you are the son of Victor de Saint-Armand? The heir to the title and castle? You were the child in the portrait?"

He nodded uncertainly, as though he did not know what to expect from her.

"Why did you not tell me?" she asked, still reeling from the news.

"I did not intend to hide it." He shrugged. "But it had been so long since I was a member of this family that I simply did not think of it at first. In truth, I don't think of myself as the baron Thomas de Saint-Armand. I refuse to be that person. I am who I told you I was. I am Thomas D'Arcy. Nothing more."

He paused then continued, his voice tense.

"Mademoiselle Villeneuve…is the name I bear so important? Does it change anything? Will you no longer talk to me of ghosts and Jane Eyre? Will you…will you no longer honor me with your friendship?"

Something in the tone he used moved Gabrielle deeply.

"My friendship? You wish for my friendship?"

"I do. Very much so."

Gabrielle's heart leapt in her chest, and warmth spread all through her. She had not been mistaken. They had indeed grown close at her father's bedside, even through the silence.

She smiled.

"It is all yours, sir."

His gaze lit up and a smile shone on his face.

"Please call me Thomas."

Dozens of butterflies suddenly started dancing in the young woman's stomach.

"Only if you call me Gabrielle."

"Gabrielle…"

Could a simple whisper provoke so many sensations? Even more than the previous evening when he put his arms around her, she could feel the effects all over her body, her blood pumping so fast that she was almost dizzy.

"Gabrielle," Thomas went on, unknowingly making the butterflies in her stomach swoop once again, "may I ask you for a favor?"

"I'm listening," she replied, her breath far shorter than the situation warranted.

"Would you read to me, if only for a few minutes?"

"I would be glad to, Thomas. For as long as you wish."

Chapter 11
Alexandra

Castle of Ferté-Chandeniers

Present day

"You again? Hell, is there no way to be rid of you?"

Such were the kind and thoughtful words that the lord and master of the castle of Ferté-Chandeniers greeted me with when I rang the next morning, after spending the night pondering Marine's revelations.

My ancestor, heir to the castle? Me, a descendant of the last baron de Saint-Armand? An aristocrat, with a title and all? I couldn't believe it.

The discovery raised a thousand questions. Why didn't Thomas bear the Saint-Armand name in the few documents I had found? Where had the name he used, D'Arcy, come from? Did Éric Lagnel know Thomas was the son of the baron? Had he deliberately hidden the truth from me in order to be rid of me sooner?

In the end, after a short night's sleep I had decided to visit Mr. Sarcasm again and bully him into letting me have access to his father's files.

Clearly, it was going to be no easy task.

"And you," Éric Lagnel added as he glared at his dog, "are a damn traitor."

As though he understood, Max let his head hang even as he pressed against my legs. Unlike his master, he had been so happy to see me that he had immediately thrown his forty-odd kilos at me, nearly knocking me off my feet.

I almost wasn't scared, this time. I'd revisited my first impressions after our initial meeting. In spite of his size, he was a truly adorable and loving dog, who only wanted everybody to play with him and pet him. I scratched him behind the ears and turned to face his master.

Hammer in hand, he glared daggers at me.

"Oh, for goodness' sake, you don't have to be that hostile, I haven't done anything to you!" I glared back.

"What do you want now?"

Straight to the point, as ever. All right, I could work with that.

"I spoke with Marine yesterday. Your cousin."

"Yeah? And?"

"She told me your father had put together some files about the castle and my ancestor was in them."

"Yeah."

"So when I told you about him yesterday, you knew Thomas was the son of Victor de Saint-Armand?"

For a second my question seemed to put him on the spot. He raised a nervous hand to the back of his neck.

"I did," he said unwillingly. "I recognized the name."

He turned back to his work as if nothing had happened and resumed banging on his nail with renewed energy, pointedly ignoring me.

"Why didn't you tell me?" I raised my voice to cover the sound of the hammer.

Had he been afraid I would take the castle from him? There was no need for that. I had no intention to claim the Ferté-Chandeniers estate as my rightful inheritance. I didn't have the means to anyway.

But I would never be able to convince him if he wouldn't listen.

No matter, I was far from done.

I deliberately set my handbag in front of him on the wooden plank he was banging on as though his life depended upon it.

"Are you crazy? That's dangerous!" he roared as he stopped immediately.

Maybe, but at least I had his attention.

Furious, Éric Lagnel drew himself up to his full height and gave me a dirty look.

"What is your problem?"

Both feet planted firmly on the ground, determined to defend my position, I looked him straight in the eye.

"Why didn't you tell me you that recognized my ancestor's name and that your father had information on him?"

It wasn't easy keeping a confident posture when I had to crane my neck to look him in the face, but I wasn't going to let that stop me.

"Oh, sorry, princess, I didn't know I had to answer to you," he mocked.

"I'd like to know more."

"You're six months late. My father's dead," he replied bitterly.

I watched him silently for a few seconds.

"Marine told me. I'm very sorry," I murmured gently.

My words seem to unsettle him.

"It's just the way it is. I told you. Life isn't a fairy tale."

"Would you let me look through your father's files? Please? It's very important to me."

His blue eyes skewered me. "Are you going to try and take the castle from me, claiming it's your inheritance?" he asked.

At least he didn't beat around the bush.

"No. I have no intention to. I can't even afford a house, let alone a castle."

"Then why are you doing this? Why do you insist so much?"

I could have tried to beat him at his own game by telling him it was none of his business. But it would have been petty, and I didn't want to start another verbal spar.

After what Marine had told me about his parents' deaths, I was starting to understand why he defended his property so aggressively; it had been his parents'. It was an unwieldly and unusual inheritance, but it was his. Maybe it was the only thing he had left of them. And given the pressure he probably had to withstand from investors, I had to admit that if I were in his shoes I too would probably have shot on sight anybody coming too close to my property.

I decided to be honest. Completely honest. I'd show him I had nothing to hide. I took a deep breath and plunged ahead.

"I wasn't lying yesterday," I began. "I just want to know where I come from. Who my ancestors were. I need to… To know who I am."

Éric Lagnel's inscrutable gaze stayed glued to me for one long moment, and I stared right back, even as I suddenly felt extremely vulnerable.

I had told no one else what I had just admitted to him. Not even Bea or Spencer.

I had realized it gradually. As I dug into my past, the hunt for Gabrielle had become a more and more important part of my life until I understood that as I searched for my ancestor, it was really myself I was looking for.

The truth was that, somewhere along the road, I felt like I had lost my way. And I didn't know where. I felt I was living a life empty of meaning, empty of everything. I spent all my time waiting for someone or something. For Spencer. Everybody around me seemed to be living life to the fullest, racing about between two flights or two parties, but I spent my evenings and weekends sketching and watching TV. I sat on my couch and dreamed of adventures I would never have, imagined feelings and emotions I would never experience. I lived inside my mind more than I did in the real world. And the longer this went on, the less I could bear it. I couldn't take it. I was suffocating. The picture had arrived at just the right time, the perfect distraction. At first it had only been a way to fulfill my curiosity, to fill in the emptiness inside. But it had come to have a symbolic importance to me—once I would finish tracing back my family tree, once I would have gone as far back as I could, I would know who I was. I was sure of it.

"Please," I begged.

Éric Lagnel stared at me a while longer, and I thought I saw something flicker in his eyes. For a moment I thought he would say yes, that he had realized I wasn't the castle thief he thought I was, even though I was an American. But the silence stretched on and still he did not reply. With a heavy heart, I finally threw in the towel.

I shook my head and sighed bitterly.

"Forget about it. I should have known you wouldn't want to. I shouldn't have come. Goodbye and good luck with your castle. I hope you find a way to save it."

I was already trudging away when his voice rose behind my back.

"Hold on. You can have a look."

Surprised, I turned around and firmly held back the hope rising in my chest.

"You mean you'll let me look through your father's files?"

"Yes."

YES!

"Follow me," he added, putting his hammer down on the table and striding off toward the building behind us. "And watch where you're going with those sandals. There could be nails lying around and I don't want to have to take you to the hospital with a hole in your foot."

"Thank you for your concern," I retorted as I followed suit, "but I mastered the fine art of walking a few years back. I think I'll manage, no need to worry about me."

"You are infuriating."

"Thank you, I get that pretty often."

Even though I was several paces behind him, I could hear him sigh in frustration.

I didn't even try to hide my smile.

I followed him into the former stables and looked discreetly around. It was surprisingly modern for such an old building: naked stone, an open floor plan, bright and airy, a bedroom mezzanine, renovated secondhand furniture that looked suspiciously like the ones at the inn—I was ready to bet Marine had had a hand in that. At the far end of the room, frosted glass walls closed a space off—probably the bathroom—while letting the light through.

An American counter separated the state-of-the-art kitchen, fully equipped, from the rest of the room. He led me there.

"Wait for me here."

"Sir, yes, sir!" I saluted.

The look he gave me could have peeled paint off the walls. I gave him my sunniest smile in reply. He shook his head and went up to the mezzanine.

"What are you doing in here exactly? Everything seems pretty much perfect," I asked, curious.

"Nothing really visible." I could hear him pulling a drawer open and extracting documents from it. "Improving the insulation. Cutting in new windows, adding a wood-burner, some solar panels on the roof. I want to save on energy."

"Oh, I see."

He came back down the stairs, a thick folder in his hands, and joined me.

"My...my father wanted to make this place into a private chalet," he confided unexpectedly. "A kind of extension to Marine's inn."

I knew it! I could tell this place had Marine's touch to it.

"What a great idea. But wasn't he afraid people would go up to the castle? You said yesterday it was dangerous."

"It is. But my father was an optimist. He was convinced that in the long term, he'd be able to get the castle classified and restored. He hoped he could make it into a luxury hotel, to host seminars and conferences, auctions and weddings. Or maybe a museum, or a writing retreat. In fact, it didn't matter to him—he just wanted to breathe life back into it, in any way he could. But he needed money for that, so he had the idea of making the stables into a luxury chalet, hoping he'd get enough income that way to start restoring the castle. He was almost done with the work when he passed away."

Which explained the top-notch, modern setup.

I couldn't help but wonder if it was a viable project. Despite the lengthy research I had done last night, I knew very little about castle restoration, but I didn't think a chalet would generate enough money to fund such a vast project.

I kept my doubts to myself. It wasn't any of my business, after all.

"My father was a dreamer," Éric Lagnel added, probably reading my thoughts. "He didn't always have his feet on the ground. Here's the file." He set it down on the counter in front of me. "This is all I have."

One thing was for sure, I thought as I eyed the thickness of the folder, Marc Lagnel had either been luckier or more efficient than I had. His file was four or five times larger than mine. Then again, not everything it contained was about my ancestors, but I was certainly going to find something that would help me uncover more information about the Saint-Armand family.

A smile stretched my lips as I mentally rubbed my hands. I could tell I was going to enjoy paging through the contents. Without further ado, I pulled my own research and my notebook from my handbag.

"I'll be outside if you want any questions answered," Éric Lagnel told me.

"Yes, thank you," I replied distractedly. I opened the folder and took out the first document, a photocopy of a newspaper article detailing the causes of the fire in February 1900. "I'll call if I need you."

I vaguely felt his perplexed look on me as I started reading the article. Then I heard him sigh, mutter something I didn't catch and, from the corner of my eye, I saw him shake his head as he exited the room.

I was alone with the history of the castle of Ferté-Chandeniers.

* * * *

Marine had not been exaggerating when she said her uncle had done a historian's job. There were all types of documents, sorted in a very organized manner: several copies of articles from the local newspaper; bibliographies; notes scrawled in an untidy, illegible hand; timelines, including one detailing the construction, destruction, reconstruction and re-destruction of the castle; building plans, some from the original construction, some more recent from the reconstruction in 1812, after the French Revolution. There was also a map of the region on which the estate was clearly marked out. I found a handful of old postcards as well as a sheaf of loose papers with lists of names and phone numbers, and pre-filled-in official forms—bank files, a registration form for the Historical Monuments with a few lines highlighted.

And in the midst of these dozens—no, hundreds—of pages, I found what I was looking for. Birth certificates. On the very top of the pile was one Thomas Victor Andrew Leroy de Saint-Armand. Also known as Thomas D'Arcy. *My* Thomas D'Arcy.

Marc Lagnel had just saved me an entire afternoon in the Chandeniers register of births.

Only barely keeping myself from jumping about in excitement, I examined it. The section pertaining to his mother was fairly straightforward—one Adaline D'Arcy Leroy de Saint-Armand, born in Plymouth, England, in 1850 and died in Chandeniers in 1880. The father's, however, was a challenge to any genealogist. The name of Victor Edgar François Leroy de Saint-Armand, born in Chandeniers in 1845 and died there in 1899, had been crossed through three times and replaced by Andrew D'Arcy, born in Plymouth, England, in 1845 and died in Amiens, France, in 1916. Just like Thomas's full name had been scratched out and replaced with D'Arcy.

I sighed over what I had just discovered, puzzled. What did that mean? Why had Thomas's name changed? The most logical explanation would be that Thomas had been adopted by this Andrew D'Arcy, but if that was indeed the case, when did the adoption take place? After his father's death...or before? Did Victor abjure his son, one way or another? Is it even possible for a father to renounce his paternity? And if that wasn't the case, if Thomas was adopted after Victor's death and thus well into his adulthood...why? And who was this Andrew, actually? An uncle? Or someone else? He probably came from his mother's side of the family, that much I could guess from his name and his date and place of birth... but that was pretty much the only question I could answer from the many ones this record gave rise to.

I skimmed the other birth certificates, but they didn't bring any clarity, as none of them pertained to the D'Arcy branch. I went through the rest of the folder in vain, until I found a loose leaf, stuck between two photocopies. At first sight it only held a handwritten note, just as illegible as the other, and I probably would have put it down again without a thought if I hadn't been able to make out one name.

Villeneuve.

I immediately dropped everything in favor of this new development. I managed to decipher a few words—it seemed to mention a bookstore, whose owner was a Maurice Villeneuve. It was apparently called *Les livres d'Héloïse*. But other than that, I could make neither heads nor tails of Marc Lagnel's handwriting. Impulsively, I rose to find his son.

I found him focused on sanding a wooden plank.

"Could you help me with something?"

He looked up, slightly startled, as though he had forgotten I was there. "What?"

"I can't read this," I explained, handing over the paper.

Wordlessly, he held it up and examined it.

"From what I can make out, the Maurice Villeneuve it mentions owned a bookstore in Angers."

I nodded to show I had understood as much, and he went on:

"Apparently, my father got in touch with a Xavier Bourgeois, the current owner of the bookstore, because he thought he might have some interesting documents."

"What makes you think so?"

"He wrote '*Journal G.*' here in the margins."

G.? As in Gabrielle?

"'*Journal*'? What kind of journal?" I immediately wanted to know. "Are we talking newspaper journal, or diary journal?"

And there I was, getting carried away again. Could there be a diary that had belonged to my ancestor? Oh God! If there was, I just had to find it.

"He doesn't say, but I suppose it must be a diary; otherwise, I don't see why he'd mention it," Éric Lagnel remarked, ever the pragmatist.

"You're right. Oh my God! Your father found Gabrielle's diary!"

"You can't be certain. He put a question mark beside it."

"Wow, you are such a killjoy!"

"It's pronounced 'realist,' princess."

"Please don't call me princess. My name is Alexandra."

He blinked.

"You know, I didn't even know your name until now."

"What do you mean? It can't be!"

"It most certainly can. You never introduced yourself."

"No, I… Oh, that's right, you didn't leave me any time. You just attacked me right away."

I held out a hand.

"Hello, I'm Alexandra Dawson."

An amused smirk flickered on his lips, disappearing so fast I wondered if I had imagined it. His gaze on mine, he grasped my hand and shook it. His palm was rough and calloused, his grip strong and warm. A shiver ran over me.

"Éric Lagnel," he said, his eyes never leaving me.

He released my hand, and for an instant I felt…strange. I jammed my hand into my pocket to give myself something to do with it, and I looked back at the paper.

"So, uh, did your father say anything else? On the paper?" I mumbled.

His gaze lingered a little longer over me before it went back to the notes.

"Nothing much. There's a phone number; I imagine it's the bookstore's."

"Hmm. Okay. I'll call, then. Just to be sure."

I plunged back inside, my heart beating slightly faster than usual.

* * * *

"So?" Éric Lagnel asked me when I hung up a few minutes later.

Surprised, I glanced up. Nonchalantly leaning against the doorjamb, he looked at me blandly.

"I hadn't realized you were there."

"I was curious. So?"

"So, I spoke to an employee, not to Mr. Bourgeois. He couldn't tell me much. He said the bookstore was opened in 1876 by Maurice Villeneuve. Probably either Gabrielle's father or an uncle. I won't know until I find her birth certificate. And he confirmed that Xavier Bourgeois does have several historical documents dating back to the bookstore's foundation, but he didn't know anything more. 'I'm new, you see, and Mr. Bourgeois isn't here today!'" I repeated, mimicking the young man's nasal voice.

Éric Lagnel chuckled, and so did I.

"In any case, I asked when I could speak to M. Bourgeois, after telling him who I was, so he wouldn't think I was a trespasser or a busybody and summarily throw me out...."

I gave Éric Lagnel a pointed look. He raised an eyebrow, but I didn't give him time to interrupt.

"He told me Mr. Bourgeois would be there on Monday, and then he would be traveling and the bookstore would be closed for three weeks starting Tuesday evening. Which means there is only one thing I can do."

"What would that be?"

"Go to Angers first thing Monday morning."

I smiled teasingly.

"Want to come with me?"

"Let me think about it...no."

Chapter 12
Gabrielle

Castle of Ferté-Chandeniers

November 1899

The next morning, after a very brief night's sleep and a frugal breakfast by her father's bedside, Gabrielle gratefully accepted Hélène's offer to stay by Maurice's side. She was impatient to return to the library. Her father had approved her mission—carry out the library inventory until his health improved.

She hummed on her way there, retracing the previous night's steps up and down the galleries. The memory of the evening—or rather, the night, she thought with a blush—still lingered in her mind...and in her body.

She had read for a long time after Mr. D'Arcy—Thomas—had asked her to. For obvious reasons, she had chosen *Jane Eyre*. She had cracked the book open and flipped pages toward the middle, choosing her favorite passage, and in her lilting voice had narrated the unusual yet moving story of these two solitary souls brought together by fate. Once she had fallen silent, he had stared deep into the embers of the fireplace and asked her, "Do you think Jane was right?"

"What about?"

He'd shifted his attention to her.

"Do you think beauty is truly in the eye of the beholder? Do you think one can really love...a monster?"

"A monster? What do you mean?"

"People who have a repellent appearance, who are misshapen. People who make others recoil in horror. Monsters."

For the second time that evening, the way in which he had intoned these words had deeply upset Gabrielle. She had wondered whether he really saw himself as such—as a hideous man. As a monster.

"Of course she was right! I believe with all my heart that each and every one of us deserves to be loved!" Her fervor had taken even herself aback. "I believe that we do not love faces, but what is behind. Take Jane, for example." She'd waved the book. "She does not fall in love with Edward's looks. She falls in love with him because she can see beyond appearances. She sees his heart, and his soul, and she recognizes that they mirror her own. She sees him as the one who completes her, who is the light to her darkness and the darkness to her light, both her opposite and her equal. She sees him as he is, with no adornments. She sees his flaws, his imperfections, and only loves him more. He might be imperfect, but he is perfect for her. Because in the end, there are more things that they share than there are that drive them apart. They may not be from the same world, he may be rich and she poor, he may be someone while she is no one, but beyond that, they are the same. Soul mates. Better still, they are one soul. In *Wuthering Heights*, Catherine declares that she *is* Heathcliff, because she loves him so that she can no longer tell the difference between herself and him. It is the same for Jane. She *is* Edward. And…is that not what love is? Accepting the other unconditionally, wholly, both the good and the bad, and wanting the same in return?"

She'd broken off, cheeks pink, aware that once again she had let herself be carried away by her romantic ideals. One day, she would learn to restrain herself.

One day.

"My apologies. I did not mean to sound so passionate. You really should not raise such topics with me," she had added self-deprecatingly. "You would be well within your rights to call me unhinged and far too romantic for my own good. You would not be the first."

"I would never say such a thing."

She had glanced down then back up again.

"I know," she had said softly. "But to answer your question… Yes, I believe that even those who think they are monsters can be beautiful and deserving of love to the right person."

Thomas had nodded silently, a gleam in his eyes. The strange swooping feeling in Gabrielle's stomach had come roaring back and had refused to leave—neither when they had talked for hours, nor when he had walked her back to her room, their hands brushing against each other.

* * * *

When she reached the library, Gabrielle paused in front of the door. She had not felt so feverishly excited in a very long time. With a deep sigh, she gripped the door handle and pushed the heavy panel.

In the daylight, bathed in sunlight pouring through the vast windows, the library seemed even more impressive than it had been a few hours ago. Once again, Gabrielle walked in and spun on the spot, unleashing her enthusiasm, laughing wholeheartedly.

This place was simply perfect.

And for a time, it was hers and hers alone.

She decided that the first thing to do was to explore every nook and cranny.

Thus, she proceeded to do so. She leafed through botanic and medicine books, grimacing at some of the images. She examined a bestiary of fantastical creatures, each more astounding than the last. She read her way through a few of Perrault's fairy tales that she hadn't opened in years. She recited Shakespeare monologues, Baudelaire poems, Ronsard sonnets....

Once her curiosity was, if not sated, at least quenched a little, she moved toward the shelf where Maurice had left off and took down the next books. And so, stepping lightly with her arms loaded with culture, she took her father's chair in front of the huge oak desk, opened the first book in the pile, a gorgeous ornithology study, and went to work.

Quietly and utterly happy.

* * * *

She had been happily doing inventory for nearly two hours when there was a knock on the door and Thomas came in. Gabrielle's lips stretched into a smile of their own volition, and her heart leapt in her chest.

With as much composure as she could gather, Gabrielle rose to her feet and greeted him.

"I see you found the library again without any help," he remarked.

"I did. But have no fear. I packed supplies in case I became lost." She affected utter seriousness. "And I left a trail of small white pebbles behind me. Did you not see them?"

He shook his head. "I must have been distracted."

"Were you? And what could distract you so?" she teased, immediately falling back on the banter they had exchanged the previous eve.

"I was thinking of what I am about to tell you." He smiled imperceptibly. "I have something to show you. I think you will enjoy it."

"Did you meet a friendly ghost?"

"No. Don't try to guess; I will say no more," he added with a mischievous smile when she opened her mouth. "You shall have to follow me and see for yourself."

It was freezing outside.

Gabrielle shivered and hugged herself in a poor attempt at warming herself up, following behind her host.

Seeing her tremble, Thomas took off his coat and laid it over her shoulders.

"Put this on. It will keep you warm."

"Thank you." She slid her arms into the sleeves. "I should have taken my shawl when I left the library."

She reflexively turned the collar up and hunched into the coat. Every centimeter held Thomas's smell, the heat of his body. She closed her eyes for a second, discreetly breathing it in. It almost felt as though she was in his arms again.

"Are you warm enough, Gabrielle? Do you want to return inside?"

She opened her eyes immediately, meeting Thomas's gaze under his frown.

"No, no, I'm perfectly fine." She turned the collar even further up to hide her pink cheeks. "Lead the way."

Side by side, they crossed the inner courtyard, the bridge over the frozen moat, and walked up the snowy path to a small cluster of trees. There, Gabrielle turned, curious to see the castle from the outside.

Her breath caught in her throat.

Covered in snow, the castle rose in all its magnificence against the pale blue sky. It was a dream vision. A painting by one of the great masters. A picture straight from the fairy tales her parents used to read to her as a child.

"It's beautiful," she breathed, awestruck. "Absolutely beautiful."

Realizing she had stopped, Thomas turned back and came to stand behind her, his presence enveloping her even more surely than his coat did. Her senses suddenly on alert, Gabrielle could feel Thomas's breath on her hair, his body against hers. And she had to check herself not to lean back against him.

Everything around was calm and quiet. She could almost hear their hearts beating.

She felt good in that moment, so good. Her father's health was improving, she literally had her hands on a collection of amazing books, she had met some exceptional people and, for a little longer at least, she lived in what had to be the most beautiful place on earth.

She breathed in deeply, savoring the moment, committing every rock, every tree, every snowflake to memory so she would always recall it when she had to leave this place and return to her everyday life.

The idea cast a shadow on this gorgeous day, and she immediately put it aside.

That day had not come yet.

She breathed in again, focusing on the crisp, cold sensation in her lungs, on Thomas's presence behind her.

"Doesn't this make you want to stay?" she asked.

He was silent for a few seconds.

"Yes, but no," he finally replied.

"Hmmm. It's a shame but...I understand."

"Really?"

Gabrielle nodded gently.

"I don't know what estranged you from your father, but for you to leave for England, it must have been serious. Stones and paintings, precious though they may be, cannot be enough to forget what has harmed you."

She turned to him. The light in his eyes told her she had struck true and that he suffered greatly.

"You are very discerning," he murmured.

He gazed at her in consideration for a second, wordlessly. Then he changed the subject so fast she almost reeled in shock.

"Shall I show you my surprise?"

Chapter 13
Alexandra

Chandeniers-sur-Vienne

Present day

The Chandeniers cemetery was surprisingly large for a town of this size. Lined with massive trees that were probably at least a hundred years old, it was a peaceful place that seemed to stand outside of time. Solemn silence reigned, barely disturbed by my footsteps on the gravel and leaves rustling in the wind.

I had woken with the sudden idea of visiting my ancestors' burial vault. Probably from spending too much time digging through the birth register of the barons de Saint-Armand.

The previous day, after leaving Éric's house—or after he more or less kicked me out, same thing—I had returned to the inn, where I had spent part of the afternoon working on my genealogy, trying to fill in the blanks with the information from Marc Lagnel's files. Very reluctantly, Éric had agreed to loan me the precious documents as long as I promised that I would watch over them like a hawk. I had sworn, hand over heart, that they would not leave the inn. I'd even suggested he could ask Marine to supervise if it comforted him. He'd grunted that there was no need, but the look on his face kind of undermined his words.

So I'd gone to work in the inn's garden, laptop in front of me and documents spread all over the table, with a pitcher of iced tea beside me, courtesy of Marine. I had plunged into the past, carefully entering the names of the various barons de Saint-Armand into my family tree.

Once done, I had returned to the note I'd found that morning and leaned back into my chair thoughtfully. Now that Éric had "translated" his father's handwriting it was easier to decipher. I'd reread it, especially the part about the journal. Did it really exist or was it just a hypothesis? Did "G." mean Gabrielle? Was Maurice her father?

There was a way to check, but it meant forgoing the pleasure of digging through the archives in person, a small treat I had been saving for my visit in Angers. I had hesitated—for thirty seconds at least. Then I had given in to my curiosity and looked up the birth register on the town's website.

After very, *very* long minutes of research on a several-hundred-page PDF written in chicken scratch, I had finally located Gabrielle's birth certificate, which immediately confirmed my suspicions—Maurice Villeneuve was indeed her father. I had almost jumped for joy right there in my chair. I had only barely held back from driving straight to Angers, even if I had to sit in front of the bookstore until Mr. Bourgeois arrived.

Restraining my impatience with great difficulty, I'd screenshot the document and written down the reference and page number, determined to retrieve a copy on Monday after I visited the bookstore.

I had closed my laptop, mind reeling. I felt jittery and yet I knew that I was probably building my hopes up. The diary might not even exist, and I was especially afraid that it might have been written before Gabrielle met Thomas, in which case it would hold no information about him. Even if I was very interested in knowing more about my ancestor—she had been, after all, the entire reason my search had begun—I was growing ever more curious about the mysterious Thomas D'Arcy every time I uncovered a new section of his life.

Who was he? What lurked behind the scratches and blots on his birth certificate?

Marine, returning from a date, had put an end to my wonderings. Impatient to share my findings, I'd invited her to sit down with me. She'd eagerly accepted and we'd spent the rest of the evening together, laughing and chatting away. We'd spent a fair bit of time talking about my ancestors, obviously, and about the hypothetical diary—she told me Marc Lagnel had never mentioned it to her—but also about local art and history. I'd asked about the celebration that was to take place next week, which had led to her briefing me about the history of Chandeniers. The town had been built a thousand years earlier, at the same time as the castle, by a rich lord, and it had grown over time from a hunting lodge to the charming little town it was today.

As we had grown pleasantly tired, she'd told me, in a voice full of nostalgia and longing, how Éric's father had come to own the castle.

It was both a tragic and romantic story, one that had begun many years ago when Marc Lagnel had met Laura, Marine's aunt.

Laura had always had a passion for the Chandeniers castle. And Marc had quickly come to have a passion for Laura. So one August night with shooting stars streaking through the sky, Marc had asked for Laura's hand in the ruins of the castle.

Laura gave it to him, and they lived happily for many years after...until one winter night, a few years after Éric's birth, their car had skidded over a patch of black ice. When Marc woke a couple of days later, he was a widower and Éric had lost his mother.

Years had passed, and Marc had begun to gamble at the lottery every week. Laura had loved gambling, so he'd taken up her favorite number combination—their birth months and years, their wedding date, the birthdate of their son Éric. And one day the incredible had happened—he'd won the jackpot. He'd used the money to buy the castle and stop investors from making it into a holiday resort. And he'd started to do anything he could to save it. He'd pieced together the castle's history with some help from Marine and a few other people. Unfortunately, he'd passed away before he could accomplish his mission, leaving his son with the heavy task of saving the castle.

"And we're not even close to finding a way yet," Marine had admitted unhappily. "Éric enrolled in Doctors Without Borders a long time ago—he's very good with children, you know, he's a great pediatrician"—I'd raised an incredulous brow—"so he's rarely ever here, and all the lottery money got swallowed up by taxes and inheritance. There's almost nothing left."

I'd stayed quiet for a time, taking in all that Marine had just told me. Sadness had washed over me, making me rail quietly against the tragedy and unfairness of life. *Poor Éric,* I'd thought.

But before I could say anything, Marine had changed topics abruptly, steering the conversation toward lighter subjects. The evening had resumed its pleasant course, full of laughter and banter.

But deep inside, I kept thinking of Marc, Laura and Éric, and my heart was heavy on behalf of these people I didn't know.

Voices next to me brought me back to the present. A family was laying a bouquet on a tiny grave a few steps away. My heart clenched when I saw the dates. Barely two years apart.

I walked away as quietly as I could, unwilling to disturb them. I looked around for the Saint-Armand family vault. It wasn't difficult to find—given its size, it was rather a challenge to miss it.

It was a white stone building, a sort of small square tower. The Gothic architecture echoed that of the castle.

I automatically flipped my sketchbook open and started to draw, detailing the sculptures on the mausoleum, the moss creeping on the walls, nature slowly asserting its rights over the place. And as my hand flew over the paper I let my mind wander to my ancestors, the castle and Éric.

A part of me still couldn't wrap my mind around the fact that I was descended from French aristocrats. Aristocrats who had owned a real castle, had experienced wars, balls and French History with a capital *H*. It was incredible, and not at all the kind of thing that usually happened to me. And yet it had. I had the proof right here in front of my eyes and in the thick file waiting back at the inn.

I wasn't sure yet what it meant to me, or even if it was going to change anything about my life. But somehow, I had the feeling that this discovery gave my life a new value. As though all of a sudden I deserved my place on earth because I had famous ancestors.

A familiar voice and bark rose from a few alleys over, bursting my bubble. I looked up to see Éric and his dog Max stop in front of a gravestone. Éric crouched down, broad shoulders hunched under an invisible weight, and remained there before what I guessed was his father's grave.

His shoulders bent lower and lower, his head hung down and the air seemed to fill with sadness. In this instant, the emotion emanating from him was so pure, so raw and intense that my throat tightened. My conversation with Marine came rushing back, and the pang I had felt upon hearing his story ran through me again.

Instinctively, I flipped to a blank page in my sketchbook and drew the moment—his lowered head, the curve of his shoulders, his messy hair, his hand on the dog's head as though to draw comfort.... With every line, my heart clenched tighter, as though I absorbed part of his emotion.

Éric brushed a hand over his face. I knew I should have looked away, but I couldn't. I was...hypnotized. My fingers had paused, pencil poised over the paper, and I had almost stopped breathing. The emotion was that strong.

But the moment suddenly shattered as Éric got to his feet and walked straight toward me, signaling for Max to follow.

Panic rose in me. I suddenly felt guilty for spying on him, albeit unintentionally. I had an inkling he would not appreciate being caught in a moment of weakness. So, of course, instead of doing what any normal

and sane person would do—move one step to the left and stand in front
of the Saint-Armand mausoleum—I did the only thing that could possibly
look even more suspicious than staring at him. I dove behind the nearest
gravestone and hid there.

Raging at my own stupidity, I folded my meter fifty-one body behind
the gravestone into the smallest pretzel I could and hugged my sketchbook.
I crossed my fingers, hoping he would walk straight by.

My plan would have been perfect, if not for Max's reliable nose. Ideal
hiding spot or not, the dog soon sniffed me out and alerted everyone within
a range of 150 kilometers to my presence, leaping at me with his usual
enthusiasm. If my back hadn't been against the gravestone, he probably
would have knocked me over.

And what had to happen, happened. Éric appeared behind his dog
and found me unsuccessfully fending off Max's affectionate attack. The
surprise on his face quickly gave way to suspicion.

"I don't believe it! Were you *spying* on me?"

Pushing Max back, I stood up and tried to gather the tattered remains of
my dignity under his master's hostile eye. Éric, of course, made no move to
help me. I smoothed my white blouse, now with added pawprints, tugged
at my A-line flower skirt and met his gaze dead on.

He had the red eyes of someone who hadn't slept in three weeks, or
who had recently cried. There was an immense world-weariness in his
blue gaze. Mindful of the emotions he was probably trying to mask behind
his aggressiveness, I choked back the withering comeback rising in me.
Instead, I summoned my most radiant smile and declared with just a touch
of mischievousness:

"Why, good morning to you too, Mr. Lagnel! How do you do? What
a lovely day, isn't it? Such perfect weather! Ideal for drawing," I added,
brandishing my sketchbook.

I kept it shut, naturally. I could only imagine his reaction if he saw what
I had just been sketching.

"Oh. You...came to draw?" He seemed slightly embarrassed.

"I came to visit my ancestor's graves, actually," I explained. "And I took
the opportunity to sketch a little. I love drawing; it's my hobby."

"I thought genealogy was your hobby?"

"That too. But I can't remember a time when I didn't draw, whereas I can
very much remember having a life before getting interested in genealogy.
It's fascinating, but boy is it time consuming."

"I can guess."

"But really, you can't imagine how much you can discover when you start looking up your past."

I had somehow become a real chatterbox and couldn't stop.

"Look at me, for instance. I never would have guessed that my ancestors were noblemen when I started researching! Have you never wanted to find out who you descended from?"

"No. I'd rather focus on the present and future. You can't change the past."

"But studying the past is the only way to understand the present and avoid making the same mistakes all over again," I insisted.

"I don't know what kind of world you live in, princess, but I think very few people give a damn about the past, and most are rushing to make the same mistakes all over again, the same people forgotten, the same sins committed. This world is corrupt, and rotten from the inside. It's every man for himself, and to hell with the others!"

I didn't know how to answer such a rant. It gave me a glimpse into how dark his view of life was. Was this man unable to see any form of kindness around him? He appeared to carry the weight of the world on his shoulders.

"Was it Africa that made you this cynical?" I couldn't help asking.

"Who told you I went to Africa?"

"Marine did."

"Marine should know when to keep her mouth shut."

"It must have been an amazing experience."

"It was an eye-opener for sure."

"I can imagine."

"No, you can't. Nobody can imagine it, and that's the problem. It's beyond imagining."

Silence fell, and I wondered how we had drifted from talking about my drawings to poverty in Africa. The air around us was oppressive.

"I'm sorry." Éric sighed. "I'm a little on edge."

"It's okay. I know things are hard for you right now."

"That's no reason to snap at you."

He sighed again.

We started walking toward the gate. Heedless of the respect due to the dead, Max bounded merrily around us. I caught sight of a stick by the side of the alley and picked it up, waving it at Max then throwing it away.

"You shouldn't have done that," Éric commented.

"Why? Are you going to tell me playing isn't allowed in graveyards?"

"It probably isn't. But I actually meant that Max will never leave you alone now."

"That's all right, I don't have anything planned after this outing."

"I do."

I glanced sideways at him, eyebrows raised.

"Oh I'm sorry, I forgot you had a busy schedule," I teased, grabbing the stick Max had just returned to me.

"I actually have an appointment set up." I turned my attention back to Éric. "I'm meeting with an architect specializing in restoring ancient buildings. For the castle."

"I thought you had given up?" I threw the stick again, and Max ran to fetch it with endless enthusiasm.

"The meeting was set up a long time ago, so I didn't cancel it. Don't expect any miracles, though. I'll never find the funds to restore the castle without help. He might have some suggestions to raise money, but I'm under no illusions."

"I'm sure there are solutions."

He shrugged.

"We'll see."

We'd reached the cemetery gates. I threw the stick one last time, and Max galloped away as fast as he had the previous times.

"How did you come?" I asked. I couldn't see any other car.

"I rode my bike." He jerked his head toward a bicycle rack next to the wall.

"What about Max? Did he ride in the little pink basket in front?" I joked, pointing to a cute little-girl bike.

"Very funny. He runs beside me, he needs the exercise. There's a shortcut through the forest not far away. We can avoid the road and there's no risk of him being run over by a car."

"I see."

"What about y—"

I never knew what he wanted to ask me, because just then, Max came straight at me, stick in his mouth, and rammed right into me, knocking me clear off my feet. Pain spiked through my ankle as I fell flat on my back in the gravel.

"*Ouch! Oh fudge, that hurts!*" I swore between gritted teeth, instinctively reverting to English.

"Down, Max!" Éric growled. "You know you're not allowed to jump at people like that!" He rushed toward me. "Are you all right?" he asked, extending a hand.

I grasped it and pulled myself up.

"I think I'll live."

But the instant I shifted my weight onto my foot, the pain in my ankle blazed up my leg. I dropped back down heavily, grimacing.

"*Ouch!*" I moaned.

I barely had time to look up before Éric knelt in front of me.

"Let me see," he ordered, summarily taking hold of my foot.

"Don't worry, it's just a sprain," I assured him.

"So you're a doctor too?" He raised an eyebrow, examining my foot.

His hands were startlingly gentle as he slowly rotated my foot, checking my reactions. In spite of myself, feeling his hands on my skin made my heart race and my cheeks flush. Marine's words came back to me—"*He's very good with children.*" I'd been skeptical, but I no longer had any trouble imagining it.

"You sprained it," he announced, releasing my foot. "You need to bandage it and keep your weight off it for a while. I can prescribe painkillers if you want some."

"It's okay, I'll be fine. But I'll have to put some weight on it. I'm going to Angers tomorrow, remember?"

"Out of the question. You have to let your ankle rest."

"It's nonnegotiable. Tomorrow's the only day I can go to the bookstore before it closes."

"You can't drive with your left ankle sprained," he protested.

"I'll figure something out."

"You're really stubborn, you know that?"

"It's pronounced 'determined,' mister," I told him.

He blinked as he processed the callback to our last conversation, and then he almost smiled.

"You're going to make it worse if you walk on it."

"I told you, I'll figure something out."

"Oh, hell."

He closed his eyes and shook his head, rising to his feet and lifting me in his arms.

"What are you doing?"

"Helping you onto the bench. I think you'll be more comfortable there than on the ground."

"Thank you," I mumbled ungraciously.

"Wait here. I'll take Max back to the castle and return for you."

"Don't bother. I can find my own way back."

"How did you get here?"

"On foot." I grimaced.

It had seemed like such a good idea earlier. The cemetery was thirty minutes' walk from the inn, and I'd thought it would be a pleasant stroll along the Vienne River. I'd planned to buy lunch on the way back and have a picnic by the riverside.

The idea of walking back was no longer quite so appealing. Yet I got to my feet and bravely limped a few steps under Éric's sarcastic gaze, trying not to wince at the pain.

I was going to need all day to get back at that rate.

"Come on, you know you can't walk. Just sit down and wait for me. I'll be back in ten minutes."

I sighed and gave up, sitting back on the bench.

"Come on Max, you've done enough for today. Let's go home!"

He mounted his bike and rode off into the forest.

* * * *

I was sketching again when I heard a low thrum. I didn't pay much attention, focused on my drawing. The sound grew louder and louder, until I looked up to see a big black motorbike stop in front of me. The rider wore a full black bodysuit. He kicked down the stand and turned to me, pulling off his helmet.

My breath caught in my throat, and my heart missed a beat.

Éric.

I can say this about Éric, he filled a motorcycle outfit *very* nicely. He exuded a rugged, almost dangerous aura. Heck, I wasn't expecting him to be so...sexy.

I pulled myself together—more or less—and raised an eyebrow.

"Showing off, Mr. Lagnel?"

"Absolutely not," he retorted, smiling slightly. "I don't own a car. Here, I brought you a helmet." He held out an old-fashioned round helmet. "Hop on. I'm taking you back to the inn."

I limped across the fifty centimeters to the motorbike and fastened the helmet on, grumbling internally. Who the hell looked sexy with this kind of helmet? Clearly not me. Not that I was trying to be, let's be honest, but I did have a little self-esteem and this helmet would make even the most gorgeous model look ridiculous. Or at least it made *me* look ridiculous, as far as I could tell from the amused gleam in Éric's eyes. He'd probably done it on purpose, I realized.

I took the bait. I posed like a pinup girl, pouting and batting my eyelashes at him, determined not to let him get away with it.

"So, Mr. Life-isn't-a-fairy-tale, do I look ridiculous enough?"

"You're stunning. Come on. Do you need help to climb on?" he added, eyeing my skirt.

I fired my most dazzling smile at him, and with a sultry look, lifted my skirt high up on my thighs to straddle the bike as gracefully and provocatively as I could, wrapping my arms around him.

I pushed down a satisfied smile when he swallowed and quickly pulled his helmet back on before kicking the bike into life.

"Hang on, princess, this is going to be a rough ride."

* * * *

When Éric halted in front of the inn some ten minutes later, my heart was still beating wildly.

He hadn't lied about the rough ride. I had been rattled and shaken, and I had no doubt he had done it on purpose. I felt as though I had just stepped off a roller coaster.

And yet I had not felt endangered for even a second. I had never been afraid he would lose control of his ride. I had never doubted him.

I didn't know why he'd decided to put me through the wringer. Maybe out of spite. But the truth was…I had loved every minute of it. For ten glorious minutes, I had felt more alive than ever before. I had only one thing in mind—go for another round as soon as possible.

But I would never admit it to him, of course.

Éric kicked out the stand, leaned the bike against it and pulled off his helmet. To my great surprise, as I did the same, Marine exited the inn holding a pair of crutches.

"Look what I just found!" she called out.

"Perfect," Éric replied.

How did Marine already know about my ankle?

I was so surprised I didn't even protest when Éric took my helmet out of my hands and carried me into the inn. He put me down on a chair next to a table where Marine had spread out a medical kit.

"Éric called me to say you had a little accident with Max," she explained, seeing my surprise. "So I took out my first aid supplies." She smiled.

"You shouldn't have, it's really nothing."

"Maybe not," Éric cut in, "but you still need to take care of it."

He didn't leave me any time to reply, kneeling in front of me to undo the straps of my sandal and bandage my ankle. Again, his hands were both firm and extremely gentle. An uncontrollable shiver ran over me, and I prayed to God he didn't notice.

"You shouldn't move too much," he said as he pinned the end of the bandage. "Be ready at eight a.m. tomorrow. I'll come get you."

"Get me?" I repeated, taken aback.

"You're still going to Angers, aren't you?"

"Yes, but—"

"Then I'm driving you. There's no way you can take the wheel with a sprained ankle. I'll drive your car."

I was about to protest when he added, his voice final: "It's nonnegotiable."

Chapter 14
Gabrielle

Castle of Ferté-Chandeniers

November 1899

"We're here," Thomas announced a few minutes later when they walked into a snowy clearing.

A low gray stone building rose in front of them. She could hear horses whinnying inside.

Gabrielle raised her eyebrows and said, mock seriously: "It's very kind of you to give me the tour of the estate, Mr. D'Arcy, but should I remind you that my father and I do not have a penny to our names with which to buy it?"

"You are in error, Mademoiselle Villeneuve, what I wish to show you is inside the stables."

"I am sure Tornade would be right at home in the middle of our bookstore," she went on, "but I do not think I have the means to ship him back to Angers, either."

"That's not it, either. Come in, you'll see."

"Should I close my eyes again?"

"No need." He smiled.

She followed him toward the building.

"Why is the architecture here so different from the rest of the castle?" she asked.

"This used to be a hunting lodge, back when the first castle was built. It was made into a stable in the early eighteenth century. It's all that is left of that period, since the castle was destroyed during the Revolution. Just this and a vast barn a few kilometers away."

"This is the second time you mentioned the castle being destroyed. What happened?"

"Nothing extraordinary for the time. The castle belonged to a marquis who was in Paris when the Revolution started. He and his wife were imprisoned and guillotined a few days later, and the castle was looted and torn down."

Gabrielle's eyes were wide and horrified.

"Dear Lord... What about your family? Did they also suffer through the Revolution?"

"Nobody was beheaded, if that's what you mean. The Saint-Armand family fled overseas as soon as the Revolution was ignited." Thomas recited the facts dispassionately, as though he were reading from a history book. "Their belongings and title were seized while they were in exile. Henri, the eldest son and heir, returned to France as soon as he could and managed to be appointed equerry to Napoleon, who returned his title as thanks for good and loyal services. He bought the castle for a steal—or the ruins, at least—in 1812. And since he was a humble and modest man, he rebuilt it twice as large and dug the moat deeper, as well as buying a few acres more of land and woods."

He paused as they came up to the great wooden door of the stable, pushing it open for Gabrielle. Several horses neighed and stomped, trying to attract their attention. Gabrielle's nose wrinkled as the strong scent of manure wafted closer.

"Come around, they are just here," Thomas urged her, drawing her toward an empty stall.

"Who is?"

"They are," he replied, moving aside to let her see.

She peered into the stall and could not hold back a cry of delight. Five tiny puppies snuggled up against their mother's belly. Their coats ranged from black to brown through white and golden, while their mother was snowy white with a heart-shaped black spot on her muzzle. Upon hearing Gabrielle's footsteps, she raised her head and gave her an imploring, fearful look, seemingly exhausted.

"Oh my God!" Gabrielle exclaimed, falling to her knees in front of the puppies without a care for her dress. "They are adorable!"

"Guillaume found them this morning," Thomas declared behind her. "She probably whelped during the night."

"She's gorgeous, but so thin! She must be starving!"

Hesitantly, Gabrielle reached out to the dog, muttering soothing nonsense under her breath. Too weak to move, she closed her eyes and allowed Gabrielle to stroke her without protest.

"I asked Céleste to prepare something for her to eat," Thomas told her, crouching down next to her. "We'll get them inside where it's warm. I sent Guillaume to fetch the veterinary in town."

His hand came to rest next to Gabrielle's on the dog's head, gently scratching her ears, and all of a sudden, the bubble that had enveloped them the previous night rose again. Thomas was so close to her that their shoulders touched and their hands brushed against each other. Their fingers were inches from tangling together. All noise faded away, and time slowed to a crawl around them. She closed her eyes, and for a fraction of a second, prayed for it to stop altogether and let them stay next to each other for all of eternity.

Then a voice rose behind them and reality reasserted its grip.

"I found this in some of your father's old belongings," Céleste explained, joining them inside the stall.

Gabrielle swallowed a disappointed sigh and turned toward the new arrival, who deposited a large wicker basket lined in blankets on the ground.

"I don't know if you remember, sir," she told Thomas, "but the family used to have a very sweet dog, Gypsie, when you were a child. This basket was hers; it used to be in the kitchen. She loved to lie in it while I cooked. She was a glutton, always hoping I would feed her some tidbits!"

"I remember," Thomas murmured reluctantly, getting to his feet.

Cold broke over Gabrielle, and she rose in turn as the cook went on:

"It's not exactly new, but I'm fairly certain neither mother nor pups will object."

"Thank you, Céleste. It will suit perfectly. You can return to the kitchen; we will follow shortly."

Céleste gave a little nod of acknowledgment and left, leaving the litter to her master and Gabrielle's care. When Thomas tried to move the mother to the basket, he discovered the cause of her distress—her left hind leg was injured and in dire need of attention lest it got infected. In her weakened state, the poor dog probably wouldn't survive.

Within minutes, Thomas and Gabrielle had moved the puppies, settled the mother in the basket and replaced the puppies against her. They then quickly went to the kitchen, cradling the precious burden in their arms.

While Céleste busied herself preparing some food for the mama, Thomas carefully cleaned her wound, keeping up a steady stream of reassuring words to soothe her. Every time the poor animal whined in pain, Gabrielle's heart clenched and she prayed the dog would make it. Who would take care of her babies if she did not survive?

Thomas was almost done by the time Guillaume swept into the kitchen, wind tousled and red nosed, announcing that the veterinary was busy on the other side of town and would not be able to come for several hours.

"That will be too late." Thomas frowned. "She can't wait that long."

He and Guillaume conferred for a few moments before deciding they would ask help from an old hunter living a few kilometers away. The man's knowledge of dogs was legendary. He would know what to do. Within minutes, they had strode out of the room, leaving Gabrielle reeling and a little unsure what to do with herself while she waited for them to return.

"Here, sit and drink this," Céleste commanded, sliding a steaming bowl of hot chocolate across the table. "You must be freezing."

"Thank you," Gabrielle replied as she lowered herself onto the bench.

She wrapped her hands around the bowl and sipped it. As the dog resumed whining, Gabrielle leaned down and petted her head, murmuring soothingly. Unlike Thomas's talk, however, her words remained without effect.

"You know," Céleste confided, "if there is one person who can take care of that dog, it really is Mr. D'Arcy."

"I don't doubt it for a second," Gabrielle replied, still stroking the dog. "He seems to have a gift with animals."

"He was always that way. He loves animals, and they can feel it. As a child, he used to save all the lost frogs and tortoises he would find, long before he could even walk. He carried earthworms in his pockets and brought back injured squirrels in boxes. I remember one day he found a fledgling fallen from his nest in the forest. He put it in his pocket and climbed all the surrounding trees until he found the nest and returned it to its mother. He must have been seven or eight...."

She paused.

"You know, he always was more at ease with animals than with people. He was an only child, and he had few friends. He almost never left the estate. It made him...shy, I'd say. He filled the void with animals."

"I understand."

"But he's different, these days. I haven't seen him so carefree in a very long time. I think..."

She hesitated before going on.

"I think it's thanks to you, mademoiselle."

Gabrielle did not answer, but she could feel her cheeks heating up, and an involuntary smile crept across her face. Céleste's words pleased her far too much for her to hold it back entirely. She cleared her throat and simply stated, "He's a good man."

"Oh, he is that," the cook agreed, a touch of pride in her voice. "More than he lets on."

"You seem to know him well."

"I do. I've worked here since well before he was born. His father hired me shortly after he married Adaline D'Arcy. Even if he's been living in England for almost twenty years, I think I know him better than anyone."

"What was he like as a child?" she inquired, unable to restrain her curiosity. "If it's not too private?"

"I don't think it would be for you." Gabrielle turned even redder. "If you really do want to know, he was a devil of a child."

"Surely you must be teasing me. I can't imagine it! He's always so somber and serious!"

"He wasn't so as a child. On the contrary, he was always getting into one spot of mischief or another. How many times did I see him slide down the bannister of the great staircase? He could have broken his neck, and he always received a wallop for it, but it didn't stop him. I remember when he started reading tales of knights. He read all of the books in the library he could find on the subject, and he made himself a sword. He would run about crying 'Surrender, miscreant!'"

She paused, nostalgia etched into every line of her face.

"It was such a joy to see him so carefree. He was so full of life then."

Gabrielle could clearly hear the regret in her voice, and it made her heart clench. What had happened for Thomas to change so drastically?

"You love him very much," she realized.

Céleste nodded.

"As though he were my own grandson, and just as much as when he was a child, if not more so."

Silence fell as each of the two women retreated within their thoughts. Gabrielle kept on stroking the dog's head mechanically, praying for Thomas to return soon. He seemed to be the only one able to reassure the animal.

"Mr. D'Arcy implied that he did not get on well with his father prior to his death," she began after a few moments, curious to know more about him. "What happened?"

Céleste sighed.

"It's a complicated story."

To Gabrielle's disappointment, she did not expand. Gabrielle did not insist, steering the conversation toward another topic.

"I saw his mother's portrait, the one outside the library. She was a stunning woman. He looks much more like her than he does his father, I think."

"Indeed. He has her hair and eyes."

"And her smile."

"Yes, that too."

"He seems to have adored her."

"He did. Everybody loved Adaline D'Arcy. She was a wonderful woman, very sweet and kind. Sometimes she would come down to the kitchen with Mr. D'Arcy and bake biscuits for them to have a picnic in the park. They were very close. She was the center of his world. Her death was very hard on him."

"It was an accident, I believe?"

A shadow stole over Céleste's face.

"Yes. She…she tripped and fell down the stairs. Almost right at Mr. D'Arcy's feet."

Gabrielle clapped her hands over her mouth.

"Oh Lord…," she breathed. "You mean he saw—"

"Yes."

"How horrible."

Céleste nodded and went on: "It was a tragedy for all, but it was worse still for Mr. D'Arcy. The merry, loving child he had been vanished that day, and he became only a shadow of his former self. He no longer smiled or laughed. He was a sorry sight. I did what I could, but…it wasn't enough."

Deep within her chest, Gabrielle's heart beat a violent tattoo against her ribs as she imagined the horror he had lived through. So many things were suddenly cast in a new light. His abrupt change of mood when she had talked of tragedies and ghosts. The glint of pain in his eyes when he had spoken of his mother.

She wished she could take back her words that evening, the stupid jokes she had made. She wished she had never exhumed the painful memory.

A sigh rose from deep within her chest. "What a tragedy… I feel so sorry for him."

"So do I, mademoiselle. So do I. He suffered greatly because of it."

"Is…is the scar on his face connected to his mother's death?"

Once again, the cook's answer was evasive.

"Not directly, no. That too was a traumatizing story."

"Even more than seeing his mother…?"

Céleste nodded. "I'm afraid so."

Oh Lord…what had happened to him?

"It is a period of his life that he does not speak of," Céleste continued, "but it has left considerable scars upon him. He no longer trusts himself or others. It is as though he no longer expects anything from the outside world. As though his light has gone out."

To her deep regret, Gabrielle could not find out any more—the door swung open to reveal Thomas, followed by Guillaume and an unknown man. It was the veterinary, whom they had run into on their way. He carefully examined the dog and finally declared that the wound was serious but that with a bandage and appropriate care, she would live.

The relief in the kitchen was unanimous.

* * * *

That evening, once everyone had taken their leave and retreated to their rooms, Gabrielle remained awake for a long time. Despite her exhaustion, born of a short night and too many emotions, sleep eluded her. Her conversation with Céleste kept replaying through her mind, always ending in the same question—what could have happened in Thomas's life that would be worse than the shock of seeing his mother lie dead before him?

Unable to settle, she rose and slipped on a dressing gown, silently padding toward the only place she knew could soothe her—the library.

She crept in noiselessly, carefully shutting the door behind her. The fireplace was still lit, bathing the closest shelves with a warm glow and outlining the shape of the man sitting on the nearby love seat.

"Thomas? You're awake?"

"So are you."

"Sleep eludes me. I came to find some reading. Do you...wish for me to leave you alone?"

"No, stay. Please."

She carefully sat beside him.

"I can't stop thinking of that poor dog," she said after a few moments' silence. "Do you think she belongs to someone? That they could be looking for her even now?"

"I don't believe so. She seems too underfed."

"She's so handsome, though. And the puppies are very cute!"

He laughed. "They are, yes."

"You know," she continued, "I think she has adopted you as her master."

"You think so?"

She nodded.

"You only need to see the look of adoration in her eyes whenever you are near. And I think you have adopted her in return. You fell for her instantly."

He smiled slightly without answering and looked down.

"If she belongs to no one, are you going to keep her and the puppies?"

"I can't cast them out in her state. But...I won't be able to keep them."

"Why is that?"

"Because..." He paused. "I am leaving for New York."

Gabrielle froze in shock.

"New York? You're not returning to England?"

"No. I... Everything is ready. I was about to leave for America when news of the baron's death reached me."

"Oh."

Gabrielle kept quiet, processing the information, a hollow feeling in her stomach.

The news shouldn't affect her so deeply. It was absurd. Be it England or America, it did not change anything for her. Their ways would part after this short period of their lives. It had always been that way.

So why did she feel so sad all of a sudden? Why did the United States feel so far?

"When are you leaving?" she asked, ignoring the lump in her throat.

"As soon as the castle has been sold."

"Oh. I see."

She paused before plunging on, circling back to her initial topic. She longed to know more about his departure, but she needed a little more time first.

"Can't you... Can't you take the dogs with you, then?"

"Not all of them. I can't take care of that many animals. Maybe I could take just the mother, though. To do so would mean I'd need to wait for the puppies to be weaned and placed in new homes."

A sudden ray of hope warmed Gabrielle's heart. "How long does it take to wean puppies?"

"Several weeks, perhaps a couple of months. I'm not sure precisely, I'd have to ask."

"Do you think...do you think you could stay that long?" she hesitantly asked.

Thomas turned to Gabrielle, upon hearing the tone of her voice, no doubt, and plunged his gaze into hers. The firelight illuminated the scarred half of his face, but Gabrielle did not see it. She only saw Thomas's shy smile, his eyes light up with a mixture of surprise, joy and something she could not identify. She saw the man who had cared for the puppies and held them against his heart. The man who had made her own heart tremble more than she cared to admit over the last few days. The man who had been shattered by life, but still stood tall and defiant.

She saw him, all of him.

"I might be able to, yes," Thomas finally answered. "If she insists."

Relief washed over Gabrielle.

"I think she would really enjoy having some more time here. With you," she heard herself reply over her thundering heartbeat.

"Then I will stay a little longer. For her."

She smiled at him, he smiled at her, their gazes still linked.

"Gabrielle?"

"Yes?"

"Would you read to me again?"

"With pleasure, Thomas."

Chapter 15
Alexandra

Angers

Present day

"So," I asked as I fastened my seat belt, "how did it go with the architect?"

True to his word, Éric Lagnel had parked his motorcycle in front of the inn at eight o'clock sharp. I had been waiting, file in one hand, crutches in the other, full of energy and impatience.

"Okay."

He might have had many faults, but using too many words wasn't one of them, I had to give him that.

"Very well, but what else?" I insisted. "Did he understand the problem? Give you any ideas? Solutions? A zero percent interest rate on a hundred-and-fifty-year loan? Half a billion euro?"

"He's an architect, not a banker. He said he would think about it, make a few phone calls and get back to me within a couple of days."

"Do you think he's going to help you?"

"I don't know."

"But did he make a good impression on you at least?"

"I wouldn't go that far. He seemed competent, but not overly interested. I imagine the castle isn't famous enough for him."

"But he can't do that! He can't just pick and choose which castles deserve to be saved!"

"Come back to earth, princess. He's a famous architect, and very sought after. Of course he can. Life—"

"Life isn't a fairy tale, yes, I know," I interrupted. "But you have to admit it's infuriating!"

Seriously? What entitled this man to judge *this* castle uninteresting? It might be a small one, but it had its own history, it held memories, some people had lived through its highs and lows! He couldn't just wave all of that away and shrug, saying, "Who cares? There are a lot more just like this one."

"Of course it's infuriating, but it's not your problem. Don't get worked up over it. How's your ankle?" he asked abruptly.

"It's fine," I sighed, tamping down my frustration. "I'll live."

"I don't doubt it for a second. You would survive the world ending if only it would allow you to get your own way."

I wasn't entirely sure how to interpret that.

"I'm going to take that as a compliment," I finally decided.

He shrugged and didn't reply, his gaze fixed on the road. The only sound in the car was the jazz music on the radio.

"You didn't have to come with me, you know," I told him quietly.

"I can't let you drive with a sprained ankle. You'd be a danger to yourself and to others."

"I meant I could have taken the train."

My remark seemed to unbalance him, and he kept quiet for a few seconds, seemingly determined to not look away from the road stretching ahead.

"Yeah, you could have."

And that was all.

It looked like I would never understand that man.

* * * *

We drove the rest of the way in near silence. I talked, but true to form, Éric kept his replies monosyllabic. It really was more of a monologue than a dialogue. An hour later, he parked in front of a small shop on a street lined with cobblestones at the heart of Angers.

"We're here," he announced as he cut off the ignition.

A wave of excitement broke over me.

At last! I thought.

I mentally ran over the speech I had prepared for Mr. Bourgeois one more time. I hoped he would be easier to convince than Éric. While he waited for a break in traffic to exit the car on the driver's side, I hauled myself gingerly out of my seat, desperately trying not to trip over my crutches and end up on my derriere for the umpteenth time. Once I had managed this demanding task with no damage to either myself or the car, I took a few moments to admire the shop in front of me.

It was an adorable little bookstore, quaint and old fashioned. The shop window was framed in black, with hand-painted gold letters on the glass that read *Les livres d'Héloïse*. I could see shelves groaning under a heavy load of books, bright colors both warm and cozy, with antique furniture that gave the impression you were about to step through a window to another world, another time.

"Are you coming or are you just going to stare?" Éric grumbled with his usual tact and delicacy. "I sure didn't come all this way to stand outside all day."

"You know, it wouldn't kill you to be pleasant once in a while," I complained as I followed him inside.

The bookstore might have looked cramped from the outside, but stepping inside definitely gave the lie to that idea.

"It's the *best*!" I gasped in delight as Éric closed the door behind us. "It's much bigger on the inside too!"

"I have no idea what you're going on about," he muttered.

"Forget it. Doesn't matter. I love this place!"

I stared around in wonder, utterly starstruck. I took in every detail: the ancient shelves that ran from one side to another, the paintings on the walls, most of them old book covers, the beanbags scattered in the corners and at the ends of the aisles, beckoning readers to sit and leaf through their selections. A tantalizing aroma of coffee and freshly baked pastries mingled with the incomparable smell of leather-bound books. I searched for the source and discovered a little 1900s-style café corner, adorned with brown oak tables, matching chairs and high shelves filled with old leather-bound red and brown books. A golden-red chandelier dangled from the ceiling and bathed the room in soft light.

Completely charmed, I limped up to the counter at the back of the bookstore, trailing Éric. The man behind it was paging through a catalog.

He looked up as he heard us approaching and smiled politely. He must have been in his early forties.

"Good morning, how may I help you?"

A glance from Éric let me know that this was all up to me.

"Hello!" I offered my sweetest smile. "I would like to speak to Mr. Xavier Bourgeois. I called on Saturday," I added as though it would magically smooth the way.

"I am Xavier Bourgeois. What can I do for you?"

Instantly, the speech I had rehearsed flew straight out of my mind and I let my excitement take over.

"Pleased to meet you. I'm Alexandra Dawson. You're going to think this is totally insane, but here it is. I'm descended from the man who built this bookstore, and I recently found out that you might have some documents dating back to the creation of the store. Including some personal papers belonging to the Villeneuve family."

I paused, slightly short of breath, and waited, heart hammering. I felt Éric draw closer behind me and I wondered if, in spite of the aloofness he pretended, he *was* interested in the content of the diary after all. Who knew what it could hold if it did exist? We might even find something that could help save the castle.

I hoped so at least. I really did.

Across the counter, Xavier Bourgeois looked at the both of us.

"I do. It's a funny coincidence; you're not the first to ask me that. A while ago a man called me, asking to see these documents. I never heard back from him, though. He must have changed his mind."

"Was it Marc Lagnel, by any chance?" Éric queried.

"I think that was his name. Do you know him?"

"He was my father."

"Was?"

"He died six months ago."

His voice was toneless, but I could feel the same pain, the same heartbreak as I had in the graveyard the previous day, and my own heart wept for him. I almost wanted to reach out and squeeze his hand, just to show him he wasn't alone.

Of course, I did no such thing. I wanted to leave the store in one piece.

"My sincere condolences," Mr. Bourgeois told him compassionately.

"Thank you."

He turned to me.

"Mr. Lagnel didn't tell me his daughter-in-law was a descendant of Maurice Villeneuve."

My eyes went wide in amazement as I understood what he meant, and I immediately blushed scarlet, hastening to set him straight. At the same moment, Éric protested.

"Oh no! No, no, no! Mr. Lagnel wasn't my father-in-law."

"We're not married!"

"He can barely stand me!"

"I've only known her two days!"

"I'm sorry," Xavier Bourgeois apologized. "I thought—"

THE CHÂTEAU BY THE RIVER

"You were mistaken," Éric said harshly.

"Really, I'm sorry." The poor owner seemed embarrassed. "I didn't mean to offend."

"Don't worry about it." I glared at Éric. "Would you be willing to let me look at those documents? I'm doing some genealogy research and I might find some useful information."

"Of course, it's no bother at all. I'm happy to help. Follow me!"

I thanked him with my widest smile.

* * * *

Mr. Bourgeois led us to a small office off the bookstore's main room. Darker and simpler than the rest of the store, it held a desk, a chair and a few cabinets. We patiently—more or less—waited for him to rummage through one of these. A few moments later, he pulled out a large file box and set it on the desk.

My excitement level skyrocketed.

This was it.

"Everything is in here," Mr. Bourgeois told us. "Maurice Villeneuve's correspondence, both personal and professional, and everything I could find and preserve when I bought the store ten years ago. A number of documents were unfortunately lost over time, so this is all I have. I hope you find something helpful."

"It's very kind of you, thank you," I assured him.

Just then, the bell over the door rang out.

"Please excuse me, duty calls. I'll be right next door if you need anything."

"Thank you."

He left the room, leaving us alone with the past.

"How do you want to proceed?" Éric asked.

"I'm not sure. I didn't plan this far ahead. I think I'll just look through the contents and see what's relevant for me."

"What about me?"

"You? What do you mean?"

"How can I help?"

I raised an eyebrow, surprised. "You want to help? I thought you weren't interested in the past?"

He shrugged. "Since I'm here, I may as well be useful."

"Admit it, you're just curious to know what I'm going to find out," I teased.

"What of it?" he parried defensively.

"I'd like that. I was thinking earlier that if we're lucky, we might find something that could help save the castle."

"That's not very likely."

"But not impossible."

"But not impossible," he conceded, before adding, "Don't get your hopes up, though. Nothing is ever that easy in life."

I heaved an exasperated sigh.

"Do you ever see the glass half-full?"

"It's not a question of a glass half-full or half-empty. I'm a realist, that's all."

"Yeah, well, if you ask me, your realism looks dangerously like pessimism," I fired back as I cautiously opened the file box.

Mr. Bourgeois was as orderly as Éric's father had been. Loose sheets of paper had been placed in thematically and chronologically organized binders. I examined the first one. A label on the front read "Professional correspondence, 1880–1942." I set it aside for later. I pulled out a second, much lighter one, entitled "Personal correspondence." I flipped it open and began to page through it while across from me, Éric picked up another document.

The first letters, I quickly realized, did not seem relevant to what I was looking for. I thumbed through the pages until a name at the top of one letter caught my eye. "Chandeniers."

Heart beating impossibly fast, I bent lower to decipher the content. No easy task, since the writer's cursive was near as illegible as Marc Lagnel's.

> *My dear Gabrielle,*
>
> *I have reached the castle of Ferté-Chandeniers. My journey here was uneventful—as arranged with Mr. D'Arcy, Guillaume was waiting for me in Saumur. You will have guessed already that I asked to see the library immediately upon arriving, in order to weigh the task I had been entrusted with. Gabrielle, if only you could see it. It is unimaginable! Books by the thousand, everywhere, piling two stories high, from ground to ceiling and on every wall! If she were still with us, your mother would have leapt for joy.*

I stopped reading the instant I understood what I was holding.

Wow! Had there really been that many books in the castle? I had known that the fire had destroyed many valuable works of art, but I'd had no idea of the scale of the loss. Scanning the rest of the letter, I realized that

Gabrielle's father had described everything he had seen of the castle since his arrival, and I unthinkingly called out to Éric.

"Éric, come see, I think I found something you're going to be interested in!"

He rose and came up behind me, one hand on the desk and the other on the back of my chair, his face exactly two inches from mine, and the fragrance of his skin suddenly enveloped me.

All at once, butterflies began to flutter in my stomach even as a strange sensation of pins and needles crept over my body. The feeling disturbed me so much that I lost my train of thought. Strangely, it was the sound of his voice near my ear that helped me gather my thoughts after a few moments of blankness.

"What is it?"

"A letter," I replied, relieved to hear my voice did not quaver. "From Maurice Villeneuve to Gabrielle. He describes the castle the way it was in…" I checked the date at the top of the letter. "November 1899. Listen to this."

I read the rest of the letter out loud, Éric helping me sound out the words I had trouble with. We discovered the castle as it was just before the fire: a library to rival the one in Alexandria, paintings of great masters, precious tapestries. A magnificent collection of jade statuettes. Egyptian statues, Japanese armors, Turkish scimitars. A gallery lined with mirrors and another populated with medieval armor.

A few names were repeated throughout the letter: Hélène, Guillaume, Agnès…the castle staff, apparently.

The binder held several other letters in the same vein, Maurice describing castle life to his daughter. From what I could tell, he had been hired to inventory and sell the contents of the library. It seemed the castle was to be sold following the death of Victor Leroy de Saint-Armand.

I remained speechless upon reading this.

"But why? Why would Thomas want to sell the family castle? It makes no sense!"

"It might seem hard to believe," Éric drawled, "but not everyone has the means or the desire to live in a castle, even if it belonged to their ancestors."

"Okay, but why would he want to sell everything? Maybe he was already planning to leave for America…."

"Or his father was too deep in debt, and the only way to pay off the creditors was to sell the castle."

"I think I like your theory even less than mine."

"It's not a question of liking, but of seeing whether it proves true. You might not like what you find out."

I sighed wearily.

"I know…I know. But something isn't right. If Maurice was the one to go to Chandeniers while Gabrielle stayed behind in the bookstore, how come I have a photo of her in the library? Why did she go there?"

"There are no other letters?"

I flipped a few pages over, but none of the other letters mentioned Chandeniers or Gabrielle.

"Doesn't look like it," I said, disappointed.

"There might be some information in here, then," Éric hinted, holding out the thick red leather-bound notebook he had been leafing through. "I found something too, and I think you're going to like it." He laid it on the desk in front of me.

My heart leapt.

"Is that what I think it is?"

"I think so."

"Why didn't you say anything?" I cried, seizing it at once.

I opened it feverishly, flipping through the pages. The yellowing pages were covered in narrow, feminine handwriting, a little untidy in places, as though the writer's thoughts had occasionally wandered away from her. And among those lines, names jumped out at me: Papa, Hélène, Agnès, Guillaume…and Thomas.

Heart thumping in my chest, I returned to the first page. The diary seemed to begin sometime in 1898. The flyleaf and the first few entries confirmed what I already instinctively knew.

It was Gabrielle's diary. It was real.

I raised my eyes to meet Éric's. He was so close to me I could see the tiny gleam that seemed to shine just for me.

"This is it," I whispered.

"This is it," he agreed.

I lowered my gaze back to the diary, and for a few moments I simply stroked the cover lovingly.

"You're going to make fun of me," I admitted softly, "but part of me thought this was going to be a false trail and that I shouldn't build too much hope on this diary. I think you might be rubbing off on me!"

"You haven't read it yet, you have no idea what's inside," he remarked.

"You've seen it too—it mentions the same names as in the letters, and the castle, as well as Thomas. I'm positive it has the answers I'm looking for."

"And what are you looking for? Apart from your roots?"

I smiled and looked guilelessly up at him.

"A beautiful love story."

I giggled when he rolled his eyes, visibly appalled.

* * * *

An hour later, when Xavier Bourgeois looked in on us, I still hadn't uncovered the love story I had hoped for. But then again, Éric and I had only skimmed the first pages of the diary, relating the months prior to Gabrielle and Thomas meeting. From a purely historical and cultural point of view, my ancestor's diary was a treasure trove of information of the society and way of life of the time, a historian's dream.

Not so much on the romantic and glamorous aspect, though, I thought.

I was going to have to be patient. I didn't know when exactly Gabrielle and Thomas had first crossed paths, but I had reached October 1899. I knew my ancestors had been married in July 1900. Any moment now I would turn a page and read about the day of their first meeting and uncover why she had journeyed to the castle, I was sure of it.

If I could be left alone to read in peace.

"Did you find anything interesting?" Mr. Bourgeois asked.

"I did! Exactly what I was looking for—my ancestor's diary!"

"Good for you! Can I offer you a coffee or something to eat?"

I was about to refuse when Éric straightened and massaged his neck.

"I would love a coffee, if you don't mind."

"Come, I'll brew some."

"Go ahead." I gestured at the door. "I'm going to keep reading."

"Are you sure?" Mr. Bourgeois insisted.

"Yes, thank you!"

"The diary's not going to vanish, Alexandra," Éric interrupted. "And I need a coffee."

"Go and get one, then."

"So do you."

"No, I'm fine. And I don't care for coffee, anyway."

"I have tea too," Mr. Bourgeois offered.

God, couldn't they leave me alone? I just wanted to read!

"Come on, don't be stubborn, just come along!"

"What, are you scared of going on your own?"

He raised an eyebrow, but refused to answer. That question, at least.

"You asked for it. Don't come complaining."

"Complaining about what?" I asked, naively thinking he was at last going to let me read in peace.

Instead of following Mr. Bourgeois out of the room like I expected, he came up to me, smiling mysteriously, and unceremoniously lifted me into his arms. And under the amused gazes of the owner and the few patrons hunting through the shelves, he bodily carried me into the café, deaf to my protests.

"You didn't need to do that," I grumbled as I smoothed my clothes, sitting on a chair.

My cheeks were crimson. I hadn't been that embarrassed in a long, long time.

Éric sat across from me.

"If I'd had to convince you, we'd still be back there. My method is quicker."

"And a lot ruder."

"You've already told me as much, princess."

"What would you like to drink?" Mr. Bourgeois asked us.

I peered at the board and chose a chai latte. Éric ordered an espresso.

"Coming right up."

I walled myself in stony silence, examining my fingernails so my displeasure would be obvious even to Mr. Sarcasm.

"All right, I'm sorry," Éric finally said. "I was a little out of line."

"A little?"

"Okay, a lot."

I considered, then sighed, resigned. Éric smiled, and the butterflies in my stomach took off for another loop-de-loop. What the hell was wrong with me?

"Here you are!" Mr. Bourgeois announced, depositing two cups in front of us.

"Will you join us?" I hastened to ask.

"If you'd like me to, I can spare a few minutes."

I promptly put those minutes to good use interrogating him about the bookstore and how he'd come to own it.

He told us he had found the documents in the attic of the apartment above, which had come with the bookstore. He wanted to show them to a historian to find out whether they had any value other than the one they held for him, and use them to create a section in the bookstore about its origins. He had only lacked the time to take care of it.

"You know how it is. You manage the most urgent matters first, thinking you'll do the rest later, and days and months go by and you still haven't found the time."

"I know exactly what you mean," I assured him with a smile, gulping at my—delicious—chai latte.

Somewhere around the middle of the conversation, Éric's phone rang, and he excused himself to answer, muttering that he absolutely had to take this call. He stepped outside the store, and I couldn't help watching him through the window. A shadow had stolen over his face when he had seen the name of the caller and his smile had vanished. Now he paced up and down the sidewalk, gesturing wildly, his shoulders tight with frustration.

Seeing him so downcast, I couldn't help but think he sorely needed a little levity in his life. Just to change his mind.

My gaze slid absently over the posters on the walls, and one of them caught my attention. It featured a hot-air balloon flying over a vineyard, a castle in the background. A headline at the top of the picture read: "Discover the Loire valley from a whole new angle." An idea blossomed into my mind, and I turned to Mr. Bourgeois.

"Can you really go ballooning around here?"

"Yes, one of my friends runs the tour."

"Do you think he could take us?"

"Of course! When?"

"This is kind of last minute, but do you think tonight might be possible?"

"I'd have to ask. Let me call him."

"Thank you."

Mr. Bourgeois pulled out his cell phone and made the call. He explained the situation, waited for a reply, then covered the phone with one hand and said:

"He can't tonight, but somebody just canceled for tomorrow morning, is that okay?"

I thought as fast as I could and decided that yes, it was doable. We just needed to find a hotel to spend the night in Angers.

"That would be perfect."

Two minutes later he hung up.

"He'll be waiting for you tomorrow at five a.m. You can watch the sun rise. I'll give you directions to the meeting point."

I swallowed a grimace, realizing the ungodly hour we would have to awaken, and thanked him.

The bell over the door rang, and Mr. Bourgeois excused himself to attend to the new arrival. I immediately jumped on my phone and searched for a place to spend the night. Two minutes later I had booked two rooms in a nearby hotel. Only one thing remained—tell Éric about the change of plans.

* * * *

His reaction did not disappoint.

"It didn't cross your mind to wait for me to be done with my own phone call so you could ask my opinion?"

"If I had, would you have said yes?"

"No!"

"Yeah, I thought so too. So I followed your example and made an executive decision to save some time." I paused. "You need to have a little fun, Éric. Once in a while wouldn't kill you."

"And what if I had plans for tomorrow?"

"Then I would have sent you home and I'd have taken a train and taxi to return tomorrow. But you don't seem to, so relax and live a little. It'll do you good."

"We can't spend the night in Angers anyway. I didn't pack any clothes."

I raised my eyebrows, dubious before his increasingly desperate excuses.

"France is a civilized country; I'm fairly certain we can find something."

"Maybe you're rolling in money, but I have a broken-down castle to save. I can't afford to spend money on frivolities."

"I'm certainly not rolling in money, despite what you seem to believe, but I think I can afford to buy you a pair of briefs if that's your only argument. Unless you're a boxer man?"

This time he was the one to roll his eyes.

"This conversation is unreal. I wasn't talking about the underwear but the hotel and the balloon!"

"That's no issue. My idea, my funding. You won't need to pay for the room, the trip, or your spare underwear."

"I refuse to let you pay for me! Out of the question."

"So if I let you pay your half, will you climb into the balloon with me?"

"You're insufferable, you know that?"

I summoned my sunniest smile for him and leaned close to purr: "It's pronounced 'determined.' So, Mr. Lagnel, tell me everything—boxers or briefs?"

Chapter 16
Gabrielle

Castle of Ferté-Chandeniers

December 1899, one week later

Pale light bathed the library on this cold and wet afternoon, lending an otherworldly air to the room.

Gabrielle sat at one end of the great oak desk, working.

Or at least, that's what she was supposed to be doing. But it would be closer to the truth to say that she was playing, experiencing some of the most extraordinary and precious moments of her life in this library. Every book she inventoried seemed to be a new treasure to uncover, a new world to explore. The work she was examining just then was an antique, richly illustrated edition of the *Roman de Lancelot du Lac*, written in French so ancient she had trouble deciphering it. It had been published by Antoine Vérard in 1494 in Paris. It was, she realized, the oldest book she had ever come across.

Smiling slightly, Gabrielle held the book close to her face, closed her eyes and inhaled its smell. It was a ritual of hers. She reveled in the scent of books the way others might with flowers. The aroma of leather, paper and ink brought comfort like no other.

Sighing happily, she opened her eyes and carefully, reverently, cracked the book open and got to work, listing every detail and characteristic on the notecard in front of her.

She finished her examination, jotting down a few final notes in clear, legible print, and tried to estimate what such a rare book should be valued at for sale. What price would be fair? She soon gave up the attempt. A sharper eye and greater knowledge than hers were required for such a rarity—published less than fifty years after the invention of the printing press! She set it aside with a few others to bring to her father that evening.

She yawned and stretched, rising to her feet and going over to one of the high windows, admiring the landscape stretched out in front of her eyes.

Snow had fallen again during the night, and the vast gardens around the castle were so blindingly white she could not tell where the land ended and the sky began. She could have been in a Hans Christian Andersen fairy tale.

Two silhouettes appeared at the foot of the castle, a few feet from the moat. One was tall and broad, its dark coat a sharp contrast to the surrounding white, throwing a stick that the other shape, a beautiful dog almost as white as the ground, leapt after, joyfully plunging into the powdery snow. After a week of tender care, she was brimming with energy. Gabrielle watched the taller silhouette bend down to pet the dog; her heart filled with emotion at the sight.

Many would have judged the scene ordinary or even uninteresting. What could be more common than a man playing with his dog?

But it wasn't any man, and it wasn't any dog. They had found each other. It could almost be said that the dog had saved the man as much as the man had saved the dog. Thomas seemed different with her. Happier. He radiated joy such as Gabrielle had rarely seen in him, and each day, his smile grew larger, his shoulders became straighter. Light reasserted its rights over him and cast the shadow away from his face.

And the happier he was, the happier Gabrielle became.

She wished time would stop.

She wished she could stay forever.

Stay with these people who made her so happy.

Stay with him.

With the man to whom her heart now clung.

* * * *

A week had gone by since the puppies and their mother had been saved, and Gabrielle's life had fallen into a quiet routine. She split her time between the inventory of the library, the care she provided for her father with Hélène's help, the moments of pure bliss she shared with the puppies…and this bubble out of time and space that emerged when night fell and firelight replaced daylight.

Her secret.

Their secret...

Every night, after all had retired to their bedrooms and silence had fallen over the castle, another life began for Gabrielle. She put away the diary into which she scrupulously noted the detail of her days and tiptoed out of her room up to the library, oil lamp in hand, to join *him*.

They had never really agreed on this, but it had become a habit, something they both awaited impatiently throughout the day. Every night, they met up in secret in the library. Every night, she pushed open the door, heart hammering, wondering whether he would be there. And every night, when Thomas saw her come in, when his gaze caught hers, he lit up and seemed to glow from the inside, making her heart beat a little faster.

And in this moment in time that belonged only to them, when they would read, talk or simply sit side by side in the comfortable silence of two people who do not need to speak to understand each other, Gabrielle could feel new emotions welling up within her. She did not attach any words to them, but they grew stronger by the day, tying her closer to these intimate, carefree moments. Closer to him.

* * * *

Voices from the gallery of portraits outside the library reached Gabrielle through the open door, bringing her back to the present. She glanced out the window. Thomas and his dog—Duchesse, they had named her—had vanished.

Curious, she cocked her head to listen, hoping he would be the one to come in, as he sometimes did to borrow a book, ask a question or her opinion.

Her hopes were soon dashed.

"My dear friend, please photograph this gallery of portraits. It is perfect. Come over here, the light is ideal."

Gabrielle grimaced as she recognized the nasal voice.

Mr. Choiseul, the auctioneer, had arrived that morning to evaluate the hundreds of works of art in the castle with his own photographer, one Arnaud Colin. He was affected and obsequious and obviously had a very high opinion of himself. Gabrielle had come across him as she made her way toward the library after breakfast. He had burst into the great hall like a messiah ready to dispense his great science and superior knowledge to the poor ignorant wretches of the castle.

Gabrielle had loathed him on sight.

She cast about for a hiding place in case he had the sudden fancy to enter the library. Listening carefully, her whole body poised to spring behind the curtains at the slightest suspicious sound, she suddenly relaxed upon hearing a familiar gait in the gallery.

Her heart suddenly beat faster, and a smile came to her face. He was here.

"Gentlemen," a deep voice intoned.

Gabrielle heard the photographer greet Thomas; then Mr. Choiseul's grating voice rose.

"My lord baron! I was hoping to see you!"

Gabrielle shook her head, appalled at the man's attitude. Thomas had told him at least fifteen times that he did not wish to be addressed as such. From the safety of her window, she could almost sense his exasperated sigh as he tensed.

"I must say that you have some truly *extraordinary* pieces here!" the pompous fool continued. "Simply *marvelous*! It really is an *immense* honor to be the one to estimate such a priceless collection!"

"I have told you before, Mr. Choiseul, that I do not carry the title of baron," Thomas replied coldly. "I would thank you to call me D'Arcy as all others do."

"Of course, anyone in my profession knows your late father's reputation as a learned amateur of art," the auctioneer prattled on bombastically, seemingly deaf to his employer's remark. "I would venture that many an expert wishes he were me in this moment. But you were right to call for the best. Art is a serious matter."

Gabrielle silently rolled her eyes, convinced that just then Thomas would much rather have chosen anyone other than "the best." How could he be so full of himself? She wondered how his photographer friend, who appeared both shy and quiet, could stand to be with him all day long. Truly, it was remarkable.

Mr. Choiseul carried on with his own accolades, telling Thomas at length of his many accomplishments, singing the praises of his wonderful patrons and boasting of his many friends in the Paris auction house of the Hôtel Drouot, relentlessly asking Mr. Colin to confirm while never pausing to let him do so.

He went on for so long that Gabrielle finally took pity on Thomas and decided to step out of her sanctuary to try to pry her friend from the detestable Mr. Choiseul's claws. She walked up to them, head held high, and cleared her throat. All three turned toward her.

"Mademoiselle Villeneuve." Thomas greeted her with a slight nod and a relieved gleam in his eyes.

"Mr. D'Arcy. Gentlemen."

Mr. Colin nodded to her while Mr. Choiseul graced her with his usual condescending sneer. Gabrielle raised her chin a little higher, ready to do battle.

"What is it, my dear?" Mr. Choiseul asked patronizingly. "We are dealing with serious matters here."

Breathe, Gabrielle, stay calm. She swallowed the cutting jab rising in her throat. She pasted her most professionally polite smile onto her face.

"Please forgive me for interrupting, gentlemen, but would you have a few minutes to devote to me, Mr. D'Arcy? I have something to show you. It is an unusual work that—"

"Come now, can't you see that the baron is busy?" Mr. Choiseul interrupted. "He has no time for such nonsense."

Gabrielle's eyes met Thomas's, and she saw that he was about to reply. She motioned for him to keep quiet. She was here to help him, after all, and not the other way around. And it was a battle she was perfectly qualified to lead. Men like this one, who took pleasure in looking down on her because she was a woman and thus witless, were unfortunately too common.

"Of course, sir," she replied with her sweetest voice. "I'm very sorry for overstepping myself."

"You're a darling little thing," Mr. Choiseul told her, visibly satisfied. "I will be magnanimous—"

"But please allow me to remind you that what you call 'nonsense' are works painstakingly collected by several generations of bibliophiles, the very same ones as those you have been lauding for hours. These are books written by learned people who have mastered French perfectly. Books that were put together with the greatest care by equally passionate publishers and printers. And no matter what you may think, sir, a great number of these books are truly works of art. And now, if you will excuse me, I was not speaking to you, but to Mr. D'Arcy. And unless he dismisses me himself, I do not intend to leave. With all due respect."

Out of the corner of her eye, Gabrielle saw Mr. Colin smothering an amused smile and Thomas looking at her proudly.

Mr. Choiseul did not appreciate her little speech quite as much.

"You impertinent wretch!" he sputtered. "How dare you talk to me in such a manner! You have no idea who you are dealing with!"

"Believe me, sir, I have had more than enough opportunity over the last few hours to hear you introduce yourself. The issue rather seems to be that *you* do not know who you are dealing with."

Mr. Choiseul's face was so red she thought for an instant he would burst.

"You little—"

"That is enough!" Thomas stepped in between them, throwing a frosty glance Mr. Choiseul's way. "I would advise you to think carefully on your next words, Mr. Choiseul, if you wish to keep the honor you have not stopped raving about for the past few hours. Mademoiselle Villeneuve is my guest, and I will not stand for her being insulted under my roof. Is that clear?"

The man seemed to fold in on himself, while Thomas drew himself to his full height.

"Crystal clear," he simpered, lips pressed together. "Please accept my apologies, young lady," he added to Gabrielle. "My temper got the best of me."

She accepted his apology with a gracious nod.

"I believe you have everything you need to begin your appraisal?" Thomas declared.

"Indeed, Mr. D'Arcy."

"Very well. Begin, then." He turned to Gabrielle. "Mademoiselle Villeneuve, if you would show me the book you spoke of..."

"With pleasure, sir."

And they left Mr. Colin to his amusement and Mr. Choiseul to his frustration, fleeing toward the safety of the library. Blithely transgressing propriety, Thomas closed the door behind them and leaned against it.

"Thank you for providing an excuse to leave. I did not know how to get rid of him."

"My pleasure. I wouldn't wish him on my worst enemy."

"I am sorry you had to bear his disrespect."

"Oh, don't worry about me. This is not the first time I have had to listen to such meaningless drivel, nor will it be the last."

She smiled impishly.

"Thank you for standing ready to defend me. But I can manage on my own."

"Of that I have no doubt. You can stand your ground before anyone. You are the strongest person I know. But I could not bear to hear him insult you so. It was beyond me."

His words moved her, and she averted her gaze before glancing back at him.

"My thanks, gallant knight," she teased, curtsying to disguise her turmoil.

Thomas smiled at her, their eyes catching each other's for a fraction of a second. As she so often did, she felt as though she could lose herself in his gray gaze. Her heart swelled in her chest until it seemed to her that her body could not possibly be large enough to hold it.

"Tell me, was there really a book you wanted to show me?" he asked.

"You doubt me, my lord?" she mocked, falsely outraged. "Let it be known that there are actually several."

She strode toward the desk and seized the pile of books she had set aside a few hours earlier to show to her father, then retraced her steps, setting it down in the nearest armchair.

Smiling, she waited for him to come close and opened the hardcover book at the top of the pile—*Paradise Lost*, from the English poet John Milton. Spreading the book flat, she fanned the pages so a magnificent fresco appeared on the edges where there had only been a golden gilt.

"Incredible," Thomas breathed. "I've never heard of such a thing."

"It's called a fore-edge painting," Gabrielle explained. "It's common enough in Anglo-Saxon countries, but I'd never seen one before. It's extraordinary to find one in a French library. Your ancestors must have been very widely traveled to acquire such beautiful books!"

"They were." He immediately changed topics, as he often did whenever Gabrielle brought up his ancestors. "How do you achieve such an effect?"

Gabrielle did not insist. She explained how a very thin slice of the picture was painted just next to the actual edge of the page so that it would appear when the book was fanned open. Some books, she added, actually had a double fore-edge painting, each picture visible according to the way the pages were fanned.

"And this is far from the only treasure in here!" she enthused, setting the first book aside to seize the one she had been examining earlier. "This one was printed in 1494. It's the oldest book I've ever seen! I make discoveries like this every day." She hesitated. "And…I found something else this morning."

She returned to the desk and picked up three thick volumes bound in brown leather. She went back to the armchair and held the first one out wordlessly to Thomas. He took it and read the title and author on the cover. For a long moment, he did not speak, gaze fixed on the golden letters.

François Leroy de Saint-Armand.

"I skimmed through it," Gabrielle said gently. "These are the memoirs of your grandfather. He narrates his life, but also the history of the Saint-Armand family, from Louis XVI ascending the throne to the last years of the second empire. A piece of French history told through your family's memories."

Thomas kept silent, his eyes on the book.

She went on.

"I wondered…if you wouldn't want to keep it."

"No." His reply was prompt. "Sell it with the rest."

Gabrielle hesitated.

"I heard what you said about debts and about not wanting to keep anything of your father's. I can understand you not wanting to know anything about him and refuse his legacy. But...Thomas... These books... They are the history of your family! Your ancestry!"

He closed his eyes, but not before she caught a flash of pain. He suddenly seemed tense, and she almost regretted showing him the books. Yet she could not understand. Why forsake his entire lineage when it had been only his father he had been estranged from? Why not keep at least a memory of this place, of the castle, of his roots?

She remained silent, keeping her questions to herself.

After what seemed like an age, Thomas opened his eyes and looked straight at her.

"They... They are not my ancestry." His voice was tense. "It is not my history."

Gabrielle froze, uncomprehending.

"What do you mean, it is not your history?"

Thomas hesitated in the face of her reaction.

"What I mean," he said finally, "is that Victor de Saint-Armand was not my father."

Chapter 17
Alexandra

Angers

Present day

Rrrrriiiiiiing!
Rrrrriiiiiiing!
Rrrrriiiiiiing!

Huh? What?

The earsplitting sound brought me back to earth so abruptly that I nearly fell off the bed upon which I had been reading Gabrielle's diary.

I blinked and looked around for the source of the noise.

The hotel room was sparse enough; I quickly identified the wall phone next to the door as the culprit.

Slightly dazed, my mind half in the past and half in the present, I rose and grimaced as my full weight came to rest on my sprained ankle. I cursed the person who dared disturb me in the middle of a confession worthy of a *Dallas* episode and limped toward the phone, still thinking of what I had read in Gabrielle's diary.

Not his father? Was that what the scratchings on his birth certificate meant, in the end? Who was Thomas's father, then, if not Victor de Saint-Armand? It couldn't be Andrew D'Arcy. I still needed to search the records in Plymouth to confirm my supposition, but my guess would be that Andrew D'Arcy was his uncle. So...was Thomas an illegitimate child, then? What was his story? Was that the reason why he was adopted by Andrew? Curiosity consumed me, and questions spun inside my head.

This was the going to be one of the shortest phone calls in history.

I barely had the time to pick up the phone before a male voice started screaming at me.

"What the hell are you doing, princess?! I've been waiting for you for TWO HOURS! You think it's funny to stand me up?!"

I froze, suddenly noticing the crowd of details that had escaped me so far: the darkened room, my strangely empty stomach and my numb legs. I checked my watch. Nine p.m.

Oh crap! Crappity, crappity crap!

Éric and I had been supposed to meet at seven.

"I'm...I'm sorry, Éric, I lost track of time," I stammered. "I'll be right there."

"Get moving. The cook's not going to wait and neither am I. It's been long enough already!"

He hung up. I grabbed my mini makeup bag and rushed into the bathroom.

* * * *

Earlier, upon leaving the bookstore, Mr. Bourgeois had allowed me to make photocopies of some of the letters and, in a rush of generosity that had taken me completely by surprise, had offered to let me keep Gabrielle's diary, explaining that it was too personal for him to expose in the store and that I would make better use of it. Touched, I had thanked him from the bottom of my heart, clutching the precious document to my chest like the Holy Grail.

Éric had immediately suggested we go to the department archives. French administrations closed early, so if I wanted to have the time to rummage about we should go as soon as possible.

In the end, we could have spared ourselves the trip. The manager, a very nice and polite lady, had let me use the computer available for visitors. I'd retraced my research from two days previously and found the document I wanted. A couple of clicks later, I had a printed copy that joined its little friends in my file. To my great satisfaction, the file was growing ever thicker.

I'd taken advantage of another of Éric's mysterious—and apparently unsuccessful—phone calls to keep researching. An hour later, Éric was still on the phone and I had managed to unearth copies of Gabrielle's parents' wedding certificate as well the birth and death certificates of Maurice. I was about to start tracking down Héloïse's when Éric returned, looking embarrassed.

"I need to go see someone," he'd abruptly announced. "Can I borrow your car for a few hours? It's really important."

"Uh... Sure. Of course. Can you drop me at the hotel first?"

"If we leave right away, yes. I'm sorry, but I'm really in a hurry."

It must have been important for him to just abandon me without a car while I was on crutches in a town I didn't know. I didn't really mind. I would have time to read Gabrielle's diary, and continue my research from my laptop. I didn't actually need to be in the archives.

"It's fine." I smiled. "This seems to be important."

"It is. I... It really is. Very important."

Éric had apologized again and dropped me in front of the hotel, holding my handbag and crutches. We'd agreed to meet in a nearby *brasserie* for dinner. He'd jotted down the address on a piece of paper for me.

Once in my room, I had cautiously extracted Gabrielle's diary from my handbag and settled comfortably on the bed to continue reading—with the aforementioned consequences....

In my defense, my ancestor's story was fascinating. Her meeting with Thomas was epic, and the circumstances in which they had met again were both tragic and romantic, not to mention how they had drawn closer to each other by the firelight in the library.

Gradually, as I deciphered as best I could without Éric's help my ancestor's sometimes untidy or crossed-out handwriting, a strange feeling had come over me. A certain something that made my heart go tight; there was something in Gabrielle and Thomas's story that made me both very happy and deeply envious.

When Thomas had asked Gabrielle if you could really love a monster, his manner so shy and fragile that Gabrielle had melted before him, I had stopped reading, my breath caught in my throat, tears in my eyes as a sudden and awful truth hit me hard.

My own story with Spencer was nowhere near as romantic.

Until now I had always been content with it. I knew, valued and loved Spencer deeply, for many reasons; he was my best friend, the one I could tell everything and who would give me the best advice. He was a very smart man, and I could rely on him to keep me cool when I was about to get carried away. He was my anchor to reality when my mind wandered too far into the clouds. But he was not one for grand gestures or romantic openings.

Take his marriage proposal, for instance. We'd been living together for a year when one day, watching TV on the couch after our traditional Saturday night sushi, he'd asked me between two episodes of a show:

"It would be a good idea to get married, don't you think?"

Taken aback, I had stammered something like: "Uh... Yeah... Uh, sure, yeah, it'd be neat."

Spencer had smiled one of his irresistible smiles. "Great!"

And his attention had returned to the new episode just starting. I had leaned against him, not quite sure what had just happened. Had he proposed to me, or was it just a general question as to my opinion on marriage?

"Of course it's a proposal!" he'd confirmed later, kissing the tip of my nose. "We'll choose a ring as soon as possible."

Eight months later, there was no ring in sight.

The reason for that was simple—he'd been very busy with work, and I had been hesitant to bring it up, knowing he had concerns far more important than an engagement ring.

It wasn't that big a deal. It didn't matter how he'd proposed so much as the fact that he had, and that he'd been sincere. He really wanted us to get married. The rest was secondary and could wait.

Or so I had convinced myself.

But I no longer knew what I believed. Maybe I was just tired. Maybe I missed him. I had no reason to feel slighted. I was happy with him. The rest would come in good time.

As though to apologize for these dark thoughts, I had sent Spencer a cheerful message, telling him about finding Gabrielle's diary and that I was thinking of him. I hadn't waited for an answer—I knew there wouldn't be one for several hours—before plunging back into my reading, losing all sense of time before the phone ring jarred me back to reality.

* * * *

The restaurant we had agreed to meet in was by the river, in an old building that dated back at least a century. The inside was both ancient and modern, gray stone walls decorated with a sepia-toned painting of Angers, black wooden furniture and steel lamps that gave off soft light. Because it was late, the restaurant was nearly empty.

I found Éric sitting in a corner. *He started without me,* I thought as I caught sight of a half-full glass of wine in front of him. I couldn't blame him if he'd been waiting for me for two hours....

"I'm really very, very sorry," I apologized again as I sat across from him. "I was reading Gabrielle's diary and I lost track of time. Please forgive me."

I dropped my crutches on the ground and smiled apologetically. He glared at me, but I thought I could detect something besides annoyance in his eyes.

Had he been worried about me?

"I hope you learned something interesting at least," he grunted.

"Apart from the fact that Thomas and Gabrielle had a love story that was as romantic as it was epic and so sweet it would probably give you a toothache, nothing that can save the castle just yet. But I discovered a momentous family secret right before you called."

"A secret?"

"Apparently Thomas wasn't Victor de Saint-Armand's true son."

He raised an eyebrow.

"So the baroness was unfaithful. What a surprise!" he commented sarcastically. "Who was his father, then?"

"I don't know yet. I was about to find out when you called."

The waiter approached.

"Would you care for a drink, miss?"

"A glass of white wine," I answered. "What do you have that's local? I haven't had the chance to look at your wine list yet."

The waiter listed a few names from Loire valley domains, and I chose among them.

"Very good choice, miss. Would you like to order or should I come back?"

"Can I have a few minutes?" I asked.

"Very well. I'll be right back with your glass."

He departed, and I scanned the menu, feeling Éric's gaze on me.

"Do I have some parsley between my teeth or am I just that irresistible?" I looked up and met his eyes.

"You chose a very good wine," he said, surprised.

"And you're wondering whether I knew what I was doing or if it was just luck."

"A little," he admitted.

"Is it because I'm a woman or because I'm an American?"

"Because you're American. I'm not sexist."

"Well that's a start. But it's really discriminating on your part to think that the French are the only people to know anything about wine. There is a life outside France; I'd have thought you'd know that, having traveled the way you have."

"Touché."

"And just so you know, I work for a Californian vineyard and I probably know more about wine than you do."

"I had no idea," he confessed. "I don't know anything about you, in fact. Apart from you being an incurable romantic and as bad-tempered as I am," he added slyly, a surprising, teasing gleam in his eye.

"Hey! I'll have you know that I do not, in fact, have a temper." I pretended outrage. "I am the soul of diplomacy. You just bring out everything bad in me. And the reason you didn't know anything about me is that you never bothered to ask."

"Fair enough. So who are you, Alexandra Dawson?"

Just then, the waiter came back with my glass, which he set in front of me. He asked again if we wanted to order.

"Give me just a couple minutes more."

He inclined his head and left.

"Have you chosen already?"

Éric nodded.

"I had more than enough time to learn the menu by heart while I was picturing you being mugged in some side alley," he remarked.

"Why didn't you call earlier?"

"I did. You didn't answer."

I winced.

"I didn't leave the room, though."

"You have no idea what went through my mind. I didn't dare leave the restaurant for fear of missing you."

"I'm really sorry for worrying you. I swear I didn't hear the phone ring. Are you still mad at me?"

"I'm not mad. I was just worried." He glanced away then added, "Sorry for yelling at you."

"It's okay. It was my fault really." I reached across the table "Give me your cell."

He frowned.

"What are you going to do with it?"

"I'm not going to steal it, relax. I just want to give you my number; it might spare you a few gray hairs next time."

He pulled it out and unlocked it then slid it across the table. I dialed my own phone and waited for it to ring before hanging up.

"Let's hope you actually answer this one," he grumbled.

"Come on, will you stop being so negative?" I protested as I returned his phone.

"I'm not negative."

I raised my eyebrows.

"Okay, maybe I'm a little sarcastic," he acknowledged.

"That's the understatement of the century. I'm pretty sure if I looked up 'killjoy' in the dictionary I'd find a picture of you."

He smiled. "Nah. I'd be under 'irresistible.'" He gave me a flirtatious look.

Hot damn, he was even more attractive when he gazed at me in that sultry way, and he knew it. My heart stuttered slightly.

"Yeah, right. Watch your feet, I think you're getting too big for your boots and I'm not sharing my crutches," I retorted, hastily hiding behind my menu.

I barely had the time to see a satisfied smile spread across his face, and my heart began to beat faster in spite of myself.

Chapter 18
Gabrielle

Castle of Ferté-Chandeniers

December 1899

"He wasn't...your father?" Gabrielle repeated, astounded.

Thomas shook his head.

"Neither in blood nor in spirit... Not in any way, in fact, except on paper," he amended bitterly. "He never wanted me, and upon my mother's death he hastened to send me away. I was a thorn in his side, a burden he did not want and that he discarded as soon as he could. The black, monstrous stain on the pure lineage of the Saint-Armand."

Speechless, Gabrielle took in the enormity of Thomas's confession. She had expected many things, but not that. Yet if she thought about it the clues were all there: the utter lack of resemblance between Thomas and the other barons de Saint-Armand, the fact that he changed his name to his mother's, the apparently irreconcilable issue between him and Victor de Saint-Armand, the way he had cast away his inheritance...

Thomas was not the son of the baron, and the man had known and made him pay for it.

"I am sorry, Thomas."

"I am not." His tone was cutting. "He was not a good man. I would rather not be related to him."

Gabrielle nodded and steered the conversation away.

"Do you know who your real father is?"

Thomas inclined his head.

"His name was Frederick Andrews. He was English, like my mother."

Gabrielle froze.

"'Was'?"

"He...died too. Around the same time as my mother did."

How could the universe be so cruel to one person?

Gabrielle's heart bled for him, and she only just held herself back from throwing herself at him and holding him tight.

"I am so sorry," she breathed. "It is very unfair."

"Life is rarely fair, you know."

Gabrielle sighed. "I know...." She hesitated. "May I ask you something?"

"Go ahead."

"How did you find out that the baron wasn't..."

"My father? By happenstance, a few years after my mother's death."

"Was that also when you were...injured?" Gabrielle asked.

He paused.

"Yes." He looked away, as though his scar were a mark of shame he had to hide.

Gabrielle thought she could feel a hand close over her heart and squeeze it, and along with it her chest, throat and soul. A deep-seated, fierce need to protect him arose from within her.

"Would you... Would you like to talk about it?" she offered.

"It is not...a pretty story," he said after a pause. "I do not think you really want to hear it."

"The question isn't so much whether I want to hear it as it is whether you wish to tell it," she gently replied. "It is said that a burden shared is a burden halved. And with all my heart, I wish to help you. Maybe...maybe it would relieve you to speak of it?"

"I do not know whether I can."

"Why? Do you not trust me?"

"Of course I do. More than any other. But..."

He broke off, and Gabrielle could read in his eyes his inner struggle. Part of him wanted to tell her, she could see. Yet something held him back, some measure of fear that she could detect in his gaze.

"What are you afraid of, Thomas?" she whispered.

His eyes searched Gabrielle's, hesitant, unsure.

"No one has ever looked at me the way you do," he confessed, with the vulnerability he only exposed when he was alone with her. "And when you know I will lose that. You will no longer look at me the same way."

"Why? Why do you think that? Are you going to tell me you killed the baron?"

She immediately regretted her poorly thought out words when silence greeted her words. It lasted for so long she began to wonder whether she had somehow uncovered the truth.

"No," Thomas finally murmured, "but I have often wished to over the last twenty years."

Gabrielle drew closer.

"Thomas, we have all one day dreamed that someone who hurt us would...disappear. A few minutes ago, I would have thrown Mr. Choiseul to the wolves. That does not make you a monster! It makes you...human."

In that moment, his gaze was undecipherable, full of emotion, hesitation, vulnerability and something Gabrielle could not identify. Her heart clenched a little tighter.

He averted his gaze.

"I have never told this to anyone. Even Céleste does not know the details."

He glanced up, and Gabrielle nodded at him encouragingly.

He motioned for her to take the love seat, and she did so, transferring the books to the floor. But instead of sitting down next to her as he so often had over the past few days, he stood next to the fireplace and laid a hand on the mantelpiece. The expression on his face grew distant, as though he were trying to detach himself from what he was about to tell her. Gazing into the flames, he began his tale.

"Once upon a time there was a prince. He was fair of face with sky-blue eyes and a perfect smile, and all of the young princesses in the world wished to be his lady love. He was also a skilled wordsmith, on par with the best poets of the kingdom. He had ascended the throne early, having lost his father when he was little more than a child, and ruled as sole lord and master over his domain.

"In a nearby kingdom, a rich cloth merchant had several sons who ran his business, and a daughter. Adaline was the light of his life and his greatest pride. She was beautiful, kind, loving and generous. She was a romantic, dreaming of her Prince Charming. She had been protected by her father and brothers all her life and knew little of the real world. She was sweet and naïve, and wondered at everything—a butterfly, a flower, a snowflake. It was said that she had the sweetest smile in all of creation.

"One day, the cloth merchant traveled to the prince's kingdom. When the prince saw Adaline, he immediately wished to marry her. Not because he had fallen in love with her at first sight, no. He wished to marry her because her beauty was without equal and underneath his fair appearance, the prince hid a dark soul and heart, rotten with vanity, pride and an insatiable desire to possess everything beautiful and precious on earth.

"He coveted Adaline from the moment he first saw her.

"Adaline believed his smooth words, his promises and vows, allowing his handsome appearance to fool her. She fell in love with him, and begged her father to let her marry him. But she did not know that once he had obtained his heart's desire, the prince soon grew bored with it.

"Soon after their wedding, young Adaline discovered her prince's true nature. He was violent, easily brought to anger, and instead of the fairy tale she had dreamed of, Adaline's life became sadness and disappointment. Fearful of displeasing him and suffering his wrath, she obeyed his every whim, fading to a shadow of her former self. She lost her smile, the light in her eyes, her joie de vivre. She came to eagerly await the times when he would leave in search of a new treasure, for solitude was a thousand times sweeter than living with her prince.

"Adaline kept her torment silent. She kept the weight of her unhappiness and sadness to herself, hiding the breadth of her misfortune from her father and brothers, assuring them she was the happiest of women.

"And as time went by, she slowly withered, like a flower deprived of water and sunlight.

"One day, a fancy struck the prince; he decided to have his castle expanded. He called for a renowned architect from his wife's country. He was a strong, tall man, as dark of hair as the prince was fair, and his soul was as light as the prince's was black. While the architect worked on the castle, the prince continued his travels, searching for treasures he immediately discarded.

"Adaline soon came to develop true and sincere feelings for the architect who reminded her of her homeland. She could speak her language with him, and he shared her love of books and poetry. His feelings were equally passionate. She could feel herself come alive again. Like a fire that burns and lays waste to all in its wake, she loved him as she had never loved before.

"Blinded by his arrogance, the prince saw nothing. And when the architect left the finished castle, he took young Adaline's smile with him, but left her part of him in exchange. Nine months later, Adaline gave birth to a boy as dark haired as his father. She named him Thomas and loved him even more than she had loved her architect. And when the prince saw how little the child resembled him, his joy upon learning he had an heir vanished along with his interest for the woman who had carried him."

Thomas's face hardened, and his jaw clenched.

"Whether he confronted her and forced her to admit that the child was not his or whether he nurtured doubt within him for the following years is not known. But in the salons he attended, he began to hear unpleasant rumors behind his back that fed his raging temper and turned his disinterest into hatred. He was satisfied with nothing and held his wife responsible for his fall from grace, beating her often. To protect her child, Adaline endured without a word. And the child grew. He began to notice the silent tears on his mother's cheeks, the grimaces of pain she would allow to escape when she believed herself alone. And his heart broke anew every time."

Gabrielle's own heart cracked in her chest, and she thought she could feel the cracks up to her throat. "Dear Lord...," she breathed. Céleste had told her that Thomas's story was grim and tragic and that the events of his childhood had left scars upon him, but she had been far from imagining the truth of it.

"And so it went for ten years. Then, one January day, everything came tumbling down. Adaline received from a trusted friend of her architect a letter announcing the death of her beloved. Upon reading the words she turned pale and clutched her child to her so hard he thought he might suffocate. Then she locked herself in her bedroom while the cook, who was her sole friend and confidante, took her son into the kitchen. The news had broken Adaline's last resolve. Unable to bear the hell in which she lived any longer, Adaline decided to seek shelter with her family and impulsively began to pack a suitcase, taking only the barest necessities for her son and herself. But the prince caught her in the act and grew angry. No one knows what happened exactly, but the prince and Adaline left the room and continued to argue in the corridor. The child suddenly heard his mother cry out and ran out of the kitchen. When he reached the foot of the stairs he found her lying there in a pool of blood."

Oh Lord! Gabrielle almost could not breathe.

"The prince claimed she had tripped and fallen, that he had tried to catch her but been too late.

"Yet there was neither tears nor regret in his eyes.

"Adaline was buried a few days later in the family vault to preserve appearances, and the following week, the prince had the boy shipped to a boarding school. And he forgot him there. The child never returned to the castle.

"Three years went by in total solitude; three years during which the boy dreamed of his mother's bloody face every night. He withdrew into himself until the other children nearly forgot he existed.

"Life had almost become bearable when one day a new boy came to school. He was the son of a neighboring prince, an odious brat very full of himself. He recognized the child's name and began to proclaim that he knew his shameful secret—that the boy was nothing but a bastard that no one wanted, a disgrace to his rank. That he was only a monster, too big and too ugly. That it was no surprise his mother had preferred to die rather than live with him and that his father could not bear the sight of him. He was nothing and no one. A reject.

"And the school laughed at the child.

"For days, weeks, the child endured the mockery and jeers in silence. But one day, when he could bear it no longer, he challenged the young arrogant boy to a duel. Just like in the books his mother had loved, old-fashioned combat at the break of day. He secretly stole the antique swords the fencing master kept in his study and waited for his adversary at dawn.

"The boys fought. The child was strong with uncontrollable rage and anger, and he won, only barely holding back from running his opponent through. But the prideful boy would not admit his defeat and waited for him to lower his guard to slash at his face. The wound grew infected and the child almost lost an eye.

"In three years, it was the only time the prince deigned to come and see him, not out of worry, but to beat the urge to duel with higher-ranking people such as the other boy and his family out of him. Thomas's wound reopened. And as blood poured down his face, the boy looked at the man he still called Father then and asked for the truth.

"'Is it true? Am I a bastard, a reject and a monster?'

"The disgust he saw in the prince's face was all the answer needed. The instant his face was healed, he did as his mother had tried to do. He sailed to England to find an uncle whose address he had received from the cook. The uncle took him in and gave him a home and a family, and over the years, a job and a position of trust in the family trade."

Thomas blew out a breath and fell silent, still staring at the fire, his hands on the mantelpiece, clenched so hard his knuckles were white.

"For seventeen years there was no contact between the prince and the young man. Until one June day when he received a letter from a notary informing him that the baron Victor de Saint-Armand had passed away.

"And despite all of his hatred, despite everything his mother had suffered because of him, the young man cried that day. Maybe it was out of relief or sadness. He did not know. And because it was his duty, he retraced the steps he had taken seventeen years earlier to stand before his mother's grave and cut once and for all the last ties to a past he could not forget, no matter how he tried."

Tears streamed down Gabrielle's cheeks. She could not tell when she had lost the battle and ceased to hold them back. All she knew was that she was distraught, horrified and utterly furious all at once.

A sob shook free from her throat, catching Thomas's attention. Realizing her distress, he rushed toward her and knelt in front of her, cradling her face in his hands. He wiped her tears with his thumbs and gently brought their foreheads together. Eyes closed, Gabrielle relished the proximity, laying her fingers on his wrists as though to keep him there.

"I am sorry," he whispered. "I did not mean to make you cry. I should not have told you."

"You should!" she immediately protested, her voice hoarse. "You should. I just…feel so hurt for you. So very, very hurt."

"It's in the past now," he murmured, his gaze on Gabrielle's. "And it is a past that does not deserve your tears. I am all right, Gabrielle. Everything is all right."

She wasn't so sure. He still carried the scars of Victor de Saint-Armand's abuse on his soul, and she hated the baron for it. So much that her rage almost suffocated her. She was not a violent person, but she would have made an exception to protect Thomas.

"I know it is in the past, but I cannot help it. I feel so…angry. I wish—"

Thomas laid a finger over her lips and gently shook his head.

"Do not. He does not deserve your hatred or your sorrow. Do not stain your beautiful soul with such a man. Dry your tears, Gabrielle. I do not wish you to weep because of me, and even less so because of him. He is not worth it. *I* am not worth it."

"Of course you are worth it!" she cried. "You are worth everything in the world. You—I—"

And in that moment, as she groped for words to defend Thomas's worth to him, a truth that she had known deep inside for some time revealed itself to her. She had fallen utterly and hopelessly in love with him.

"Thomas—" she began, not entirely sure of what she was about to say. Everything in her head was awhirl. Emotions, desires, thoughts.

She wanted to kiss him, feel his lips on hers, his hands on her body, his chest against hers. But she also wanted to hold him in her arms and comfort him. Comfort the child he had been, who had suffered so much. Tell him that he was no longer alone. That she was here.

She wanted to tell him she loved him. To kiss away the sadness, the bitterness that darkened his life away.

She plunged her gaze into his, hoping he would see everything she had in her heart and mind that she did not have the words to express.

"You are worth it," she whispered fiercely, hoarse with emotion. "You are so very, very worth it.… Can't you see it?"

The air in the room shifted, charged with electricity, and some deeper, more primal emotion blazed in Thomas's eyes. His hands were still on her face, gentle and reverent, his thumbs rubbing circles into her cheeks, but millimeter by millimeter, their lips were drawing closer.

"Gabrielle…," he murmured.

She felt her heart expand in her chest and almost feared it might burst.

All of a sudden, there was a knock on the door, and the bubble burst. Again.

Gabrielle closed her eyes.

"What?" Thomas barked, jerking back as an uncertain Agnès slid her head through the door.

"M–Mr. Choiseul says he needs to see you, sir," she stammered.

"Not now," Thomas snapped, while Gabrielle rolled her eyes, grimacing. Even when he wasn't there, the auctioneer managed to ruin her day.

She rose and moved to the window, hoping to calm her wild heartbeat. Everything was calm outside. The wind was barely a breeze. The sun shone. The pure white snow seemed to beckon.

An insane idea flitted through her mind.

"Tell him I've seen enough of him for today," she heard Thomas say.

"He's insisting, sir."

"I said not now!" Thomas was almost shouting.

Gabrielle's eyes went wide, and she spun around. She had never heard Thomas speak in such a manner to anyone.

"Very well, sir," Agnès said, staring at the ground and visibly ill at ease.

Thomas sighed and shook his head. "I apologize, Agnès. I shouldn't have shouted. Tell Mr. Choiseul I am busy and I will see him tomorrow at the earliest hour if it really is important."

"Yes, sir. I'm sorry for disturbing you. Mademoiselle," she added, nodding toward Gabrielle.

She left, closing the door gently behind her. Thomas turned to Gabrielle and tried to meet her eyes. "I'm sorry," he said to her.

"It's not your fault."

"I…maybe…maybe I should leave you alone."

"No, I don't want you to leave!"

I want to show you that you deserve to have a life. That you deserve to have someone make you happy.

He seemed hesitant to draw nearer.

"Do you trust me, Thomas?" she asked quietly.

He nodded.

She smiled at him. "Then come with me. I promise you won't regret it."

Chapter 19
Alexandra

Angers

Present day

"You didn't answer my question," Éric said once we had ordered.
"How did your meeting go?" I asked at the exact same moment.
Éric's shiny new good mood vanished instantly.
"Not well," he replied unhappily.
"Sorry. Do you want to talk about it?"
"No."
Yet he seemed to change his mind almost immediately. He toyed with the knife in front of him and, without looking at me, began: "An acquaintance of an acquaintance helped me get a last-minute meeting with someone who might have been able to help me finance the castle's restoration, or at the very least give me a breather so I could find a more permanent solution... but it didn't work out."
"What exactly didn't work out?"
He shrugged in a thoroughly disillusioned manner.
"It's always about the money. Investing in a castle isn't interesting enough. The return on investment is neither quick nor big enough for him. He'd rather pay for a casino on the coast."
"What?" I protested. "He said that? What about the preservation of history, of heritage? Doesn't he care about that either? Doesn't anybody care?"

Éric sneered. "You really think anybody is still interested in that? Money is the only thing that matters. History doesn't bring in cash. Only the poor and the intellectual care about heritage."

I sighed. "I'm sorry."

"Not as sorry as I am."

"We'll find something," I assured him. "There must be a way to save the castle."

Éric blew out a long, slow breath.

"There isn't, princess. I've run out of options. That man was my last hope."

I could feel the bitterness and despair he did not manage to hide as he gulped his wine down, and my heart clenched. I opened my mouth to say something, anything, and he drove on, speaking to himself as much as to me.

"I've banged on every door. I've set my pride aside to beg the banks and sponsors and heritage organizations. Nobody wants to take the financial risk to restore the castle. And those who are willing to take it don't have the money."

He paused, looked up at me as though to weigh his next words. "I have to sell it."

"You can't do that!" I cried.

"I don't have a choice."

"There's always a choice. There has to be! You can't sell! You have to fight! Don't give up!"

"I've told you. I tried everything. This is the end, princess. I don't have the means to keep the castle anymore. The inheritance tax swallowed what little money was left from my father. I don't even know if I will be able to finish restoring the loft. I'm penniless. I have to accept it. I failed, and everything my father fought for over the years is going to disappear."

The sadness and guilt in his eyes twisted something deep inside me. I wanted to hold him close and comfort him. Barely aware of what I was doing, I reached out and laid a hand on his.

"Don't say that," I reprimanded him gently. "We'll find a solution. I haven't finished reading Gabrielle's diary. Give me a week before you decide to do something you might regret. One week."

He stared at my hand on his. When he spoke, his voice was bitter. "You really think that diary holds the key to saving the castle? I wouldn't put too much faith in it."

"I don't know if there's anything inside that can help, but I'll look. And I'll find something. Trust me. Didn't you say that I was the most stubborn person you'd ever seen and that I never give up?" I tried to make my smile reassuring.

I didn't really know why saving the castle had suddenly become my top priority. Maybe it was because I had spent the entire day immersed in Gabrielle's tale, picturing it in my mind. Maybe it was because it was important to her and Thomas, and therefore to me.

Or maybe because Éric looked so lost that I wanted to help him save his father's dream.

One thing was for sure—I wasn't ready to give up yet. I would find a way. I had to.

My determination must have been written all over my face. A glimpse of hope came back into Éric's eyes, and he nodded. "All right. One week."

"One week," I repeated. "Thank you."

As though he could tell this was a good moment, the waiter came up with our plates. I realized my hand was still resting over Éric's and pulled it back, blushing under the waiter's knowing gaze. I thanked him as he laid my plate in front of me.

We ate in silence for a few minutes, cutlery clinking. The atmosphere had become heavy, and I cast about for an idea to lighten it. Something came to me, and I smiled.

"My name is Alexandra Dawson."

Across the table, Éric paused, fork in the air, icy-blue gaze questioning. Before he could interrupt I went on.

"I'm an only child of two parents who love each other very much, or at least who probably once loved each other very much but don't show it too often. I'm a commercial assistant for a large wine company from the Napa Valley trying to implant itself in France, and I shamelessly took advantage of a business trip to go on holiday here and do my genealogical research—I never could have afforded it on my own."

I thought of what else I could tell him that would lighten the mood.

"I have two cats, Milady and D'Artagnan—don't laugh," I ordered, seeing the amused glint in his eyes. "I like the colors pink and black, eggs Benedict, french fries, tea and dessert. All kinds of dessert. Hmmm. What else? I'm a great romantic, but you know that already. I love reading and I've grown to love genealogy, but my number one hobby is drawing. It has brought me a few reprimands, but also some small amount of fame."

Memories came back to me, and I smiled.

"In middle school, I was often alone, so I drew between classes and during recess. I would sketch anything in front of me. Teachers, students, the staff. I'd do caricatures, manga-style—tiny body, big head, huge eyes."

He nodded to indicate he knew what I meant, and I continued.

"One day, a classmate saw one of my drawings. I don't remember what it was, maybe a teacher. He thought it was funny and talked about it. It snowballed and all of a sudden, I was a popular kid. I loved it. My drawings grew more and more provocative. The other kids loved it and encouraged me. It all blew up in my face in the end. A teacher caught me caricaturing him in class and confiscated my notebook. He didn't like the contents. I was summoned to go see the principal. He called my parents, and I received detention for the rest of the year. And I was also grounded at home, because my parents believe in enforcing a sentence. It was kind of an eye-opener."

"But you didn't stop drawing, did you?"

"No, I couldn't. Drawing is second nature to me."

"I would have been surprised if you'd said you had. You don't seem like someone who allows themselves to be stopped so easily."

"I don't know. Maybe I fight harder for the things that are really worth it."

Maybe one day I would think about what that sentence meant exactly.

One day.

Not now.

"So there it is. You wanted to know me, well, you know just about everything there is to me. Your turn."

"Where did you learn to speak French?"

"You're cheating! It's your turn now!"

"There's not a lot to say."

"There's always something to say," I retorted. "Come on, you're being unfair; one question each. I've already told you a lot, now you need to tell me who you are."

"All right, but this will be over pretty quick. I work for Doctors Without Borders, I'm an orphan and penniless. The ideal catch for a young woman of good standing, in short."

He was joking, but I could tell that he really believed he wasn't worth any more.

"Don't say that! You're a good person. Any woman would be happy to be by your side."

His eyebrows rose as though he doubted me.

"They would, believe me!"

"So I'm no longer rude and a killjoy?" he alluded.

"Of course you are. But a lovable killjoy," I teased.

He smiled, and his sincerity had a strange effect on my stomach.

"Why did you choose Doctors Without Borders?"

"It's a long story."

"I've got time."

His eyes went distant.

"In the late eighties, there was this earthquake in Armenia. I was six or seven, and I was in my father's class—he was a schoolteacher, did Marine tell you that?"

I shook my head and propped my chin on my hand, motioning for him to continue.

"It was in all the newspapers, and the next day my father spoke about it in class to answer a question from a student. And one of the other students, Pierre, said that his father was with Doctors Without Borders and he was leaving for Armenia a few days later. Of course, my father then had to explain what that was. I remember being fascinated. I wasn't very chatty at the time and even less so after my mother's death, but I listened a lot. That evening I asked dozens of questions. My father replied to each one." He paused. "I think that's when I began to consider it. Hearing my father talk of these people with so much respect and admiration, seeing that what they did was both generous and indispensable, impressed me. I used to want to be a firefighter and emergency responder, because I was convinced that if they had arrived earlier my mother would still be alive. But I changed that day. I had found my calling. It never changed. I studied medicine, specialized in pediatrics, and as soon as I was qualified I enrolled. I went on missions, came back to see my father in between, and after a few days or weeks I would leave again."

"Wow. What a beautiful story!"

"I don't know. It seems kind of ordinary."

"Believe me, it's not."

"How did you choose your profession?"

"Hmmmmm..."

For a second I wanted to lie and invent a story. But I decided against it. I wanted to tell him who I really was. "My parents chose for me."

"How so?"

"Well, I wanted to be an artist."

"Yeah, I can picture you as a trendy comic artist, writing stories about women and female empowerment."

I gaped. *How...?* "Well...I wanted to do that. But after the whole caricature thing, my parents and I had several long conversations. They told me I couldn't make a living that way. That it was too risky. Anyhow, I still hadn't gotten over the lecture from my teachers, my parents and the principal, so I just went with it. I didn't know what to do with my life, so any opinion was worth as much as another.... I took some commercial assistant classes, I studied in Montréal to improve my French, and when I came home my father helped me get a job at the wine company. That's it."

Éric stared at me dubiously for a long while.

"Are you disappointed?" I finally asked him.

"No. I just can't really imagine you as the person you describe, that's all."

"That's because you don't really know me."

"Maybe. But I can't help but feel I've met the real you. Not the one who just gives in to others."

I looked down, more troubled than I wished to admit by what he had just said, and sipped my wine to regain my composure.

"What was the country you preferred?"

He kept gazing at me for a little longer, and I thought he was going to accuse me of changing the subject so I wouldn't have to answer.

Which was absolutely what I was doing.

But he didn't mention it, reaching for his glass instead. "Kenya."

"Why?"

"It's a beautiful country, with incredible animals. I had extraordinary colleagues there, who were both interesting and passionate about what they did."

"Did you stay long?"

"Several months. My turn. Do you like your job?"

"It might surprise you, but I do. I learned to love it. My chief is nice even though she drives me hard. We often have wine tastings, and we see a lot of people; it's fun. And I have enough time to do what I want in the evenings."

"And what do you do?"

"What do you think? I draw!" I beamed at him. "I read, I watch television. And these days, I search for my ancestors."

"I see."

I waited for him to continue, to tell me that my life was empty of meaning, that all of these hobbies only hid the absence. That I had no purpose.

I was all too aware of it, especially now that I knew his own life. As if knowing that the man across from me had truly earned his place in paradise made me feel even more acutely how little I had accomplished. How much I meant nothing.

But I didn't want to think of it. Not then, not that evening. So I tried to change subjects.

"Are you going to leave again?"

"I don't know. It depends on what happens with the castle. If we can find a way to save it, I'll stay. Otherwise..."

Otherwise he would leave.

It was silly really, but the mere idea made my stomach feel hollow.

It was ridiculous. We barely knew each other. We didn't even like each other.

"I understand. But if we find a way to save it, can you practice medicine in France?"

"I could. I have a university friend who would let me work with him in Angers."

"But you don't want to."

It wasn't a question. I could see it in his eyes.

"No. I feel like I'm stagnating here. I'm not useful, and there are so many places that need me far more than Chandeniers, Saumur or Angers do. There are more than enough doctors here. I feel more useful overseas. At least the people there really need me. And I like to travel. If I had to stay I would miss it. And yet...the castle is the last thing I have left from my father. It might be troublesome, but it was his dream and my mother's, so I want to achieve it. But if not for the castle, I don't have any reason to stay."

"What about your cousin? Your niece? Aren't they reason enough?"

"Of course they are. But...I can always see them when I come back."

"Oh. I get it."

I could understand his desire to leave, to exist for somebody. Not to be just a face in the crowd, but to make a difference. To do good.

I read somewhere that it's addictive.

I thought of his situation and his dilemma. If we managed to save the castle, his father's legacy, and he chose to stay, he would slowly wither away. I didn't know him very well yet, but I could tell he took his responsibilities very seriously and that he would feel obliged to stay in France permanently. And supervising the castle restoration while he practiced medicine wouldn't be enough for him. He wouldn't be saving lives. He wouldn't be making a difference in his own eyes.

But if he left, he would be abandoning everything he had left from his father to greedy entrepreneurs. If he failed, he would lose his father all over again.

Whatever his decision, he would have to forsake something precious to him. It was sad, in a way.

I sighed, then tried to lighten the mood.

"You know, the ideal solution would be to save the castle and find someone trustworthy you could charge with supervising the restoration.

You save your father's legacy, and you can swan off to Africa or wherever your heart takes you."

"Hmm, not a bad idea."

"Not bad! Come on, it's a *perfect* solution! But you'd have to be thorough in your choice. You'd need someone devoted, who loves history and heritage, and who cares about serving your best interests and the castle's. Someone determined, unafraid to stand their ground if they need to. Someone independent enough to make decisions without calling you all the time."

A knowing smile stretched his lips.

"Someone like you, in short."

"Really?" I feigned surprise. "You're absolutely right! You need someone like me! A pity I'm going back to the States soon, huh?"

Silence greeted my words; then, gently, Éric said: "Yes, it's a pity."

For a few seconds, his gaze caught mine, heavy with something different, something new. My heart suddenly started beating faster while time seemed to stop.

"Alexandra—" Éric began.

"Is everything to your satisfaction, ladies and gentlemen?"

The waiter's question shattered the dangerous bubble that was rising around us.

I turned to him.

"Perfect, thank you," I hurriedly replied.

Éric returned his attention to his plate as though he hadn't eaten in days. The waiter left, visibly satisfied.

The rest of the meal was a little off. In appearance, nothing had changed, yet the air was subtly different. I teased him and he provoked me, but something had shifted. It was as though I had abruptly become very aware of him, of his movements, of his gaze. As though there were a new link between us, born of the secrets we had shared.

We left the restaurant at midnight. Éric had insisted on paying as thanks for lending him my car.

When we reached the hotel, the night warden informed us that the elevator was out of order and the repairmen would come the next day.

"I hope we're not on the last floor," Éric remarked.

"Not quite," I grimaced, "but we are on the fifth."

Climbing four flights of stairs on crutches was going to be no bed of roses. I was tired just thinking of it.

"Only one solution, then," Éric declared.

I stared at him uncomprehendingly.

"I'll carry you."

And he scooped me up the way he had the day before. Before I could protest, he had already started climbing the steps.

"I could have managed, you know," I told him, trying to ignore my traitorous heartbeat that seemed to double with every step.

"I know."

But he didn't set me down before we reached our rooms, right next to each other.

"Her Royal Highness's bedchamber. If her Royal Highness would…"

"Thank you, milord. You are too kind."

"At your service, Your Royal Highness."

We smiled at each other, and for a fraction of a second time seemed to stand still. Eyes locked together, shining in the semidarkness of the corridor, he was so close I felt his breath. My heart was going wild inside my chest.

"Thank you, Alexandra," he murmured.

"Thank *you*, you paid the restaurant."

"No, thank you for being here. For believing. I can't tell you how much it means to me."

I lost all control over my heart rate while a swarm of butterflies invaded my stomach.

A smile identical to Éric's made its way unbidden over my face.

"You're welcome."

"Good night, Alexandra."

"Good night, milord."

He smiled again, and the butterflies somersaulted.

"Good night, princess."

Once the door had clicked shut behind me, I leaned against it, a silly smile on my face. I hadn't felt so alive, so light in ages. I wanted to laugh. To dance.

I tipped my head back and closed my eyes, rewinding the movie of the evening. Éric's smile. His eyes. The moments we had shared, the secrets we had told each other. All the things we hadn't spoken of.

That *I* hadn't spoken of.

And my eyes suddenly flew open as two disturbing realities collided with my horrified mind.

First, I was attracted to Éric. Way, way too attracted.

And second…

I hid my face in my hands, wracked with new guilt.

I had deliberately failed to mention Spencer.

Chapter 20
Gabrielle

Castle of Ferté-Chandeniers

December 1899

"I often wonder what our lives would have been if my mother had not fallen down the stairs that day," Thomas confided that evening when Gabrielle joined him as usual in the library.

Gazing into the fireplace, she considered her reply. Ever since he had opened up to her, Thomas seemed lighter, less withdrawn, less somber even. As though talking to Gabrielle had torn down the last walls around his soul. Nothing could make her happier than to be the one he had chosen to confide in. In the time they had left together, she would do her best to help him overcome his past and find his smile once and for all. She promised herself as much.

"I do not think you should ask yourself that kind of question," she said kindly. "Nothing good will come of it, and it will only make you suffer more. You can't go back. All you can do is turn the page and move forward, toward the future."

"I know."

"You should concentrate on the good things in life." A teasing smile made its way across her lips. "You could...I don't know.... Focus on improving your snowball-throwing skills. You really are a very poor shot."

To her great surprise, Thomas burst out laughing. And it seemed to her it was the brightest sound in the world.

* * * *

They had played in the snow that afternoon. And it had been unforgettable.

Gabrielle had carefully concealed what she had in mind and had convinced Thomas to follow her back outside with Duchesse. And while he looked at the dog frolicking in the snow, she had taken a few discreet steps back and crouched down to fashion a handful of white powder into a ball with her gloved hands.

And without warning, she had hurled it at Thomas's back.

He'd whipped around, surprised. Smiling widely, Gabrielle had waved then thrown her second snowball straight at his face.

It marked the beginning of an epic war that ranged all over the grounds, to Duchesse's great delight as she jumped around them and barked harder than Gabrielle shouted.

And for the first time since she had known him, Gabrielle had heard Thomas laugh—a clear, carefree sound. Suddenly he no longer was Mr. D'Arcy, the broken man, but Thomas, a happy, teasing man.

Gabrielle and Thomas had played for over an hour like children, heedless of their wet clothes, uncaring for propriety or decorum.

They had ended the battle exhausted, lying in the snow, faces turned to the sky and hand in hand, blissful smiles upon their frozen lips, eyes sparkling.

At first, Gabrielle's intent had been to give Thomas some happy memories, memories he could carry in his heart and that would bear him through future hardships. But as they lay next to each other, she realized that she had also created some for herself. And in her heart, she knew that no matter what happened, she would always cherish the memory of this afternoon when Thomas had laughed.

* * * *

"You must work on it, Mr. D'Arcy," Gabrielle said, smiling. "It is unacceptable—how will you ever teach your children to throw snowballs if you are unable to hit a target three feet away?"

Thomas gave her a strange look, and shyly asked, "Do you truly believe I could have a family one day?"

"I am convinced of it." A stone seemed to settle over her heart at the thought. "Across the ocean, in America, you will find a woman who will love you more than anything in the world and you will love her just as much. You will build a big, loving family together. Because you deserve one, Thomas."

He gazed at her for a long moment, face expressionless, a kind of affection in his eyes that Gabrielle felt right down to her soul. For half a second, she thought he was about to speak and she hoped that he would ask her to be that woman. To be his wife. She would have said yes. Of course she would have said yes. She probably would not even have let him finish asking before she accepted eagerly.

But he averted his gaze, seeming to change his mind.

"You know, a few years ago I tried to track down my father's family."

"Did you find them?" Gabrielle couldn't quite hide her disappointment at the change of topics.

"Yes."

He confided that he had needed time to gather the courage for such a task. He had hesitated, unsure of his welcome. He was a child of sin, an unwanted, disfigured monster. Yet his curiosity had been too strong. He had wanted to know. Needed to. He had done his research and found where his father was from. Before he could change his mind, he had traveled to the small town where Mrs. Andrews, his father's mother—his grandmother—lived. But upon seeing her face when she had opened the door, he had abandoned the idea of revealing himself and had merely introduced himself as the son of a friend of Frederick Andrews, come to deliver late condolences. And he had left.

"I could tell from the look in her eyes that my scar, my size scared her," he explained. "She was a frail, lonely old woman made unhappy by her only son's death. I couldn't bring myself to impose upon her."

Listening to his confession, Gabrielle felt her own heart break for him.

"Did you ever think..." She hesitated, fearful of rubbing salt into the wound. "Perhaps... If she had known you were her grandson, she would have embraced you?"

"I do not believe so. She was afraid of me."

"Did she say so?"

"She did not need to. I could read it in her eyes."

Gabrielle chose her words with care.

"What happened to you was horrible, and I do not know how you lived through the combined pain of all these tragedies. But...Thomas...what happened in the past must not hinder you from living today. Or loving."

Thomas stared at her in bemusement, and she went on.

"Not every person is like your...like Victor de Saint-Armand, or your adolescent bully. They are not all waiting to reject, abandon or betray you.

You must learn to trust again. Otherwise... In a way, you are letting them win. If I were you, I would return to see your grandmother and tell her the truth. I am sure she will accept you."

"Do you really believe so?"

"Of course I do! You are her own flesh and blood. Of course she will love you. You are a wonderful man, Thomas. You are not the monster you imagine. You have a scar, it's true, and? You are more than that. You are a man who survived his past and built himself into who he is. You are worth a hundred of those who hurt you. Accept it once and for all—you deserve to be happy. And you deserve to be loved."

She fell silent, short of breath, and bit her tongue. Her outburst had not been planned. The words had escaped from her before she could hold them back.

"I am sorry," she hurried to add. "I should not have said that. It is none of my concern...."

Gabrielle knew her speech had troubled Thomas, even hurt him a little. She could see it in his face. Yet she did not regret her words. There were some truths that needed to be said. And she wasn't done. Looking him straight in the eye, she solemnly inquired, "May I ask you something?"

He nodded slowly.

"Promise me that you will no longer hesitate to open up to others. That you will live your life head held high and ready to be happy, the way you did this afternoon. Do you regret trusting me?"

He hesitated. "No, I don't."

"Then promise me you will heed my advice," she insisted. "I have faith in you. If you give me your word, I know you will keep it."

He took a deep breath.

"I promise."

* * * *

The next day, Gabrielle was in the library again. Pen in hand, an open book in front of her, she was daydreaming, remembering rolling around in the snow with Thomas. She was jarred back to reality by the deep voice of Arnaud Colin, Mr. Choiseul's photographer.

"Dear God, you scared the living daylights out of me!" she exclaimed, startled, clutching at her heart.

Discreetly, she peered around to check that the odious auctioneer was not in the room. She inwardly sighed in relief when he failed to appear.

"My apologies, Mademoiselle Villeneuve. I thought you had heard me."

"You know, when I am focused on a book, the world could fall to pieces and I would never even notice," she replied.

It was true, though she hadn't quite been focusing on a *book* when he had startled her.

"I feel the same way when I am photographing," Mr. Colin agreed, gesturing to his camera.

It was different from the one he had used the day before to take pictures of the castle, Gabrielle noticed. That had been a bulky black box on a tripod, twice as big as her head. This one was much smaller, a black leather rectangular case with a lens on the front. She had never seen the like.

"So?" he repeated. "Would you let me photograph you?"

"You...you want to photograph me?" she parroted, surprised. "But why? There are several thousand more interesting subjects in this room!"

An enigmatic smile flickered across the photographer's face.

"Let's say it's a matter of personal preference. People...are what make a photograph interesting, in my opinion. They breathe life into it. Otherwise all pictures are just still life. And I have always found that life was a thousand times more interesting."

Gabrielle's eyebrows rose. It was the most she had heard him say since he had come to the castle.

"I see. Well, after such a speech, I can only accept. What should I do?"

"Be yourself, and everything will be just fine."

"I think I'll grab a book, then; I'll be more at ease."

"As you wish."

She selected a book and lowered herself into the love seat by the fire, waiting for the photographer to finish setting up his camera.

"Are you ready?" he asked, glancing up. "You need to stay still until I give you the all clear, otherwise the picture will be blurry."

Gabrielle nodded, opening the book to a random page and pretending to read. A few seconds later she heard familiar footsteps in the gallery of portraits and the door swung open. Disregarding Mr. Colin's instructions utterly, Gabrielle looked up and saw Thomas on the threshold.

Their gazes met and suddenly, the world vanished. A smile bloomed upon her lips while her heart began to race. Somewhere close by, she heard the shutter of the camera go off.

She soon realized, however, that something was wrong. Thomas's gaze was grim and he was unsmiling, staring at her with new intensity, as though he wanted to carve her face into his memory. Gabrielle's smile vanished as dread rose within her.

The sound of a throat clearing reminded her that they were not alone. But she could not tear her eyes off Thomas—nor he off her.

Mr. Colin seemed to feel the shift in atmosphere and rose to his feet, stating that he had the picture he wanted and that he would take his leave.

"Thank you, Mr. Colin," Thomas said. "Could you wait for me in my study? I have a request for you."

"Of course, sir. Should I call Mr. Choiseul? He is in the armor gallery."

"No, just you."

"Very well, sir."

He nodded to Gabrielle and left. Thomas turned to her.

"What is it?" she immediately asked, moving closer to him.

"I must return to England."

The words hit her like a blow.

She could feel her knees and hands begin to shake.

No-no-no-no-no-no-no! He couldn't leave. Not yet. Not so soon.

She wasn't ready to leave him, to say goodbye to him.

"But…," she stuttered. "You will come back, won't you? You won't leave for America without coming back here first? Without…without saying goodbye?"

His smile was humorless.

"I will come back, I promise you."

Her hand rose to her chest as though to calm her wildly beating heart, and she released the breath she hadn't realized she was holding.

"How long will you be away?"

What if he only returned after several weeks, long after she and her father had left? What if this was the last time she saw him? What if…

"I do not know yet."

Gabrielle's knees almost gave way under her, but she somehow managed to regain control over herself.

"When will you leave?"

"Today."

Oh Lord! She closed her eyes, unable to bear the pain in her chest.

"Gabrielle?"

She opened her eyes and met Thomas's hesitant, worried gaze.

"Could you… Would you promise me something yourself?"

"Anything," she breathed.

She meant it. She would have said yes to anything, even leaving for England with him.

"Will you wait for me? I mean… Will you wait for my return before you depart for Angers?"

"I will wait for you as long as necessary," she replied without a moment's pause, without even thinking of what such a promise implied.

The door swung open again, admitting her father. Gabrielle tried to collect herself.

"Mr. Villeneuve," Thomas greeted him. "I am glad to see you up and about. You seem in better health."

"Much improved, sir. Thank you for your kindness. And thank you for everything you have done for my daughter and me. I am in your debt."

"Your health is restored, that is all the thanks I need."

"Thank you, sir."

"I am glad you are here. I wished to see you. I must leave for a time, and I was asking your daughter whether you would object to waiting for my return before departing."

"Of course not, sir. Gabrielle and my employee can man the store while I remain here."

"No!" Thomas exclaimed. "I mean…," he continued, ill at ease. "I would like for the both of you to be here when I return. I would like to thank you properly for what you have done."

Surprise painted itself on Maurice's face, but he did not insist.

"As you wish. I imagine Étienne can manage for a little while longer."

"Thank you, Mr. Villeneuve. I must leave you now. I have…many things to prepare before I leave."

* * * *

An hour later, the entire castle staff had gathered before the main entrance, each wishing Thomas a swift and safe journey.

"Would you walk with me to the gate?" he asked Gabrielle as she lingered while the others hastened to return to the warmth inside.

She nodded, and they silently made their way up the path, Duchesse romping through the snow around them.

The sun was high in the sky, and the light reverberating on the snow was so blinding Gabrielle had to squint. A gust of icy wind slithered under her shawl, and she shivered.

"You are cold," Thomas said. "You should go back inside.…"

"No," she immediately replied. "I don't want to go in."

Not yet…

She wanted to savor every second of his presence.

They walked slowly, silently, as though to postpone the moment of their farewell. Of their goodbyes.

It was only goodbye. He would come back. He had promised. And Thomas wasn't the kind of man who reneged on his promises, Gabrielle knew that much.

So why am I so choked up? she wondered. *Why does my heart feel so heavy?*

And if she was so distressed when she knew she would see him again, how would she react when they had to bid each other farewell for good? It was best not to think of it for now. She could barely hold back the tears rising in her eyes as they drew closer to the castle gate where Tornade waited. Closer to the moment he would leave.

"You do know that there are more modern ways to travel, don't you?" she remarked with a forced smile as she gestured to the black horse, trying unsuccessfully to lighten the mood. "In a few weeks we will be in 1900 and you still ride on horseback."

Images of their ride through the countryside in the middle of the snowstorm flashed through her mind.

It felt as though an eternity had gone by since that day when he had come to fetch her in the bookstore. So many things had changed....

"I do know that there are more modern means of transportation," Thomas replied, "but I prefer Tornade."

Gabrielle smiled. Of course he would rather take his horse.

He would always prefer animals to machines. And to men, she was convinced of it.

As though she could feel something in the air, Duchesse came up to Thomas and slid her head under his hand. Gabrielle felt a pang of envy.

"She will miss you," she murmured, stroking the dog's side.

She wished she could imitate her and cling to Thomas, bury her face in his neck, slide her hands into his hair. And never leave him.

"I will miss her too," Thomas said softly, and looked at her. "But I will miss you more."

Gabrielle's heart skipped a beat.

"Not as much as I will you," she whispered, throat tight.

It happened in a fraction of a heartbeat. Before she knew what was happening, Thomas cupped her face in his hands and pressed his lips against hers, first gently, then more forcefully, as though he wanted to seal an unbreakable bond between them.

Half a second later, he was gone. He'd leapt onto his horse and galloped away without a backward glance.

Chapter 21
Alexandra

Angers

Present day

Neither the sun nor the birds had risen yet when my phone's alarm rang a few—too few—hours later.

Exhausted, I had fallen into bed without opening Gabrielle's diary in spite of my raging curiosity. I had slept fitfully, plagued with dreams I preferred not to recall. As a result, I felt more tired upon waking up than I had the previous evening.

Still half-asleep, I fumbled for my phone and stopped the alarm.

Could someone remind me why I had thought a balloon ride at the break of dawn was a good idea?

Yawning, I staggered upright and into the bathroom, hoping a good shower would wake me up and turn me into something remotely alive.

Once I'd brushed my hair and done my makeup, I was as presentable as I ever would be under the circumstances. I limped down into the hotel entrance to meet Éric. He was already waiting for me, comfortably ensconced in his seat and reading the newspaper. His hair was wilder than ever and his five o'clock shadow more pronounced than usual.

He got up when he saw me.

"Hello!" he greeted me with a smile when I came up to him on my crutches.

"Hello." I muffled a yawn.

"Ready to go up?"

Where did he get his energy?

"Is it just me, or are you as excited as a child on Christmas morning?" I teased. "You can admit that you're happy I bullied you into this, you know."

"Yes," he confessed. "I think I'm even somewhat impatient."

"Really?"

"Here you go," he went on, handing me a tall cup. "This should tide you over. Chai latte, is that okay? You said you loved it yesterday."

Seriously? One whiff of the delicious aroma and I almost jumped into his arms. Only my cumbersome crutches preserved my dignity.

"*Oh God...* Thank you!" I moaned. "I could almost build an altar and worship you for this!"

"Only 'almost'?" he questioned, one brow raised.

I snorted and literally fell upon the cup like a ravenous beast.

"Hold on, it's—" Éric warned me as I took a large gulp.

"Ouch!" I cried, spitting out the searing liquid almost immediately.

"—hot," he finished. "Are you okay? Did you scald your tongue?"

"A little, but I'll live."

"Want me to have a look? Check if it's all right?"

"No, no need. Don't worry!" I hastened to reply.

That was the last thing I needed. If he started to examine me, I might not make it out in one piece. Not so early in the morning, anyway.

"Fine, but tell me if it doesn't fade."

"I will."

Not on your life!

"I also brought a few croissants," Éric continued. "In case you're hungry."

So many attentions made me a little suspicious.

"Thank you..."

"You look surprised."

"I'm not used to you being so thoughtful."

"Hey, you said it yourself." His smile was sardonic. "I'm not *just* rude."

That's kind of the problem.

"Are you hungry? Or do you want to save them for later?"

"I'd rather keep them for later, if you don't mind. I'm not awake enough to eat anything right now; it's too early for me."

"No problem."

He leaned down to pick up his jacket from the back of his chair. He paused when I spoke.

"Éric?"

"Yes?"

"Thank you. For the tea and croissants. It's...really sweet of you."

He dragged a hand through his hair, embarrassed.

"You're welcome, princess."

He smiled at me. It was almost shy, with a sidelong glance, and it reverberated through every cell in my body, startling the butterflies in my stomach awake.

Crap.

As much to collect myself as to avoid his eyes, I stared down into my tea.

"Let's go," he said. "I brought the car up in front so you wouldn't have to walk too far."

Okay. So, to recap, he'd gotten up even earlier than the ungodly hour we had to rise at, just to fetch me from who knows where some tea and croissants and bring the car closer. For me.

Crappity crappity crap.

I stifled a sigh and sternly ordered the butterflies in my stomach to stop their shenanigans. And because I did not know how to react to this new, attentive, pleasant and way too attractive Éric in front of me, I reverted to the only type of interaction with him that I knew.

"Who are you and what have you done with Éric Lagnel?" I joked. "Are you trying to butter me up for something?"

"Absolutely not! Can't even be nice without being told off for it," he groused. "Next time you can fetch your damn breakfast yourself."

"Phew, it is you! I was worried for a second that you'd been body-snatched and replaced with a polite pod-person!"

His gaze was deep and inscrutable but suddenly, against all odds, he smiled.

"You really are a piece of work, aren't you? Come on. You're not going to succeed in making me angry today, so there's no point trying."

Without asking permission, he snatched up my chai latte and my handbag and held the door for me. He escorted me to the car and helped me sit inside, folding the crutches into the trunk.

"Do you have the address?" he asked as I switched on the GPS in my phone.

I nodded.

"I programmed it when we were in the bookstore."

"Good idea. It'll save us some time."

I selected our destination, and the dulcet tones of my fake Jamie rang out. Éric gave me a sideways look, one eyebrow raised, and I scrambled to switch into French.

"What accent is that? Irish?"

"Scottish," I corrected as I raised my cup. "We all have our fantasies."

"Really? Redheads in skirts are what make you fantasize?" he said, mockingly. "Good to know."

Crap! I'd missed an opportunity to keep my mouth shut. I was so not going to discuss my fantasies with him in an enclosed space.

I hid my embarrassment with a shrug and gulped down my tea, now at a more acceptable temperature.

Éric barely contained a laugh, and we drove on in silence. The streets were empty, only a few bakeries and cafés open. On the horizon, the first rays of daylight were pushing back the night.

My cup of tea radiated gentle warmth that wrapped me in a cocoon. Head tipped back, lulled by the car's rumble, the GPS's voice and Éric's presence at my side, I felt my eyelids grow heavier and heavier.

I fell asleep.

* * * *

"Alexandra? Alexandra!"

I felt a hand gently shake my right shoulder. I cracked an eye open and met a sky-blue gaze. A blissful sensation engulfed me, and I smiled. The face smiled back, and the blue eyes sparkled.

"Hey," said the owner of that beautiful pair of eyes.

"Hey," I replied hoarsely, still lost halfway between the blue and Morpheus's arms.

"We're here, princess."

His words cut through the fog and sparked something in my brain.

I sat up, blinking, and looked around. I was in a car with an open door, and Éric was crouching in front of me. Everything came rushing back.

The balloon ride! I had fallen asleep on the way!

"I'm so sorry," I said. "How long have I been asleep?"

"No more than an hour."

The last dregs of sleep immediately vanished.

"*What?* Why didn't you wake me earlier? I—"

"Relax, princess. I was kidding. It was barely twenty minutes. I let you sleep while I looked for our balloon among the others and talked to our pilot. Everything is ready. He's waiting for us."

"'The others'? There are other balloons?"

Éric's eyes lit up again, and he smiled.

"A whole field of them."

He stepped aside and opened the car door wide, clearing my view to the field we were parked in.

Dozens of brightly colored balloons rose proudly, their envelopes straining toward the sky, ready to soar up like a flight of exotic birds. In the background, on the horizon, the sun's soft orange glow stretched shadows impossibly long.

I was spellbound, eyes wide with wonder.

"It's magnificent," I breathed. "I didn't expect so many! I thought it would be just us."

"So did I."

"I love it!"

"Okay, princess, ready to have the time of your life?" Éric asked as he leaned down to help me out of the car.

"Sooooo ready!"

I grasped his hand in mine and hauled myself out of the car, smiling like a little girl in front of Cinderella's castle.

"Do you want your crutches?" Éric asked. He was still holding my hand. I shook my head.

"They'll be in the way. I can do without."

"That's what I thought. Let's go, then?"

"Let's go."

* * * *

Our hot-air balloon was a rainbow of pastel colors, from pink to green to red and blue. The pilot, Franck, introduced himself and explained the safety rules for takeoff and landing. Then he described the gear he would be using and how it worked. Since we hadn't been there when he'd inflated the balloon, he summarized the proceedings.

Then came the moment for us to climb into the wicker basket. Franck explained that since there were only two of us, we had enough gas for a two-hour trip. We'd be able to go somewhat farther than he usually did if we wished, a favor he granted us on behalf of Xavier Bourgeois being the one to send us. I immediately asked him if he knew Chandeniers and whether we could fly over it.

"I do know it, and if the winds are with us, we should be able to range that far."

"That would be amazing! Thank you!"

"It's time to take off," Franck decided. "Ready?"

Next to me, Éric shot me a questioning glance. I nodded.

"Ready," he replied.

"Hang on, then. Off we go!"

And he opened the gas valve, beaming. A flame shot out and heated the air inside the balloon. Gently, the basket began to rise into the air. Several of the aircrafts around us had already lifted off. It was an incredible sight.

A feeling of freedom and elation gripped me, submerging me as we inched away from the ground. I felt like I was flying. The basket was small and the sides were high, yet I could fancy myself standing on a rope, completely exposed to the elements. A cool breeze ruffled my hair.

As we climbed higher I swiveled my head around, trying to take everything in, not wanting to miss a fraction of the experience: the ground falling away, the people shrinking to the size of ants, the slowly expanding view as we cleared the trees, the cluster of balloons gradually breaking apart as they cruised at different speeds and in different directions, reaching for the sun, dozens of tiny shadows in the morning light.

And suddenly everything was silent. Total silence, without a bird or a gust of wind. We were higher than everything else, above the forest and the fields.

We were at the heart of a swarm of hot-air balloons and yet we were utterly alone, in the muffled silence of altitude and soft morning light.

It was astounding, magical. I felt excited, dizzy and incredibly serene all at once.

I turned to Éric, my eyes and smile full of wonder.

"It's fantastic," I whispered under my breath, not wanting to break the spell of the moment. "Absolutely fantastic."

"It is," he agreed, the same expression on his face.

His gaze captured mine for an instant. My heart was pounding in my chest, and my head was spinning slightly. I was suddenly very aware of him by my side, of his shoulder touching mine, of the sound of his breathing, of his dazzling smile. He too looked relaxed. As though a weight had been lifted off his shoulders.

He seemed happy. At peace.

It was the first time I had seen him look that way.

And it made *me* happy. Very happy.

It had been what I had been aiming for, after all.

"Enjoying yourself?"

"I am. Very much. Thank you, Alexandra."

"You're welcome, Éric."

* * * *

And so over the next hour and a half, Éric and I discovered the Loire valley as we had never seen it before, admiring the silvery ribbon of a river snaking through the countryside, the vineyards that stretched as far as the eye could see like great stripes on the land. From time to time a cloud caught on a clump of trees, wrapping the treetops in unraveling white strips of cotton.

Then we flew over the first châteaux: Brissac's square chimneys rising from the slate roof, Saumur's geometrical towers and pointed rooftops, Montsoreau at the heart of the town on the banks of the Loire. Franck masterfully controlled the air currents and the balloon's temperature so we could fly as close as possible, offering us an incomparable view of these majestic monuments.

Then our pilot steered us toward the Vienne River, and shortly before we reached Chinon, the castle of Ferté-Chandeniers appeared in all of its splendor.

"Look!" I cried as soon as I caught sight of it. "We're here! We can see the castle! It's beautiful from up here...."

"It is."

Before I could even ask, Franck swung down as low as he could the way he had with the other châteaux, bringing us just over the fire-ravaged west wing, half crumbled, the dovecote in the inner courtyard, the square tower that marked the entrance to the castle. The path that Gabrielle had ridden up to the castle in Thomas's arms. The old stables where they had found the puppies.

From up here, the plants that had overrun the castle were even more obvious, green and lush. They spilled out of the windows, creeping over every surface, be it horizontal or vertical, coiled over the walls, disappeared into every crack.

And in my mind's eye, the landscape flying beneath us superimposed itself on the plans I had found in Éric's father's file, on the images I had pictured as I read Gabrielle's diary.

Here was the ballroom, and the balcony that looked over the moat at the back of the castle. In this vast wing, the largest of all, was the library that had sheltered so many precious works. There, in the wing that was still standing, had been the servants' quarters where Maurice had remained bedridden for so long. If I called upon my imagination, I could almost see Gabrielle and Thomas come and go in the snow-filled courtyard, watch the snowflakes fall through the window, fall in love little by little.

So many lives, so many memories, so many moments of happiness that were in danger of disappearing a second time, and this time for good.

No.

It couldn't be. I refused to accept it. Today more than ever, I refused to accept all of this could disappear. I would fight for this castle to survive this hardship the way it had all of the others.

For once in my life, I would leave my mark upon something.

For once in my life, I would do something truly useful.

Out of the corner of my eye, I saw Éric's face darken, and impulsively slipped my hand into his.

"We're going to save it, Éric," I murmured as the balloon glided away from the castle. "I swear we will."

He didn't reply, but I saw his slight nod, and his hand tightened around mine.

For long seconds we remained silent.

Then, as we coasted by the town of Chandeniers, Éric pointed to a building.

"See that big building there?"

"Yes, what is it? It looks like a huge barn."

"It's a kind of art gallery, halfway between a museum and an exhibition center. I don't know if they're still there, but there used to be a few pictures of the castle dating back to before the fire."

My breath caught in my lungs.

Oh my God!

Photos of the castle as it was in Gabrielle and Thomas's day!

"There weren't a lot," Éric went on, "maybe four or five."

"Why didn't you tell me earlier? I have to go there!"

"I didn't think of it. I haven't…I haven't been there in a long time. Once we went there often with my father. It's…it's where he met my mother. She was head of the gallery."

"Oh. I see. Marine told me about your parents. Their story was… beautiful," I murmured.

"It was. A shame it ended in tragedy, right? Like all beautiful stories."

My heart clenched.

"I'm really sorry about your parents, Éric."

He only nodded, his gaze faraway.

* * * *

The landing was smooth—almost. At the last minute, just as Franck was going to complete a perfect maneuver and alight like a leaf gliding on the surface of the water, a treacherous gust of wind rocked the basket and made it bounce one, twice, three times. We'd all been crouched down, but somehow, I ended up in Éric's arms, my back against his chest, sitting sideways across his legs.

His arms closed around me as though to keep me from being tossed about. And if I didn't pull away, it was only because I was safety conscious. Very conscious of my safety. It had nothing to do with the feeling of warmth and contentment that suffused me. When at last the aircraft fell still, the weight of the envelope and the inertia tipped it over, pushing me even farther into Éric's arms.

"Sorry," Franck apologized, pushing himself up onto one elbow and switching the last machinery off. "Sometimes the landings are a little rougher than planned."

"No harm done," Éric assured him. "That wasn't so bad."

His arms still around me, his voice a low, throaty purr in my ear, he asked, "You all right, princess?"

A shiver ran up my spine.

"Fine." I was short of breath.

"How's your ankle?"

"No worse than before."

"Okay. Think you can get up?"

"Yeah, no problem."

He didn't let go of me.

"You can stop holding me now," I risked, trying to ignore my frantic heartbeat while Franck dragged himself out the basket. "I'm not going to fall."

It was the adrenaline of the landing that had made my heartbeat skyrocket, it had to be.

"That's true," Éric's voice said in my ear.

But he didn't move. And after a few seconds, I realized I wasn't moving either. It seemed to me that every cell in my body was hyperaware of Éric's proximity. I felt his breath upon my neck, his chest against my back, the small of my back pressing—involuntarily!—against the front of his pants.

My head spun, and this time, there was no wine to use as an excuse. And deep down, I knew it had nothing to do with a lack of sleep either.

It was him, and him alone, that set my senses afire.

And for an instant, I wanted more than anything for him to kiss me. I wanted it so much that it scared me.

Fudge. Fudge fudge fudge.

I had to move. Fast.

I was about to do just that when a small twitch on Éric's part informed me that he wasn't indifferent either to the closeness of our bodies. The sudden desire that blazed in my lower stomach was almost painful in its intensity.

Just then, Franck popped his head over the edge of the basket.

"You all right in there? Need any help climbing out?"

"We're fine, thanks!" I rushed to reply.

Clearing my throat, I broke free of Éric's arms—he released me without protest—and crawled out of the basket.

Once the envelope had been folded and the gear packed away in the van Franck's assistants had been following us in, we joined them for the traditional celebratory drink. We toasted our first balloon flight with a delicious glass of wine right where we had landed, in a field before a picturesque vineyard and its manor. We lazed about in the sun for over an hour, talking and reliving the high points of our experience.

As usual, Éric was taciturn and I was chatty enough for two, asking everyone about their jobs or why they had chosen to do this.

Time fairly flew by and soon enough, it was time for us to return to our starting point, where we had left my rental car.

We drove in semisilence, Franck's team talking among themselves while I listened, half lost in thought. As for Éric...I wasn't sure what he was doing. He seemed...unsettled. And I couldn't help but wonder whether it was due to us flying over the castle and talking about his parents...or something else.

Several times, I felt his gaze rest on me. And each time, I tried to ignore the quivering sensation in my stomach.

Back at the car, we drove back toward Angers without a glance toward the pastries still waiting inside. After checking out of our hotel, we left for Chandeniers.

And during all this time, we didn't exchange a single word.

"Do you want me to put on some music?" I asked after a while.

"If you want to."

I reached for the radio, then changed my mind.

"I have a better idea. I could read the next part of Gabrielle's diary to you. I don't know about you, but I'm dying to know who Thomas's father was."

"If you want to," he repeated.

"Gee, contain your enthusiasm," I grouched.

He shook his head and stole a glance toward me.

"Sorry. I think the lack of sleep is catching up to me."

"Want me to drive?" I immediately offered. "I can, you know. My ankle barely hurts."

"No, I'm fine. And I don't believe you. I saw you grimace earlier when you were walking. I'll drive, but please read, it's a great idea." His smile was strained.

I raised my eyebrows but didn't push it. I took out Gabrielle's diary and flipped to where I had left off the day before, summarizing briefly for Éric's benefit—who was who, who did what, who flirted with whom. I introduced him to the dogs, explaining that Thomas had found them one morning in the stables and had taken them in. I teased him for his resemblance to Thomas.

Then I plunged back into the story, discovering the truth behind Thomas's father through Gabrielle's eyes.

I had to stop often, throat tight, when I read what Thomas had suffered. I shared Gabrielle's rage as she heard those horrors.

My wrath vanished as soon as Gabrielle realized her feelings for Thomas, and I allowed the butterflies in my stomach free rein. My heart beat to the same rhythm as hers when their faces drew close. Hands clenched on the diary, I had to force myself not to skip lines, whole paragraphs, and shout, "Just kiss her!" And like Gabrielle, I could have strangled that loathsome Mr. Choiseul for interrupting *their* moment.

And when Gabrielle and Thomas played in the snow, the sheer absurdity of the situation almost made me laugh out loud. And I probably would have burst into laughter if tears hadn't been streaming down my cheeks.

I felt ridiculous, stupid, completely off course.

A sob wrenched itself free of my throat, surprising me.

"Hey, Alexandra," Éric said gently, wrapping an arm around my shoulders.

I didn't know when we'd grown familiar enough with each other that it seemed natural for him to do such a thing.

"I'm okay," I sniffled, wiping the tears away. "I'm just…I'm just tired, don't worry about it. It'll pass."

But the tears didn't pass, not right away at least. Éric pulled me toward him and hugged me, one hand stroking my hair, letting me cry my eyes out. I almost thought I felt his lips on the top of my head, but I must have been mistaken.

When my tears ran dry, I was painfully aware of his hand running through my hair, a gesture that was both soothing and electrifying, of the warmth of his body, of his heartbeat against the hand that had curled on his chest as though it had a mind of its own.

It felt so *right* there, nestled in his arms. Like Gabrielle in Thomas's arms, I felt…cocooned.

I didn't want to leave the comfort of his embrace.

But I *had* to leave the comfort of his embrace.

I couldn't go there. I couldn't let my body react to Éric the way it did. It was a mistake. Éric wasn't for me. I had Spencer. I loved Spencer. With all my heart. I was going to marry him.

So why did the thought of spending the rest of my days with him seem like a jail sentence just then?

I had to move away from Éric. Immediately.

Seizing my courage, I cleared my throat and pulled away, ignoring the sensation of heartbreak that gripped me.

"I had no idea—" I said, looking down at my folded hands. "I knew his past was dark, but I had no idea how dark. I thought…I thought those kinds of things only happened in books."

"I know. Life…life is unfair sometimes."

"So you've said, often enough."

"I'm sorry."

"I'm glad he had Gabrielle to bring him some measure of happiness."

"Some women are the redemption of men. They are…a bright light in a dull and drab existence. Gabrielle was one of those."

His words moved me, and I found I still had a few tears left. I hurriedly wiped them away.

"God, I'm so stupid. Crying over a story that's a hundred and twenty years old."

"It's not a hundred and twenty years old to you. You threw yourself into this story like it was your own, so it's only natural for you to be emotional."

I sat straighter and gaped at him, surprised yet not that he had once again seen straight to the core of the matter. He reached out and wiped the lingering tears on my cheeks, exactly like Thomas had done for Gabrielle.

His fingers burned like fire on my skin, and yet I had to fight not to nuzzle into his palm.

"Are you all right?"

I nodded. "I'm okay. Thanks. Sorry about that. You really must think of me as a kid."

"Not at all. I understand. But we should get out of the car now, before Marine starts wondering what we've been doing for the past ten minutes in here. And judging from the barking, Max is eager to greet us."

I then became aware that we were parked in front of the inn. Once more, I had been so consumed by my reading that I hadn't noticed anything going on around me.

I hastily checked that my little crying jag hadn't made a mess of my face and cursed inwardly when I saw that it had. As Éric stepped out of the car, I pasted a smile on my face and opened the door.

It was time to get back into the real world—and draw away from Éric before I was no longer able to.

Chapter 22
Gabrielle

Castle of Ferté-Chandeniers

December 1899

"Where should we put it?"

"There." Gabrielle pointed to a pedestal table in the corner of the ballroom.

"Very well."

Wordlessly, Guillaume and Arnaud Colin set the huge gramophone down. The photographer turned to her.

"Anything else? A grand piano, a double bass, an organ, the entire symphonic orchestra from Vienna?"

Both of Gabrielle's eyebrows rose high into her flyaway hair. Arnaud had clearly loosened up since he had come to the castle, and he sometimes even bantered with her. She had been the first one surprised.

"Well,"—she pretended to think—"now that you mention it, there is the piano in the billiard room...."

Seeing his eyes widen, she hastily added, smiling: "It was only a jest! The gramophone should be enough. Thank you for your help. Now remember, not a word. I want this to be a surprise!"

Both men nodded.

"Perfect! Again, thank you both."

"At your service, fair maiden," Arnaud declared before he followed Guillaume out of the room.

He has *changed,* Gabrielle thought. *There's no stopping him now.*

Especially when his unbearable friend was not around, as was the case today. Mr. Choiseul had had to leave for "urgent business that required his immediate attention."

Such a shame, Gabrielle lamented, *we will not be able to ring in the New Year with him. I do not believe I shall ever get over it!*

Chuckling at her own jibe, Gabrielle turned to the gramophone. She had better check now that it was in working order, rather than discover it was broken that evening once everyone had gathered in the ballroom. She deposited a record on the turntable and cranked the handle to wind it up. As the table began to turn, she placed the stylus into the groove of the record. After a short burst of static, the opening notes of *The Blue Danube* rang out.

Gabrielle smiled in satisfaction.

The machine worked perfectly. Well, the sound was not strong enough to fill the ballroom. It did not carry further than a few meters around the horn, but the dancers would not be many. It would do well enough.

Gabrielle was delighted. She knew her surprise would enchant everyone, her father especially. Maurice loved to dance, and he'd had precious little chance to since Héloïse's death.

A familiar wave of nostalgia washed over her, and she swallowed the lump threatening to form in her throat. She usually managed to deal with the absence and the void left by her mother. She had grown used to it. But today the pain flared stronger than ever.

And Gabrielle knew exactly why.

She missed Thomas. She missed him so very much. She missed his eyes, his smile. She missed their conversations late at night in the library. She missed his very presence, the sound of his footsteps on the carpet, the way he said her name, with a barely detectable hint of an English accent. The look on his face when he was with Duchesse and the puppies, his gentle manner with them, with her. The light in his eyes when their gazes met... She missed every part of him, so much that at times she couldn't breathe.

She wished she could confide in her mother, ask her whether it was normal for her to feel such a gaping emptiness when he was parted from her, as though half her soul had been cut out. But she could not. Héloïse was no longer there to hear her talk of her first love and provide her with wise advice. So Gabrielle kept her questions to herself and filled the emptiness as best she could, pouring her hardships into her diary instead.

Eyes closed, heart and mind overflowing with melancholy, Gabrielle swayed to the waltz's gentle melody. Carried away by the music, she gathered her skirts in one hand, eyes still firmly shut, and spun as she hummed, the world fading away.

As though her prince, the man of her dreams, were not hundreds of kilometers away but on her arm.

Thomas had been gone three weeks already, and it had been seven days since she had last heard from him.

She missed his letters. They had filled a little of the loneliness that his absence had created in her life and heart.

Gabrielle had been the first one surprised when Hélène had handed her a small envelope, three days after Thomas's departure. She had been in the library with her father, assiduously working on the inventory, when the governess had come in to deliver the daily reports Étienne sent from the bookstore to Maurice. But instead of returning to her usual tasks afterward, she had headed toward Gabrielle, and, with a knowing smile, had deposited the letter in front of her. Gabrielle's heart had leapt when she had read the name of the sender.

Blushing, she had slipped it into her pocket. Anticipation ate her alive, but she wanted to be alone to read it. She'd waited all day, and in the evening, once Maurice and the others had retired for the night, she had padded to the library and sat on *their* love seat. She'd unsealed the letter and pulled out an ivory-colored sheet of paper folded over an exquisite dried white-and-red rose. Its scent was still fragrant. There had been a few words on the paper.

It made me think of you. ...

Gabrielle's heart had begun to race.

So he thought of her. ...

Laying the letter over her heart, she had released a deep sigh. She thought of him too. Always. Whatever she did, he was always at the back of her mind. She often recalled his kiss, both brief and intense, and she wondered...did he love her as much she loved him?

The first letter had been followed by a second a few days later, then a third, and a fourth. They reached the castle every three or four days, like a ray of sunshine in Gabrielle's day. They often only held a few words, a handful of lines, a dried flower, a different one each time, always beautiful, but she needed no more.

Then a week had gone by without messages. Not a word, no news. Gabrielle had grown worried. No matter how she tried to rationalize, repeating to herself that there could be dozens of reasons for his abrupt silence, that he was a busy man, with an important job in his family's company, she could not help but imagine the worst. What if something had befallen him? Or what if he regretted the kiss, the letters, everything that had happened between the two of them?

The days had crawled by, each one similar to the one before, and Gabrielle's anxiety had risen. To avoid losing her mind, she had plunged headfirst into her work. From dawn to dusk, she drowned her thoughts, questions, doubts and hopes in paper and ink.

Of course, with such dedication on her part, she and Maurice had soon finished the inventory. Now there only remained to add the date of the auction, and the document would be ready to be sent to the printing press. Already Maurice had begun speaking of returning to Angers and the bookstore, their customers, their trade and books. He paged through Étienne's reports with increased interest, planning visits to their patrons, drawing up his schedule. Gabrielle's zeal had turned against her. The end loomed nearer than ever, and, caught between their impending departure and Thomas's silence, her spirits were at an all-time low.

She put on a brave face, though, enough to fool the inhabitants of the castle. But not her father. The previous evening, as they put away the last books, she had released a sigh that spoke volumes as to her true state of mind. Maurice had immediately taken advantage of the opening.

"What is it, my darling?"

"Nothing, Papa. Nothing at all."

Maurice had raised his eyebrows. "Gabrielle, I know you better than anyone. I can see something is amiss. You haven't been yourself in days."

"It's nothing, Papa, it will pass. I just…I don't think I want to leave. The castle, the books… I will miss all of this."

Her father had gazed at her for a long while before he had replied. "Is it the castle you will miss? Or its lord?"

Gabrielle had been so taken aback she was momentarily struck speechless. She should have known her father would see right through her.

"You love him, don't you?" Maurice had insisted.

She could only nod, a sad, resolute twist to her lips.

"Does he return your affection?"

Gabrielle had sighed.

"I believe so, but I do not know for certain," she'd admitted. "I hope he does."

"I see."

Maurice had fallen silent for a few seconds, as though thinking of what to say and how to say it.

"You do know he is leaving for America."

She'd nodded again without replying. She knew it only too well. Just as she knew that it would be wiser for her not to dream too big, in order to avoid disappointment. After all, he would be sailing across the ocean in a few weeks...leaving her behind. She should not forget that.

For once in her life, she should keep her feet firmly on the ground. Rein in her overactive imagination before it could run away with her. For once, she should...keep herself from dreaming.

"Be careful, my darling," her father had warned her. "I would hate to see you suffer."

"Don't worry about me, Papa. I can take care of myself. And of you." She had winked at him.

Maurice had smiled and sighed in nostalgia.

"I know. Time flies by so quickly! It seems to me that it was only yesterday that I healed your scratches with magic kisses, and today you have become a beautiful young woman, clever and talented, making her old father very proud indeed."

"Thank you, Papa."

Silence had reigned again for a time, troubled only by the rustling paper between Maurice's hands as he gathered their notes.

"What about you?" Gabrielle had asked, glancing sideways at him.

"What about me?"

"Will you not miss the lovely Hélène?"

"Why do you think that?" he deflected, trying to look casual and busying himself with his papers.

"Don't pretend, Papa. You may know me better than anyone else, but the reverse is true also. I've seen the way you look at her. You're fond of her, aren't you?"

He hadn't replied, but the dreamy look on his face and his involuntary smile had been all the answer she needed.

"I don't know," he'd finally said. "A little, maybe."

"'A little'? 'Very much,' I think. And she is fond of you too."

"Do you think so?"

"Papa! How can you not see it?"

"I don't know. I am not that young anymore."

"Neither is she, and I do not think she would be interested in a younger man."

Maurice had glanced at her hesitantly.

"Do you...do you like her?" he had asked, almost timidly.

That was when Gabrielle had abruptly understood what held her father back from publicly courting Hélène. He needed to know that his beloved daughter, the light of his life, approved his choice, that she did not regard his feelings for the housekeeper as treason toward her mother.

He wanted her consent.

Touched, Gabrielle had risen and put her arms around her father, standing on tiptoe to kiss his balding head.

"You have my blessing, Papa," she had murmured.

She was sincere. She truly loved Hélène, and she knew she would make her father happy without ever trying to replace Héloïse in her husband's or her daughter's hearts. Yes, Gabrielle's heart ached a little at the thought of her father rebuilding a life with another woman, but her mother was no longer here. After so many years, Maurice deserved to find happiness again. Héloïse would have wished that for him. And so did Gabrielle.

That was one of the reasons she had decided to throw this impromptu ball—a grand word for what she had planned. She wanted to give her father a chance to reach out to Hélène before it was too late.

One of them at least should have a chance at happiness.

* * * *

Still the music filled the vast ballroom, and Gabrielle spun and twirled, eyes closed, gliding across the marble floor between her imaginary partner's arms, dreaming he was at her side, calming her doubts and quieting her fears, drying her tears.

And suddenly, a very real hand grasped hers and spun her around, pulling her toward a body whose scent was very familiar. A second, slightly possessive hand slid over her waist to the small of her back.

Gabrielle's eyes flew open as her heart raced. She hardly dared to hope. With a gasp of surprise, she met a silvery gray gaze that she knew better than anything in the world.

Relief filled her entirely, and she threw her arms around Thomas's neck, heart bursting with joy.

He was back.

At last.

Chapter 23
Alexandra

Chandeniers-sur-Vienne

Present day

With the exception of a couple of details, the castle of Ferté-Chandeniers in 1899 was exactly as I had pictured it from Gabrielle's descriptions—sumptuous.

I examined the few yellowed photographs in the museum Éric had told me about with no little awe. There were only six—the rest had probably been lost or destroyed over the past century. They all featured a different room of the castle. From left to right, the visitors of the museum could admire a long gallery lined with mirrors, and a vast ballroom with a checkered marble floor and wonderfully sculpted columns. Then came a picture of a study filled with dark-colored furniture, decorated with armor from all over the world and scimitars hung over the imposing mantelpiece. A dining room adorned with painting and wall hangings, as well as a magnificent crystal chandelier was next. The following picture depicted an endless gallery of portraits featuring proud-looking men with a distinct family resemblance. I could only suppose they were the various barons de Saint-Armand.

And the last picture of the collection was of the library.

The library.

The one that had brought Gabrielle and her father to the castle. The one that had been witness to so many discussions, confessions, intimate moments. It was a room built lengthwise, pierced with high windows hung with heavy velvet curtains. The walls and columns were lined with bookshelves two stories high.

Gabrielle had compared it to Captain Nemo's in her diary, but it came closer to the one in *Beauty and the Beast*.

I admired the picture. It was one thing to read about it in my ancestor's diary, and quite another to see it "for real." I was almost...moved.

Impulsively I took out my singed photo of Gabrielle, the one that had sparked all of my research, and compared it to the one on the wall. The shelves were identical. So was the large oak desk. Even the love seat was the same.

There was no doubt about it, her picture had been taken here. And if her journal could be believed, by the same photographer, Arnaud Colin.

I put the picture away and gazed back at the photographs on the wall, letting my mind wander, picturing Gabrielle and Thomas (in my mind's eye, he was a mix of Gerard Butler, Channing Tatum and Captain Harlock) sitting in the library talking, or standing in the portrait gallery gazing at the only picture of Thomas's mother. From there, my thoughts leapt toward the revelations Thomas had made to Gabrielle, and suddenly something occurred to me. I hadn't thought of it until now, but if Thomas was not really the heir of Victor Leroy de Saint-Armand, then neither was I a descendant of the Saint-Armand family.

I lingered on the thought for a moment. I didn't have any blue blood, despite what I had thought for a time. My ancestors were ordinary folk, with ordinary lives. Did that change anything for me?

Absolutely not. After all, before I'd come here, I'd had no idea that Thomas had owned a castle, or that he was—officially, at least—a noble. So yes, I'd been proud for a time of my elevated origins. Who wouldn't be? It isn't every day a random American finds herself descended from French aristocrats. But reading Thomas's account of Victor, I could only rally to his opinion. I would much rather be nobody than be related to such a man.

I thought of what I had told Éric shortly after my arrival. That knowing where I came from was key to knowing who I was. I now realized how mistaken I had been. I was now far more aware of my roots, knowing what I did of Gabrielle and her life's story; but contrary to my earlier belief, I was nowhere near knowing myself, and even less where I was bound for.

To tell the truth, I was more lost than ever, both in real life and inside my mind.

Yes, I had learned a lot about myself during this time, and I had changed, that much was for sure. The Alexandra of today was clearly not the same as the one who had found the photo, but it wasn't uncovering my ancestors' identity that had wrought that change. It was everything else. It was the fact that I had found a project to pour all my energy into. It was that I had done everything in my power to come here. It was my wish to save the castle at all costs.

This jaunt had upended my life and my every certainty. Or perhaps it wasn't just the adventure that had turned me inside out, I thought as Éric's azure gaze came to mind.

One person had changed everything. A single person full of sarcasm, with a dog and a too-rare smile and piercing eyes that seemed to see right through me. Someone who managed to make me feel like the person I had always wanted to be with a single glance, whose simple presence made me feel at peace with myself. Someone who seemed to turn my heart, my head and my every sense upside down. Someone who attracted me like a magnet, in new and primal ways.

God...

I sighed.

And here I was thinking of *him* again.

I hadn't stopped in three days.

Since Angers, the restaurant and the balloon ride.

Since I had lost all control.

It had been an insidious, sly process. A feeling that had sneakily made itself at home in my chest. First a dream, a mindless drawing sketched out with a distracted hand. Then a feeling of loss in a corner of my heart, diffuse, vague but very real, growing each day. And the impression that my entire body was reaching for *him*, that my heart went crazy every time I caught a glimpse of him.

And see him I did. I couldn't miss him, in fact. I had never seen him around as much as I had since I'd decided to distance myself. He was everywhere. I saw him in town when I went for a walk. I saw him at Marine's inn repairing the tap or having coffee with her. At the cemetery where I had left flowers on Adaline's grave, that I had found since I was there last. On the path along the river, running with Max.

He was in my thoughts, my dreams, my life, every day, all the time, without fail. And despite my efforts to cut our conversations short, pretend I had a thousand things to do to avoid his company, doing everything I could to kill this fledgling, forbidden attraction, I couldn't stop my heart from beating faster when he was near, my knees from going weak or my body from being irresistibly attracted to him.

I was becoming crazy. Literally.

And I felt terribly guilty because of Spencer.

I loved Spencer, I truly did.

So even if a single glance from Spencer had never set me ablaze the way Éric's did, that was no reason to betray him. He deserved better. I had promised him my heart and my hand, and I had to reassert control over myself. I had tried calling him, hoping that hearing his voice would rekindle my feelings for him and help me sort out my emotions. But he had never been available, and his answering machine was no longer enough.

I absolutely had to erase Éric from my mind, to stop thinking of the way he looked at me, of how I had felt in his arms, of the sound of his voice....

Oh, hell!

I stifled an annoyed sigh and shook my head to clear it of these dangerous thoughts. Rummaging in my handbag, I pulled out my sketchbook, determined to busy my mind and hands. I opened it and flipped through it in search of a blank page, slowing as I stared at the last few days' drawings. They were all of the same person.

Oh.

I hadn't realized I'd drawn so many. I'd sketched everything of his, his face, his sharp blue eyes, his square jaw, his smile, his messy hair, his hands, his silhouette...his ass.

Oopsie...

My face turned bright red as I lingered over the last picture. I was ashamed of it, but I had drawn his muscled ass, clad in the ripped jeans he was wearing when I'd visited him last Saturday.

I turned the page over quickly, trying to limit the damage, and started copying the photos of the castle faster than light. I was so absorbed I only realized I was no longer alone when a voice rose next to me.

"You must be Alexandra Dawson."

I looked up to meet a pair of hazel eyes on a smiling face. Both seemed strangely familiar, though I could not recall where and when I had seen their owner before.

I smiled.

"I am. How did you know?"

He shrugged.

"Chandeniers is a small town, and I know everyone."

"And you are?"

"Bruno Lepic," he introduced himself, offering his hand to shake. "I'm the mayor and also, as it happens, the curator for this little museum."

"A pleasure."

My memory suddenly spiked.

"You were coming out of Marine's inn last Friday as I arrived, weren't you? That's where I saw you."

"Yes, that was me."

"You had a little boy with you."

"My son."

"I knew your face was familiar! Has anyone ever told you you look like Tom Hiddleston?"

"A couple of times," he admitted, chuckling embarrassedly. "I see you're admiring our castle," he added, nodding toward the photographs.

I followed his gaze, returning to the pictures I was reproducing.

"I was. It really was magnificent. It's a shame it's in such a state. When you see the way it used to be..."

"Tell me about it," he agreed. "We do all we can to maintain the grounds and ruins in the hope that we can restore it one day, but I don't need to tell you it's a thankless task. And every day that goes by, it breaks down a little more. One day the damage will be irreversible, and it will be too late."

I shook my head. "That's really sad. I'm trying to think of solutions, but I've had no luck so far. Not for lack of trying."

"I was told you have some historical documents about the castle?"

Gossip travels fast around here.

"I do. Thanks to Mr. Lagnel's research, I found a diary belonging to one of my ancestors that lived for a time in the castle, at the turn of the century. Around the time these pictures were taken. I could give you the name of the photographer if you're interested."

"Yes, I am."

He explained that he'd been interested in the castle's history for many years now, and that he'd helped Marc Lagnel with his research on several occasions.

"Anything you can tell me could turn out to be very useful for my own research," he concluded.

"Then let's strike a deal—your information against mine."

He beamed.

"Done!"

* * * *

Half an hour later, I was sitting in a café with the charming mayor of Chandeniers, discussing our common interest—the castle.

We hardly strayed from that topic throughout the meal. Bruno, as he had told me to call him, turned out to be a treasure trove of information, and I scribbled note after note, fascinated, listening to tales of sixteenth-century parties that were as splendid as they were opulent.

"How do you know all of this?" I finally asked, when the waitress brought us desserts. "Have you ever thought of writing a book on the castle? It could help save it."

"I've thought of it, yes. But by the time I finished writing it, it would be too late. And how I know this… I'm very interested in history, especially my city's. I have big plans to develop tourism and try to find the means to help Éric save the castle."

"Do you know Éric well?"

"Well enough, we were in school together. When I was in university, I read his mother's work on the history of the region. I was so impressed I took over her museum as soon as I could."

"I see. In that case, forgive me for asking, but…why don't you help fund the restoration?"

He sighed.

"I've tried to find a solution, and I even offered to buy a share of the castle from Éric, but he won't hear of it. I talked to him about it only yesterday and he refused again."

I was surprised.

"Why? It would be a solution to all his problems. Or most of them, in any case."

"He told me he was waiting. That someone had promised to help and that he wanted to wait. I don't know who," he added with a knowing glance, "but I can tell you that it's very unusual for him. When I offered to buy a share, I thought he'd leap on the opportunity to return to Africa, but…it seems this person impressed him very much."

I felt my cheeks turn scarlet and my heartbeat ratchet up. I tried to look innocent and composed.

"I was ready to negotiate with the banks and throw in my own savings," he went on, "even if I had to mortgage my house."

"If that was the condition, I think I would also have refused," I said. "I don't think Éric would want anyone to be ruined because of him."

"But it would have bought us some time."

"Maybe. Maybe not."

"Hmmm."

As the waiter came to take away our plates, neither of us spoke. Leaning back on his chair, Bruno swirled his glass of wine idly, admiring its clear ruby color.

"You know, not many people are aware of this, but the castle used to have its own vineyard back in the eighteenth century. It disappeared when the castle was torn down during the Revolution, and nobody ever replanted the vine stock, but at one time there was a Chandeniers vintage."

I froze in my seat.

"A vineyard?"

"Yes," Bruno repeated. "There are no traces left today, but I have evidence that there was one."

I pulled out the plans I had copied from Marc Lagnel's file and spread them over the table.

"Do you know where exactly the vineyard was? How big it was?"

"Let me think about it...." He studied the plans. "I think it was around here."

He pointed to a patch of land at the back of the grounds, a smallish area, but not inconsequential.

A plan began to form in my mind. The plot of land was smaller than what we were looking for, but if I presented things right, I might be able to make that seem meaningless compared to other points, including the fact that it came attached with a castle. A significant detail concerning marketing, not to mention the philanthropic aspect of our investment that could be emphasized.

Excitement almost overtook me. How had I not thought of this before? The answer was obvious! It was *the* solution we had been looking for!

"What is it?" Bruno asked, perplexed.

I raised shining eyes to him.

"I know how to save the castle."

Chapter 24
Gabrielle

Castle of Ferté-Chandeniers

December 1899

If Gabrielle's impulse surprised him, Thomas did not show it. On the contrary. She felt his powerful arms close around her without hesitation as he buried his face against her neck. A second later, he had lifted her clear off the ground. He held her so tightly she could barely breathe, but it did not matter. Why would she need to breathe when she had the man of her thoughts holding her?

"You came back!" she exclaimed.

"I promised I would," he murmured against her neck.

His English accent, more pronounced than it had been when he left, made her shiver. She closed her eyes and savored the feeling of his arms around her, a sensation both foreign and familiar.

It was so good to see him again.

He set Gabrielle down but did not release her from his embrace.

"Welcome back, Mr. D'Arcy." She beamed.

"Thank you, Mademoiselle Villeneuve."

"Did your trip go well?"

"Well enough."

"Are you sure you are all right?"

"Now that I am here, I am just fine."

Gabrielle scrutinized him for a minute, then nestled against his chest. She could hear his heartbeat, strong and powerful. She loved the sound of it. More than any other, maybe even more than his laugh.

"I am so glad to see you," she breathed. "I…I worried. I was afraid something had happened to you. There were no more letters."

She felt his arms close a little tighter around her, and Thomas's lips brushed her hair, stopping just shy of a kiss. Just a touch, a tender gesture. She closed her eyes.

"I am sorry I left you without news this week. I was…embroiled in family matters."

She pulled away again and tried to meet his eyes, frowning.

"Is your family well?"

He nodded. "Yes."

She smiled, relieved. Abruptly, as their gazes met and stayed bound to each other, an intense emotion washed over Gabrielle and, unable to keep quiet, she confessed with a sigh, "I am so very happy to see you. You have no idea how much I have missed you."

The world was not the same without him. The castle was not the same. *She* was not the same.

"I have missed you too, Gabrielle."

Thomas's hands slid up to her face, uncertainly, hesitantly. His smile vanished, and his face grew more serious. And when his eyes rested on her lips, time seemed to slow. Millimeter by millimeter, Thomas's face drew nearer to hers. Her heart began to beat faster. Her body stretched and leaned toward his, and she instinctively clutched the lapels of his jacket. She burned with anticipation and desire. She may be crazy, for part of her loved this sweet, sweet torture. She wished this moment could last forever, and yet she yearned for Thomas to end this wait that drove her insane, for him to kiss her at last, to—

There was a knock on the door.

Please tell me I'm dreaming, Gabrielle thought, closing her eyes in frustration as Thomas leapt away from her. *Not again!*

How many times was history going to repeat itself? Was the castle not big enough? Could someone tell her where her fairy godmother was when she needed her? Flirting with the local wizard? *Lord!*

With a deep breath, Gabrielle tried to collect herself.

"My apologies, sir, mademoiselle," Agnès stammered as she came in, more embarrassed than ever. "Céleste sent me to tell you that supper will soon be ready."

"Thank you, Agnès," Thomas replied. Gabrielle could only admire his calm and self-control. "Tell her we will be there shortly."

"Very well, sir."

Agnès curtsied and promptly left, undoubtedly delighted to get off so lightly this time.

Thomas turned to Gabrielle, an apologetic look on his face.

"I believe we are expected."

"I'm afraid we are," she said, hiding her disappointment behind a smile.

"Will you do me the honor?" Thomas asked, offering her his arm.

She tilted her head gently and slipped a hand in the crook of his elbow.

"With pleasure."

* * * *

Two hours later, after a meal fit for kings, the party was well under way. To Gabrielle's great satisfaction, everyone seemed to be enjoying themselves, dancing to the heady tune of Ravel's *Boléro*—Gabrielle with Guillaume, Maurice with Céleste, Thomas with Hélène, Arnaud with Agnès, social hierarchy abolished for a time.

The last notes of the crescendo rang out, and Gabrielle thanked her partner with as gracious a curtsy as she could manage, then proceeded to the gramophone to place what would certainly be the last record to play before midnight.

"This party was an excellent idea," Arnaud declared, drawing near to her as she replaced the *Boléro* with *The Blue Danube*. "Everyone seems enchanted."

"It certainly looks like it," Gabrielle replied, turning toward the crowd, record in hand. "Dancing is always a good idea."

She observed the small clusters tenderly for a time. Guillaume and Agnès were chatting animatedly. This evening did not mark an end for them but rather a beginning—they had both chosen to leave with Thomas for New York. Maurice and Hélène were talking close by. Gabrielle's father seemed...tense. A stranger would not have noticed, but she could tell from the way he fiddled with the buttons of his jacket. She grinned to herself. She thought she knew what made him so nervous.

Gabrielle's gaze left him and slid over to Thomas, who was listening attentively to a beaming Céleste. Their eyes met, and they smiled as though they were the only people in the world. Gabrielle's, however, were full of melancholy. As the evening went by, a thought had crept into her heart, darkening her mood, chipping away at the joy Thomas's presence created.

Now that he was back, the time to say their farewells would soon be upon them.

"Indeed," Arnaud agreed.

It took Gabrielle a few instants to realize that he had not read her mind and was still talking of the dance. Tearing herself away from Thomas's gaze, she turned to him.

"What will you do once Mr. Choiseul no longer requires your services?" she asked, laying the record on the gramophone's turntable.

"I will be leaving for America."

Gabrielle froze. She must have misunderstood.

"I'm sorry, I thought you said you were leaving for America."

"I am."

"You too?" she exclaimed, unable to mask entirely the hint of despair in her voice.

Was everyone leaving to rebuild their life elsewhere? Would she be the only one left behind, to return to her old life? To stay where she was, unchanging?

"I had been thinking about it for some time, but speaking with Mr. D'Arcy earlier helped me make my decision. I will try to become a journalist there. He can help me receive the necessary paperwork quickly."

She couldn't help but envy him for his dreams, and the freedom he had to pursue them. She wished she had the same liberty and the opportunity to make such a choice. She wished she, too, could leave with Thomas.

"It is a beautiful project," she said, busying herself with the gramophone. "I hope you will be happy there."

"So will you, I hope."

"Oh, I am going nowhere," Gabrielle replied, a touch bitterly. "I will be returning to my quiet little life among my books, in my father's store, with my father's employee who awaits only one thing, for me to swoon into his arms."

She loved her life; to pretend otherwise would be a lie. She had always loved it, as far back as she could remember. Like her mother, living among books had always been her dream, and she counted herself lucky that she could earn a living with a job she very much enjoyed. God knew all women did not have such luck, and many had to endure conditions far worse and with much less freedom.

Yet it was no longer enough. She wanted more; she wanted the entire world.

Her eyes flitted back toward Thomas, and he smiled at her, as though he had only been waiting for this. Nostalgia welled up inside her.

She wanted him. His life, his world. His heart.

Out of the corner of her eye, Gabrielle saw Arnaud grin in that mysterious way of his. But before she could ask him what amused him so, he bowed and took his leave, claiming he had photographs to take. Thomas came over to her.

"Would you do me the honor of this dance, Mademoiselle Villeneuve?"

Setting aside the melancholy that threatened to spoil the precious time she had left with him, Gabrielle pasted a smile onto her face and sank into a deep curtsy fit for a king.

"It would be my pleasure, Mr. D'Arcy."

Chapter 25
Alexandra

Chandeniers-sur-Vienne

Present day

Bruno stared in astonishment as I haphazardly flung my things into my handbag and tossed enough money to cover my share of the bill and a tip onto the table.

"What do you mean, you know how to save the castle?" he asked. "What are you thinking of?"

I paused just long enough to reply.

"It's just an inkling. I need to work through it, so I'd rather not say just yet. I need to check a few things and discuss it with Éric."

"Sounds good."

Bruno did not insist but rummaged in the inside pocket of his vest and pulled out a notebook and pen. He scrawled a phone number and tore the page away, handing it to me.

"Call me. When you find something and you're ready to talk about it, call me. Tell me if I can help."

I nodded and hesitated.

"Sorry for ditching you like this. Thanks again for everything. I'll keep you posted."

I was about to leave when Bruno called me back.

"Will you be there tomorrow?" he asked. "At the costume ball?"

Crap. I had totally forgotten about that.

"I... Yes. I don't have a costume, but I'll come."

"Ask Marine. She's head of the events committee; she'll find you something. See you tomorrow?"

I nodded again and was about to leave for good when he called one last time.

"Alexandra?"

"Yes?"

"Thank you. I don't know why you're doing all of this, but thank you."

I grinned.

"I'll keep you posted."

And I left the café without a backward look, impatient to start drawing up plans.

* * * *

I had already mentally listed several arguments in favor of my idea when I parked in front of the inn a few minutes later. Still mulling it over, muttering to myself about what I'd need to put together a rock-solid case, I limped in without noticing the motorbike in front. I was about to climb the stairs toward my room when a sharp voice coming out of the kitchen stopped me dead in my tracks.

"There is no way on earth you will convince me to put on a skirt."

I froze just outside the room and out of sight of its occupants, recognizing Éric's voice. My heart promptly started beating double-time, and that keen edge of loss pierced me through and through.

I stifled a sigh, thinking that I had better sneak up to my room to work on my project, but my legs refused to move and I kept skulking there, ears pricked to find out exactly what kind of skirt Éric refused to wear.

"It's not a skirt," Marine explained patiently, sounding like a mother placating a sullen child. "It's a kilt. All Scotsmen wear one, and they don't make a fuss about it. Sean Connery, Gerard Butler, David Tennant, Ewan McGregor…they all wear kilts, and let me tell you, they wear them well. So will you, I'm sure."

"Seriously, what is it about you women with the Scottish?" Éric exclaimed.

I blushed as the memory of our brief conversation upon hearing my GPS's voice popped up. My brain helpfully supplied me with a load of images from that day. Images I had tried to forget. Unsuccessfully.

"The Scottish are sexy," Marine's voice said, "and their accent makes any woman melt on the spot. Read *Outlander*, or watch the series, you'll see what I mean."

Éric grunted something incomprehensible, and Marine replied, "Look, the kilt is the ultimate fantasy of just about every woman right now. Forget about tall, dark vampires; muscular Scottish redheads are in. Get used to it."

"I'm not a redhead. And I have no wish to prance about in a skirt just because it's 'in.' I'm going to look utterly ridiculous."

"You're not going to look ridiculous, you're going to be sexy. And sexy is just what we're aiming for. Anyway, there was nothing else left in the costume shop, so..."

"I don't believe you. I'm sure there were a lot of costumes that wouldn't leave me half-naked or in a skirt."

"Nothing as attractive as this, believe me. I wanted the leather pirate costume for you. It would have been perfect with your dark hair and stubble, but somebody else had already rented it. I wonder who dared. I should have asked them to save it for me. Anyway, the only thing left in the "Sexy Man" category was the kilt. Deal with it."

Images of Éric in pirate costume and in a kilt danced in front of my eyes. If he was as irresistible as he was when dressed up as a biker, a lumberjack or just in plain clothes...I was as good as dead.

I really shouldn't be thinking about it.

I heard Éric sigh. "This is a bad idea. I shouldn't have said yes."

"Look, Éric, I'm doing this for you. For you and the castle. All of this, the party, the costume ball, the auctioned dances, it's for you and Marc. So the castle can stay in the family. So it wasn't all for nothing."

I didn't catch his muttered reply, but I guessed it was something about hitting below the belt. I couldn't help but agree that Marine was targeting all of his weak spots.

"You won't be the only one. Bruno, Maxime and Benjamin will be with you."

Bruno? The mayor? What did he have to do with this? And who were Maxime and Benjamin? Obviously I lacked the necessary elements to understand all of this conversation, but one thing was clear—it would be better for my health and my sanity if I did not go to this ball.

I wasn't sure I'd survive Éric in a kilt.

"Oh goody," Éric drawled with his usual sarcasm. "Everything's so much better all of a sudden."

"You could at least be grateful I didn't go with Mrs. Grenier's idea. She wanted to auction off an evening and a night with each of you."

WHAT?

Éric's reaction mirrored mine.

"What? She's crazy!" he protested. "Out of the question!"

"She's not *that* crazy, you know. We could have collected a lot of money that way. You're the most attractive man within thirty kilometers and you own a castle. You're the local Darcy; every woman talks about you and they just about swoon when you go by. Find one that wouldn't want you under those circumstances!"

"I can name at least one," Éric muttered.

I felt myself turn red.

Just about then, a small furball rubbed itself against my ankles and I started with a gasp, betraying my presence.

The kitten had already scampered when Marine called out to me.

"Alex! You've come at the right moment. Come help me convince my stubborn cousin that he will be sexy as hell in a kilt."

Sure! No problem, my pleasure! Easy as pie!

My eyes met Éric's, bright blue and shining with something unidentifiable. An invisible hand closed over my heart, sending a shock wave rippling all over my body.

God...

It was worse every time I saw him.

I took a step back and tore my gaze away from him. His eyes seemed to see right through me. It was way too dangerous.

"I'm sorry, I...I have to go," I stammered. "I—my friend Beatrice—I have to call her. Right now. Sorry."

And I beat a hasty retreat—though not quick enough to avoid hearing Marine ask in a puzzled voice, "What's wrong with her? She's been weird for the past few days."

"I don't know and I don't care," Éric snapped back.

The hand around my heart crushed it to bits, and I fled to my room, short of breath.

* * * *

I stayed there for several hours, music blaring in my headphones to avoid hearing anything from the inn below. I hoped that Kings of Leon, my favorite band, would help me forget all about him.

It didn't, of course. I went through my entire playlist without being able to erase Éric's parting jab from my mind. But I still managed to focus enough to do a first draft of the proposal I would send to my boss, Elizabeth.

The plan was so simple and obvious it was a wonder I hadn't thought of it before.

On the one hand, my company wanted to buy or rent a vineyard in France. On the other hand, I had access to a plot of land. Sure, it was a little smaller than the criteria required and it had no known history of production, or maybe no history at all...but it came with a real castle attached, and that was a hefty argument in its favor.

This wasn't going to be easy, I was aware of that, and I was going to have to bring out the big guns if I wanted my proposal to be taken seriously, but it was worth a try. Unless I was mistaken, our research hadn't yet moved on to the decision stage, and the choice had to be approved by the board of directors as well as by operations management and our new international operations management. I still had time to submit a proposal, but only just. I had to work fast.

Alone in my room, I spent the rest of the day working, tallying the advantages of my plan for the company and finding counterarguments for each negative aspect. The area was small? We'd produce exclusive vintages we could sell for a hefty price. The castle was broken down? What better way to gain the collaboration of all local parties than to help restore a local piece of history?

I reviewed every detail carefully, estimating the surface area from the plans, lining up my arguments in a way that would have made Spencer proud.

Several hours later, the only things missing were pictures from the castle and the estate, and I would be just about ready.

I had the weekend to add in the details I might have forgotten and fine-tune my arguments.

And, incidentally, convince Éric it was a wonderful idea.

Something told me he might not be that easy to convince, but I was hoping that just this once, he would listen to my arguments and agree with me. I wasn't asking him to sell his castle—only to rent part of the grounds to a handful of Americans so they might produce some wine there.

Chapter 26
Gabrielle

Castle of Ferté-Chandeniers

December 1899

Gabrielle set the stylus on the record and, once again, the first notes of *The Blue Danube* rang out. Slipping her hand into Thomas's, she spun to the gentle melody. They danced with their eyes on each other, wordlessly, as though the world around them no longer existed.

Mesmerized by his gaze, Gabrielle did not realize they were the only ones to waltz, nor did she see Céleste's loving look or the conniving wink she exchanged with Arnaud. In that instant, Gabrielle's world came down to Thomas, and she was not aware of everyone leaving the ballroom, Maurice and Hélène through one door and Céleste, Arnaud, Guillaume and Agnès through the other.

When the music stopped, Thomas bowed to her and, with exquisite gallantry, kissed her hand without ever taking his eyes off hers. He did not kiss the top of her hand, as propriety and every etiquette book would have it, but rather her palm. She could feel the press of his lips and their warmth though her satin glove. It was a caress so intimate, so personal and gentle that it sent a shiver down her spine.

"Turn around," Thomas murmured softly.

Heart beating, Gabrielle obeyed and took in the empty room, realizing only then that they were alone and that Thomas had led her to the balcony. She had seen nothing, noticed nothing, neither their companions departing nor the sudden cold.

Blinking as though emerging from a long sleep, she contemplated the view.

Perched on the fifth floor of the southern wing, the balcony overlooked the vast park behind the castle. Crystalline snow stretched out as far as the eye could see, flecked with half-buried trees.

Gabrielle looked up to the ink-black sky. Little by little, as her eyes adjusted to the darkness, thousands of tiny stars appeared, twinkling against the sky like so many minuscule diamonds hanging from the canopy of heaven. Behind her, the full moon bathed the landscape in radiant, surreal light. She felt as though she were in a fantastic, magical world.

"I have never been on this balcony before," she breathed, turning to Thomas. "The view is magnificent."

"It is," Thomas agreed, his eyes on her.

She felt her cheeks turn crimson while an irrepressible smile bloomed on her lips. To collect herself—and maybe a little to impress Thomas—she stepped closer to the balustrade and recited in her very best English:

"Oh Romeo, Romeo, wherefore art thou Romeo? Deny thy father and refuse thy name, or if thou wilt not, be but my sworn love and I'll no longer be a Capulet!"

"Shall I hear more, or shall I speak at this?" Thomas replied.

He leaned onto the balustrade next to her, his back to the view but his eyes never leaving hers.

Gabrielle glanced at him from under her lashes, smiling slightly.

"I was not aware you knew *Romeo and Juliet* by heart!" she teased him.

"I saw the play a few years ago in London with my aunt and uncle," he explained. "A little tragic for my taste, but my aunt insisted and so I accompanied them."

His mouth quirked up into the half smile she loved so well, the one that always made her stomach behave so strangely.

"I was not aware you spoke English," he continued.

"I can read it, but speaking it is another matter entirely. I can make myself understood well enough, though my accent is dreadful."

"Your accent is absolutely charming."

Gabrielle reddened, flattered. A handful of butterflies flitted around the inside of her chest.

"My father felt I should be able to at least understand his correspondence with other bookstores in England and Germany," she explained.

"You speak German too?"

"A little."

"You are so full of surprises," Thomas murmured, admiration clear in his voice.

The butterflies swooped. Gabrielle glanced down then up again.

The wind unfurled around them, rustling through the branches of the trees, billowing under Gabrielle's petticoats, stroking her bare neck. The icy breeze against her skin, still warm from the dance, made her shiver. The cold was biting, but she did not feel it. Only Thomas's shoulder against hers was real as he turned and gazed at the view at her side. His presence was both troubling and reassuring.

For how long? a little voice in Gabrielle's head questioned.

No. Enough. She would not dwell on her sadness or melancholy, or their upcoming parting, she suddenly decided. Tomorrow could wait. For now, she was here and so was he, and that was all that mattered. She refused to spoil these precious moments with thoughts of the future.

Carpe diem, Gabrielle. Carpe diem.

There would time enough to think of tomorrow when it came.

She tilted her head back, offering her face up to the wind, sky and stars.

"Look," she exclaimed as a white blaze trailed through the sky, there and gone in the blink of an eye. "A shooting star!"

She smiled as a sense of peace, a conviction that all would be well, rose up within her.

Thank you, Maman, she thought, closing her eyes. And she made a wish.

"Did you see it?" she asked Thomas, still gazing up, searching for another.

"Yes."

"Did you make a wish?"

"No."

"No?"

"No," he repeated. "I do not believe in such things. Shooting stars, fate, God... I do not wish to believe in them."

"Why is that?"

But even as she asked, Gabrielle regretted her question. She knew the answer. And she did not wish to remind him of the pain. Not tonight.

She bit at her lip. One day, she would learn to think before asking questions. Or before speaking. She was far too prone to saying whatever flitted through her mind.

His gaze faraway, Thomas replied just what she feared he would.

"Because it would mean that somewhere out there, there is a being that decided that my mother would be unhappy all her life and would meet a tragic ending. And I cannot bear the thought. I would rather blame the man she married than believe it was her fate to suffer so."

His hands had clenched on the balustrade, the knuckles white. Unthinkingly, wishing only to comfort him, Gabrielle reached out and closed her hand over his. It was only when Thomas laced their fingers together that she realized what she had done. She could feel his heat radiate into her even through her glove. Their eyes met and clung, and for a second she forgot what she wished to say. She looked up toward the sky without tugging her hand free.

"As for me," she said, untangling the thread of her thoughts, "I wish to believe that my mother is among these stars. And that whenever one of them falls, it is her way of telling me 'I am here, and I watch over you.'"

She broke off as Thomas's thumb automatically stroked the inside of her palm. A small touch, but one that set her entire body ablaze. For a moment she closed her eyes, unable to think.

"I am sure your mother is up there too," she went on, careful to conceal her turmoil. "And so is your father. The man she loved, I mean. I am positive that they found each other beyond death and they now dwell together in happiness. And from the sky, they watch over you and they are proud of the man you have become."

A faint but unmistakable smile stretched Thomas's lips.

"I do not know why, but tonight I wish to believe you. Tonight, I would believe that wherever she is, my mother is happy and at peace."

"She is. I am convinced of it."

Silence fell as Thomas gazed out at the horizon.

"I may not have wished upon a star," he began, "but I decided something while I was in England. Does that count?"

"Of course! What did you decide?"

"I will follow your advice. Upon leaving for America I will be turning over a new leaf, starting from scratch. I will build my life anew with new people. People I trust."

Gabrielle could almost hear the pop of the bubble bursting, washing away all the spell of the moment, leaving only cold, loneliness and harsh reality.

The reality she had tried so hard to forget.

He was leaving.

In her stomach, the butterflies turned to stone.

"Thomas, that is wonderful!" she cried with an enthusiasm she did not feel. "I am so glad for you. You deserve to be happy."

"I do not know if I deserve it, but I decided you were right and I should make a fresh start."

She nodded feebly, lowering her gaze.

How ironic! Until now, it had been her heart's desire. For him to be able to start over and be happy. Until a few weeks ago, she only wanted his happiness, and she had been content to be the one to help him shed his past. Truly, she had been honored.

And then he had kissed her, and as unexpected and unplanned as it had been...it had changed everything. For her, at least.

Now she was no longer content with standing in the shadows. She wanted more. She wanted everything.

But she did not wish to impose. She did not want to guilt him into anything or force him to bring her along if he had not planned to. If his plans did not include her.

"When are you leaving?" she asked, a knot in her stomach.

"As soon as possible. I... There is something I must do first, but I hope to leave in early February."

So soon...

A gust of icy wind buffeted her, and she shivered again. She pulled back her hand and rubbed her arms. She felt empty, all of a sudden. Lonely. Sad. So very sad.

Wordlessly, Thomas removed his jacket and, as he had done before, draped it over her shoulders, his arm lingering a little longer than necessary. Gabrielle had to gather all her strength of will not to nestle against him, to remind herself that she had to let him go. That she was not his destiny.

"I have decided something too," she declared impulsively. "I will make something of my life. I have had enough of waiting for something to happen and give it meaning. I will do it. I will make my mark somewhere. I want to count. I do not know how yet, but I will."

She abruptly needed to have projects, something to fill her life...after. Once he was gone. To avoid going insane. To have something to cling to.

How strange that the world can change so fast. A single person, a single meeting, a single glance...and everything has changed.

"You count, Gabrielle," Thomas said gently. "You are important."

She laughed briefly.

"I meant for someone other than my father."

She bit her tongue the moment the last word left her mouth. She felt pathetic, fishing for a confession. Hoping so hard to hear Thomas protest and tell her that she counted for him.

For a long moment, Thomas gazed at her in silence. She could see a thousand and one emotions in his eyes. A strange feeling rose up within her. Her heart sank into her feet—and lower still when Thomas sighed, hesitant.

Suddenly she knew.

He was bidding her farewell. There and then. The dance, the balcony, the stars…all of this was his way of saying goodbye. And speaking of his decision was the ideal introduction.

Oh Lord…

She could almost hear her heart shatter.

"Gabrielle—" Thomas began, then broke off.

Gabrielle's eyes clung to his.

Tell me I count for you, she begged. *Tell me you will not forget me when you are far from here.*

Yet despite her fervent plea, her prayer remained unanswered. Her fairy tale was breaking apart tonight. Perhaps her fairy godmother had abandoned her. Or perhaps, despite what her mother had so often told her as a child, she did not truly have one, and she was fated to a lifetime of disappointments.

"I went to see my grandmother when I was in England," Thomas abruptly said.

"Did you?"

These were not the words she had hoped for, but neither were they the ones she had feared. If this conversation could make the specter of their parting recede for a moment, she would welcome it gladly.

"That was why I could not write to you," he went on. "I spent the week with her."

"I understand."

"I told her everything. Who I was, how her son and my mother had met, what had happened next…."

"And what did she say?"

"Nothing. She put her arms around me and told me she was sorry. Then she thanked me. She wept. I think—I think that for a moment, I gave her son back to her."

"Thomas, that's wonderful!" Gabrielle cried out sincerely. "How did you feel?"

"Well. Very well. Relieved. As though a burden had finally been lifted from my shoulders."

She smiled. She had always known that it would be a good thing both for Thomas and for his grandmother if he told her the truth.

"We spoke at length. I told her…about America, about what I would do there. She had many questions; she wanted to know everything."

Gabrielle's heart clenched so tightly it felt painful.

"She must have been very proud of you."

"I think so. I also told her about my other projects."

"Your other projects? You have other projects?"

"Yes. I only had the idea very recently, I have not yet worked out all the details, but...I have decided that I will use everything left over from the Saint-Armand heritage after the castle is sold to fund an orphanage. To give what my uncle once gave me to those children who have no one. A place they can call home and a person to love them as they deserve."

The last few words were a final blow. How could any woman not fall in love with him? He was simply perfect.

But he was not meant to be hers. Or rather, she was not meant to be his.

She closed her eyes, the pain in her chest so sharp she could barely breathe.

"Gabrielle."

She felt Thomas move beside her, shifting to face her.

"Gabrielle, my darling, look at me."

Her heart stuttered at his use of the endearment. Surprised, she turned to him.

"All of this is because of you."

"Me?"

Thomas's eyes plunged into hers, a mix of tenderness and intensity shining in their depths. The light from the ballroom illuminated his profile, his scar, and Gabrielle became aware that she no longer found him handsome *despite* the scar—she found him handsome *because* of the scar. It was the symbol of who he was. A phoenix that had risen from the ashes. A man who had risen above adversity, head held high. A man who had overcome hatred to keep the beauty and generosity of his soul and heart.

The man she loved with all her heart.

The wind tugged a curl of her hair free and made it dance in front of her eyes. Infinitely gentle, Thomas pushed it back and slipped it behind her ear. His finger lingered over her skin, tracing the shape of her face.

Gabrielle's heart beat like a hummingbird's.

"You inspired me to do all of this," he whispered tenderly. "Your words convinced me to seek out my grandmother; you gave me the idea to build an orphanage. You have changed my life, Gabrielle."

Thomas's gaze tracked his fingers, caressing the curve of her lips. His jaw clenched, and he breathed in deeply, then out. He was so close to her that she felt his warm breath on her cheek. His face filled her entire field of sight.

"Me?" she repeated.

She no longer knew who she was, where she was. She no longer felt the biting cold of the wind that pulled at her. She only heard the beating of her heart, only felt the touch of his fingers on her skin.

"You," Thomas confirmed. "You have opened my eyes, Gabrielle. You have made me understand what kind of man I wish to be, and you have made me into that man. You have given my life meaning. You are...the most beautiful thing that has ever happened to me."

Oh Lord...

Gabrielle closed her eyes, savoring the effect those few words had on her. Her heart beat so fast that she feared it might burst out of her chest any moment. She felt Thomas's hands settle on her face, felt his fingers twine into her hair, his thumbs stroke her temples as he tilted her face toward his.

"Gabrielle, open your eyes," he murmured. "Look at me."

Throat tight with emotion, she obeyed. Every emotion he felt was apparent on his face in that moment: hope, tenderness, reverence, admiration. And something else, something stronger yet. He kept their gazes linked a few moments more, until he was sure he had her full attention. Then, his voice solemn, he spoke the words she had so hoped to hear.

"I love you, Gabrielle. From the first day, from the very first moment."

And thus, with the stars and moon as sole witnesses, he kissed her at long last. As light as a butterfly landing on the petals of a rose, his lips claimed Gabrielle's in a tender kiss that made her heart melt. His hands slipped free of her curls and lost themselves on the planes of her face, caressing the curve of her chin, the velvety softness of her cheeks. As one, their breath grew short, and as their bodies flowed together, Gabrielle's hands mirrored Thomas's and traveled up his chest toward his neck, his face, sliding full of emotion along the scar that symbolized who he was and losing themselves in his thick hair as she had so often dreamed they would, and she held him tightly, so tightly, to her.

In his arms, she rose from the ground, flew somewhere far, far away, beyond sky and stars, toward an elsewhere in which tomorrow no longer existed, where they only existed for each other, only existed *through* each other.

No matter what tomorrow may be made of, Gabrielle decided. No matter what her life would be after tonight.

Whatever happened, whatever would become of her, of them, she would always have this magical moment, these few seconds of happiness and the words he had spoken. *"I love you...."* A single tear rolling down her cheek, Gabrielle let go of the world and of reality, and lost herself in the kiss she had hoped and waited for so long.

* * * *

Later, when Thomas broke away and leaned his forehead against hers, Gabrielle could not hold back a sigh.

"Thank you," she murmured against his lips.

"What for?"

"For everything. For this kiss, for telling me I changed your life, that you loved me. Thank you."

"Does this mean...?"

She nodded.

"I love you too, Thomas. So much...you have no idea..."

He kissed her again, tenderly, full of love and awe, and she melted anew.

"There are worse ways of saying farewell," she sighed under her breath. She bit her tongue, but it was too late. The words had escaped her.

Thomas froze.

"Farewell?"

"Is that not what we are doing? Saying farewell to each other?"

Thomas jerked away from her.

"No!"

"No?"

"No, not at all! Why would you think such a thing?"

"You said so yourself not a minute ago," Gabrielle replied, surprised. "You will be leaving shortly, to rebuild your life across the ocean. I thought you were saying goodbye. I understand, Thomas," she hastened to add as he opened his mouth to protest. "You need not answer to me."

"No, Gabrielle! You do not understand! I will be leaving soon, yes, but I did not mean to imply—I do not—I am not saying farewell! On the contrary!"

A spark of hope kindled in Gabrielle's heart, and Thomas sighed. "This is not how I meant for things to happen," he said, half to himself, shaking his head, and fished into his pocket. "Not at all."

He pulled out a square of crimson velvet.

"I had planned everything out," he went on, unfolding the cloth. "I wanted to speak to your father first. And I meant to give you a beautiful speech, the kind that you deserve. But I think...a change is in order."

Gabrielle's heart had started beating fast again as her mind deciphered the meaning behind Thomas's words and actions.

Was he...? Oh Lord!

Eyes wide open, she stared as Thomas finished unfolding the cloth to reveal a magnificent ring, an opal set in a bed of rubies and diamonds, and held it out to her. His gaze never leaving hers, he knelt and declared: "Gabrielle, these three weeks away from you have been the longest in my life. You have not only changed my life, you have made it more beautiful. My days without you are gray. I have had time to think while I was in England, and forsaking the past is not the only decision I made."

He paused then carried on, hoarse with emotion:

"Gabrielle Adélaïde Hortense Villeneuve, would you do me the immense honor of becoming my wife and sailing with me to America?"

Chapter 27
Alexandra

Chandeniers-sur-Vienne

Present day

I slowly closed Gabrielle's diary, my hands lingering over the leather cover, and switched off my reading lamp. Sighing, I tilted my head back, gazing up toward the sky and stars. Once I was sure the coast was clear, I had left my room in the evening to have dinner and resume reading. Night had fallen, and small solar lamps bathed the garden in a soft glow, casting shadows over the green grass, the trees and the hedges around the inn.

Everything around me was peaceful and quiet.

Inside me, however, was another story. My heart beat a violent tattoo against my ribs and my throat was tight with emotion.

I was happy, deeply and sincerely happy for Gabrielle. Even though I already knew that she and Thomas had gotten married, that they had lived happily ever after in the US and had four children, reading about how they had finally revealed to each other their pure and beautiful love was…intense. I was overwhelmed.

I almost could have cried.

But that had not been my only feeling upon reading about Gabrielle and Thomas's reunion, their dance and this tender, beautiful proposal. Something deeper, more complex stirred within me. An emotion that was not quite envy—it was much more than that.

We English speakers have a word to which I have not yet found a strict equivalent in French—*longing*. It means a kind of desire, more or less rational, generally difficult or impossible to fulfill, one that grips you and does not let you go. Desire mingled with want and a touch of regret sometimes, for something that you do not or no longer have, and crave more than anything in the world. A desire so strong it is physical, felt in every cell of your body, in your heart and in your mind, a sense of void in your existence. Like a hand gripping your heart and stomach, clenched so tightly you wonder if you will survive. Like yearning for something, but stronger.

That was what I felt in that instant. It filled me entirely. A single sentence ran through my mind and looped, again and again, punctuated by my frantic heartbeat: *I want that too.*

I, too, wanted to know that unconditional love. I, too, wanted to feel such passion in real life, in my life. And I wanted it right away.

A face, always the same, floated in front of my eyes, mimicking Thomas's movements, his hands stroking Gabrielle's face, his lips on hers, on mine, his arms around her, around me…this yearning, this desire rang so deeply in me then that I felt almost…oppressed.

My vision blurred, and the stars vanished.

Crap. Crappity, crappity, crap.

Just then, my tablet buzzed, announcing a message on Skype. Blinking to clear the tears from my eyes, I set aside the diary and read the message— or messages.

Alex?

You there?

No news! I'm worried….

Call me if you're there! I miss my best friend!!

Aleeeex?

And I realized that I had neither written nor spoken to Beatrice since the day I had arrived at Chandeniers, after my first encounter with Éric. She had written and texted several times since, and each time I had promised myself I would reply soon. And I had been swept away by something else, and for the first time in my life, I had completely forgotten to write to my best friend.

I used the camera to check that my face revealed none of my inner turmoil. I blessed the darkness of the garden and clicked on the call symbol.

"Alex! There you are! I was going out of my mind here! We haven't talked in ages, and you didn't reply to my emails or texts. If I didn't hear from you, I was going to call Spencer! Is everything all right? What happened? Why weren't you answering? Is it nighttime already in France? I can hardly see you!"

She spoke so fast I had trouble following her.

"I'm so sorry, Bea!" I reassured her. "Everything's okay! It's just been crazy these last few days and—"

"Crazy how? Good crazy or bad crazy? Tell me everything!"

"How long do you have? This could take a while."

"Long enough. Spit it out. And it better be worth it if you want me to forgive you for neglecting me for so long."

Over the next half hour, I told her everything—nearly everything.

I told her about my conversation with Marine and about Marc Lagnel's file, the information I had found there, the bookstore in Angers, how I had decided to go there. About going to the graveyard, coming across Éric, and my misadventure with Max. How Éric had decided he needed to take me to Angers, probably out of guilt. I explained that I had found Gabrielle's diary, the phone calls Éric had received and the fact that he was going to have to sell the castle that meant so much to his parents. I relived for her the balloon ride, the view, the châteaux. I summed up what I had learned from the diary about my ancestors' story.

"It's strange how close I feel to Gabrielle. I read her diary like a novel, but at the same time, she feels so real that it sometimes seems to me she's somewhere around and that I could meet her here in Chandeniers."

"You know what they say—some people have a personality so strong that even after their death, they leave a trace of themselves behind."

"You're going to make fun of me, but just this afternoon I wondered whether she hadn't been the one to guide me to her picture so I would come here and save the castle."

"Who knows…maybe you were destined to retrace her footsteps. To go back to where she came from."

"Nah, you know I don't believe in that stuff. But I do think I've found a way to save the castle."

I told her about my visit to the museum, lunch with Bruno, and his revelation that there had been a vineyard on the estate in the eighteenth century. Then I told her about my plan to suggest the place to my boss, Elizabeth.

"But that's amazing! Alex, you know you're brilliant, right?"

"Let's not get carried away...nothing's certain yet; first I have to get Éric to agree to the plan, and then I have to convince Elizabeth and the other managers. It's a long shot."

"You're going to nail it, I know you will. And your grumpy old castle lord may be a grouch, but why would he refuse if his situation is as desperate as you say it is?"

"I don't know. I don't think he's very fond of Americans in general, so he might not like the idea of renting out part of his estate to an American wine company."

"He might not be overly fond of Americans, but a vineyard on part of his estate is better than disrespectful tourists everywhere and a razed castle. If he's smart, he'll make the right choice."

"I hope he will. I'll talk to him tomorrow."

"I expect you to call me the very minute you return to the inn."

"It's a promise."

"And think about it—my theory is growing more solid by the minute!"

"What do you mean?"

"It really was your destiny to go there. You can't deny that it's a lot of coincidences. Out of all the people descended from your ancestor, you were the one to find her picture. And you work for a wine company that is trying to establish itself in France. And boom—right when you need it, you discover that the castle used to have a vineyard and that you have the perfect solution to save it. You can't *not* see the signs!"

"Yeah, well, that *is* a lot of coincidences. But it's not *that* extraordinary."

"It seems so obvious—you were destined to follow in your ancestors' footsteps, to save their castle. How was it destroyed exactly?"

"Apparently there was an electrical fire."

A thought flashed through my mind.

What if the article I had found was incomplete? It mentioned no victims, but such a large fire must have inflicted serious damage. What if some of the castle's inhabitants had been injured? My gut twisted as I imagined one of them with third-degree burns or worse—they had all grown so real to me that should I learn that one of them had been hurt, I believed I would truly mourn them.

"Alex?"

"Yeah?"

"What is it? You look weird all of sudden."

"Nothing. I was just thinking of Gabrielle's diary, and of the people she met while she was here. Sometimes I have trouble remembering they've been dead and buried for a long time. I kind of expect to come across them in the market square or the castle gardens. Hey, speaking of the castle grounds, did I tell you that Éric wanted to make the old stables into a bed-and-breakfast? His father also came up with the idea to rent the castle out for a wedding venue once it had been restored. I really think it could bring in quite a lot of money."

"Mmmh."

Bea stared at me.

"You are coming back, right?" she asked. "When your vacation is over?"

"Of course I'm coming back! Why wouldn't I?"

"I don't know. A hunch. The fact that you're so wrapped up in the castle's future, as though it's your responsibility. Or maybe because you've been speaking of Éric nonstop for the last hour. Have you noticed you haven't mentioned Spencer even once?"

I froze.

Her words were a knife twist in a wound, and guilt crashed over me again.

Bea's eyes were serious all of a sudden and as I failed to reply she went on: "You like him, don't you? You've completely changed your mind about him since the last time we spoke."

"Yeah," I admitted, hanging my head. "I—I've gotten to know him. He's not as—rough as he looks on the outside. He's just—frustrated and powerless. He wants to save his father's castle, and it seems like the entire world is against him. But he's someone good deep down. He's sensitive and generous, but he's also grieving and adrift. Which is understandable, given his situation."

"Mmmh."

"But that doesn't mean I'm going to stay. There's nothing for me here; I don't belong. It's not my life, not—"

I broke off as the truth slammed into me—I wanted to stay. I didn't want to return to my old life. To my day-to-day routine. I wanted...I wanted to feel useful. To do something that mattered.

Like saving the castle while its owner saved the world, one child at a time. To let him leave with his mind at peace, to do good where he was needed.

Longing.

God, I was pathetic.

"And my job is in California. So are you and Spencer. And my cats. I have to go back."

"I see. Can I ask you something?"

"Sure."

"Have you told Éric about Spencer?"

Her question caught me by surprise.

"Uh—no, not really," I mumbled. "It didn't come up and—"
I didn't finish my sentence.

"'It didn't come up,'" my best friend repeated dubiously. "Of course it didn't. Alex...are you in love with Éric?"

"No, of course not!" I all but fell over myself to reply. "What do you mean? I love Spencer! I'm going to marry him!"

Bea stared at me wordlessly for a long while.

"Are you really sure you love him?"

"Of course I am! You know that!"

"That's kind of the problem. I don't. I know you, Alex, and I have a feeling everything is not all nice and tidy inside your head right now." She paused. "Do you want me to tell you the truth?"

I swallowed and waited.

"Spencer is a good man."

"But?"

"But he's not the right person for you. I know you think you really love him, but I don't think your feelings for him are true love."

I was about to protest when she raised a hand.

"Let me finish! I know you care for him, I have never doubted that and the two are not mutually exclusive. But, sweetheart, you have to face the facts—you're not *really* happy with Spencer."

"Of course I am!" I argued. "I'm happy! I'm very happy! Look at me, I positively glow!"

Bea shrugged my protests away.

"Just tell me this—when was the last time you felt completely and utterly fulfilled with him? When was the last time you told him you loved him and felt it right down to your gut? When did you feel like weeping with joy just because he was at your side?"

I feverishly searched through my memory for an answer, but none came.

"When was the last time you did something crazy and unplanned like the balloon trip?"

Again, I was silent. There had to be something!

"When was the last time you told him about the little tidbits of your life and our bouts of fun? Office gossip, what happened while you were standing in line at the movies, men flirting with us in bars...or even just telling him about going out for a drink with me after work? When was that, Alex?"

Once again, my brain stalled. It wasn't for lack of searching. I couldn't believe I couldn't find a single answer to any of her questions. But the truth was plain to see. There was nothing to find.

Bea was right.

At some point over the last few months, the last few years maybe, Spencer and I had stopped talking to each other. He couldn't tell me about work, and he didn't have time to anyway, and I…I felt that my little worries and thoughts were too ridiculous and small compared to his, and didn't rate a mention.

Little by little, I'd grown used to not talking to him, focusing instead into my genealogy research, my drawing, my books. And now I realized that some evenings we barely exchanged two or three words, each lost in our own world and thoughts, unaware that the other wasn't a part of them. We had grown apart, and neither of us had noticed it.

Panic washed over me.

"Bea—" I began, unsure of what I was about to say.

Her words rang inside my head. I felt feverish and lost. Utterly lost. I needed to think. To pause. To understand.

But Bea wasn't done yet.

"Alex, I think it's time you stopped lying to yourself. You're bored, you're not happy with Spencer. You're not doing anything. You're…faded. Believe me, you need someone different. Someone who can follow you in your passions, who can fuel them and not stifle them like he does. The light in your eyes tonight, the enthusiasm in your voice, your inner fire—I hadn't seen those in forever."

"You're wrong," I protested. "You—"

"I don't think I am, Alex, and what's more, deep down, you don't think so either."

I shook my head, but she continued, relentless.

"I'm going to ask you one last thing, Alex, and I want you to be honest. Not with me, but with yourself. Promise me."

"Promise."

"If you really loved Spencer as profoundly and sincerely as you wish to believe you do—do you think you could fall in love with Éric? And don't pretend you don't care about him. The only one you're fooling is yourself, sweetheart."

"But I barely know him! I can't be in love with him! I don't want to—"

"I'm not saying he's the one, or that you should drop everything for him! I'm just saying—you don't fall in love with another man, even a little, even just for the summer, if your relationship is strong. Just think about it, please. It's not too late to change your mind. You deserve better than the life you're leading. And I know you don't want to hurt Spencer's feelings, but I don't think it's fair to him, either."

I didn't even try for an answer this time. I was too unbalanced by everything she had said to be able to string two coherent thoughts together. Her words found an echo within me, reflecting my own guilt, the feelings that had awoken deep down, the realizations I had experienced over the last few days and had tried to push away.

I wasn't ready. I needed to think. To assess. I needed time.

"Bea, can I call you back? I need to—to think. To be alone."

"Of course. Whenever you like. I'm sorry, Alex, but what kind of friend would I be if I didn't tell you those things?"

"No, it's fine. I'm grateful you did. I just…need to take it all in. And try and decide what to do."

"I'm here if you want to talk it out."

"Okay."

"Good night, sweetheart."

"Good night, Bea."

I disconnected the call and put the tablet down.

It felt like talking with Bea had made the very foundation of my life crumble. Yet I knew she had been telling me the truth. I had probably known for a while, but I hadn't wanted to face it.

I wasn't happy. Spencer meant a lot to me, and I didn't want to hurt him or have him walk out of my life. But—over the last few days, the idea of spending the rest of my life with him seemed less…thrilling. The thought of going back to California and resuming the life I had carved out for myself, the one I had chosen and that had seemed so reassuring, felt like a death knell.

Everything was mixed up inside my head. I no longer knew what I wanted, where I was at.

I was utterly lost.

* * * *

I hadn't gotten any further the next morning when I drove over to the castle after a sleepless night. Max's enthusiastic barking greeted me as soon as I got out of the car, and I had barely reached the former stables when he jumped at me, tail wagging frantically.

He had missed me, apparently.

It felt good.

I crouched and petted him.

"Hey, buddy! You look good! I missed you too, you know." He licked my hand cheerfully. "I hope you haven't done anything reprehensible with that tongue before you slobbered all over me!" I half laughed but didn't pull away.

"What are you doing here?" a voice behind my back asked.

The curt tone was easily recognizable—and irritating. I felt cracks splinter across my heart as I rose to my feet to turn and face Éric. His eyes were cold and almost disdainful.

Was he upset I had fled the day before? He had been very clear, however, that he didn't care what happened to me.

A lump formed in my stomach.

It felt like our first meeting all over again, when he had been as rude as possible. I should have been glad. It would make pulling away that much easier. Yet his reaction filled me with unbearable sadness.

I still pasted a smile onto my face.

"Hello to you too," I chirped with feigned enthusiasm. "I'm good, thanks, how about you? Didn't sleep well? Oh, I'm sorry to hear that. Must be why you're so grumpy on such a beautiful morning. Don't worry, though, I have good news that will put the smile right back on your face. Guaranteed or your money back."

He raised an eyebrow.

"Good news?"

"Uh-huh. I have a plan to buy you some time before you have to sell the castle."

His face relaxed into a softer expression that suited him so much better. *Longing...*

"You found a solution?"

"I promised, didn't I?"

"You did, but I thought—" He hesitated, and suddenly he seemed so very fragile, as if he had lost all self-confidence. "You always seemed so eager to leave each time I came across you these last few days, I thought you'd changed your mind. That you weren't interested anymore."

If only he knew.

"I just took advantage of my last few days to play tourist." I couldn't help but add, without really knowing why, "And I gave you my number. You could have called if you wanted an update."

"Yeah, I could have. I just—didn't want to bother you."

"You wouldn't have bothered me," I said gently. "Not at all."

What was the matter with me? Why the heck had I said that? *Alex, what is wrong with you!*

Yet when I saw the sudden grin lighting up his face, I couldn't help but feel a glow of contentment spread through me.

"Can I offer you something to drink while you tell me about it? I have tea."

"I thought you didn't like tea?" I remarked. "Changed your mind?"

"Absolutely not. I bought it for you."

* * * *

Ten minutes later we were sitting in the former stables with a cup of coffee in front of him and a chai latte for me—he hadn't just bought tea, he'd chosen my favorite—as I prepared to give him the details of my plan.

"Okay, first of all, you have to let me finish before you interrupt, and you should think about all the aspects involved before you react."

"All right."

His attentive gaze rested on me. I cleared my throat and launched into my prepared speech.

"So, I told you how I work for a wine company that wants to implant itself in France, right?"

He nodded.

"Yesterday I went to the museum you told me about, and I met Bruno Lepic. We spoke at length of the castle and its history. He mentioned that there used to be a vineyard in a northern plot of the estate, up until it was destroyed during the French Revolution."

I could tell from the gleam that suddenly lit up Éric's eyes that he understood where I was going with this. Yet he remained silent and motioned for me to carry on.

So I did.

"With your approval, what I'd like to do is submit that land to my employer as a plot to be rented for a new vineyard."

Éric sat up slowly and leaned forward.

"Why would they accept?" he asked, dubious. "I imagine they've probably found bigger and better located places, ones that would be more interesting for them. Why would they care about this one?"

"Because I'm going to give them arguments that they can't possibly refuse."

"Such as?"

Ever the skeptic. I raised my chin. Okay. He was as tough as Elizabeth, so if I could convince him, I had a decent shot with my boss.

"Well, first of all, I want to offer up the possibility to re-create an old variety of vine. If you accept my proposal, I'm going to call the National Institute of Agricultural Research and ask them if they have old stock, and what it would take to re-create some if they don't. I want the vineyard to be unique, which would make my company have to consider it in spite of its smaller size. The sites we've shortlisted so far are larger and should allow for large-scale production, and some of them even already have live vine stock, but I want to gamble on the limited area to promote a more reduced output. Preferably we'd create a vintage. We could attract another category of consumers, higher up the social ladder, such as luxury restaurants or wine collectors."

I'd unwittingly slid into commercial and professional mode. Éric's eyes were glued to me, but I had difficulty reading his expression.

I rolled on. The sensitive part was coming up, and it was the one I was most nervous about. I had no idea how he would react.

"I also want to emphasize the...shall we say...philanthropic side of the endeavor."

Unsurprisingly, Éric frowned.

"Which is?"

"I want to insist on the fact that if they invest in this vineyard, the company will be helping save an important monument of French cultural heritage. And that, in the eyes of consumers and local inhabitants, is one hell of an asset. It will be much easier for them to settle in and work with the local population if their activity helps rebuild a ruined castle and develop a city by creating jobs and promoting the region, even on a small scale."

"You want to tell them that saving the castle is a good deed that will get the locals on their side. Is that what you're telling me?"

I eyed him for a few moments before I replied.

"That's kind of a harsh way of putting it, but yeah, that's exactly the button I want to press, because I know it's important. You can't tell me it's not. Bruno himself told me that the town needs money, that he has a lot of projects to develop Chandeniers. Imagine how many jobs will be created, the taxes raised, the wine tourism. You'd have the money to create the association your father wanted to restore the castle. If this works, it could be the start of a huge change in the region, for the castle and for you. You could go back to Africa or Asia or wherever you want, because the association would take care of your father's inheritance for you. You'd be free, Éric! Isn't that what you wanted? To have your cake and eat it?"

"Can I get the baker girl too for good measure?"

"Huh?"

"Forget it. Anyway, all of this is only if your boss says yes, right?"

"Yes. But if you don't want me to, I won't say anything. I won't do anything without your agreement."

He gazed at me for a few seconds.

"And if I agree," he said slowly, "and your boss okays this little social experiment, we're all good?"

"Not quite. We'd have to check a few parameters first to see if we can use the land."

"Such as?"

I briefly summed up the process. We'd take physical and chemical samples to check the nature of the soil, the presence of bacteria, the agricultural potential—all things that would help with the choice of compatible vine stock and the preparation of the soil. I also detailed the profitability surveys and market studies we'd have to do.

"If all the results indicate that we have a chance of success, then my boss will strike a deal with you, and together you will mark off the plot reserved for the vineyard. We'll then be in charge of preparing it, as well as building the wine storehouse. This means there would be a team on-site to supervise. Once that's done, we'll plant the vine stock. Of course, we'll need a few years before we can start making wine, but I have a few ideas to use the facilities in the meantime."

"Okay."

"This means," I pointed out, "that if you accept, you'll probably feel overrun with Americans often enough. They will consider they are at home, because it will be their land. You'll be entitled to have a say on some matters, but they will be the ones in charge. Not you."

"Understood. I accept."

"I know it's a lot to ask, and you're going to have to compromise on some things you won't like, but—what did you say?"

"I said I accept."

"Really?"

He nodded.

"I can tell this is the best chance I'm going to get to save the castle. So I'm willing to compromise where needed."

I almost leapt for joy. Nothing was guaranteed yet, but I'd just cleared the first hurdle—and probably the most important one to me.

Over the next hour, Éric and I went over the project together. Before she'd left for the US, Elizabeth had left me the phone number of one of her friends working at the Institute of Agricultural Research in Paris. Luckily, he was a workaholic and I managed to get hold of him right away.

He couldn't answer then and there, but he promised to look it up and get back to me as soon as possible. In the meantime, I'd have to do without.

Éric and I then went out to take a few pictures of the castle, the plot of land I intended to submit and the grounds. I'd add them to the file I would show Elizabeth as soon as I was back.

Lunchtime had long since come and gone by the time I decided I had more than enough for my purposes.

"Are you free right now?" Éric asked just as I packed away my camera and file, ready to return to the inn to search for the costume I was still missing for that evening's ball. "There's something I would like to show you."

You should go, the voice of reason whispered.

"Sure," I heard myself reply.

His smile practically lifted me clear off the ground.

Longing...

"Follow me."

I trailed him through the grounds. The sun blazed overhead, not a trace of the torrential rain of the previous day in sight. Slightly behind him, I walked in silence, lost in a daydream. From time to time my eyes wandered over his broad shoulders, his hips, his ass...and I blushed, thankful he couldn't see, remembering my sketches.

You're pathetic, I chided myself. *Stop it this instant. You're playing a dangerous game.*

A dangerous game I couldn't seem to resist.

"Alex...are you in love with Éric?" Bea's voice echoed inside my head.

I was going insane.

Lost in thought, I didn't really pay attention to where I was walking and twisted my ankle. Again.

The same one, of course.

"*Ouch!*" I grunted. "Oh, heck! I must be cursed!"

Éric turned back.

"Are you okay?"

"Yeah, yeah, everything under control. I think the ground is trying to murder me," I joked, "but I'm tough, so it's going to need to step up its game."

"You twisted your ankle again?"

"Yeah, but I'm fine. It just rekindled the pain, but it's okay. It's gone now!"

"Is it the same ankle?"

"Yes, but I'm telling you, I'm fine! Look!"

And I hopped up on one foot to prove it—but I couldn't hold back a grimace.

Maybe I had been just a touch optimistic.

"I can see that. Come on, princess, up you go. I'll carry you."

What? No! Bad idea! Very bad idea!

"You will not give me a piggyback ride!" I retorted.

He turned and offered me his back as if I hadn't spoken at all.

His muscled back that I had been admiring.

"Climb up," he insisted. "Or I'm carrying you like a sack of potatoes. Your choice."

"I can walk, I'm telling you!" I protested. "There's no need!"

Even to my own ears, my protests did not seem very convincing. Unsurprisingly, Éric simply stared at me over his shoulder, eyebrows raised as though to indicate that I would do better to cooperate.

After a few seconds of me refusing to move, he sighed and turned to face me fully. Smiling wolfishly, a mischievous glint in his eye, he took a step toward me.

"Very well. You leave me no choice."

"You think your caveman impersonation will convince me?" I drawled, backing up with a simmering glance. "My dear, you are very much mistaken."

"We'll see."

And he leapt for me without further ado.

Of course, I used my smaller size to dodge under his arm. A merciless game of tag followed, one that I eventually lost. Éric was much faster and nimbler than I was, especially with my still painful ankle. And before I knew it, he had hoisted me up on his shoulder like a sack of potatoes, half laughing, half shrieking and kicking, begging him to let go of me.

"*Nope.* I caught you, I'm keeping you."

"But I can walk. I'm fine. You've seen it!"

"This is for your own safety. You are the clumsiest person I have ever met, and I have better things to do with my day than drive you to the hospital for a broken leg or God knows whatever part you decide to damage next."

I giggled. I could only picture what a sight we must have made, me slung over his shoulder, his arms around my thighs, and suddenly I couldn't stop laughing.

I was still laughing when Éric set me down.

He eyed me for a few moments, half-baffled, half-amused.

"You really are an astonishing woman, Alexandra."

There was no mistaking the admiration in his voice. His words moved me despite my best efforts, sobering me up, and I felt my cheeks flush.

"You're adorable when you blush," he murmured. His gaze and his voice wrapped around me.

Time stood still for a heartbeat.

I dragged up from somewhere the strength to tear my gaze away from his. I cleared my throat and looked around.

"So, what is it you want to show me?"

"Come over here."

We were deep in the park, on a slightly elevated point, near the forest that curved around the estate and had probably been hunting grounds before the Revolution. The remains of an old wall of white stones lay at our feet.

From where we were, we had an unrivaled view of the rear façade of the castle and what I could only guess was the ballroom and balcony where Thomas had declared his love to Gabrielle. The water from the moat glistened beneath.

Longing...

"The view is magical from here," I murmured in a slightly strangled voice.

For a moment, I wished time would stop so I would stay forever frozen in this instant.

I sighed a little.

"Is everything okay?" Éric asked, drifting closer.

"Yeah, yeah, everything is fine."

I turned to him.

"So?"

"Come here," he repeated.

I followed him around the low wall and caught sight of a rosebush with a single rose standing tall in its midst. Its petals were a deep pink, so dark it was almost red. It was only just blooming, but it already seemed magnificent to me.

"My father planted this bush for my mother," Éric said quietly. "This is where he proposed to her."

"Really?"

He nodded.

"It hasn't bloomed in years. It barely broke the ground each year, even though my father had chosen a perennial flower so it would live forever. Like his love for my mother."

My throat tightened again, and I crouched, examining the flower. Out of the corner of my eye, I saw Éric kneel down beside me. My heart began to beat faster.

"For a long time, I thought it was dead. And yesterday I came here to think, and saw the rose. As though it wanted to be reborn."

I kept silent, but my conversation with Bea was playing on a loop inside my head. As though reading my thoughts, Éric turned to me.

"Do you believe in fate, Alexandra?"

"No. Surprising though it may be for a romantic like me, I don't believe in fate. I believe in choice. That everyone is the master of their own destiny."

I could hear myself speak, and with every word something quivered inside me. His presence so close to mine consumed me entirely. I wanted to lean against him. To rest my head in the crook of his shoulder.

And stay there forever.

"I didn't believe in fate either."

"What made you change your mind?" I asked without looking at him.

"You did."

"I didn't do anything."

"You arrived just when I needed help. And you found a solution."

"I haven't done anything yet. The castle hasn't been saved."

"I know that. But no one has done for me what you have, even though I'm a total stranger. You don't owe me anything. I treated you like the enemy. And you gave me hope when I was ready to give up."

I kept my gaze on the flower, like a lighthouse in the night, a solitary sign of life and hope amid the ruins. I could feel my heartbeat pulsing right up into my ears.

Gently, I reached for the rosebud. I focused on it, unwilling to show how much his words were winning me over. How much I had to restrain myself not to give in to the siren song of his arms. Not to give in to him.

I traced the still half-closed petals with a fingertip. In a little while, the rose would be in full bloom.

And I would not be here to see it.

A sob rose up in my throat, and I swallowed it down.

Éric's hand brushed against mine, a slow and deliberate caress that created a storm within me. My eyes halted on his fingers lacing with mine.

"Alex," he murmured. "Alex, look at me."

Mesmerized, I obeyed. Him using my nickname was enough to rock my world. Everything was shaking, my stomach, my heart, my lungs. And then our gazes met again, and I drowned in his eyes.

I couldn't think. I knew I should have said something, done something, but I couldn't remember what. I had lost all power of speech and thought. I could only think of, only wish for one thing—for his hands to hold my face and his lips to brush against mine, for him to end the torment that was flaying me alive.

He seemed to read my thoughts. His hand left mine and framed my face, fingers sliding into my hair, thumbs stroking my cheekbones, blue gaze searching mine for a sign, for approval.

He must have found it. I could no longer struggle, not even against myself. So I let go.

Our faces drifted gently closer until we were only a hairsbreadth apart. The expectation made my senses and emotions grow raw as I slipped closer to insanity.

At last, his lips brushed mine. Gently at first, almost chastely, shyly. Then one of us—which one, I had no idea—opened their lips and the kiss grew deeper, fiercer. His tongue searched for mine and started a slow dance. His hands gripped my face tighter, drawing me closer until I was glued to his chest. I almost toppled over, unbalanced, and clung to him like an anchor, throwing my arms around his broad shoulders while my body melted against his.

I lost all sense of time. I was dizzy and I wanted more. Much more. Too much.

A voice inside my head repeated that I should stop, but I chased it away, kissing Éric even more fiercely, hiding from reality, forgetting everything that wasn't him, me, us. Then the voice grew louder, and I was suddenly aware of what I was doing.

With great difficulty, I pulled my lips and body away from his. I reclaimed the distance I needed to think, to have control over my thoughts and actions once again.

"I'm sorry," I murmured. "I have to go."

Pain, rejection, incomprehension flashed through his eyes, breaking my heart. I should have told him it was a mistake. That we should stop there. That I had Spencer, that I was engaged. But instead I smiled and said apologetically, "I don't have a costume for tonight. I really need to find one."

Éric sighed in relief and beamed at me.

"See you tonight?" he asked almost shyly.

I nodded and wordlessly sprang to my feet before literally running away.

Without a care for my painful ankle, my legs carried me away of their own volition. With every step, a question rang in my head.

What have I done?

Chapter 28
Gabrielle

Castle of Ferté-Chandeniers

January 1900

The next morning, Gabrielle joined her father in the library as if nothing had happened, as though the world, *her* world, had not just spun right off its axis. She kept her brand-new happiness quiet—she had promised Thomas she would not say anything before he asked her father for her hand—and helped Maurice restore order to the room in light of their upcoming departure. It would be soon, now.

Careful not to meet her father's gaze lest he read her like an open book, Gabrielle tried to contain her impatience. She sorted through the misplaced books, riffled through an atlas—stopping on North America, of course—before she put it back, humming the melody to *The Blue Danube* under her breath. The memories of the previous evening danced through her mind: the waltz, the stars, the proposal…and her yes, sincere and heartfelt.

She was on her fourth iteration of the music when there came a knock on the door. At last, at long last, Thomas came in.

Her heart began to beat wildly.

This is it, she thought. *Here we are. Today is the first day of the rest of our lives.*

Their gazes met, and Thomas smiled at her. It felt as though the sun had risen behind his eyes.

It was only a brief glance, over before you could say "wedding," but enough to turn Gabrielle's knees to water.

Thomas walked up to Maurice and bowed respectfully, asking to speak to him in the most solemn of manners. Maurice accepted immediately, though not without a sideways glance toward his daughter. Begging her knees not to betray her, Gabrielle rose and excused herself with a murmur, heading for the door. She brushed against Thomas and he seized her hand.

"Stay," he whispered too low for her father to hear, and his gaze was so tender she almost melted on the spot.

Nodding, she remained by his side—he had not released her hand—and, eyes lowered, summoned all of her will to keep a cool façade utterly at odds with the smile that stretched her lips while she waited patiently for Thomas to speak.

"What can I do for you, Mr. D'Arcy?" Maurice asked as he stood.

"Sir, I have come to humbly ask for your daughter's hand in marriage."

Euphoria rose within her, and she closed her eyes. All night, she had imagined this moment. Thomas bowing to her father, asking for her hand, Maurice eager to accept, joy and happiness in his eyes. But his icy response felt like cold water thrown in her face.

"I suppose you want to take her with you halfway across the world?"

Shocked, Gabrielle looked up and stared at her father uncomprehendingly. Maurice's gaze was so hard, so cold in that moment that she almost believed he would refuse to give them his blessing. And what followed did nothing to reassure her.

"I do, sir," Thomas replied, apparently unaffected by his hostile demeanor. It almost seemed as though he had been prepared for it.

"Do you love her?" Maurice asked.

Thomas's gaze strayed toward Gabrielle's and met it.

"More than life itself."

Gabrielle was so moved she nearly kissed him there and then.

"I have two conditions," Maurice announced, reclaiming the lovebirds' attention.

"What are they, sir?"

"I want you to promise me to take care of her as if she were the most precious thing in your life. No, more than that. If anything should happen to her, or if I should learn that you have harmed her in any way, I will not hesitate to cross the seas to let you know what I think."

"You have my word, sir."

"That is not enough. Swear it to me on what you hold dearest."

"Papa!" Gabrielle cried, unable to keep quiet any longer.

She knew that her father wanted to ensure Thomas would take good care of her, but need he be so cold? She could barely comprehend it. She had thought he would be happy for her!

"Stay out of this, Gabrielle. This is a matter between this young man and me."

Gabrielle wanted to protest that she was at the heart of the matter, since it was *her* hand they were discussing, but Thomas stopped her.

"Your father is right, Gabrielle. It is only natural that he should wish to ensure that I deserve you."

She settled down, reluctantly willing to keep her peace a little longer. Thomas turned back to her father and, with utter conviction in his voice, declared, "I swear it upon my mother's grave."

"Very well."

"What is the other?"

"The other?"

"You spoke of two conditions."

"Ah, yes."

And instantly Maurice's severe attitude vanished, to be replaced with his usual kindly smile. "I would like you to call me 'Father,' since you shall become my son," he announced warmly.

Relief washed over Gabrielle, and she could not resist the urge to throw her arms around his neck, dragging Thomas with her, making him an awkward member of a three-way family hug.

"I hope you will forgive me for my little deception," Maurice apologized. He explained that he had promised his late wife he would watch over their only daughter and that it was his duty to ensure that Thomas would do the same.

"It is only natural. I expected as much."

"And I have a favor of my own to ask," Maurice added.

"What is it?"

"For you to release Hélène from her duties so I may marry her."

Gabrielle clapped with joy.

"She accepted?"

"She accepted."

"Papa, that's wonderful!" She hugged him again. "I am so very glad on your behalf!"

"Well?" Maurice asked Thomas over his daughter's shoulder.

"Hélène may leave today if she so desires. I wish you both all the happiness in the world."

* * * *

That evening, true to form, Gabrielle slipped out of her bedroom and ran through the halls to join the man who was now her fiancé. Her heart beat wildly, and her stomach was doing cartwheels. She only slowed as she reached the library. The door was ajar, and pale light filtered into the corridor. She pushed it open and stepped in.

Sitting in what would forever remain *their* love seat, his back to her, Thomas's gaze was lost to the flames. He seemed deep in thought, so deep he did not hear her approach. She tiptoed closer, smiling in mischief. Then she placed her hands over his eyes.

"Who is it?" she whispered in his ear.

"Hmmm. I know not. A fairy?" Thomas guessed playfully.

"Wrong."

"A mermaid?"

"Wrong again."

"The woman from the next castle over?"

"In the middle of the night?" She pretended offense. "Why in God's name would the neighbor's wife creep through *our* castle in the middle of the night?"

"Shall I deduce it is again the wrong answer?"

"Yes!"

"Then only one possibility remains," he declared.

"I am all ears."

"The love of my life."

And without further ado, he reached up and seized her wrists, pulling her over the back of the love seat until she tumbled into his arms, into his lap. She giggled breathlessly, but her laughter trailed away as her eyes met Thomas's. Slowly, tenderly, her fiancé's lips brushed hers, a sweet caress so soft and gentle it set her entire body to shivering.

"Good evening," he whispered, his forehead against hers.

"Good evening," she replied, twining her arms around his neck.

Of their own volition, her fingers lost themselves in her fiancé's hair— she savored the word—and she stifled a blissful sigh. So often had she dreamed of this.... She could still hardly believe she would be able to do it as much as she desired. It was a dream, a dream she wished never to wake up from.

Thomas closed his eyes under her hands, relaxing against her as she had never seen him do before. He nestled his face in the crook of her neck and sighed.

"I can still hardly believe you are here," he murmured.

"I have been here for the last few weeks, in case you failed to notice," Gabrielle teased him. She felt him chuckle against her skin.

"I did notice. I noticed you from the very first day."

"So did I."

He drew away from her, and their gazes met again. They smiled at each other. Unable to resist, Gabrielle drew his face toward hers and begged for a kiss. Her fiancé was more than happy to oblige. Then she demanded another, and another, and another—until their brief kisses, interspersed with smiles and laughter, grew more heated. Deeper, longer. Gabrielle's lips savored Thomas's greedily, lustily, surprising even herself. When Thomas's tongue found hers in a heady caress, the world vanished, consumed by sensations she had never felt before. It was as though her entire body had been set ablaze from the inside, as though a terrible need to quench a thirst she had not been aware of previously rose from within.

She felt light-headed and elated.

She did not wish to stop.

A few minutes, a few seconds later, though, Thomas pulled back and gazed at her, wordlessly, a glint of pure admiration in his eye.

"If I had the slightest artistic talent," he finally murmured, "I would paint you like this, in the firelight with your hair loose and your eyes aglow, your lips red from our kisses. You are magnificent, Gabrielle. Utterly magnificent. The most beautiful woman on earth."

Her cheeks flushed at the compliment, and she hid her face in his neck to conceal her pleased grin.

"I love you, Thomas," she whispered under her breath.

She felt his arms close tight around her, and gratitude filled her heart at the happiness radiating through her in that instant.

"I never thought I would love anyone as much as I love you, Gabrielle," Thomas confided. "I was not alive before I met you. Your smile, your kindness, your generosity, your great spirit, all of this brought me back to life. I do not know what I have done to deserve you. I still hardly believe it. It feels as though I will wake up and realize it was all nothing but a dream."

"It is not a dream. I am here, in your arms, and I have no intention of leaving. I promise you that."

He nodded gently. She could not see the look on his face, but she felt his hesitation in the sudden tension in her fiancé's frame. She drew back in concern.

"What is it, Thomas?"

"Nothing."

"Tell me."

"Are you certain—"

"Certain of what?"

"That you will not regret coming with me? Leaving your father, your bookstore, your life behind...for me?"

Gabrielle seized his face in her hands and met his eyes resolutely.

"For you? Thomas, *you* will be my life from now on. My home will be wherever you are. Of course I will miss my father, but I know Hélène will take good care of him. You are my future now. You are my family, and I do not wish to be anywhere but by your side. I love you!"

"Even—even scarred as I am?"

And Gabrielle did what she had so long secretly dreamed of. Only taking her eyes off Thomas's at the very last moment, she kissed his scarred cheek, long and sweet, almost reverently. Then she pulled back and searched his gaze.

"Does this answer satisfy you? I love you, Thomas, which means I love your scar as much as I love your eyes, your hands or your smile. No, that is not true. I love it more, because this scar is you."

She had barely finished speaking when Thomas, relief shining in his eyes and struggling with a myriad of other emotions, took hold of her face and kissed her frantically, urgently, greedily, the way he had that first time on the day he had left for England. But he did not break off after a few seconds as he had done then. He kissed her again and again, clutching her to him as though he wished to absorb her and never let go.

Gabrielle met his ardor with equal passion and urgency. And when his tongue met hers, when his hands traveled over her body, she forgot anything that was not them, surrendering to the moment, to the uproar of sensations, to the exquisite delight that his skin sparked against hers. Her whole body was afire under his hands, and she nearly vibrated out of her skin. She felt light-headed and suddenly very, *very* aware of parts of her body that apparently had a will of their own and wanted more.

Gabrielle too wanted more. Much more.

She wanted to feel Thomas against her, skin to skin, feel his heartbeat against hers, explore his body with her own.

She wanted to be one with him.

It was as simple as that.

Without hesitation, her hands began to loosen Thomas's tie, unbutton his shirt, pulling the lapels aside to venture beneath the barrier of fabric, daring and resolute, as she kept on kissing him. The feeling of her hands on his chest seemed to electrify Thomas even as it brought him back down to earth. He pulled away from her, short of breath and eyes fever-bright.

"Gabrielle—Gabrielle, I—"

"What is it?" she panted, light-headed.

"I—I think I should walk you back to your room. And dive headfirst into the moat."

"The moat is frozen; you will only break your skull. Why would you do that? Do you…do you not want me?"

His eyes gleamed.

"On the contrary." His voice was hoarse. "But I am only a man and I—I am not certain I can remain a gentleman if we—if we carry on. I—"

"I do not want a gentleman," Gabrielle cut him off fiercely.

Another person had taken possession of her body. She no longer was herself. She was another, a daring, demanding Gabrielle. A sensual Gabrielle, she hoped, as her lips teased her fiancé's. His chest rumbled, and he replied in kind, voraciously, before pulling back again.

"Gabrielle—"

"I do not want to be good, Thomas," she murmured as she nipped his ear, tearing a new growl from him. "I want to be yours tonight. And I want you to be mine. All mine."

"Gabrielle, I am already yours," Thomas protested weakly. "My heart and soul are yours always."

"Then give me your body. Thomas…please. Love me."

Unable to resist what he so desired any longer, Thomas surrendered, and they fell together as he offered all she asked, and took all she gave in return.

And more still.

I will always remember that night when Thomas and I were one, Gabrielle wrote in her diary that night, once she had returned to her bedchamber, starlight in her eyes and happiness in every part of her soul. *When I am old and wrinkled, unable to remember even my own name, I will relive those moments, those sensations, again and again. Exploring our bodies, the fire rising within us, burning everything in its wake, reason first of all. Thomas's hands on my skin, bold and heady, my own that mirrored his every move. His tongue making me lose my mind.*

I never closed my eyes. I wanted to see his every expression, I wanted to hear the growls, the sighs as our bodies merged. I wanted to carve every minute, every second into my memory.

I will admit to my eyelids fluttering shut when I felt my body explode and stars shimmer in front of my eyes, when I felt Thomas surrender to pleasure himself, whispering my name again and again like a prayer, until he could no longer speak, body taut, his arms tight around me as though to keep me there forever.

Yes, even after my mind has deserted me and I will no longer recognize myself in the mirror, I will always remember the mark Thomas left on my body, my heart and my soul. Because what I felt tonight in his arms was stronger than anything that can exist.

Our fates are now sealed, I know it. There will never be a me without him again, nor will there ever be a him without me.

Never.

Chapter 29
Alexandra

Chandeniers-sur-Vienne

Present day

Fire. Fever.

His body against mine. Our fingers laced together. His breath, his kisses, setting me ablaze, from outside to inside, to the deepest corners of my soul.

I sighed out his name.

"Éric. Éric..."

"Princess," he growled, his voice hoarse, sensual, bewitching.

A shiver ran over me

More. I wanted more.

"Your wish is my command."

His lips teased mine, his tongue played with mine, traced my lips, peppering them with little kisses then claiming my mouth feverishly, passionately, stoking the fire in my veins. His hands were everywhere: in my hair, pulling me closer, on my breasts, coaxing the raised points, at the small of my back, arching me further, pressing my hips against his, on my thighs, stroking every centimeter of my skin, exploring every curve.

Every gesture, every sigh, every murmur drove me crazy. Crazy with desire. Crazy about him.

"Éric—"

"Patience, princess."

His lips left mine and trailed kisses along my jaw, nipping my ear until he felt me lose control, until my hips lifted, begging for his body. His mouth wandered down my neck, tongue tracing the curve of my shoulder, lingering on my breasts, sucking, biting, until I throbbed with desire, head thrown back, eyes closed. He resumed his careful exploration of my body, dipped over my navel and traveled further down, where every sensation was heightened, where I wanted to feel his hands, his lips, his tongue—him—the most.

I was on the verge of eruption, the blood in my veins had turned to lava, my breath was short, choppy.

"Éric!" I screamed.

I want you, in me, right now! I wanted to shout.

He straightened until his face was level with mine, scattering kisses across my stomach as he went, and his gaze met mine.

"I love you, Alex."

* * * *

"Alex, wake up."

What?

Something was wrong.

"Alex, I found you a costume!"

Éric was falling away, the weight of his body on mine vanishing.

No, no, come back! Don't leave! I need you!

I need you....

"Alex!"

A hand shook me.

"Alex?"

I opened my eyes, and everything disappeared in a flash. Éric, his smile, his gaze, his caresses.

Everything except the weight in my stomach and the horrible, cold sensation of loneliness inside.

I closed my eyes briefly, trying to check the vast disappointment welling up within me. I shouldn't feel this way. I should have been glad it was only a dream. Instead it felt like part of me had been torn away.

"Alex?" the voice repeated.

I sighed and opened my eyes to Marine's face.

"Sorry to wake you up, but I found you a costume. And I know you're going to love it."

Upon returning from the castle earlier, heart and senses still in full turmoil, I had found Marine in the kitchen, elbow-deep in flour.

"Marine! I was looking for you."

"What can I do for you?"

"I know I'm really late for this, but I don't have a costume for tonight. Do you know where I can find one?"

"Fabrice doesn't have any left, but let me think about it and make a few calls. I'll find you something."

"Oh, don't go to a lot of trouble on my account. You have enough on your plate. I'll find something on the internet."

"I don't mind, really. I even have an idea. What's your size?"

I gave it to her, first in American standard then converted it to European sizing.

"That could work...I think I can create the perfect costume for you! You're going to be just *magical*," she'd sung. "Wait here, I need to go rummage around for a bit."

"Thanks, Marine. You're amazing."

And I'd settled in the garden to wait, hoping to forget my agitation between the pages of Gabrielle's diary, and fell fast asleep.

Still half-caught in my dream, I sat up and looked around, slightly light-headed. I had no idea how long I had been asleep. A while, surely. Shadows stretched across the garden, and the sunlight had turned molten. I stifled a little yawn and closed Gabrielle's diary in my lap.

"Don't worry about waking me up. If you hadn't, I'd have slept right through to tomorrow morning."

I still felt feverish, exhausted by several sleepless nights tossing and turning, pondering the same questions without ever finding an answer.

I tried to dispel the afterimages of my dream in vain, and tried to smile. Marine had gone out of her way for me; the least I could do was be attentive and grateful. I was about to ask to see the costume when she caught me short.

"Is everything okay, Alex?" There was a worried look in her eye. "Excuse me for asking, I know it's none of my business, but you seem out of sorts."

What could I answer? That everything was spinning inside my head because I wanted things I wasn't allowed to want, that I felt emotions I wasn't allowed to feel? That I was adrift, torn between what I felt for a man who wasn't my fiancé, and the guilt I felt toward said fiancé? That instead of thinking of him and our future together, I was consumed with desire for a man I had barely met and who had upturned my life, my certitudes and my plans? That my best friend's words had unbalanced me so badly that I didn't know where I was or what I wanted anymore?

Would I tell her all that when I didn't even dare admit it to myself?

Well, I had the answer to that at least—no.

So I made my grin a little wider.

"I'm fine, don't worry about me. Probably just a little tired, I haven't been sleeping well."

"Is it the mattress? The pillows? Is there anything I can do?"

"No, no, the room is perfect. Everything is wonderful, and you're great. I have no idea why I have trouble sleeping," I lied. "It'll pass. I'm probably just thinking too much."

Marine scrutinized me. I could see in her eyes that she didn't believe me—not completely—but she didn't insist.

"If there's anything I can do, please don't hesitate to ask," she said gently. "All right?"

"Promise. So, what did you find? A kilt for me too?"

"Ha! No, I'm sure you would have been very cute in a kilt, but I found you something more...magical."

"'Magical'? Okay, color me curious," I quipped as I took the garment bag she handed me.

I zipped it open to reveal a sleeveless blue satin sheath dress that flared out slightly at the hips, complete with a little train.

I was speechless. "Marine, it's gorgeous."

"You like it?"

"It's much too good for me! I can't wear it!"

"Nonsense! It's going to look incredible on you! And that's not all!"

She dashed inside the inn and came back almost at once, brandishing an adorable pair of iridescent wings, a mask made of the same fabric, a wand with a glittering silver star and a small Austen-like clutch bag of the same blue satin as the dress.

"You will be the fairy-est of them all!"

"You're *my* fairy godmother! How did you ever manage to put all of this together in so short a time?"

"The wings, mask and wand belong to a friend from when she danced in *The Nutcracker* in Canada."

"You have a Canadian friend?"

"Yeah. You've been there?"

"Of course, I lived in Montréal for a while."

"What a coincidence! Caroline was a prima ballerina in Montréal. She married a Frenchman and came to live here with him, but she kept a few mementos from when she danced in the great ballets."

I suddenly remembered that I was leaving again in a few days, and the dread hovering over me doubled in weight.

"What about the dress?" I inquired in an attempt to change the subject.

"It's mine. I wore it for my engagement party."

"I can't wear your engagement dress!" I protested.

"I haven't been able to fit in it since I had Océane. And…my marriage was a mistake. The only good thing that came out of it was my daughter. I don't know why I didn't get rid of the dress before."

"What happened? Not that it's any of my business."

"Nothing very special. Hugo and I married too young, and when I got pregnant unexpectedly, he realized I wasn't the one for him and he left while I was in the hospital giving birth."

"*Son of a bitch!* Sorry for being so crude, but—"

"Don't worry, I've said a lot worse about him."

"But when I arrived last week, you mentioned your daughter was with him right now. Have you forgiven him?"

"Hell no. I don't think I ever will. I suffered too much for that."

"I can understand."

"It took me years to forget him, and to be honest, I would've been happy never seeing him again. But he came back one day asking for a divorce. He wanted to remarry. And get this—his fiancée was pregnant."

"What?!"

"Yeah. I didn't take it well. But he insisted he'd changed and that he wanted to get to know his daughter."

"And you accepted. For her."

"I didn't have the right to deprive my daughter of a father who wanted to know her now."

"Tough choice."

"Tell me about it. But she's happy whenever she goes over there. He takes good care of her and she adores her little brother, so—I just grit my teeth. Her happiness is what matters."

"Haven't you met someone yourself?"

"Once bitten—"

"Twice shy, yeah."

"There is someone, though. But…I'm not quite ready yet, so…" She shrugged. "We'll see. Sorry, here I am again pouring out my life story! This is getting to be a habit!"

I smiled. I had asked the question, after all.

"Anyway, as for the dress, if it fits, please keep it. You'd be doing me a favor."

"I can't do that Marine, it's too much!"

"Then it's straight into the garbage with it. I don't want to keep it. I want to be able to move forward without having that holding me back."

Marine's words rang true in me. Too true.

If Bea were here she would proclaim it a new sign pointing out my fate, saying I should take heed and act before it was too late.

Except I was afraid. Petrified.

And anyway, I had a ball to go to. I'd think about it later.

* * * *

An hour later I had showered, dressed, done my hair and makeup, and I glittered in all of my winged glory in the full-length mirror in my bedroom.

I'd tied my hair up in a messy bun with blond locks falling free over my neck and face and just a touch of makeup, and I had to admit the result was striking.

I'd never considered myself especially pretty. My face was a little too square, and my freckles were the bane of my existence. And I was short, which hardly helped matters.

Yet in this dress I felt…different. Beautiful. Bold. Confident. Maybe it was the mask, the mysterious allure it lent to my face, but it felt like there was a new gleam to my eye, something I hadn't seen there in a long time.

"You're faded, Alex."

I shook my head to banish Bea from my thoughts.

I hadn't kept my promise to call her as soon as I had spoken to Éric. I knew I was digging my head in the sand, that at one point I was going to have to face myself and the truth. That I was falling for him.

Images from my dream kept flashing through my mind, mingling with reality until I no longer knew where real life ended and the dream began. The look in his eyes, the softness of his lips, the words he had spoken…

"Alex, look at me…."

I shivered and closed my eyes.

"I love you, Alex…."

The verdict was in. I was going crazy.

Voices drifted in through the open window. I recognized Marine's soft, cheerful accent…and Éric's deep, velvety tone. Unable to resist, I moved closer to the window, hoping to catch a glimpse of him.

Pathetic.

Stupid.

Dangerous.

"Are you really sure you love Spencer?"

"You gave me hope...."
"Alex, look at me."
"I love you."
A door slammed shut in the street, jolting me out of my thoughts. An engine purred to life, and the car drew away.

And then there was silence. Outside, at least. The racket inside my skull was deafening.

Shaking my head, I left the window and gave myself a last once-over in the mirror before stepping into a pair of stylish heels. I grabbed the clutch purse and the wand and left the inn for the center of Chandeniers.

* * * *

I saw him the minute I arrived on the church square where the costume ball was. Like I had a sixth sense that had drawn my gaze to the place he stood with a group of friends across the plaza, facing me in his ceremonial kilt.

Wow!

Even from several dozen meters away, I could feel the charisma rolling off him, his animal grace. I froze where I stood, unable to move, unable to look away, unable to control my wild heartbeat while my treacherous brain gleefully flashed all of the erotic imagery from my dream in front of my eyes.

"I love you, Alex."

For God's sake! When was it going to end?

He doesn't love me! It was just a dream!

You, on the other hand..., the little voice purred.

STOP!

I took a deep breath and tried to empty my mind by going backward through the alphabet.

As though he had felt my presence, Éric looked up from his glass and our eyes met. For a few seconds, time seemed to stand still. Sound faded away and people vanished. There was only him, and me.

Us.

Just us.

And my brain.

Fortunately, Marine, dressed as a gypsy, turned around and caught sight of me. Beaming, she waved.

"Alex! Over here!"

I elbowed my way through the crowd toward them, trying to avoid putting anybody's eye out with my wings or wand.

Marine took me by the arm and leaned down to whisper in my ear that the dress looked amazing on me, then introduced me.

"Everyone, this is Alexandra Dawson, one of the last descendants of the Saint-Armand family."

Oh, right. I'd been so busy not thinking of Éric, avoiding him at all costs, that I had spent very little time with Marine over the last few days, and I hadn't been able to share my findings with her.

"Uh, that's not actually—" I tried to say, but Marine didn't hear me and went on.

"The musketeer is Maxime, a childhood friend. And the best chef around here."

"M'lady, it is a pleasure to meet you," he greeted me, extending a hand.

But D'Artagnan didn't just shake it like anybody else would've. He removed his hat with a flourish, and with a bow fit for a Renaissance court, he kissed the back of my hand.

"You are resplendent," he declaimed, 100 percent in character. "You light up this square with your mere presence."

"Yes, uh—thank you," I replied, as flattered as I was embarrassed. "How—gallant!"

He beamed and winked at me. Out of the corner of my eye I saw Éric roll his eyes, jaw clenched tight.

"I forgot to mention he's the biggest flirt around here," Marine laughed. "Beware!"

"Marine, you break my heart. And you ruin my chances!"

"Maxime, there isn't a woman here that you haven't flirted with," Little Red Riding Hood scoffed. She turned to me and added, "We only forgive him on account of his delicious lasagna."

"And his tasty salmon tartare," Marine added. "Alexandra, this is Caroline, the Canadian friend I was telling you about earlier."

"So you're from Montréal! You still have your accent, that's wonderful! Thank you for the wings and mask, you saved my life!"

"You're welcome, they look good on you! And I tried getting rid of the accent, but every time I speak with my family it comes back in full force. Marine told me you'd lived in Montréal; did you stay there long?"

"Two years. It's a hard place to leave."

"That is very true."

Marine then introduced me to Paul, the magician who had pulled Caroline away from her city of birth, and Benjamin, a.k.a. Robin Hood and police captain of Chandeniers.

"And I think you know Bruno, our mayor," Marine concluded, waving at him.

I eyed the delicate blush spreading across her cheeks and wondered whether he was the "someone" she had mentioned earlier. Which would explain his presence at the inn on the day of my arrival...

"I do. Good evening, dear mayor, how do you do?" I simpered dramatically.

"Very well, how about you, Alex?"

"Wonderfully! I see you stole the pirate costume out from under Marine's nose."

"Guilty as charged. But if I have to pick between the pirate and the kilt, I'll go for the pirate."

"Tsk. Someone needs to be schooled." Marine shook her head.

"The Scottish are the new vampires," Caroline asserted. "Just come by our book club one day."

"*Exactly!* That is precisely what I have been trying to tell them!" Marine cried. "And anyway, the kilt looks better on Éric. Right, Alex?"

I turned to Éric, whose gaze I had felt on me all through the introductions, and nodded.

"You look good," I heard myself say, our eyes locked together as if we were utterly alone.

He smiled.

"You're gorgeous," he murmured, and my heart leapt again.

"You know, we could just leave," Maxime commented. "The electricity here could set water on fire!"

I turned redder than ever before and looked down—then immediately back up at the man who had been the center of my thoughts for so long it felt like forever.

"That's enough, Max," Marine said firmly. "Come dance with me instead of making fun of them."

She tugged him onto the dance floor.

It was only then that I noticed the band on the makeshift stage a few meters away. They struck up a pop-rock tune, and people began to flood the dance floor.

"Would you do me the honor, Mrs. Levasseur?" Paul asked Caroline.

"It would be my pleasure, Mr. Levasseur."

Arm in arm, they moved away, followed by Benjamin who made a beeline toward a young woman waving at him.

"Time for me to find a partner," Bruno chimed in when there were only the three of us left. "Alex—"

"Don't even think about it," Éric interrupted without looking away from my face.

The butterflies in my stomach shuddered.

"I just wanted to wish you a pleasant evening."

"And to you, Bruno," I answered.

"See you later," Éric said.

A knowing grin on his face, Bruno slipped away, leaving us alone.

"Hi," Éric said.

"Hi."

"You're gorgeous."

"You already told me."

"I know. You're gorgeous."

I couldn't help but huff out a laugh.

"You're not so bad yourself."

Probably the understatement of the century.

"Do you want to dance?"

"Why not? I make no promises about stepping on your toes, though."

"I don't care if you step on my toes. I just want—"

To kiss you forever, eat you up, taste every part of your skin, his eyes seemed to say. Or maybe I was imagining things.

All I knew was that his gaze was so intense that every inch of me was ablaze.

"Just what?"

"Dance. I just want to dance with you," he concluded, extending a hand.

Reality returned to me all at once.

"I'm not sure that's such a good idea. My ankle—"

"Give me a second."

He strode over to the musicians and talked to them. They nodded and he returned to my side.

"What did you tell them?" I asked, even though I had a pretty good idea.

"You'll see." He smiled mysteriously.

A few moments later, the musicians cut their tune short and switched to a gentle, romantic ballad. Éric bowed, his eyes on mine.

"My fair lady, would you grant this humble human a dance?"

"With pleasure."

In that instant, I could have sworn my wings were real and I could soar.

I slid my hand into his and followed him onto the dance floor. The dancers had started to sway gently to the languid rhythm of the slow melody. Éric turned to me and placed his left hand on my waist, pulling me toward him as his right hand kept hold of mine. Wordlessly, our bodies pressed against each other and began to move as one, as if it were the most natural thing in the world. Slowly my head tipped closer to his until my temple rested against his cheek—whoever invented heels deserves an altar. Éric's hand tightened around mine. My eyes fluttered closed.

I felt so calm. At peace.

We danced for a few moments, legs and fingers entwined; then he whispered into my ear. "I've been thinking about your proposal."

I pulled back, suddenly concerned. "Please don't tell me you've changed your mind."

"I haven't."

"Phew! What were you thinking of, then?"

"If your plan works and your boss accepts...will you be part of the team coming here to oversee the vineyard?"

His question caught me flat-footed. I had thought of it, of course—heck, I'd thought of little else ever since I'd had the idea—but coming from him... I don't know. I wasn't expecting it.

"I don't know. I don't think so."

"You have to be. That's my one condition."

My pulse sped up.

"I don't—I don't understand," I heard myself reply. "Why would you want me here? You'll have gone back to Africa or somewhere else. It won't change a thing for you."

"Because I trust you, Alex. Because you love this castle as much as my father did, and I know that nothing will happen to it as long as you are in charge. Because—"

He broke off and somehow, without discussing it, we stopped dancing. I hung on his every word. Part of me wanted to hear what I shouldn't have hoped for. It was a dangerous game, I knew it, but I was unable to stop playing.

"Marine is here," I argued. "She loves the castle too. She would know how to take care of it. No one here needs me," I added, holding my breath.

I hardly recognized myself. Here I was, practically begging Éric to tell me he needed me.

It was insane. It was crazy.

"How can you say that? Alex, you—I—"

He sighed, shook his head, hesitated. His gaze searched mine. Gently, he tugged off my mask, caressing my face with his thumb. A shiver ran over me. I closed my eyes, surrendering to his touch.

Just a few moments, I promised myself. *Just a few moments.*

"Alex, look at me."

I opened my eyes, falling headfirst in the fathomless depths of blue. The bubble had closed around us. The rest of the world had disappeared. Tomorrow no longer existed. Just then, there was only this moment. Just him, and me.

Slowly, his face came closer to mine, and he rested his forehead against mine.

"Alex," he said with a sigh. "*I* need you. I think—I think I'm falling in love with you. Please don't run away from me again...."

Chapter 30
Gabrielle

Angers

February 1900

"What do you think?" Gabrielle asked timidly as she stepped out from behind the screen.

Sophie examined her with an expert eye, swooping wordlessly around her best friend, pinching the dress here and there, puffing up the skirt, tugging at the sleeves, muttering to herself, until Gabrielle began to wonder whether this had been a good idea after all and if the result would meet her expectations.

After what seemed like forever, Sophie turned to her and beamed, eyes shining.

"Gabrielle, you are magnificent. A vision. If he wasn't already absolutely enamored, your Prince Charming will fall in love the moment he sees you coming up the aisle. He will want to eat you right up, that's for sure!"

Relieved, Gabrielle blushed. It was exactly what she had hoped for.

She wanted to dazzle her future husband.

"Do you really think so?" she asked, stepping in front of the full-length mirror in Sophie's milliner shop.

The white cotton dress was medieval in cut, with flowing sleeves held tight around the elbows by wide copper arm rings and embroidered in gold around the wrists. Similar patterns decorated the neckline and sketched a belt over her hips as the dress flared out. Celtic designs ran along the hem of the skirt, etched out in the same golden thread.

It was a magnificent dress, and Gabrielle felt like a medieval princess in it, Guinevere waiting for Lancelot, Iseult sighing after Tristan, Enide following Erec to the ends of the world. But beyond its beauty, this dress was precious to her for another reason—her mother had worn it for her wedding. Maurice had given it to Gabrielle when they had returned from the castle a fortnight earlier.

"I have little I can give you for your wedding, but I know your mother would have wanted you to wear this," he had confessed, his voice full of emotion.

Gabrielle hadn't been able to hold back a few tears at this precious gift. Nothing could have made her happier or prouder than to marry the man of her dreams in her mother's wedding dress.

"I am certain of it," Sophie asserted, an answer to the question Gabrielle had already almost forgotten. "The size is almost perfect, we just need to hem it a little so as to avoid you tripping over it. We do not want you falling flat on your face in the middle of the church."

"Dear God, no! I would just as soon avoid ridicule on my wedding day...."

"I will make sure of it, I promise. I will also take in the sleeves, they are a little too long, and tighten the bodice so it hugs your figure perfectly, here and here. What do you think?"

As she spoke, she stuck pins into the fabric as markers.

"You are the professional. I trust you entirely," Gabrielle assured Sophie.

"Exactly what I wanted to hear," Sophie replied with a smile.

Their gazes met in the mirror, and she froze in midmotion, staring at her best friend, eyes shining.

"I cannot believe you are getting married," she breathed. "How amazing!"

"I know! I can scarcely believe it myself! Everything happened so fast!"

"So fast you did not even tell me about it beforehand, you sly little minx!"

Gabrielle grimaced an apology, well aware that while she had filled page after page of her diary during her stay at the castle, she had not sent a single letter to her best friend, except to briefly inform her that Maurice was out of the woods and that they would remain at the castle until he had recovered and the inventory was done. As if part of her had wished to keep her relationship with Thomas...to herself. Like a secret to be protected. A flame to be kindled and sheltered before it could be exposed to the world.

It was only when she had hurried into the shop an hour earlier, her mother's dress in her arms, that Gabrielle had told her everything. Eyes bright, she had asked her to be her bridesmaid—and to adjust the dress for her. Naturally, Sophie had accepted. The entire neighborhood had probably heard her delighted cries when she had hugged Gabrielle right there in the shop in front of the astounded patrons.

"Are you angry with me?" Gabrielle inquired timidly.

Sophie hugged her and laid her chin on her shoulder.

"Of course not. Never. I'm happy for you. You deserve this."

"Thank you, Sophie."

They held each other for a few minutes before Sophie pulled away.

"Tell me, my dear, when will I be meeting your intended?"

"Soon, I hope. He is in England, taking care of a few final details before we leave," Gabrielle explained, "but he will be back shortly, and he will come here and take me to the castle. We will be married in the Chandeniers church. Everything is ready. Hélène spoke to the priest, and Céleste will be in charge of the meal, which will take place in the castle just before it is sold next month. We will celebrate my father's wedding to Hélène at the same time."

"What a wonderful idea! How romantic!"

Gabrielle nodded, butterflies swirling in her stomach. Knowing that her father would not be alone after she left for America with Thomas made things somewhat easier. He would have someone who loved him to take care of him.

"As for Thomas, I hope I can meet him before the wedding," Sophie commented.

"I will introduce you when he comes to Angers, I promise. You will love him, I am certain of it."

"I have no doubt about it. If you love him, so will I. But why didn't you travel with him to England? Did he not offer?"

"He did."

A few days after his return to the castle, as they sat together on their love seat one night, watching the fire, just happy to be there, Thomas had confessed that he must leave again soon. He had only come back for a few days to propose to her. He would not be gone long, he promised. He only had a few more things to settle. She could come along, he had suggested, his voice hopeful. If Maurice accepted, of course.

Gabrielle had almost packed immediately, without even asking her father. The mere idea of being separated from Thomas even for a few days when they had only just been reunited was unbearable. She never wanted to be parted from him again, not for a minute. She wanted to stay with him always, go wherever he went. And she wanted to discover his life there, meet the uncle who had raised him and be introduced to his grandmother. She wanted to see all the little things that had been a part of his life: the streets he had walked, the buildings he had passed every day, the rooms where he had lived. She wanted to see the place where he had grown into...himself.

But even though they had planned a simple ceremony with only their closest friends in attendance, Gabrielle wanted to make their wedding... magical. She wanted the first day of their life to set the tone for all those that followed. She wanted to give him the fairy tale he had never had, the one the baron had stolen from him. It was a promise she had made to herself, and the reason she had insisted upon being a part of the preparations, despite Céleste's protests that she already had more than enough to deal with.

And in order to do so, Gabrielle needed some time.

So she had kissed Thomas gently and said that she would love to come with him and meet his family, but that she could not. He had understood, of course, and had promised they would detour by England before they sailed for America so he could introduce his *wife* to his family. The mere word had made Gabrielle dizzy with happiness.

A few days later, their ways had parted for now in front of the bookstore, on a kiss laden with emotion and promises.

Two weeks had gone by, and Gabrielle had been glad to be busy with the bookstore and the wedding preparations, because she missed Thomas. Very much.

"Why didn't you go, then?"

Sophie's voice pulled her out of her reverie.

"I wanted to have time to prepare our wedding properly," she explained. "I want us to be able to remember it for all our lives, even when we are old and decrepit and no longer know our names. I want to give him the most beautiful wedding I can."

Sophie considered her for a time, smiling.

"You really love him, don't you."

It was more of a statement than a question, and Gabrielle confirmed with a nod.

"From the bottom of my heart. I had never felt anything so strong for anyone. It is as if—I do not know how to describe it. I can only breathe well when he is near. My heart no longer belongs to myself but only to him. Without him, the world is gray, black and white, but it is awash with a thousand colors the instant he appears. Do you see what I mean?"

"I think I do. I envy you, Gabrielle, for having all of that."

"One day so will you. I know it."

"May you be right. Your Prince Charming would not happen to have a brother, by any chance?" Sophie teased.

"Unfortunately not. But the man of your dreams is out there somewhere waiting for you, Sophie. I am certain of it."

"I don't doubt it."

They smiled at each other in the mirror, and suddenly there were tears in Sophie's eyes.

"Oh, Sophie! What is it?" Gabrielle cried, turning around to enfold her friend into her arms.

"It's silly. You are not even gone yet. But—I will miss you so, Gabrielle! What will I become without you?"

Gabrielle felt tears well up and roll down her cheeks.

"You will become a famous milliner, very in demand! I will miss you too, Sophie. But we will come back from time to time. And you will come visit me in New York. It might not be as exciting as the *Exposition Universelle*, but—"

"Oh, I think I can live with that." Sophie laughed through her tears.

She moved away and wiped her face then Gabrielle's before adding playfully, "Maybe I will move there too!"

"Oh, please do! Come live in New York with us! We would have such fun! And perhaps your Prince Charming is there waiting for you!"

Just as Sophie was about to reply, the clock in the corner of the room struck two.

"Dear God!" Gabrielle exclaimed in alarm, sniffling inelegantly. "I must return to the bookstore! Papa is visiting the printer today and we are expecting a delivery."

"Run along, then! I have everything I need to finish your dress; it will be ready in a few days."

"Thank you, Sophie!" She rushed back behind the screen. "You are a wonder! I knew I could count on you!"

* * * *

A few minutes later, cheeks pink from the biting February cold, short of breath and somewhat disheveled, Gabrielle pushed open the door to the bookstore.

"Étienne, I am back!" she announced, the bell over the door ringing merrily as she shut it behind her.

She looked around and caught sight of him at the back of the deserted bookstore. Before she could remove her hat or gloves, he strode toward her and put his arms around her, holding her tight.

For a second she thought she felt his lips against her neck, just under her jaw.

"What are you doing?" she protested, laying her hands on his chest to shove him back.

Just then, the bell chimed again as the door opened to admit two delivery men carrying a large case full of books.

"Delivery for Maurice Villeneuve," the first declared.

"I am his daughter," Gabrielle announced at once, breaking free of Étienne's hold. "Follow me."

She guided them toward her father's study, glaring at Étienne as she went, but he only smiled smugly back before looking away. Gabrielle boiled inwardly as she showed the men where to put the case.

Étienne had been behaving very strangely ever since she had returned from Chandeniers. It was as though he had suddenly made it his mission to have her give in to his advances. His dedication could only be admired. Previously he had more or less restrained himself—though rather less than more—but now he displayed his interest openly, often taking advantage of Maurice's absences to slip increasingly unsubtle double entendres into their conversations. Sometimes he stood so close to her when he "helped" her put the bookshelves into order that she could feel his breath in her hair and his body brush against hers.

Enough was enough, Gabrielle decided as she saw the delivery men out. It had to stop, and it had to stop now.

Once she had closed the door, she flipped the sign to indicate the bookstore was temporarily closed. Feigning a calm she did not feel, she removed her coat, hat and gloves, hung them on the hook and motioned for Étienne to follow her to the back of the bookstore.

"What in name of the Lord were you thinking?" she attacked, furious. "Étienne, enough is—"

He didn't let her finish. Before she realized what was happening, he had taken her face between his hands and pushed her against the wall to kiss her.

"What are you doing?" Gabrielle cried, shoving at him. "Are you insane? Let go of me!" she exclaimed when Étienne refused to budge.

Far from obeying, he caught her wrists and moved in closer again.

"Marry me, Gabrielle," he murmured.

"You have lost your mind, Étienne! Let go of me!" she repeated, trying to tug her hands free. "This is not funny!"

"It is not meant to be, and I have not lost my mind. I want to marry you. I always have."

"Étienne, I know you think you are in love with me, but—"

"I *am* in love with you, Gabrielle."

"—but I do not love you. I am engaged to Thomas and I will marry him. I love him. Now let go of me, please."

But still Étienne did not release her. Roiling fear began to bubble up within her. There was a strange glint in his eyes, and it did not bode well.

"You are not from the same world, Gabrielle," Étienne argued, his grip on her wrists tightening. "We are. I will love you and take care of you better than he ever will. I will be by your side all your life, in your father's bookstore. It is what you always wanted. I can give you what you wanted. He cannot. He does not know you the way I do. He does not love you the way I do."

"You're talking nonsense. You do not know him. You know nothing of him. Release me, or I will scream."

"I may not know him, but I know that if he loved you as much as you say he does, he would be here with you now. But he is not. I am. I was always here, and I always will be. And I am worth a thousand times more than that monster."

Rage ignited within her.

"Thomas is not a monster!" she shouted, struggling harder.

In vain. Étienne was much stronger than she was, and he used all his weight to hold her against the wall.

"You are not even half the man he is! And he respects me far more than you do right now! Let go of me, I said!"

Uncontrollable rage seemed to come over Étienne, and his face twisted in disgust. As though a mask had fallen away and revealed his true self.

"Why him?" he yelled, red with anger. "Is it his castle? His money, is that what you want? You disappoint me, Gabrielle, I did not think you so mercenary. But I will never let you go. You are mine, do you hear? It doesn't matter how, you will be mine, whether you like it or not. I haven't waited for you for two years so you can just slip through my fingers!"

He shoved her against the wall, pinning her with his bulk, and kissed her. His tongue forced its way past her lips without any regard for her resistance.

Panic washed over Gabrielle for the briefest of moments, intensifying when Étienne grabbed one of her breasts and kneaded it forcefully, humping against her like an animal in heat. She whimpered in pain, which only seemed to encourage him. He tried to hike up her skirt and worm his way in between her legs. And just like that, her panic disappeared, replaced with rage that increased her strength tenfold.

Who the hell does he think he is? Does he really think he can use me like this? I'll show you, just you wait!

Both his hands were busying feeling her up, leaving her face free to move. She bit down viciously on his tongue and immediately pulled free from his mouth when he flinched back. Then she wrenched one of her legs free and stamped on his foot with all her strength.

Étienne jumped back with a shout of pain, but she wasn't done yet. Utterly furious, she swung up with all her might and kicked him in the crotch, then slapped him as hard as she could. The crack rang out in the silence of the bookstore.

Short of breath, eyes blazing, she dashed out of reach as he squirmed on the ground, face twisted in pain, the shape of her fingers clearly visible on his cheek, staring at her as though she were the devil.

She wished she were. She would have turned him into a worm and crushed him beneath her heel.

"Never. Do. That. Again," she enunciated furiously as he hobbled to his feet.

The fact that he was up again so soon filled her with panic, but she pushed it down, putting more distance between them.

"You are mine, Gabrielle," Étienne grunted.

"Leave. Leave now and maybe I will forget what just happened."

"I will not. Not until you belong to me."

"I will never belong to you," she retorted icily. "Now leave before I become really angry. And never set foot in here again."

Étienne smiled sardonically, predatorily, and lurched forward, a cat playing with a mouse. Gabrielle's heart was beating so hard she felt it resonate all through her body. She backed away and hit something. She moved aside and stepped into another piece of furniture.

Lord, she thought as she fought against her rising fear. *There is too much furniture in here.*

She looked around for an exit, but no matter where she went, Étienne could catch her in a matter of seconds.

Think, Gabrielle. Think.

But nothing came to her. Her thoughts were flooded with panic.

Seeing her cornered, Étienne smiled triumphantly.

"Angry, you?" he hissed. "Do you really think you can overcome me?"

He leapt at her and seized her wrist, pulling her to him. Gabrielle thrashed, but his grip was too strong.

"I think I just did," she retorted, concealing her fear. "I can repeat the feat."

"That's what you think. I won't be fooled twice."

His lips scraped against hers again, but she turned her head away, twisting in repulsion.

"Just hold still, you'll like it. Hell, you'll even ask for more," he growled as he grabbed her skirts.

"Never!" she gasped, teeth clenched.

Think, Gabrielle, she repeated to herself. *Think. There has to be something.*

The solution flashed in front of her eyes.

The dagger!

The bookstore had been robbed a few years earlier. Ever since, her father had kept a dagger hidden behind the counter. If she could reach it, she would be able to defend herself.

Summoning all her courage, Gabrielle pretended to stop struggling. She forced her body to relax, hoping his grip would loosen so she could tear free.

"You see? That's a good girl," Étienne purred, biting at her earlobe.

She shuddered in disgust and tried to breathe through it. She closed her eyes as he cupped her breast, covered her lips with his. She let him, hiding her revulsion.

Just a few seconds more. Just a few seconds.

She felt the tension in his muscles recede, almost imperceptibly at first, then for good. That was what she had been waiting for. Gathering her strength, she shoved him back and darted behind the counter. With trembling hands, she gripped the dagger and pointed it at him.

"Out. Now."

"You think you can just chase me out? This bookstore is mine, Gabrielle, and so are you! It belongs to me, as you do!"

That was too much. She could not bear his presence any longer.

Gabrielle took a deep breath and leapt at him, blade aimed at his throat.

Her heart beat wildly, blood pulsing in her temples. Her legs shook so hard it was a miracle she could stand.

Her hand around the hilt, however, had never been so steady.

She was deathly afraid, but her wrath was greater still.

She gripped the dagger tighter and pressed the point against his neck, drawing a drop of blood.

"Out, I said!" she hollered, pushing him back. "Out of my sight before I butcher you like the swine you are!"

This time Étienne seemed convinced of the seriousness of her threats. He stared at her hatefully a few seconds longer before he raised his hands in surrender.

"Very well, I will leave," he conceded ungraciously. "But you will come back to me, Gabrielle. Trust me, you will."

"Never. Especially after what you just did. Leave! I never want to see you again! Ever!"

"You say that now, but when you are alone and need me to take care of the bookstore, you will come back to me and I will have won. I will be patient. I will wait."

"OUT!" she shrieked, all restraint lost.

She kept her eyes trained on him and the dagger pointed at his throat until he was outside. Then she darted to the door and slammed every lock shut. She tracked his movements as long as she could, checking he did not double back. Once she was certain he was far away and would not return, she dropped into a corner, curled into a ball and broke into sobs.

* * * *

When Maurice returned from the printer, some two hours later, the copies of the inventory for the castle sale under his arm, Gabrielle had pulled herself together. She was still shaken inwardly, but her hands were steady and her legs supported her.

It was almost as though nothing had happened.

Almost.

She was attending a patron when her father entered.

"Is everything all right, Gabrielle?" Maurice asked in concern once they were alone. "You look ill. Did something happen? Where is Étienne?"

Of course her father would be able to read her. It was pure fantasy to think she could hide anything from him. Trying to swallow down the nausea that threatened to overcome her at the mere mention of his name, she kept her voice carefully neutral.

"Étienne was no longer satisfied with the conditions of his employment here and decided to give his notice."

Maurice laid a hand on her forearm as she busied herself behind the counter.

"What happened, Gabrielle?"

She paused and took a deep breath, looking up at her father.

"Apparently, dearest Étienne disapproved of the match between Thomas and me," she said in a voice of carefully controlled rage. "He felt that I belonged to him, as did the bookstore. I very clearly signified to him that he was delusional and that I would never wed him. When he…insisted, I showed him out."

Surprise, shock and dismay warred over Maurice's face.

"Did he hurt you?" he asked, his voice as cold as his daughter's.

Gabrielle hesitated, and he needed no more.

"I will find him and tell him what I think of his attitude," he declared, moving toward the door.

"No, Papa, he isn't worth it. He did not harm me."

"He laid a hand on my daughter!"

"But I defended myself and he left! I was not hurt!"

"It does not matter, Gabrielle. You cannot stop me. I will show him. He cannot touch my daughter and fail to suffer for it."

"No, Papa! I do not want you to face him! I object! I am fine, everything is all right. Let it rest."

"Gabrielle, I—"

"Please," she insisted. "Papa, this is my life, my decision. And I have decided it was not worth it. He is not worth it. Please."

Maurice considered her for a few seconds, then grudgingly nodded.

"Thank you, Papa."

"He had better not show up here, though, or I will not be responsible for my actions."

Gabrielle clung to his embrace, hoping with all her heart it would never happen.

"Papa?"

"Yes?"

"Do not tell Hélène about this, please. I do not want anyone to hear about it."

"Will you not tell Thomas?"

She shook her head.

"Him least of all. It would only trouble and distress him needlessly."

After all that he had been through, she feared that Étienne's actions would only bring up painful memories and drive him to confront the man in anger. And she did not wish for either. Nothing should spoil their wedding.

"Are you sure?"

"I am. Let us forget about it. I am fine, and that is all that matters."

The bell over the door chimed as a new patron came in, preventing Maurice from replying, and so the topic was closed.

Chapter 31
Alexandra

Chandeniers-sur-Vienne

Present day

A shower of meteorites could have rained over Chandeniers then and I would have been none the wiser. I was elsewhere. Somewhere we were alone, and tomorrow did not exist. Only Éric's body against mine mattered, his hands framing my face, his thumbs stroking my cheeks, his forehead against mine. My heart pounded against my ribs as my stomach turned cartwheels. My thoughts spun erratically, and contradictory feelings warred within me: joy, exaltation, the irrepressible urge to dance and skip yelling, "He loves me!" at the top of my voice. And among these soaring emotions—guilt and the insufferable little voice that kept repeating that I was engaged to another man.

Just a little longer, I begged. *Let me enjoy his words just a little longer.*

Éric pulled his forehead away from mine, but his hands did not leave my face. On the contrary, they gripped it tighter, tilting it gently toward him. And without further ado, he kissed me.

It was a magical kiss, sweet yet passionate, shy and daring, tender and desperate, intense and romantic...and totally, utterly overwhelming. A kiss that said everything. A kiss that gave and did not ask for anything in return—which was precisely why it received as much as it granted.

It was a kiss I would not get out of unscathed. I knew it, I could feel it deep down.

And I confess that when his lips touched mine, I forgot everything. Who and where I was. The crowd, the dancers, Marine. Yesterday, today and tomorrow. The little voice inside my head that just wouldn't shut up.

And before I could stop them, my hands traveled up toward his face, slid into his hair, and I surrendered to him, to us, to the spell wrapping around us.

I don't know how long we stayed like that, kissing in the middle of the crowd like we were in one of the rom-coms I'd watched a hundred times. Time stood still.

But everything good comes to an end, even the sweetest kiss in the history of kisses. His lips broke away from mine, and time reclaimed its rights. Sound resumed, and I heard music. I kept my eyes closed. As long as I didn't open them, I didn't need to face reality.

A lump rose in my throat. I suddenly wanted to cry, but I didn't know whether it was out of sadness or joy.

Sadness, probably.

A sigh escaped me before I could stop it.

"You're going to leave again, aren't you?" Éric whispered, and his voice broke my heart. "You're going to run from me again."

Our faces were so close together I could feel his breath on my lips.

"I'm not running," I lied.

Of course I was. I had been running from him for days, running from his presence, from my feelings, for fear I wouldn't be able to resist.

Éric chuckled.

"Princess, ever since Angers, the way you've been acting is textbook running. I'm pretty sure if we looked it up in the dictionary, we'd find a picture of you."

Eyes still firmly shut, I smiled sadly.

The reference to our conversation in Angers was unmistakable. Back when it had all started. Or maybe I was fooling myself, and I had fallen for him far earlier.

Perhaps on the very first day, from the moment I had seen the glint of sadness in his eyes and I had wondered what lurked behind his arrogance and belligerence.

"You're right," I admitted.

"Why? Don't tell me you have no feelings for me. Your every move says otherwise. This kiss says otherwise."

"I know."

"So what is it? Talk to me, Alex. What are you afraid of?"

"I'm not afraid. I—"

I'm engaged.

Two little words. Why was it so hard to speak them? Why did it feel like I was tearing my own heart out?

I couldn't carry on like this. I couldn't keep torturing myself—and him. I had to tell him the truth. And pull away before it was too late. Before I was no longer able to.

I took a deep breath.

"Éric—" I began, eyes still closed, then broke off.

The lump in my throat made breathing difficult, and tears were rising in my eyes. Inside my chest, my heart seemed to shatter into a million pieces. It was the right decision. It was the only decision.

I opened my eyes, looked up to him. The intensity of the emotions warring in his eyes was like a slap in the face. My internal organs curled up, screaming I couldn't do that to him.

To us.

I ignored them.

There was no 'us.' Us was me and Spencer. The sooner I reminded myself of that the better, for both our sakes.

"Is there a place we can talk? There are...too many people here."

He scrutinized me, as though to drag an answer from within, reassure himself as to what I was about to tell him. I don't know what he found there, apart from the tears I valiantly tried to swallow, but he closed his eyes, sighed and nodded.

"Come on. I know somewhere we won't be disturbed."

We'd made it less than three steps when the music stopped and Bruno hopped on the stage with a microphone. Not really listening, Éric continued to elbow his way out of the crowd, my hand in his.

"Good evening everyone, and thank you for coming," Bruno began. "First of all, I have to tell you that your costumes are all amazing. Marine and I wanted to thank you for being such good sports. Before I step aside, I would like to say a few words. Don't worry, I know you just want to dance and have fun, and you're impatient for the fireworks. I'll be short. There's something important I'd like to tell you. Actually, there's someone I'd like to tell it to first—Éric Lagnel. Éric, can you come up here?"

Bruno's words stopped us short. Éric turned to the stage, then back to me.

"Go," I prompted, guessing the question in his gaze. "I'll stay right here."

"Are you sure? Bruno can wait."

"No, he can't. I promise I won't run away."

He stared at me a little longer, as if to make sure I was not lying and would wait, then nodded and released my hand.

"Okay. I'll be back as soon as I can."

"I won't move."

He strode through the crowd of dancers, all eyes on him. He jumped onto the stage once again and came to stand beside Bruno. Two people brought forth a sort of pedestal draped with a sheet.

I stepped a little closer to see better, my distress momentarily forgotten in favor of my curiosity.

"Éric, thank you for being here tonight. I know you hate being the center of attention, so I'll keep it brief." He moved closer to the pedestal, pulling Éric with him. "As you all know, this week we will be celebrating the thousandth anniversary of Chandeniers. Precisely one millennium ago, a young knight received a gift of a few acres of forest and built a hunting lodge there. We know this because of the research of passionate historians, who sifted through the past of our town and castle. Tonight, we honor not only our beautiful town, but two of its most fervent and devoted defenders." He turned to Éric. "Your parents, Laura and Marc Lagnel."

Surprise stole across Éric's face, and he frowned.

I stepped forward, curiosity mingled with anticipation rising within me.

"You know I always admired them, even though I never knew your mother personally," Bruno went on. "But I always wished to officially acknowledge their devotion toward the town and castle, the love they felt for Chandeniers and its history. Shortly after being elected as mayor, I had this commissioned."

Bruno pulled back the sheet, unveiling an exquisite bronze model of the Ferté-Chandeniers castle. A single bronze rose in bloom lay atop. I was too far away to distinguish the details of the sculpture, but I was very aware of Éric's emotion, even though he tried his hardest to conceal it.

"This rose is from the same variety as the ones your father planted for her," Bruno explained as Éric remained silent. "I present it to you today in memory of Marc and Laura. Without them, Chandeniers would not be what it is today. Know that we all loved them, and the world is sadder for their loss."

"I don't know what to say," Éric choked out.

I could tell he was struggling not to cry. I knew how much his father's death had hurt him—still did.

My heart overflowed. With gratitude for Bruno, for this gesture that I knew moved Éric from the bottom of his heart. But also with another, powerful emotion that propelled me toward Éric and made me want to jump onstage and share this moment with him, to tell him he wasn't alone, that I was here. That we were here.

"You don't need to say anything," Bruno reassured him. "I know. This is nothing compared to what we owe your parents. I would like to suggest for this sculpture to be installed in the town hall, where everyone can admire it and read about Laura and Marc Lagnel. Once the castle is restored we will move it there, with a plaque explaining who your parents were and how they are part of the castle's history." He saw the surprise in Éric's eyes. "Because I promise you, Éric, the castle *will* be restored." He looked around until he met my gaze and added, "I don't think I'm being too presumptuous when I say that everybody here tonight will fight as long as needed for it to rise from its ashes. If you agree, of course."

Still staring at the sculpture, Éric nodded wordlessly. I guessed he was afraid to speak and be overcome with emotion.

"He didn't know," Marine said.

I jumped. I'd been so focused on the stage I hadn't heard her come up.

"What you've done for him is amazing," I whispered.

"What *we've* done," she corrected. "Bruno told me you had a plan for the castle."

"I do." I summarized what I'd told Éric earlier.

"Alex, that's wonderful!"

"Nothing is for certain yet," I warned. "I can't make any promises."

"I know. But between us, we can do it. I know we can. We'll save the castle."

"I hope so," I sighed, glancing back at Éric. "At least, I'm going to do everything I can to succeed."

"Thank you, Alex. Thank you so much."

"You should wait before you thank me."

"Whether it works or not, thank you. You didn't have to do anything."

"I know. But I wanted to."

Silence fell. Éric thanked Bruno, his voice full of emotion. My throat was tight, and my heart pounded in my chest. It was as if—as if I could feel his turmoil. As if it was mine.

I cleared my throat.

"You know, it turns out I'm not really the descendant of the Saint-Armand family," I began, trying to distract myself.

"What do you mean?"

I outlined Thomas's story for her.

"I always wondered why he'd changed his name," Marine said.

"I'll have to check a few facts to confirm my theory, but my guess is that he really wanted to get rid of any connection left to Victor after his death, so his uncle legally adopted him. It might be my romantic side talking, but I can't help thinking that Thomas wanted to officially have the name D'Arcy to give to Gabrielle when he married her, as it was too late for him to take his real father's name."

Marine smiled. "You may be right, you know. From what you told me, it seems the kind of thing he would do.

"I think so too."

"All things considered, his life really reads like a novel."

"I agree. Someone should write it, one day. I'm sure it would make a wonderful book."

There was a thoughtful gleam to Marine's eye, and she turned to me in excitement.

"Do you remember my friend in Brittany I was telling you about the day you arrived?"

"Yes?"

"She's a novelist, and one of her books was a huge success not long ago. I just know she would be the perfect person to write it. Her writing has that little touch of magic that makes any story into a fairy tale."

I turned the idea around in my head. A novel, by a real writer, that would relate everything my ancestors had gone through... It would be amazing. Really amazing. And not just for me.

"Imagine the tourism it could create for the castle if there was a best-selling novel taking place here!" I clapped my hands. "I can picture it already—'The site of the tragic and wonderful tale of the last baron de Saint-Armand.' Sounds cool, right?"

Marine giggled.

"Very cool! I think I'll call her first thing tomorrow. If you're okay with that, of course."

"I'd be honored. But are you sure she will want to write it, or have the time?"

"Oh, I know Flavie, and I have no doubt she'll want to! She can't resist a love story. And she's a historian too, so there's really no question. Whether she has the time is another matter, but there's only one way to find out."

"That would be great! Thank you, Marine. You're an amazing person, you know that?"

"So are you."

A sad smile played around the corner of my lips, and I glanced down.

"I don't know. I haven't been feeling very amazing these last few days."

I glanced at Éric and Bruno, and sadness welled up inside me at the thought of the conversation we were about to have.

"Alex, what is it? You can talk to me, you know."

I sighed.

"I know, Marine. It's nothing. I just—it's the thought of leaving. This place, the castle, you."

Him.

My gaze met Éric's across the crowd and lingered there for a few heartbeats.

"I see," Marine said gently after a few seconds. "You know… There will always be a place for you here. A friend of mine rents out a small flat over her garage, completely separate. I could get you a good price, if you ever want to come back for a few weeks. Or months. You know. For the book. Or the castle. Or any other reason."

"If only it were that simple." I sighed.

Marine fell silent and we listened to Bruno. Or at least pretended to. I couldn't hear a thing. My eyes were still on Éric's, and a thousand thoughts, a thousand emotions whirled through my mind. I couldn't even hear myself think.

"You know," Marine began, "sometimes decisions are much simpler than they look."

"They are," I agreed. "But the consequences are what's difficult."

"Alex?"

"Yes?"

I turned to her.

"Do you love him?"

I looked away.

"I don't know. I—there's something there, but I don't know what."

"What's stopping you from finding out?"

Another sigh. Another silence. But Marine was shrewd.

"You already have someone, don't you? The person you've been trying to reach for days. I heard you one evening," she explained when I looked surprised.

I pursed my lips and nodded reluctantly.

"Does Éric know?"

"No."

"You should tell him. He's always valued honesty. He hates being lied to."

"I was about to when Bruno called him up."

"Oh, okay."

"I'm lost, Marine," I suddenly confessed. "I know I should pull away, move on, but—"

"It's harder than you thought it would be."

I nodded.

"Flip a coin."

"I'm not going to just flip a coin for such an important decision!"

"Do you know *The Big Bang Theory*?"

"The show? Yeah. What does it have to do with this?"

"Have you seen the episode where Sheldon goes into a game shop and doesn't know whether he wants one console or another?"

"I don't remember it."

"Amy suggests he should flip a coin to know his true feelings."

I frowned, confused.

"It's simple," Marine explained. "Whatever the result, you will either be happy or disappointed. If you're disappointed…you'll know what your decision should be."

I considered it. The logic was pretty sound.

I was about to reply when Bruno's voice called Marine onstage.

"Duty calls. Think about it. And don't forget to listen to your heart. That's what matters most."

"Thank you, Marine."

She smiled and left me to my thoughts, joining Bruno and Éric on the stage, snagging Éric by the elbow so he'd stay a little longer. She winked at me.

I grinned to myself. I might be the fairy tonight, but she had been my guardian angel ever since I had gotten here. I would miss her too.

I listened as she outlined the program for the celebration with her usual wit and liveliness, explaining how the money raised would be used to fund an association for the castle.

"Ladies, we have put together a little something just for you—the dance auction. In a few minutes, you will be able to bid for a dance with one of the men you elected to the prestigious position of "Four sexiest men in town." Sorry, gentlemen, but the ladies have spoken: Benjamin, our classy, charming policeman; Maxime, as handsome as he is handy in a kitchen; our resident castle owner and adventurer Éric; and last but not least, our very own mayor. Gentlemen, if you would join us onstage so the ladies can admire you…"

I laughed along with everyone else when Maxime and Benjamin jumped up onstage and began to strut up and down like models on a runway. They all played it perfectly, bowing and showing off their abs to seduce the ladies of the audience.

Except for Éric, whose eyes stayed glued to mine, as though he were afraid I would run again.

I grinned at him, and he smiled back.

Marine was explaining how the auction would proceed when my cell buzzed. I rummaged around in my purse and fished it out.

I froze when I saw the picture of the caller.

Spencer.

The grin slid right off my face, and my shoulders sagged. For a few moments, I stared at my fiancé's face, the man I had chosen, searching my heart, my chest for the feelings I had for him.

To no avail.

I found nothing. Nothing at all.

The phone stopped vibrating as the call went to voicemail.

I kept staring at the screen, Spencer's picture, the notification for the missed call, wondering why I hadn't picked up. Why I hadn't found the feelings I was searching for.

A few seconds later, my phone buzzed again, the notification for a voicemail flashing across the screen. I didn't listen to it.

I didn't want to.

"You're not happy with Spencer. You're bored. You need someone who can follow you in your passions, who can fuel them and not stifle them like he does."

Bea's words rang through my mind, again and again—until in a flash the pieces clicked together. I didn't need to flip a coin to know my true feelings.

I just needed to open my eyes.

Bea was right.

I hadn't wanted to face the truth. I'd been afraid. Afraid to make the decisions that would come from knowing the truth. Afraid of the consequences. Of the unknown. But I had to stop burying my head in the sand and face it—I had gone past the point of no return a long time ago. I'd been silly and naïve to believe I could go back. That I could return to my old life as if nothing had happened. That I could just set aside everything that had happened here, everything I had done and felt and understood about myself, and resume my old routine with my job and books, my drawings and TV shows and Spencer...that dull, predictable life we had been sharing together.

My eyes had been opened to who I was and what I wanted from life.

And what I didn't want.

My heart sped up as the pieces of the puzzle fell into place inside my mind.

I had no idea what my future was; I didn't know if Éric was going to be a part of it, or if we would manage to save the castle. I didn't know where my feelings for him would lead me, or if they would lead me anywhere, or last long enough for me to find out. But there was one thing I knew.

Spencer wasn't my future. And if I had to be perfectly honest, he hadn't been in quite some time, but I hadn't wanted to admit it to myself. Yet all the signs had been there. We had grown apart without even noticing it. We had fallen into a routine that had spelled out the end of our story long before he asked me to marry him. I loved him; I probably always would, but I was now aware that it was more of a brotherly love. I loved him as my best friend or my brother, and no longer as a fiancé or a lover. I didn't get the urge to suddenly kiss him so hard I forgot my own name. I didn't long for his body, for his smile, for the sound of his voice when he wasn't by my side. He wasn't at the center of my thoughts night and day.

All of that was for Éric now, and him alone.

And I wanted to find out if we had a chance. If there could be an "us."

I looked up, instinctively seeking his gaze. His smile had vanished, worry written all over his face. He must have seen my expression change. I smiled and waved my phone, jerking my head to signify I was going to step away from the crowd for a few minutes.

He nodded to show he understood. I pulled back until I was no longer on the dance floor but still close enough to admire the show. Marine was still talking, the guys were still strutting, and Éric was still looking at me.

I typed a short message.

> *I can't speak right now. I'm at a cool costume*
> *party. Would you have time for me tomorrow? I*
> *really need to talk to you.*

My finger hovered over the Send key as I hesitated. My heart pounded in my chest. Was I sure about this? Was I making a mistake? Was I throwing away the last five years of my life for something that might not even exist? For a man who might not love me?

I was going to hurt Spencer, I knew. I was also going to disappoint his parents and mine—and I loved and respected them both very much.

I was going to have to live with my decision, and accept that I had hurt others to find myself again. After this, I couldn't go back. Did I want that? The answer was simple—yes.

Yes, I did want that. I wanted to find myself again. I didn't want this life anymore. I wanted more. I wanted Éric, I wanted the castle, I wanted freedom, adventure. I wanted the exhilaration of the unknown.

And I wanted it now.

I clicked Send, putting an end to my hesitations, to the endless days of suffering and misgivings. I might not know where I was headed, but abruptly I felt—I don't know. Free, I think. Ready to let it go, to accept anything life sent my way. Afraid, terrified—but relieved and optimistic. For the first time in a long while, I was certain fortune would smile upon me. Everything would be fine.

I was happy. At last. I knew who I was. I knew what I wanted. Everything was clear now.

Tonight, after the ball ended, Éric and I would talk. I would tell him everything. I would tell him about Bea and Spencer and my decision to shed my past and turn to the future, to the castle. To me. To him.

He would understand. I knew he would.

Our eyes reached for each other again, met, clung. I smiled at him. But this time, it was a confident smile. A smile full of promises. A smile that said I shared his feelings and I was ready to admit it and prepared to risk what it took for him.

His face lit up, incandescent with happiness, as he smiled back.

The world fell back around us, and I felt light and happy. Nothing could touch me. I had found my place. My happy ever after was near at hand.

I knew it.

I could see it in his eyes.

As I moved to join the crowd, to bid and try to win a dance with the man my heart desired, I felt a presence behind me. Two hands covered my eyes, and a voice whispered into my ear:

"The fairest of them all... May I kiss you, my fair lady?"

My smile froze, and every muscle in my body tensed.

That voice... How?

And before I could react, hands grabbed my shoulders and spun me around. Spencer closed his arms around me and, under Éric's stupefied gaze, kissed me passionately.

Chapter 32
Gabrielle

Angers

February 1900

It had been exactly seven days, twenty-two hours and forty-five minutes since what Gabrielle now called "the incident" when the letter came.

Seven painful days of grappling with the fear of coming across Étienne, which crept over her every time she went out.

Seven endless days of a lingering unease that would not leave despite her best efforts.

Seven harrowing nights plagued with nightmares as she pretended she was fine in the morning, concealing the shadows around her eyes under layers of white powder.

Seven unbearable days of waiting for a reply to her last letter to Thomas, feverishly scrawled out yet carefully edited the night after the incident.

And at last, when she had finally begun to feel better, when fear had given way to rage then anger and culminated in determination, when she thought she could almost see the sun peeking through the clouds, the letter had come.

And Gabrielle had felt herself drown.

* * * *

There had been few patrons that day, discouraged by the wind and cold that had overtaken Angers for the past week. Across the city, in the streets and in the houses, the mood was as somber as the sky. Maurice sat at the counter with his accounts while Gabrielle dusted the shelves and reordered the books in silence. Ever since the...incident, heavy, foreboding silence seemed to have become a frequent guest at the bookstore.

The mailman came in with a merry ring of the bell, greeting them with his usual cheerfulness, and, as always, headed for the back of the store to hand Maurice a small stack of letters. While her father sorted through them, Gabrielle suggested he warm up before going out again, offering him a biscuit from the batch she had baked the previous night, unable to sleep. She was halfheartedly carrying a conversation with him when out of the corner of her eye, she saw her father frown and move to his study with one of the letters.

A feeling of unease twisted her stomach, but she tried to ignore it. It was probably nothing serious. It was only a letter. Bad news always came with a telegram. And she should not worry solely because they had not heard back from Thomas, Hélène or any of their friends at the castle for over a week.

"What news today?" she asked the mailman, striving to put her fears out of her mind.

"Nothing much, Mademoiselle Villeneuve," he replied, his mouth full. "Your biscuits are delicious! Would you give me the recipe for my wife?"

"Of course. But I cannot believe you have nothing to tell me. It does not sound like you!" she teased. They both knew he was the biggest gossip in town.

"Let me see...oh yes! Have you heard about the fire at the castle some sixty kilometers away from here, a few days ago? The entire castle burned down. It was the biggest fire anyone had seen in decades!"

Gabrielle's smile froze, and her blood turned to ice.

"A fire? In a castle?" she asked, swallowing the fear in her throat.

"Yes," the mailman confirmed, unaware of the effect of his words. "A patron told me last Friday. Her daughter lives close by the castle and was visiting. Apparently the fire was so devastating it took an entire day to put it out. The entire castle burned to the ground. A tragedy."

"What castle was that?" Gabrielle gasped, panic rising within her.

She tried to calm herself as blood pounded in her temples. There were dozens of castles around here. It could be another.

It had to be another.

"Let me think...it was somewhere by Azay-le-Rideau.... Something beginning with an *S*... No, a *C*..."

No.

Gabrielle was petrified.

It cannot be Chandeniers, she repeated to herself. *It simply cannot be our castle. Impossible.*

Seconds ticked by as the mailman searched his memory for the name she did not want to hear.

And then he found it. And the ground opened beneath her feet.

It turned out that Maurice's letter had been sent by Mr. Varens, the Chandeniers notary. It informed him in cold and clinical terms that due to the fire that had ravaged the entire western wing of the castle and destroyed everything it held, Mr. Varens was sorry to write there was no longer a library to sell. A sum of money would be paid to Maurice to reimburse him for the inconvenience and financial loss, as soon as the necessary formalities had been observed.

Once Gabrielle finished reading the letter, she raised anxious eyes to her father.

"Why is the notary the one to notify us? Why wasn't it Hélène or Céleste? Or Thomas? Does he even know?"

"I have no idea," her father replied, obviously as anxious and as much at a loss as she was. *More so,* Gabrielle thought. At least she had the comfort of knowing Thomas was in England and could not have been hurt. Maurice had no such assurances concerning Hélène.

Thirty minutes later, with mere minutes to spare, father and daughter boarded the next train eastward.

Toward Chandeniers.

* * * *

The journey was long, unbearably long. Gabrielle and her father spoke little, each wracked with such dread words could not encompass it.

After what seemed like an eternity, they reached the castle, and the sight broke Gabrielle's heart clean in two. She had only worried about Céleste, Hélène and the others, and had not thought to prepare herself for what awaited her. Now they were here; it was real. The soot-blackened walls and the smoke still rising from the western wing were there to prove it. As was the snow, gray and dirty, littered with rubble: scorched papers, burnt books, objects so twisted and deformed by the heat they were unrecognizable.

For an instant, Gabrielle was speechless in the face of the disaster, one hand over her chest as though to keep her heart from bursting out.

There were no words for her pain.

She moved toward a pile of rubble among which several books stood out, somehow partially unharmed. She reached out and lifted one. What remained was sodden and waterlogged. A sob wrenched free from her throat as she recognized one of the books she had read to Thomas one night in the library. It had been one of his mother's favorites, he'd told her. *Les Romans de la Table ronde*, by Chrétien de Troyes.

A piece of paper fluttered out, miraculously nearly intact.

Gabrielle's heart skipped a beat as she stared at it. It was the picture Arnaud had taken of her the day Thomas had told her he was leaving for England. The day he had kissed her for the first time.

She had seen Thomas slip it into a satchel to bring with him to England. Terror rose within her.

Did this mean Thomas had been here at the moment of the fire? Had he been hurt? Was that why they had received no news? Had they all been hurt? Or worse?

Please, anything but that, she thought, tears in her eyes.

She rose and cast around for her father, only to startle at a familiar voice in the ringing silence.

"Monsieur Maurice? Mademoiselle Gabrielle? What are you doing here?"

Gabrielle spun around. Guillaume stood a few feet away with an empty wheelbarrow. Relief washed over her, and she ran toward him, throwing her arms around his neck, still holding the picture and book.

"Guillaume! I am so glad to see you! Is—is everyone all right? What happened? Where is Thomas? Where are Hélène, Céleste, Agnès?"

"We're all fine," he replied, pulling brusquely out of her embrace, his face dark. "Apart from the shock, we were unharmed. Agnès is with her parents for now, as the castle is uninhabitable. Hélène is staying at Céleste's house."

Guillaume's aloofness surprised Gabrielle, but she attributed it to shock.

"Oh, thank God," she sighed as Maurice came up. "What happened? Where is Thomas?"

"The fire started in the electrical circuits, five days ago," Guillaume said neutrally. "Before we could do anything the entire wing was ablaze. The moat had frozen, so we were unable to halt the fire before it ravaged almost all of the castle."

"Heavens!"

Maurice was unspeakably tense at Gabrielle's side.

"Is Hélène all right?"

Guillaume nodded.

"She is. She suffered a slight burn pulling one of the puppies out of a cupboard. But she is fine now," he added as Maurice paled. "She will recover. It was only a surface burn."

"I want to see her right away," Maurice decided.

Guillaume nodded again.

"She is waiting for you. Céleste's house is the third on the rue de l'Église. It has a blue door; you can't miss it."

"Thank you, Guillaume."

He tilted his head in acknowledgment, but his face was still cold and distant.

Something was wrong.

"What about Thomas?" Gabrielle asked again. "Where is he?"

"Mr. D'Arcy is fine."

"He—he was here, then?"

"Yes, he was here when the fire started," Guillaume confirmed.

Dozens of questions flashed through Gabrielle's mind. Why hadn't he told her he was back? Why hadn't he stopped in Angers as promised? Why hadn't he been the one to inform them of the fire?

There could be any number of answers to those questions, but for now, all that mattered was that she saw Thomas and held him in her arms so she could be certain he was unharmed.

Everything else could wait.

"Where is he? Is he here with you?"

"No."

"Where, then? I need to see him."

"I think you should speak with Hélène."

Gabrielle's panic increased, overflowing, and icy sweat trickled down her back.

"Why? Where is he? What happened? Please, Guillaume! Tell me what happened! Please!" she begged, terrified. "I have to see him!"

Something flickered in Guillaume's gaze, a hesitation, a shadow of uncertainty that stole across his cold demeanor.

"So you didn't—you mean—oh, hell!"

"What? Guillaume? WHAT IS GOING ON?"

He shook his head.

"I'm taking you to Céleste."

Guillaume and Gabrielle joined Maurice in the coach still waiting by the castle gate. Guillaume climbed up beside the driver and directed him to Céleste's house. Gabrielle's entire body was taut with tension, her heart pounding, questions racing through her mind. Why would Guillaume not tell them what had happened? What was it Hélène should be the one to say? The coach had barely reached the house before she leapt out of it, running to the door with Maurice and Guillaume on her heels. As though she had felt their presence, Céleste opened just as she was about to knock. Gabrielle threw herself into her arms.

"Céleste!" she cried.

"Gabrielle! Maurice! Here you are at last! I was starting to think you hadn't received our telegram!"

"What telegram?" Gabrielle asked. "We didn't receive any!"

"You didn't get our telegram?"

"No! The only thing that came in the mail was a letter from the notary! Céleste, where is Thomas?"

The cook considered her for an instant. "Come in, get out of the cold."

Lord... What had happened here?

They had barely stepped over the threshold when Duchesse and her puppies yipped at them in welcome. Gabrielle crouched to pet them, relieved to see that they were unharmed.

"May I see Hélène?" Maurice asked at once.

"Of course! She is waiting for you! Come, follow me. Shoo!" she added for the dogs' benefit. "You can jump all over them later. Let them through."

Gabrielle wanted to insist, to ask again where Thomas was, but she did not have the heart to refuse her father the peace of mind he so sorely needed. She swallowed her questions and dread and trailed after him and Céleste, Guillaume behind her and the dogs darting around her legs. Hélène was in a small bedroom at the back of the house, lying on the bed with her ankle and both hands bandaged.

Gasping her name, Maurice rushed to her side and embraced her so tightly it seemed he would break her bones. Gabrielle saw a tear roll down his cheek.

"Hélène," he breathed, "I was so afraid. I thought I had lost you. I thought—"

He did not finish, but merely held her tighter still. Hélène returned his embrace gingerly, relief written all over her face.

"I thought you no longer wanted me. You did not come, so I thought— given the situation—"

Maurice pulled back and cupped Hélène's face, gazing into her eyes.

"What situation?" There was emotion in his voice the likes of which Gabrielle had rarely heard. "We came as soon as we heard. I was worried to death."

Gabrielle crept closer and hugged the housekeeper with one arm, putting the other around her father.

"I am so glad to see you in good health," she murmured.

"I am all right," she replied with a sweet smile. "Merely a few burns and a bad sprain."

"Are you in pain?" Maurice asked in concern, stroking her face.

Hélène shook her head, eyes bright with emotion.

"It is bearable. It could have been worse. No serious harm was done."

Gabrielle couldn't wait a second longer.

"What about Thomas? Guillaume told me he was there when the fire started?"

Guillaume stood in a corner of the room, gazing down at the floor.

"He was, but he is fine too. He was unharmed."

"Where is he?"

Deathly silence greeted her question. Céleste and Hélène exchanged embarrassed glances.

"What is it?" Gabrielle insisted. "What are you hiding from me? Why these somber faces? Where is Thomas? Tell me where he is!"

Her dread was so overwhelming her voice rose to an octave it had never reached before. Céleste reached out and folded her hands around hers.

"Gabrielle, we understand. We will always love you, no matter what."

"Why do you say that?"

Hélène spoke up.

"You are allowed to change your mind. I have to say I was not expecting it, but you are perfectly entitled to."

Gabrielle was utterly lost. Her heart struggled as though to break free from her chest, her head spun, she had trouble breathing and she wanted someone to explain, and to do it right now.

"What in the heavens do you *mean*?" she cried, panicked.

"Gabrielle," Céleste said softly, "Mr. D'Arcy told us you had changed your mind. That you had someone else in your life and the wedding had been called off."

"*What?* But I didn't—the wedding wasn't—why would he—?"

She broke off, unable to continue.

Maurice straightened and put an arm around her shoulders, as confused as she was. He shot a puzzled glance Hélène's way.

"It is what he said when he returned from England," the housekeeper explained, frowning, as perplexed as they were. "That you had changed your mind."

Hélène's words were like a bucketful of cold water. It felt as though the ground had opened beneath her feet, plunging her into a gaping, bottomless pit.

"I don't think she knows," Guillaume said behind her.

"What do you mean, she doesn't know?" Céleste frowned.

"I don't know what you mean," Gabrielle declared. "I haven't changed my mind. This has to be a misunderstanding."

"A misunderstanding?" Céleste parroted, wide-eyed.

"What in the devil has happened here?" Maurice barked.

Gabrielle felt panic wash over her. She was going insane with dread.

"Where is he?" she asked for what seemed like the thousandth time in less than an hour. "I will speak with him. I—just tell me where he is, for heaven's sake!"

Céleste and Hélène glanced at each other in embarrassment again.

"You mean you have not changed your mind?" Hélène queried. "You have not decided to marry another man?"

"No!" Gabrielle howled in desperation. "Of course not! I want no man but him. I love him! I do not want to marry anyone else! I want to marry him!"

As she spoke, she saw Hélène's and Céleste's eyes grow wider and wider and ever more horrified.

"Tell me where he is!"

Silence grew, stretched, heavy, foreboding, unbearable, silence no one dared breach. Gabrielle felt fear rise up in her. Why didn't they answer? Why did no one answer her simple question?

She felt sick, nauseous, her very soul full of dread. Her hands shook, her heart quivered and she no longer knew whether she should shriek, weep or beg for someone to put an end to her torment and tell her where Thomas was.

"I—I am sorry, Gabrielle," Hélène whispered at last. "He is in La Rochelle. His ship sails tomorrow at dawn—for New York."

Chapter 33
Alexandra

Chandeniers-sur-Vienne

Present day

"What—what are you doing here?" I stammered, pulling back.

Spencer raised his eyebrows, smiling slightly.

"It's nice to see you too, honey," he teased, and kissed me again.

"Yeah, no, me too—but I didn't expect—how?"

"I missed you and you seemed out of sorts in your last message, so I jumped into the first plane. And here I am!"

"But that was yesterday!"

"Yeah. First plane, like I said. I was really worried. Is everything okay?" His gaze searched mine.

"Yeah, yeah, everything's fine," I replied automatically.

"Well, that's a relief."

He drew me back into his arms. Still astounded, I let him and laid my forehead upon his shoulder.

He'd dropped everything. Just like that. For me. He'd never taken off time from work like this. Especially not in the middle of a case. In five years, this was the first time he did anything so crazy and spontaneous.

And it had to be now. Just when I had decided I wanted to move on from that part of my life. Of our life.

Was this a sign that I was making a mistake? That I should give us another chance?

My heart pounded in my chest, and my mind whirred. I didn't know what to think.

"I have another surprise for you," he murmured into my ear.

Lord...what was happening?

"I'm taking you to Venice for a few days."

"Venice?"

Oh, no...it had to be Venice. I had always dreamed of going there, I'd planned a romantic trip on dozens of occasions, only to have to cancel it at the last minute because of his job.

"Yep!" he confirmed cheerfully. "I negotiated a few extra vacation days for you with Elizabeth. We fly out tomorrow!"

Whaaaat?

"You called my boss to ask for an extension on my vacation?"

I didn't know whether to find that extremely intrusive or incredibly romantic.

"Yeah, and she said yes!"

It was official, I was in the Twilight Zone. I was going to wake up any minute in my room back at the inn and realize I had dreamed up the entire evening.

There was simply no other explanation.

Spencer was still smiling at me, obviously very pleased with his surprise—and I could only stare in bafflement.

"Happy?" he asked, as excited as a five-year-old on Christmas Day.

"Yeah, of course, I—I'm ecstatic."

He beamed.

"What did you want to talk about? I saw your message right before I got here."

"I—I—" I stuttered, at a complete loss.

I didn't know what to say. Two seconds earlier I'd decided on something at last, and I'd thought my decision was final, and now everything was up in the air again, every certainty overthrown.

"Is everything all right, Alex?" a harsh voice bit out from behind me.

Éric.

Oh. Hell. Éric! He'd seen—

I turned to him.

"Yes, everything's all right. Everything's fine."

"And just who are you?" he asked Spencer.

"Her fiancé," he replied in heavily accented French. "Can't you tell?"

I closed my eyes, biting down a frustrated sigh.

This wasn't how I had meant to bring up my future ex-fiancé.

"Éric," I pleaded as I opened my eyes, hoping I could still fix this.

"Her fiancé, huh." He laughed bitterly. "I guess that explains a lot."

I could hear the blame, the pain, the implied betrayal underneath the words.

"And you are?" Spencer asked in his best lawyer voice, firm and full of authority.

Éric considered him.

"No one. I'm no one." He turned to me. "Goodbye, Alex. I hope you have a nice life. Forget about the castle. We won't need you."

And he spun on his heel, the one to run away for once.

My heart had shattered a little further with every word.

"Éric!" I pulled away from Spencer to follow him. "Éric, let me explain!"

"There's nothing to explain. I understand everything now." His pace quickened, and I started to run. I could hear Spencer trailing behind me.

"Alex, what's going on?" Spencer asked.

"Éric!" I yelled.

To no avail. He didn't stop.

It was classic comedy—Éric striding away, kilt whipping at his calves, me galloping behind, my short legs pumping as I begged him to listen and Spencer bringing up the rear, frowning in puzzlement as we all switched from one language to another.

If I hadn't been at the center of it, and if it hadn't been the flimsy house of cards that was my life crumbling around me, I probably would've laughed.

Right now I felt more like crying.

"Éric—"

"Alex!"

"Éric, will you slow down? We need to talk!"

"I thought I was the one you wanted to talk with, Alex!" Spencer protested.

Fed up with chasing me, Spencer seized my arm and forced me to a stop. "You're going to tell me what's going on! What is happening? Who is this guy?"

My usually unflappable fiancé was staring at me, at a complete loss, expecting an answer he very much deserved. I closed my eyes, breathed out and opened them again.

At the end of the street, Éric shoved his helmet onto his head and straddled his bike. I watched, powerless, as he kicked the engine into gear and fled through the night, tearing away part of me with him.

I didn't know if I'd ever see him again.

I turned back to face Spencer, who was still waiting for a reply and steadily losing patience.

"Spencer, I think—I think we need to talk."

"Yeah, so do I."

"Just—just let me make a phone call first, okay?"

Spencer hesitated, then nodded.

"There's a bench by the waterwheel a little way down the river," I indicated, pointing to a street that would lead him toward the water. "Can you wait there, please? I'll join you in a couple of minutes."

"Okay."

He looked at me for a few seconds longer, then turned and walked away.

I dialed Éric's number, knowing he wouldn't be able to reply on his bike but still wanting to try. The voicemail kicked in before it even rang. I left a message asking for him to call me back, even if I knew he wouldn't. I returned to the square and found Marine. She'd done her best to cover up Éric's dramatic exit from the stage.

"Alex, what was all that about? Where's Éric?"

"He left on his motorbike, I don't know where to. He's not answering his phone."

"What happened?"

"My fiancé decided to surprise me and just showed up," I confessed. "And—Éric saw him kiss me."

Marine didn't say anything, but I could tell from the look on her face she had understood perfectly.

"*Damn*," I swore. "I have to find him and explain, Marine. He told me to forget about the castle! I refuse to forget anything, either the castle or him!"

"Don't worry! He was angry. Give him some time to cool down and then you can explain. I think you ought to address the situation with your fiancé first. Éric's not going anywhere. He just needs some time by himself to think things through."

I didn't want to leave him alone. I wanted to talk to him. I needed to explain. Needed to tell him how I felt. Needed to see in his face that I hadn't lost him for good.

Needed to see him. Right now.

But I nodded and, sighing, agreed with Marine.

"You're right. I have to speak with Spencer."

"That's the best thing you can do right now. I promise I'll let you know if Éric calls me."

"Thank you, Marine."

As she went back to helm the party Éric's departure had more or less wrecked, I turned around to join Spencer.

* * * *

I took my time. I needed to think, to find my center and calm down—enough to have a reasonable, sensible conversation with him. I owed him that much.

I halted as I reached the Vienne and watched him for a moment before I let him know I was there. He sat up straight, as he always did, but the way his shoulders were bunched tight told me he was tense. I couldn't hold back a wave of guilt.

I slowly walked up to the bench and sat beside him. For a few minutes neither of us spoke.

I could hear the music from the party in the distance, slightly muffled. I tilted my head back and examined the starry, moonless sky, trying to figure out where to start.

It was strange. I'd never had any problems talking with him before. It was one of the things I liked about him. How easy it was for us to discuss things.

When had we stopped talking to each other? Listening to each other?

"It seems like a lot happened during your stay," Spencer said at last, staring straight ahead.

"Yes," I replied.

Silence.

He turned to me.

"Who was that guy?" he asked, with his usual calm and self-control.

I didn't think I'd ever seen him lose his cool. He was unflappable in all circumstances.

Almost all circumstances.

"Éric Lagnel," I answered. "He owns the castle my ancestor lived in. I found—"

"Did something happen with him?" he interrupted.

I sighed.

"No. Well…he—we—we kissed."

"Oh."

For one long moment, Spencer stared hard at me, taking in my confession. Then he sighed.

"Okay. I can live with that. I forgive you."

"You—forgive me?"

I didn't know if I should be surprised he forgave me—God knew I probably wouldn't have been that…understanding…if our roles had been reversed—or irritated by his paternalistic tone.

"Yes, I forgive you," he went on determinedly. "I understand. I've been neglecting you, what with the case. I've been taking you for granted. I can understand that you were lonely and that you gave in to—to his charm. I wasn't there for you, I know that. And I'm sorry. So let's forget about it, and start over again. I promise I'll take better care of you. I won't neglect you again."

"Spencer—" I began.

His admission of guilt moved me, but I had to explain that it was more than that, more than just neglect or carelessness. I wanted him to see what I had—that over the years we had taken different paths without realizing it. That our relationship as a couple had been over for a long time and that the case was just the final stop.

He didn't give me the chance to.

"Alex, I love you," he soldiered on, his voice no longer so confident, his eyes still glued to mine. "I can't imagine a life without you. I don't want to lose you. I can't lose you. So please, let's forget all this, go to Venice and find each other again. I miss you, Alex. I realize it now. I miss you so much. Let me win you over again. Please. It's not too late. I can change. I can be who you want me to be. Please, Alex."

Tears welled up in my eyes, and for a second my resolve wavered. He looked so vulnerable all of a sudden. I had seen him stare down hardened criminals with steel in his eyes, but just then, his usual poker face could not hide the concern in his gaze.

My guilt tripled, and I almost gave in to his pleas. The mere idea of hurting him broke my heart.

Through a veil of tears, I saw his face, the face I knew so well, the scar at the corner of his eyebrow from a bicycle fall when he was a boy, his straight, Roman nose, his perfect smile.

He was handsome. I truly and sincerely loved him. But it was not enough.

I had changed too much to be able to go back. To be satisfied with the life he offered me.

"I love you too, Spencer," I whispered, blinking to clear the tears from my eyes. "I always will."

"But?" he prompted hesitantly.

My heart beat like a hummingbird. This was the point of no return. Once I had said it, I could no longer turn back. I was going to give up on my life to stray into uncharted territory. Without even knowing if Éric would understand and forgive me.

But this wasn't just about Éric. It was about me, about striking out on my own and for my own sake. It was about me taking my life back in hand and living for myself. I didn't deserve any less.

I took a deep breath and stepped off the cliff.

"But I don't think I'm in love with you anymore."

There. I'd said it.

At first Spencer didn't reply, his gaze searching mine as though to find confirmation of what he had just heard.

I knew the moment he realized I was serious. He shut down, face as cold as stone. There was a new glint to his eyes, flinty and hard.

"You really think that," he said at last.

I assented.

"I'm sorry," I murmured.

"This it, then. This is how it ends."

I nodded again.

Spencer let out a bark of bitter laughter.

"Talk about a surprise," he muttered, looking away.

His jaw clenched—he was angry.

Angry was better than hurt, right?

I couldn't help but feel a little stung as I realized he wasn't going to fight for me, that I wouldn't get anything more than the short plea in his favor he'd given me. He talked a good game, but he was giving up pretty fast for someone who had professed he couldn't live without me only minutes ago.

Make up your mind about what you want, girl, the little voice inside my head grunted.

It had a point. It was better this way. He would soon realize that he hadn't loved me either in a long time.

"I'm sorry," I repeated. "I didn't want to hurt you. But I can't lie to you either. I owe you the truth."

"How long have you felt this way?"

"A long time, I think. I didn't want to acknowledge it, because—because I care for you. But I believe it would be a mistake for us to get married. You deserve better than me. You deserve someone who will love you three hundred percent and—"

"Don't give me that crap about 'it's not you, it's me' and 'you deserve better'! That never helped anyone."

I looked down wordlessly. I felt my phone vibrate in my clutch purse.

Spencer must have heard it too, because there was bitterness in his voice when he spoke again.

"Is that him?"

"I don't think so. I'm pretty sure he doesn't want to speak to me right now."

"So he didn't know about me?"

I shook my head.

"Great! You didn't even tell him about me! So you're wrecking five years of our life and a wedding for someone you barely even met and who you lied to. You disappoint me, Alex."

His words hurt. A lot.

"That's not—" I protested, hating the idea he could be disappointed in me.

"Please don't insult me with excuses you don't mean."

I fell silent. He wasn't going to listen either way. It was over for me anyway. Spencer had always had what I called Darcy syndrome—once lost, his trust could never be regained.

And I had betrayed and disappointed him.

It was his right to leave me the way I had left him. Maybe it was better this way.

A clean break.

Silence reclaimed its rights. I could still hear the faint music from the ball, apparently in full swing. Marine must have managed to salvage the evening.

The river flowed with a soft gurgle, peacefully. Completely at odds with my state of mind.

After a few minutes, Spencer stood up.

"Look, I'd rather be alone right now."

"Where are you going to sleep?"

"I don't know. Probably in the car."

I dug around in my purse.

"Here are the keys to my room." I held them out to him. "You're not going to sleep in the car. Go to the inn. I'll find somewhere else."

"At his place?"

"No. Somewhere else."

I didn't know where. Maybe in my own car.

"I don't want your keys anyway," Spencer snarled. "I don't need your charity."

His words were meant to wound. I'd hurt him, hurt him badly, and he resented me.

It broke my heart, but I also knew it was for the best. Because I really did believe it—he deserved someone who would truly love him for who he was.

I hoped one day he would realize it and forgive me for the pain I had inflicted upon him.

Perhaps that day we could be friends again.

"Spencer—"

"Goodbye, Alex."
He left without another glance.

* * * *

I stayed rooted where I was, watching him walk away, walk out of my life, for many long minutes, long after he had disappeared from sight. Silent tears ran down my cheeks, a farewell to an entire part of my life.

A page had been turned, revealing a vast blankness that almost made me dizzy.

I was alone now.

I would miss Spencer, I knew. I had begun to miss him from the moment he had understood I was serious and had pulled away.

But at the same time—I felt free. Relieved. Not happy yet, no. But that would come.

One day I would be. I promised myself as much.

I sat back down and waited for my tears to dry, gazing up at the starry sky. I wondered how Gabrielle would have behaved in my place.

She would have been honest with Spencer. She would have told him the truth, the way I had. And then she would have left in search of Thomas. She would not have stayed where she was, lamenting her fate. She would have gotten to her feet and would have found him and made him listen by any means necessary.

Yes, underneath her sweet, gentle demeanor, Gabrielle was a woman with a backbone of steel, who knew what she wanted and did everything in her power to attain it. And I was her descendant.

A plan began to take form in my mind. I dried my tears. Strangely, crying had always helped me collect myself. Now I could think without being overcome with emotion.

I fished my phone out of my purse. No calls from Marine or Éric. The text had been from Bea, asking about my talk with Éric earlier. I made a note to reply later and typed out a message to Marine.

I'm going to look for him.

I didn't care if he didn't want to speak to me. I just wanted him to listen.
I pressed Send and walked to my car purposefully.
I had a stubborn man to convince.

* * * *

"Éric?" I called out, hammering on the door to the old stables. "Éric, stop sulking. We need to talk!"

Unsurprisingly, the only reply was Max's barking.

I insisted, calling out again, then circled the building and noted his bike wasn't there. He hadn't come back.

He hadn't gone to the peace and quiet of the graveyard, or so I guessed. I hadn't seen his bike by the gate as I drove by.

But Max was here. Éric would return sooner or later, if only to take care of him. I just had to wait.

I settled down gingerly at the foot of the door, careful not to damage the dress. I was determined not to move before he let me speak my piece. I waited.

And waited some more.

The night grew darker and darker and colder and colder. I regretted not taking a shawl. I curled in on myself and finally slid into an uneasy sleep.

* * * *

The sunlight tickled me awake. The sunlight—and Éric's cutting voice.

"What are you doing here?" he barked.

I jolted, instantly awake.

"Éric! There you are!" I exclaimed, staggering upright.

I didn't dare picture what a sight I must be, with my dress crumpled, my makeup probably smudged, my hair wild and my eyes still full of sleep. I tried to repair the damage by tugging on my dress and dragging a hand through my hair.

"What are you doing here?" Éric repeated without a care for my appearance.

He wrenched the door open the second I stepped away.

"I need to speak to you," I insisted, following him inside.

As soon as he saw us, Max bounded toward us, barking loudly. At least someone was happy to see me.

"Enough, Max!" Éric roared.

Surprised by his master's tone, the poor dog fell quiet at once, dropping to the floor with a sad whine.

"Max didn't do anything," I rebuked him.

"Why don't you mind your own business."

"Yes. I need to talk to you. Is that my business?"

"I don't have anything to say to you."

"Then don't say anything. Just listen to me."

"I'm not interested in anything you have to say."

God, he was so stubborn!

He'd reverted right back to the rude jerk he'd been on our first meeting. But I wasn't going to let him get away with it. I knew he was being aggressive because he was angry. I could deal with his anger.

Yes, I was clinging to whatever excuse I could find.

"Well you're going to listen anyway."

He ignored me and climbed the stairs to the mezzanine, pulling out clothes and tossing them into an army duffel.

I followed.

"What are you doing?" I asked, dread twisting my insides.

"Isn't it obvious? Packing."

"You're leaving?"

"Aren't you a regular Sherlock Holmes."

"Where are you going?"

I had a bad feeling about this. A very bad feeling. My heart began to pound in my chest as I waited for his answer.

"Africa."

I felt like the ground was opening beneath my feet and I was tumbling down, down, down, with nothing to hold on to. *This must have been what Gabrielle had felt when Thomas had told her he was leaving for England,* I thought. Lost, so full of dread she could no longer breathe. I had never felt so close to her as I did in that moment.

But she had known she would see him again. I had no such guarantee.

"How long?" I choked out.

There was a lump in my throat. All the air in the room seemed to have fled.

"I don't know." He didn't look at me. "At least a month."

"When?"

"Tonight."

Oh God.

It felt as though he had just torn out my heart and lungs and shredded them with his bare hands in front of my eyes.

But there was no way in hell I was letting him go without a fight.

"So you're just going to leave?" I attacked. "What about all your pretty words? What were those? Just smoke? Who's running now?"

At least I sparked a reaction. He stopped, a half-unfolded T-shirt in hand, and whirled around to face me. He glared daggers at me. "Don't twist this around. You're the one who lied right from the start."

"I didn't lie!"

"Oh, are we being literal now? What about him? That was a lie, right? Why'd you never tell me about him? God, I'm so stupid. I believed it. I even—"

He shook his head and turned his back on me, stuffing the T-shirt into his bag.

"His name is Spencer and yes, we were engaged. But we broke up. I broke up with him. Because you were right. The person I was with him—it wasn't me. And if you would just stop for a second and let me explain, you might understand instead of just assuming things!"

But he kept on shoving clothes haphazardly into his duffel bag.

"It doesn't matter," he snarled, still not looking at me. "It doesn't change anything. It's too late."

"Don't you understand? I love you, Éric!" I blurted out, laying myself bare before him. "I'm in love with you!"

He froze, seemed to hesitate, and for half a second I almost dared to hope. To hope he might listen, might climb down from his damn fortress of solitude, might lay aside his bag and hold me in his arms. To hope he would say he was glad to hear it and that it changed everything.

But he did no such thing. He wrenched his bag closed and shouldered it, turning around to face me.

"Please don't leave," I begged, my eyes on his.

I wanted to lay a hand on his chest and feel his heartbeat under my palm. But I didn't dare touch him for fear he'd push me away.

"Give me a chance. Give us a chance, Éric—"

"It's too late, princess. I—I can't trust you anymore."

It felt as though a blade had pierced me through. I could feel it ram right into my heart.

"It never would've worked anyway," he went on. "I'm not cut out for a life chained to someone. I need to be free. I need to travel. You should go home. Go back to your life and forget about me. It's better for the both of us."

With one final glance, he stepped around me and descended the stairs.

"Max, come here," he called.

There was a bark of reply, and I caught a few murmured words. A farewell to the dog. Then the clink of a leash and the sound of a door swinging shut.

The click startled me out of my daze.

No! I raged to myself. *No, no, no!*

I ran down the steps and after him. I found him tying Max to his kennel.

"All right, you're mad at me," I panted. "I should have told you about Spencer earlier. I hurt your feelings, and believe me, I'm sorry. But you can't just leave! It's madness! What about the castle? What about Max?"

"I called Marine. She'll take him in. He's used to it."

"And—the castle?" I hesitated.

He clipped the leash, patted Max's head and straightened. He didn't meet my eyes.

"I've decided to sell it."

And he walked toward his motorbike.

"You can't do that!"

"And who's going to stop me? You?"

"If I have to! Éric, that's your father's legacy! What he fought for all his life. You can't give up just because you're angry at me."

"It's got nothing to do with that. I just don't have the means to keep it, that's all."

"Of course it does! I gave you a way to keep it. Why wouldn't you want it anymore, unless it's about you being angry with me?"

"Because. I'm leaving. I can't keep it. That's it."

"Okay. You're leaving. I got that loud and clear, believe me. But if you do, you have to sign over power of attorney to Marine or hire a notary to represent you. Don't sell on a whim. It's too important to the people around here. If you don't want me to talk about the vineyard to my boss, fine, I'll respect your decision," I added bitterly. "But at least think about it. This isn't just about you. It's the entire town that's at stake. It's about Marine and Bruno and all the people who moved heaven and earth to raise the money to help you save it. For your father. For you. So put a lid on your pride and make the right decision."

We'd reached his bike. He put down his duffel and hesitated for a second, helmet in hand.

"Please let me try to save the castle," I begged. "I can save it. Please."

For a long moment, he was silent, eyes on the forest. His jaw clenched, and I could see the heartbreak on his face. Finally he sighed.

"I'll think about it."

And he picked up the bag and pulled on his helmet, straddled his bike and roared away.

Without a glance for me.

Without even a backward look.

Chapter 34
Gabrielle

Angers

February 1900

> *How I wish I could write, as Jane Eyre did: "Reader, I married him."*
> *How I wish I could say that I reached him in time, that when he saw me on the dock, Thomas jumped from the ship as the sailors pulled away the gangway, abandoning both luggage and future aboard to enfold me in his arms. That we explained everything and every misunderstanding was cleared. That we married and had many children.*
> *Life is no fairy tale, as I have had the misfortune to learn.*
> *I missed that ship—if only by a handful of minutes. It had already left the harbor, the town, France, sailing away with the tide toward the other end of the world when I ran onto the dock, demanding shrilly where the liner for New York was. One gruff sailor took pity upon me, guessing I was about to have a fit, and replied that it had already sailed, pointing it out on the horizon. And I collapsed on the ground in despair, unable to hold back my tears, with only one thought in mind—I had missed him. He had left.*
> *Without me.*

* * * *

As she wrote those lines, Gabrielle's throat closed, and she stifled a sob. Forsaking her pen, she rose and pressed her forehead to the icy glass of her bedroom's window, hoping it would cool the fever burning within her.

Three weeks.

Three weeks since Thomas had left. She was sick with waiting. She could scarcely sit still.

The wait was killing her. Inaction ate her alive.

She needed to see him. Needed to understand why he had left without a word, without an explanation. Needed to know what had happened for him to sail away rather than confront her.

None of the excuses she could dredge up quite managed to explain his decision—and God knew she had thought on it long and hard over the last three weeks. It had been the only thing on her mind, night and day.

She no longer slept but lay awake at night or paced her bedroom over the bookstore, listening to the minutes ticking past, to the hours counting down, the days passing by. Conflicting emotions warred within her: anger, powerlessness, impatience.

And above all—fear.

It lurked in every part of her being, in every feverish and painful heartbeat. It haunted her trembling hands. It crawled all over her until Gabrielle fancied herself nothing but a ball of dread. She was afraid it was too late, afraid that her fairy tale with Thomas had been no more than an illusion, a dream, a house of cards buckling at the first gust of wind.

Afraid she had lost him once and for all, and without even knowing why.

A tear rolled down her cheek, heavy with the weight of her grief, of the lump in her throat, of all the feelings inside her.

She wished it were tomorrow. For at dawn tomorrow, when the plains grew bright, she would go, just as Victor Hugo had written.

It seemed so far away still. An eternity of waiting.

She wanted to be there. In New York.

She wanted to have found Thomas already, to hold him in her arms and read in his eyes that his feelings for her were still true.

She wanted to hear his voice comfort her, reassure her that he had not given up on her.

Of course, she intended to let him know exactly what she thought of his cowardly flight without a word, without an explanation. She was angry at him, and she very much meant to let him know. But that would come afterward.

After she had told him that she loved him more than anything else, more than she loved herself, more than she loved life. After she had made him understand that there was no living without him, that she only wanted to see the world through his eyes and that she would do anything for him.

That he was the one her heart longed for.

That he was a part of her.

That he was she and she him, as Jane was Mr. Rochester.

That he was the one to give her life meaning. To give the world meaning.

That she missed him every second of every minute of every hour of every day she had to spend apart from him.

That she never wanted to be parted from him again for as long as she lived.

"Thomas...why did you leave? Why?" she lamented.

A knock on the door brought her back to the present. She hastily dried her tears.

"Come in," she called.

The door swung open, but Gabrielle did not move, her gaze fixed on the street below and the people scurrying to return to their warm homes.

She felt cold all of a sudden. So cold.

"Supper is almost ready," her father said.

"Thank you, but I am not hungry."

She had swallowed almost nothing over the last three weeks. Her throat was too tight.

"You should still eat. You will need all your strength for the journey; if you fall ill it will solve nothing."

Gabrielle swung around to face her father, asking him the same question she had already posed a thousand times before.

"Why did he leave like that?"

Maurice came up to her and sat on her bed, gesturing for her to join him. She complied.

"Men are sometimes a little stupid, you know," he told her once she had nestled by his side. "I am sure everything will become clear once you have spoken. He loves you, that much is obvious."

"He has a strange way of showing it," Gabrielle grumbled. Then she sighed and added, "I am angry with him. I am angry and yet I miss him, and I am afraid it will be the end of us before we ever had a chance."

"It is not the end," her father promised, putting an arm around her shoulders and drawing her close. "It will not be."

"How can you know?"

"I am your father. Fathers know everything."

Gabrielle laughed humorlessly.

"I should come with you to New York," Maurice complained. "I warned Thomas that I would not hesitate to cross the ocean if he hurt you."

"Out of the question! Hélène needs you here. I will handle this. I am a grown woman. Everything will be fine."

"I know you are a grown woman, but in my eyes you will always be my child. Promise me you will write if you need anything."

"I promise."

Maurice held her tight, and she nestled her face in the crook of his neck as she had so often done when she was a little girl. She closed her eyes.

Tomorrow, she thought, everything would change. Nothing would ever be the same. She would leave her father, her bookstore, her best friend, her life, in search of the man she loved. A page of her life was being turned. And it was not happening *at all* in the way Gabrielle had imagined.

The lump in her throat grew, and she swallowed her tears. She would not break down now. It would only make things harder.

Her gaze landed on the small suitcase she had prepared for her journey, at the foot of her bed. She had packed only essentials: a couple of changes of clothes, the copy of *Jane Eyre* Thomas had given her, the photograph of herself she had taken from the ruins of the castle, a map of New York she had bought in La Rochelle and the addresses where she hoped she could find her fiancé.

She had asked Thomas's secretary in England for them when she had traveled there the previous week. Yes, she had gone to England alone, with nothing but an address Céleste had given her. She had found Thomas's secretary and calmly explained that she was his fiancée and needed the addresses he could be reached at in New York. Fortunately, he had been most agreeable.

Everything was ready for her departure. Now she only had to wait.

"I am sorry I will miss your wedding," Gabrielle whispered. "How I wish I could be there...."

"Do not worry about it." Maurice's arms closed a little tighter around her. "Hélène and I have decided to wait for her full recovery before we marry, as well as for news from you. Who knows? Perhaps you will return to be wed alongside us once you have found Thomas."

Tears slipped free from the corner of her eyes, and Gabrielle bit down on her lip to contain her emotion.

"I will miss you, Papa."

Chapter 35
Alexandra

Paris airport

Present day

I slowly let Gabrielle's diary snap shut. For a second I just gazed at it, my fingers mechanically tracing the cracks in the leather and toying with the straps. There was a lead weight on my shoulders.

He had left.

Or rather, *they* had left. Thomas like Éric. When faced with a problem, instead of fighting for the women they loved—*or at least claimed to love,* I thought bitterly—they had both elected to flee and go lick their wounds across the world.

Cowards.

Both of them. As bad as each other.

I sighed, slowly releasing a breath I hadn't realized I had been holding as I read, my heart still pounding against my ribs.

I knew exactly how Gabrielle had felt. Powerless and disappointed. Frustrated and afraid at the idea of never seeing him again. Full of doubts and uncertainty.

How could Thomas ever have questioned the feelings she had for him? How had he not understood that Gabrielle had loved him, for better or for worse, and that she had chosen him and none else? She had given him everything, her heart, her body and her soul, her love, her friendship and her hand. Her life.

And he'd run away without a word. Without even a warning or an explanation.

If there had been no fire, how long would it have been until Gabrielle learned he had left on a whim? She didn't even know *why* precisely he had left!

It was cruel on Thomas's part to act in such a manner. Cruel and unthoughtful. Gabrielle did not deserve it.

I pulled out the picture of my ancestor and considered it. She looked so happy, so confident, so in love. As though she had just been handed the moon and stars as a gift.

Her happiness had been short-lived, that was for sure.

I pursed my lips.

What a waste. They had been so close to happiness, almost touching it, and he had ruined everything.

And now, 120 years later, my heart bled for Gabrielle. I was angry on her behalf. And I was angry at Thomas.

I sighed. In truth, I was angry at myself—and my reaction to what I perceived as Thomas's betrayal in the distant past was nothing more than a mirror of my own frustration and anger, an outlet to what I felt deep down and did not know how to process.

Because the truth was that I was responsible for the unraveling of my own life. It was my own damn fault Éric had left. And I could only blame myself for where I had ended—alone in an airport with a broken heart and no idea how to repair it. I had fucked up, and royally so—and managed to mess up the lives of other innocent bystanders by the way.

I was lucky Marine didn't hate me after all of this.

I reflexively checked my phone for the billionth time in the last two days. Nothing.

The screen remained empty, the phone was mute, and I sighed. Again.

I should have told Éric about Spencer. I should have been honest. I didn't know why I'd kept it quiet. If I hadn't, if I'd been up-front about it from the beginning, I wouldn't be here right now. I didn't know what would have happened, but things would obviously have gone differently. He wouldn't have left for Africa, not so abruptly in any case, not the way he had.

And he wouldn't hate me the way he did right now.

I had messed up, I had lost his trust, maybe forever, and that hurt. A lot.

There was a heavy weight over my heart, and I suddenly realized tears had begun to roll down my cheeks. I hurriedly wiped them away.

* * * *

Chandeniers-sur-Vienne

Two days earlier

Éric had barely been gone a minute when Marine's car appeared at the end of the alley.

I was still standing there in my crumpled fairy dress, empty-handed and staring at the place where Éric's lights had disappeared.

He couldn't be gone, I repeated to myself. Not like this. He couldn't just take off on an impulse, leaving everything behind—his cousin, his friends, the castle, Max.

I mean, who the hell just ups and abandons their dog like that? Abandoning me I could get—it was painful, but it was understandable. But Max hadn't done anything wrong!

I could hear the dog's plaintive whine, the impatient scratch of his nails on the gravel. I didn't need to see him to know that he too was staring at the road, alert, ears pricked for the slightest sound that might indicate his master was turning around. Changing his mind. Coming back. For him. For me. For us.

But the seconds ticked by, and he still didn't return.

Then his cousin appeared at the end of the lane.

I don't think I've ever been so disappointed to see someone I genuinely like.

She parked her car and got out. Wordlessly, she put her arms around me. Just like that. Like Bea would've. Still in shock, I let her. She stroked my hair, and the steady, repetitive motion seemed to draw me out and bring me back to reality.

"He's gone," I said vacantly.

"I know."

"I'm in love with him."

"I know."

Later that day, as I lay in bed turning our conversation over and over in my mind, regretting saying this instead of that, doing this rather than that, endlessly rewinding the scene and every one of our many conversations dozens of times—in short, brooding and wallowing in self-pity—Marine knocked on the door and came in with a tray laden with pastries and biscuits.

"Tea, biscuits and chocolate, that's exactly what you need when you're a little depressed," she announced. "This'll make you feel better."

She put the tray down on the floor by the end of the bed and turned to me.

"Come on. Let's enjoy the feast together."

I settled down beside her on the floor, leaning back against the bed. Marine poured us some tea and offered me a cup. For a few moments, the only sound was the crunch of the biscuits beneath our teeth.

I was the first to speak.

"I've ruined everything."

"Everybody makes mistakes."

"You must hate me."

"Why would I?"

"I've messed up everyone's lives.... Because of me, Éric is gone, he wants to sell the castle, and you have to pick up the pieces. I never should've come here."

"I don't agree. Okay, the last few days have been a bit wild, but it's nothing we can't fix. And I like having you here."

"Éric's gone," I reminded her. "You think you can fix that?"

"He was always going to leave. He just postponed his departure to take care of the castle, but he'd already arranged to go back. And it's not like he left forever."

No. Just until I'm gone too, I thought.

"He's going to sell the castle," I insisted miserably.

"Not if I have anything to say about it. And believe me, I've had plenty to say. Several times. That's not on you."

Oh.

"I didn't bust my ass, we didn't all move heaven and earth for him to just throw in the towel and sell," Marine went on. "He knows that. And I've reminded him of it."

I hoped she was right. I was having difficulty being as certain as she was.

Éric's words still rang through my mind—and he sounded as determined as he had when he'd said them out loud.

I bit into another biscuit, hoping to drown my sorrows in butter and chocolate chips.

"I also told him to stop being such a child and grow up," Marine added. "And that you were the best thing that has ever happened to him. But he's going to need a little time to reach the same conclusion as I have."

I almost choked on my biscuit.

"You told him what?"

"I told him you were the best thing that has happened to him," she repeated. "And I believe that. You push him out of his comfort zone, and you don't give in to him. He needs a woman like you in his life. Someone who can stand her ground and smooth out his cynical edge. A dreamer who can bring a touch of kindness and craziness to his life. He could use some."

"And what did he say?"

"Nothing. He changed topics."

Of course. It would have been too easy. I sighed.

"Do you think he'll forgive me?"

"He'd better."

"He didn't even give me time to explain. He just left without listening."

"Men..."

"Yeah."

Marine nibbled a square of chocolate thoughtfully.

"Can I ask you something?"

"Sure," I said from behind my cup of tea.

"Why didn't you say anything?"

I looked down. I'd been expecting it. It was a legitimate question.

"I don't know," I replied, truthfully. "Maybe part me was starting to enjoy being...just me. Not Alex, the fiancée of brilliant lawyer Spencer Ashford. Not Alex the nice girlfriend who cooks for her boyfriend's colleagues and fades into the background for fear of disturbing. I just— wanted someone to see me. Wanted Éric to see me. And—I don't know, I didn't do it on purpose. I didn't plan to fall in love with him. *Gosh,* he was so unpleasant on the first day! I had no reason to tell him about my fiancé. And afterward...I didn't want to. And then—it was too late."

"I get it now."

"I felt guilty too. I love Spencer. He's a great man and I didn't want to be unfaithful. I was lost."

"I can imagine. What made you change your mind?"

"My best friend, Bea. She said Spencer wasn't the one for me. That he had made me fade away and that Éric had woken me up."

"I don't know Spencer, but—I think I agree with your friend. I've seen you dance with Éric, and you're made for each other, anybody could tell you that."

"Maybe. But he left."

"He'll come back. Nothing is ever easy in life, but some things are worth fighting for."

"You mean I have to travel to Africa and find him?"

"No, that's not what I mean!" She laughed. "I suppose he needs to think for a while. And realize he misses you."

"Hmm."

I took another biscuit and sipped at my tea.

"You know," Marine said, "nothing ever happens by chance."

"I really need to introduce you to Bea."

"Oh yeah? Why?"

"She thinks I found Gabrielle's picture because I was destined to come and save the castle. And its owner."

"You don't seem to agree," Marine pointed out.

"I never really believed in fate, so I don't know. And I'd need to have a really inflated opinion of myself to think I can succeed where you, Marc and Éric all failed."

"Not necessarily. Sometimes it's the smallest of things that tips the scales. Someone who knows someone who knows someone else."

"I'm not so sure. I have enough trouble saving myself from my own stupidity, let alone a castle. And anyway, Éric doesn't want my help."

"I told you, I'll take care of Éric. Trust me, he's going to change his mind."

Just then, my phone rang with a message. From Éric.

"Speak of the devil," I murmured, hastily clicking on it.

I'm keeping the castle. You can tell your boss about the vineyard.

Nothing more. No declaration of love, or regret, not even a signature. Just a few curt, emotionless words.

Okay.

* * * *

I spent my last day in Chandeniers glued to my laptop, fine-tuning the business proposal I planned to submit to Elizabeth. With Bruno and Marine's help I streamlined a couple of points, adding what other perks the town could offer to my company. All three of us were determined to do everything we could for my plan to succeed.

Now that I was a little less self-centered, I noted a crowd of details that led me to believe that there was something between Marine and Bruno: the glances they exchanged, Bruno's attentiveness, the way his manner changed, almost imperceptibly, when she entered the room. Marine's dreamy little smile whenever she looked at him without his notice. My suspicions seemed to prove true, and I was delighted for Marine. Bruno was a good, considerate person. He would know how to build back her trust in men and love.

It was a blow having to go back to California without being able to see their story unfold…but I couldn't stay any longer. I had a castle to save. I was going to prove to Éric he could trust me.

* * * *

Paris airport

The next day

I reflexively checked my phone again. Nothing.

My gaze lingered on the door to the boarding gate and the people streaming through. Every glimpse of black hair or a muscular build made my heart beat a little faster.

But it was never him.

Of course it wasn't. He was in Africa.

And this wasn't a romance novel. He wasn't going to run through the airport yelling for me not to board the plane and begging me to marry him.

Those things never happen in real life. Especially not to me.

A chirp from my phone made me snap to attention. An email. From Flavie Kermarrec!

Marine had informed me that her friend was interested by Gabrielle's story and that she'd given her my email so she could reach out to me.

> *Dearest Ms. Dawson,*
>
> *Let me introduce myself. I am Flavie Kermarrec and I'm a novelist. I think Marine Clément has already mentioned me. She relayed the story of your ancestor to me and told me about how you wanted to make it into a novel. I have to admit I'm very interested. It's a fascinating tale and if you'll let me, I would love to be the one to write it.*
>
> *I'm enclosing a digital copy of my most recent novel so you can get an idea of my style and whether it suits your expectations. I can also mail you a paper copy if you would prefer that.*
>
> *Please don't hesitate to reach out if you have any questions.*

A series of email addresses and phone numbers followed.

I glanced at my watch. I still had some time before boarding, so I decided to call her right away.

She picked up on the first ring.

"Hello?"

"Mrs. Flavie Kermarrec?"

"Speaking."

"Hi, this is Alexandra Dawson."

"Oh, hello! I wasn't expecting you to call so soon. I only emailed you a couple of minutes ago!"

"Well, I had a little time on my hands so I took the opportunity.... I hope I'm not interrupting?"

"Not at all! The chapter I'm working on is proving stubborn, so I'm ready for any excuse to procrastinate. I'm very happy to speak to you, Mrs. Dawson. I haven't been able to think of anything but your ancestor's story ever since Marine told me about it. It was all I could do not to write to you straightaway on Sunday. But I didn't want to overwhelm you, so I managed to restrain myself. For two entire days, as you just saw!"

Her enthusiasm made me smile.

"You could have written on Sunday, you know," I informed her.

"Ha! My father and husband keep telling me I'm too impatient. That all things come to those who wait. So just this once I tried to follow their advice."

"Well, I don't know the meaning of the word 'patience,' so I wouldn't have blamed you."

"Oh, let me hug you!" Flavie laughed. "On a more serious note, though, I want to say again how honored I would be to write this story. I suppose you didn't have the time to check out my novel yet?"

"Not yet, no, but I was planning to during my flight."

"Oh, are you returning to America already?"

"Unfortunately yes, but I had to go sooner or later."

"True. It's not too hard? Going back home after...all that?"

I wondered whether "all that" meant the castle...or something else. Like the castle owner, or the fact that meeting him had turned my life upside down. Had Marine told her more than just Gabrielle's story?

"To be perfectly honest...it's *very* hard," I was surprised to hear myself admit.

"I know the feeling. You go somewhere thinking you're just leaving for a few days' holiday and your entire life is changed, and you're left wondering how to fit back into your daily routine."

"That's...more or less exactly it."

"It happened to me when I met my husband and my in-laws. In a few days I fell in love with him, with them all, and I didn't want to come home again…but never mind me, you didn't call to learn the details of my meeting with Romaric. Tell me, do you have any questions?"

"Well…not yet really, I was hoping we could just chat a bit."

"All right, Mrs. Dawson—"

"Please, call me Alex!"

"Okay. So, Alex, why don't you tell me more about Gabrielle and Thomas? Marine didn't go into details, and I've been dying of curiosity for two days now…."

I smiled. "It would be my pleasure."

We talked for a long while. So long, in fact, that it was the boarding call that made me hang up. I think I can safely say that I developed a full-on friendship crush on Flavie during the hour we spent on the phone. She was funny, kind, spirited and romantic. The way she spoke, the way she looked at things, her unending optimism were like a breath of fresh air.

I revealed everything I knew about my ancestors in the utmost details. Once my tale was done, I asked Flavie whether it inspired her. Her answer was unequivocal.

"You can't imagine what it's like inside my head right now! The entire story is unfolding, into a full romance. A castle blanketed by snow, a mysterious scarred castle lord with a tragic past, and the woman with a luminous smile who will bring him out of the darkness and into the light…a wonderful love story—just the way I adore them!"

We then discussed the ending, since I didn't have any clue as to what had happened. Gabrielle's last diary entry was dated on the eve of her departure for New York.

I hypothesized that there might be a letter from Gabrielle to her father that I could have missed in the bookstore in Angers. But unfortunately, I no longer had the time to call Mr. Bourgeois before boarding. Flavie, however, was as eager as I was to solve the mystery and offered to look into it herself. Apparently she was also a part-time historian.

The final boarding call for my flight rang out then. I assured Flavie I would scan the diary for her and send her Mr. Bourgeois's contact details, and I thanked her before hanging up.

When the plane took off, I was so immersed in the pages of Flavie's book that I almost failed to notice my heart breaking clean in half.

Éric hadn't reached out to me. In any way.

I had held out hope until the last minute. But now I had to face the truth. Our story ended here.

Chapter 36
Gabrielle

New York

March 1900

The sun was rising behind the *Empress of New York*'s stern when land came into sight. Despite the freezing cold, despite the strain from the ten endless days at sea during which she had been violently ill, Gabrielle had been determined to be on deck for their arrival.

She wanted to be among the first ashore.

Gripping her suitcase's leather handle, staring resolutely ahead, Gabrielle watched the city melt out of the darkness and grow larger as the ship drew closer.

And despite the lump that had settled in her stomach and stayed there ever since she had learned of Thomas's departure, she couldn't help but admire the landscape as it revealed itself to her: the towering Statue of Liberty at the forefront, greeting travelers and immigrants, the Brooklyn Bridge behind spanning the Hudson River with its brown brick pillars, and at the very back, the skyscrapers of Manhattan, stretching so impossibly high they seemed to reach for the clouds.

It was both similar and different to what she'd expected—identical to the pictures she'd seen in newspapers, but far beyond what she had imagined from Thomas's descriptions.

The thought of the one she had come so far to find made dread rise in her stomach.

Would she manage to find him? Would she be able to convince him that she loved him more than anything else, that he was her past, her present and her future?

She dearly hoped so. She did not know what she would do if he refused to believe her.

No, Gabrielle, she chided herself. *You didn't cross the Atlantic to fall prey to bleak spirits now.*

She raised her chin.

She would find Thomas and make him see sense.

Failure was not an option.

She ran through her plan in her mind again. Her suitcase held a notebook into which she had jotted down three addresses: the building where Thomas's company was to set up its office, the address he would be staying at until he found lodgings of his own, and a young women's guesthouse she could board at.

During her time on the ship, between two bouts of sickness, Gabrielle had located all three addresses on her map of the island of Manhattan, and had traced her path there from the harbor for hours. She knew the names of each of the streets she should take by heart, the crossings she should turn at, the monuments and buildings she would have to use as landmarks.

As soon as she was on dry land, she would set out for the office first. It would only be early afternoon by then, and Thomas had already been in New York for a month. She was fairly certain he would already have started working. If she struck out, she would go to his lodgings. And she would wait there. As long as she had to.

One thing was for certain—she would not leave until she had found him.

* * * *

The ship docked at Ellis Island shortly after. Hundreds of passengers crowded together and jostled each other, eager to leave what some had termed a "floating coffin" and feel the ground under their feet. As she stood in line for the checkpoint, Gabrielle caught sight of Olivia, with whom she had shared a cramped cabin between two decks. The other woman waved exuberantly, and Gabrielle mirrored her more timidly. Heedless of the other passengers, Olivia crossed the room to join her.

"Here we are, Gabrielle! New York! A new life!"

"Here we are."

Gabrielle did not know yet whether it would be a new life for her. Her fate was in Thomas's hands.

"Oh, before I forget, here's my address," Olivia clucked, shoving a sheet of paper at her. "If ever you need something."

"Thank you, Olivia."

The queue moved forward, and Olivia scurried back to her place with a parting "I hope we'll see each other again." Soon enough Gabrielle stepped up in front of the customs officer.

"Papers, please," he drawled authoritatively, his accent so pronounced she had to guess rather than understand what he asked.

Intimidated, she wordlessly proffered all the documents she had—the very same Thomas had had drawn up for her in January, and that she had recovered from his secretary in England.

"What brings you to New York?"

This time she had no choice but to speak.

"I am reuniting with someone."

"Family?"

"My fiancé."

"Are you carrying anything dangerous?"

"Just clothing."

"Any animals?"

"No."

He finished his interrogation, checked her documentation, then smartly stamped it and handed it back to her, calling out:

"Next!"

Two hours, several dozen checkpoints and a ferry across the Hudson later, Gabrielle stepped on the island of Manhattan and set off resolutely, suitcase in one hand and map in the other.

It was time to reclaim her fiancé.

* * * *

Her first attempt met with little success.

Preferring to be thrifty with the money she had changed on Ellis Island, Gabrielle had not dared hail a cab and decided instead to walk there. But though her map steered her with little difficulty toward Thomas's office, she had not realized how large the city was and how long it would take her to reach her destination.

By the time she arrived, she was chilled to the bone, her feet ached and her suitcase seemed to weigh a ton. But she soldiered on, propelled by a resolve that suffered no hesitation. She pushed the heavy door open and cast about for someone to help her. A kindly man pointed her to the floor she was looking for and even offered to escort her there.

Gabrielle thanked him but declined, moving toward the stairs.

At the designated floor, she found two men in suits and gathered her courage to interrupt.

"Excuse me," she queried in her best English. "Where can I find Thomas D'Arcy?"

"And you are?"

"Looking for him."

Her reply seemed to amuse them, as they both smiled at her.

"He is not here," the first answered. He was tall, blond and brown eyed. "He had business elsewhere today. I think he planned to meet a partner and scope out some workshops."

"Do you know when he will be back?"

"As far as I know, he did not intend to return here today," the other man said.

Disappointment washed over her, but she swallowed it down. She had received two valuable pieces of information: Thomas was alive and in good health, and he worked here. She could return the next day if necessary. And the day after that. Every day until she saw him, spoke to him. Until she understood.

"Would you like to leave a message?" the first man suggested.

"Yes, please." Then she changed her mind. "No, don't tell him; I would rather…surprise him."

Or avoid giving him a chance to flee again before they could talk things through.

"Are you certain?"

Reflexively, Gabrielle fiddled with the ring she still wore on her finger. Certain?

In that moment, Gabrielle was many things: lost, overwhelmed, intimidated by this immense city she did not know, enthralled by it yet afraid. Exhausted by her journey, depressed, anxious at the thought that Thomas might have decided to forget her. Alone and torn between contrasting emotions: pain, loss, uncertainty, anger.

Yes, Gabrielle was many things—but certain was not one of them. Not in the slightest.

She did know one thing, however. She could not live without Thomas. She did not *want* to live without him.

So she put on her bravest face.

"Yes, I'm certain."

* * * *

After this first partial failure, Gabrielle proceeded to the second address Thomas's secretary had provided her with. Upon reaching it, however, she hesitated and gazed at it in bafflement. It was a large house, almost a manor, on a broad avenue a few streets west of Central Park. It could have fit two or three times the apartment and bookstore she shared with her father with room to spare. Four stories high, it boasted a red brick façade and a porch framed by two bay windows. It looked...opulent and bourgeois in a way that resembled Thomas very little, and was far from the bachelor pad she had expected. She double-checked her notebook for the address.

It was the correct street and number.

It was probably a temporary address. She shrugged and climbed the steps to lift the heavy lion-headed doorknocker.

A few moments later she jumped as a young maid opened.

"Yes?"

"Good afternoon. I apologize for the inconvenience, I am not certain this is the right address. I am looking for Mr. D'Arcy," Gabrielle stammered, her English suddenly unwieldy despite her many hours of study.

The maid pulled the door wide open and stepped to the side.

"Come in," she invited laconically.

At least Gabrielle understood her easily enough.

She shook the snow from her shoulders and hood, stamped her feet on the welcoming mat to wipe the clinging chunks of ice away and walked into the manor. The instant the door swung shut, she felt intimidated. The inside was as refined as the outside had been, complete with a grand staircase and golden rail, checkered black-and-gray floor and exquisite wall tapestries. Gabrielle decided to stay where she stood for fear of splattering water all over the clean interior.

"Who is it, Olivia?" a woman's voice inquired.

Well, this was a day for surprises. Who was this woman? Had Thomas already turned over a new leaf and settled with a house and family here? In only a month?

"A guest for Mr. D'Arcy," Olivia replied.

All right, Gabrielle reasoned, if Thomas were the lord and master of this house the maid would probably have said "Sir Thomas." She would not have used his full name. Unless things were different here, of course.

A very distinguished-looking woman in her thirties came up to Gabrielle, smiling.

"Come in, come in, don't stay by the door, you will catch your death! My husband and Mr. D'Arcy are out for a few visits of workshops and warehouses, but they should be back soon."

She spoke so fast it was all Gabrielle could do to follow.

Painfully aware of the water she dripped with every step, Gabrielle moved toward her.

"I am sorry to drop by unannounced," she began. "I hope this isn't an inconvenient time."

"Not at all! I am Lauren Montgomery."

"Gabrielle Villeneuve," she introduced herself, tugging off her damp glove to shake her hostess's hand.

"Heavens, you are frozen!"

"I walked a little way."

Lauren Montgomery considered her, puzzled.

"With your suitcase? In this snowstorm?"

Gabrielle grimaced and nodded.

"Take off your coat. Olivia?"

"Yes, ma'am?"

"Bring us some tea in the small living room."

"At once, ma'am."

She turned to Gabrielle.

"Come, follow me."

"Oh, no," Gabrielle protested at once. "I will leave water everywhere! I can wait here!"

"Nonsense. You will catch your death! There's a fire in the living room; you can warm yourself right up."

And she unceremoniously threaded her arm through Gabrielle's to take her to a tastefully and elegantly decorated room down the corridor. She pulled an embroidered armchair in front of the fireplace.

"Here, have a seat, I will be right back."

And she bustled away down the corridor, leaving Gabrielle with her head spinning. She cautiously approached the armchair, unwilling to sit. Her feet and back ached, and after such a long walk she really needed to be off her feet, but she did not want to damage the rich fabric with her wet dress. In the end, she compromised by perching carefully on the edge to examine the room.

The walls were hung with masterpieces, and the furniture was made of precious wood, exquisitely carved and gilded. The sculpted marble mantelpiece over the fireplace and the ornate carpet made it a magnificent room, a clever blend of distinction and good taste in clear, harmonious colors.

Not quite her style, however, and certainly not the kind of setting she could imagine Thomas in—the most glaring fault, in her eyes, being the obvious lack of books.

A shiver ran over her, and she extended her hands toward the fire. A few seconds later the door opened and Olivia came in, carrying a tray laden with a teapot, two teacups and a plate full of scones. She departed as silently as she had arrived. Lauren Montgomery then swept back in with a thick woolen shawl.

"Put this on; it will keep you warm." She offered it to Gabrielle, who wrapped it around her shoulders. Somewhere in the corner of her mind, it sparked the memory of her first moments in the castle, when Hélène had had the same gestures for her. It all seemed so far off, and she suddenly felt very alone. Shrugging the memory away, she turned to her benefactor.

"Thank you. I apologize for the inconvenience."

Lauren waved her protests away.

"No, no, do not worry about it. I will not have one of Thomas's acquaintances go cold inside my home."

She poured as she talked, and handed Gabrielle a steaming cup of tea that she accepted gratefully as Lauren lowered herself into the chair across from her. Gabrielle sipped at the scalding drink, savoring the strong aroma and the warmth slowly seeping into her bones.

"Thank you."

"Are you warm enough? I can call for more logs for the fire."

"No, no, everything is fine. Thank you for your kindness."

They nursed their tea in silence for a few moments.

"This is the first time we have met an acquaintance of Thomas's, and I for one am delighted!" Lauren declared, setting her teacup down on its saucer with a delicate *clink*. "He is so lonesome and withdrawn I had begun to fear he was all alone in this world."

"He is merely a little shy and ill at ease in company," Gabrielle retorted, perhaps a tad more defensively than she meant to.

"Oh, I know! Do not mistake me! I am very fond of him, and I am glad to see my theory proven wrong—and to meet you by the same occasion."

"Oh. Well, so am I. Is your husband Thomas's partner?"

"Indeed he is. Edward and Thomas have known each other for years. From the beginning of this endeavor, in fact." She smiled. "Your accent leads me to believe you're French?"

"Yes. In fact, I came straight off the ship. Hence the suitcase."

"You must be exhausted. The journey is not exactly peaceful."

"I am."

"Gabrielle, was it?"

"Gabrielle Villeneuve."

"Thomas should have told us about your arrival; we would have sent a car to meet you at the harbor and save you the trip."

"Thomas does not know I am here. It is…a surprise."

"A surprise? Oh, I love surprises! I am sure he will be very happy to see you."

Gabrielle couldn't hold back a sigh.

"I hope so."

"Is everything all right?" Lauren frowned. "Why would Thomas be unhappy to see you?"

"He seems to be angry with me for some reason. That is why I crossed the ocean. To tell him there must have been a misunderstanding."

Lauren's expression was puzzled.

"I am sorry. I arrive here unannounced and I speak in riddles; you must be at a loss to understand," Gabrielle apologized.

"I have to admit to being confused."

"In short, I am Thomas's fiancée," Gabrielle explained, motioning toward the ring on her finger. "But he seems to believe I wish to marry another. I came here to prove otherwise."

Lauren was speechless for a handful of seconds before her eyes lit up and she beamed.

"This sounds like a fascinating story! Please, tell me more."

* * * *

And surprising though it might be, that was exactly what Gabrielle did. She barely knew this woman, but Lauren had been so kind and generous to her after her eventful journey at sea and the long hours walking through the snowy streets of New York that Gabrielle told her everything—almost everything.

In her halting English, she described the bookstore, the library, the castle, the evenings by the fire. The feelings that had grown between them, little by little. The dance and the engagement.

Then she told her about the fire and her bafflement upon learning that Thomas had left.

"And you sailed across the ocean for him! How romantic!" There were tears in Lauren's eyes.

"I hope he will agree with you. What if he has forgotten me?"

"You know him better than I do, but I do not believe Thomas is the kind of man who forgets easily. I think he is a one-woman sort of man. And you are that woman."

"How can you be so certain?"

"He has not been himself ever since he arrived here. He is...more somber and closed off than is his custom. Now I know why. I am sure he misses you and regrets leaving so hastily. I am very good at detecting those kinds of things, you know. And you made the right decision, coming so far. Sometimes men need a little nudge."

That was when the door swung open to admit two men. Gabrielle only saw one.

Thomas.

Her heart began to race. She had to exert all of her will not to leap into his arms then and there, everything else be damned.

She had thought she knew loneliness and loss when Thomas had left for England, but that had been nothing compared to what she had just lived through.

And now that she had found him, Gabrielle's relief was a mirror to the torments she had suffered—indescribable. Suddenly there was only one thought in her mind. She never wanted to be apart from him again. Ever.

Their eyes met at once, as they had always done, and Thomas froze.

He looked tired, she noticed, and more somber than he had been even on their first meeting. Lauren had been right. She wanted to hold him and comfort him. To bring the light back into his eyes, the smile onto his lips.

But first they had to talk.

"Thomas, look who sailed from France to come and see you!" Lauren exclaimed. "You never told us you had such an irresistible fiancée!"

His eyes still on Gabrielle's, Thomas did not reply.

"Thomas," Gabrielle murmured, taking a step closer to him.

"Gabrielle..."

"Well, I think we shall give you some privacy. Come, Edward, our lovebirds have many things to talk about."

Gabrielle heard rather than saw Lauren leave the room with her husband. She took a deep breath.

"Thomas, I—"

"What are you doing here?"

The curtness of his tone, underneath the surprise, broke her heart.

This would be no easy conversation, but she would not let herself be deterred. She had not come so far only to be turned away.

"I came to have a row with you. Among other things," she retorted.

"You came here to have a row with me? Why?"

"Because that is what couples do, Thomas, and as far I know that is still what we are. When there is a problem, couples quarrel, explain things and make up again."

"You crossed the ocean for us to quarrel?"

"No, I crossed the ocean to tell you that I love you and that I do not want to live without you. But if we must have a row first, then so be it."

"I do not want to quarrel with you."

"Then let's not quarrel," Gabrielle said gently. "And please explain to me why you left so suddenly without a word, without an explanation."

"It seems obvious."

"And herein lies the problem, Thomas. It may seem obvious to you, but it is not to me. Can you imagine my shock when I learned that not only had the castle burned down, but that you had also left alone, without even a goodbye? One day we are engaged and the next you jump on a ship for America without a word!"

"I did not think you would mind, on the contrary."

Gabrielle raised her eyebrows.

"Well, Mr. D'Arcy, to my regret, I must tell you that you thought wrongly."

Thomas did not reply, and Gabrielle's patience was abruptly spent.

"Won't you tell me?" she cried, weary of this fruitless conversation. "What happened? How did you come to believe that I wished to marry another?"

"Because he told me so, Gabrielle!"

"Who? Who told you what?"

"Étienne."

WHAT?

"You spoke to Étienne?"

Thomas nodded.

"I was coming back from England," he explained. "I stopped in Angers. You were not there when I came to the bookstore, but your—*he* was there. I asked when you were expected to return, and he told me you were trying on the dress you would marry him in. And before I could add anything, he said that he knew who I was, and that I was fooling myself if I truly believed you loved me. That you had only been enticed by the castle and my money."

Gabrielle's eyes were wide.

"And you believed him?"

"Not at first, but when he kept repeating that you loved him, that the two of you had always been in love and that you had returned to him upon coming back to Angers, I...began to doubt."

Gabrielle could not believe her ears. It was a joke. It had to be a joke. He could not have believed such a thing! Not after what had happened between them!

"Because, of course," she intoned bitterly, "I am only a cheap whore, easily bribed."

"No! Of course not! Gabrielle! I would never think that of you!" he exclaimed, aghast.

"Yet that is what you are telling me, Thomas. That I bedded you for money."

"No, Gabrielle! Not at all!"

"So what is it?" she insisted. "What is it, Thomas? What made you believe such horrors even for a second?"

She wanted to push him to talk, to explain. She wanted him to tell her how he could have believed Étienne's lies and left without even attempting to talk to her.

He glanced away, but not before she caught sight of the flash of pain in his eyes, and abruptly she knew.

"Thomas—"

He was silent for a moment, then confessed: "I cannot blame you for preferring someone like him. He is young, handsome—"

Gabrielle's heart and stomach seemed to drop down into her heels.

"Dear Lord, Thomas... If only you knew—"

"Look at you, Gabrielle!" he spat, despair in his voice. "You are beautiful, kind, generous. You are the best thing that this world has created, and I—" He laughed bitterly. "Who could love a man such as I?"

"I could, Thomas! *I do!*"

It broke her heart to see the scars his childhood had left, to see that in spite of everything they had shared, Thomas still did not believe she could truly love him. That he found it easier to believe her feelings had been nothing but an illusion, rather than accept that she could be sincerely in love with him.

"Why did you not wait for my return and ask me?" she demanded again.

"I stayed, Gabrielle. I saw you."

"You saw us," she repeated uncomprehendingly.

"I did."

And suddenly she froze. The incident. Thomas had mentioned her trying on her wedding dress. This had to be it. He must have seen Étienne hold her in his arms. And after the lies he had been fed, it had been an easy jump to the wrong conclusion...

Lord...would it never stop? Would that man's actions keep ruining her life forever?

"I was outside," Thomas explained, confirming her assumptions. "I was waiting to ask you the truth. Part of me did not wish to believe it," he added resentfully. "So I decided to wait and went for a walk to clear my head. When I came back to the bookstore...you were in his arms. I saw everything."

"You did not see everything. Believe me, you did not."

"I saw enough. Two delivery men came in, and you pulled away from him, but his gaze met mine afterward. His smug, self-satisfied gaze. You were with him. So I left. I did not see the point in remaining any longer when the message had been very clear."

Gabrielle swallowed painfully, wounded to the quick, the bitter taste of anger in her mouth. She was angry with Étienne for leading Thomas astray. She very much regretted not slapping him harder that day, or cutting him more deeply with the dagger.

But she was also angry with Thomas. His lack of faith in her felt like a knife in her heart.

"Well," she said sharply, "if you had stayed a little longer you would have realized you were wrong. Étienne lied to get rid of you and engineered that whole scene to convince you that I did not love you, and you believed him because you did not trust me enough. I do not love him, Thomas, and I never will. And if you had stayed instead of fleeing, you would have seen me stand up to him to stop him from taking what I did not wish to grant. You might even have enjoyed the sight of that little creep on his knees, sobbing with pain from my well-placed kick before he slithered away as I threatened him with a dagger."

She sighed and wasn't quite able to conceal the reproach in her voice when she added, "Heavens, to think you believed the horrors he had told you about me!"

As she spoke and Thomas evidently realized the extent of his error, his face had turned white as emotions flickered across it: puzzlement, incomprehension, anger, guilt, regret. He closed his eyes, and his jaw clenched. Gabrielle could almost feel the tension rising off him.

Then he opened his eyes and stared hard at her.

"Did he hurt you?" he asked.

His voice was flat and emotionless, but Gabrielle could hear the barely contained rage underneath.

"I am fine. I did not let him do anything."

"I should have been there. I should have been there to defend you."

"You are wrong, Thomas. I do not need you to defend me. I can take care of myself just fine. I needed no one to defend me against Étienne, nor did I need anyone to help me sail across the ocean to come tell you what I think of your cowardly flight."

He opened his mouth to protest, but she did not let him speak.

"I do need you, however, to love me and make me happy. I need you to fill the gaping void in my life when you are not here. I need you to trust me. I need you to never question again the fact that I love you and that I chose you. Yes, you should have been there, but not to defend me, Thomas. To marry me, like you promised."

For a long time, he merely gazed at her, his eyes on hers. Gabrielle could almost feel the emotions struggling behind his mask. And suddenly it seemed as though his barriers were dropped. He grabbed her and enfolded her tightly into his arms.

She had missed him so much. Gabrielle clung to him with equal fervor and despair. She was still angry with him, but the feeling of loss and the relief at having found him superseded every other emotion.

"Forgive me, Gabrielle," he whispered brokenly. "Forgive me. I am nothing but a fool."

"You hurt me, Thomas," she murmured. She felt tears rise in her eyes.

"I am sorry. So sorry. I do not deserve you."

"It is not about deserving, Thomas," she said gently. "I love you, that is all."

He shook his head.

"I am poisonous, Gabrielle. I hurt all those around me. First my mother, now you…and when the castle burned down, I thought it was an omen. You should leave me and run far, far away."

She drew back and framed his face with her hands.

"No, Thomas, you cannot think that. It is not true! Should I remind you that you do not believe in omens? I do. The fire had nothing to do with you. You are not poisonous, Thomas!"

"It was because of me that my father was so brutal with my mother. I was the cause of her suffering. And I made you suffer too!"

"The baron is the only one responsible for your mother's misery. If you had not been there, he would have found another pretext. You are not poisonous, Thomas. On the contrary, I am certain that you brought your mother great joy, as you do to me."

"I love you, Gabrielle. I love you so much. My life has no meaning when you are gone."

"I love you too, Thomas. Never forget it again."

"Never," he agreed, clutching her tighter still.

They stayed in each other's arms a moment longer.

"Forgive me," he whispered again into her neck.

His warm breath on her skin made her shiver.

"I am still angry with you."

"I know. Be angry as long as you like. But please forgive me. Please."

"On one condition." She backed away and met his gaze. "I want you to promise me something."

"Anything you want."

"I want you to promise me that whenever you have a problem, no matter what it is, you will tell me about it."

"I will."

"Swear it."

"I swear I will tell you about it."

"Good. And never forget I love you."

"I promise."

"Very well. I forgive you."

Of course, the pain from his flight would take some time to fade, as would her anger. She could not simply forget the awful weeks she had lived through with a snap of her fingers. But she had not come all this way to make things more complicated. She had crossed the Atlantic to understand and to convince Thomas she loved him. To find him, because she could not picture her life without him. And now that everything had been laid bare, that he was in her arms, she was at peace at last.

They were together. That was all that mattered. It was time to turn over a new leaf and look to the future.

So she smiled and said:

"Well, Mr. D'Arcy, haven't you waited long enough? Isn't it time for you to kiss your fiancée?"

She saw relief bleed from his eyes into his smile and he leaned down, laying his forehead against hers to whisper:

"I cannot believe you crossed the ocean for me."

"I would do anything for you, Thomas. You are my entire life. I never want us to be apart again."

"Never," he confirmed.

Then he kissed her.

Their fairy tale could begin at last.

Chapter 37
Alexandra

From: Alexandra Dawson <a.dawson@lolasvineyards.com>
To: Éric Lagnel <eric.lagnel@msf.fr>
Object: Vineyard

Éric,
Great news! The vineyard project has been approved!
I will mail you the contracts shortly, I just need you to give me
an address to send them to. My boss has also appointed me
manager, so I will be on-site to supervise operations.
Since I will be your main contact, I've included my professional
contact details below.
I hope you're doing all right in Africa and saving the world one
child at a time.
Take care,
Alex

From: Éric Lagnel
To: Alexandra Dawson
Object: RE: Vineyard

Thank you.
I've given Marine power of attorney. You should deal with her
from now on.

From: Alexandra Dawson
To: Éric Lagnel
Object: RE:RE: Vineyard

Marine just informed me and I've added her to our files. I'll
deal with everything through her. Do you want me to send you
the monthly reports anyway?
Alex

From: Éric Lagnel
To: Alexandra Dawson
Object: RE:RE:RE: Vineyard

Do as you like. I'm not sure I'll have time to read them.

From: Alexandra Dawson
To: Éric Lagnel
Object: RE:RE:RE:RE: Vineyard

I'll send them. It's your castle. You can read them or not.
Take care,
Alex

From: Alexandra Dawson
To: Éric Lagnel
Object: Chandeniers Vineyard—September report
Attachment: Chandeniers_Vineyard_September_Report

Éric,
As agreed, here is the monthly report on the project's
advancement for September (enclosed). As you will see, we've
selected the companies that will be doing the building. We've
chosen the ones who offered the closest match in structure and
materials to the castle.
We're in talks with the INRA to find some vine stock dating back
to the first vineyard. As soon as we have news to share, I'll send

it along.
Take care,
Alex

From: Alexandra Dawson
To: Éric Lagnel
Object: Chandeniers Vineyard—October report
Attachment: Chandeniers_Vineyard_October_Report

Éric,
Here is the October report.
Just so you know, construction should begin at the end of the
winter. I've added the blueprints approved by Marine and my
bosses at the end of the report. I hope you're okay with them.
I've petitioned Bruno for a construction permit and I'm waiting
on his reply.
We've identified the vine stock; now we only need to prepare the
soil with our experts. Full details are in the report.
I hope you're doing well. Marine told me you came back to
Chandeniers for a flash visit. Max must have been happy to see
you.
Take care,
Alex

From: Alexandra Dawson
To: Éric Lagnel
Object: Chandeniers Vineyard—November report
Attachment: Chandeniers_Vineyard_November_Report
Chandeniers_Cocktail_Invitation

Éric,
Here is the November report.
Everything is fine, proceeding on schedule.
The next report will be sent from Chandeniers. I'm leaving to
supervise the construction, which will start in February, or
March if the weather is not on our side. I will also be managing
the preparation of the soil and the planting of the vine stock.
Enclosed is an invitation to the presentation cocktail party

*where we will officially present the vineyard to the town
officials, the press and professionals. Michael Davis, CEO of
Lola's Vineyards and Elizabeth Chadway, operations manager
and my boss, will be there. It's an important occasion for this
project, and it would be good if you could be there. It's your
land, your castle.*

See you soon, I hope,
Alex

* * * *

Chandeniers-sur-Vienne

December

He wasn't there.

I examined every face as carefully as if I were playing Where's Waldo, scrutinizing every guest, thinking I might have missed him the first fifteen times, or that he might have arrived in the meantime, but there was nothing to it.

I had to face the truth.

He hadn't come.

That stubborn son of a bitch *really* hadn't come.

At least if he had been in Africa saving the world, I could have understood. But I knew for a fact that he had returned to Chandeniers for the holidays. And despite that…he wasn't here tonight.

Disappointment washed over me, with a tinge of anger, and my throat and heart grew tight. I shook my head, ashamed at myself.

He had answered none of my emails for months, had ignored me utterly ever since he had left, and still I hoped for a gesture, a word from him, like a lovesick schoolgirl.

It was pathetic. *I* was pathetic.

When was I going to finally get a clue and stop waiting for the impossible?

I sighed again and glanced down at my champagne flute. Anyway, I repeated to myself, I hadn't organized the cocktail party for his benefit. It was for Marine and Bruno, for the town and region officials, for the restaurant owners and wine merchants and the press. To celebrate the birth of the vineyard and the rebirth of the castle.

Had I hoped that it would make him come out of the woods and give me an opportunity to see him, maybe even talk to him? Of course I had. But to be perfectly honest, part of me had always known he wouldn't come. Éric Lagnel was as stubborn as they came.

"Alex, are you listening?"

"Excuse me? Sorry, I—er, I was thinking of my speech."

I smiled apologetically and mentally shoved Éric to the back of my mind to focus on my companions. Bruno and Marine were staring as though expecting me to reveal the secret to the philosopher's stone, while my boss Elizabeth stood on my left and Michael Davis, CEO of Lola's Vineyards, on my right. They had flown straight in from California this very morning, just in time for the vineyard's opening night.

"What were you saying?" I asked.

"That you have outdone yourself," Michael repeated. "This cocktail party is wonderful."

"Absolutely," Elizabeth agreed. "Everything is perfect. Have you tasted the canapés? They are to die for!"

"Thank you," I said. "I'll let the caterer know."

"But beyond tonight's party," Elizabeth went on, "I want to thank you for the work you've done over the last months. Your investment is amazing, and I have no doubt that with you at the helm, the vineyard will be a success."

I felt myself blush. Coming from someone as demanding as my boss, it was a flattering compliment.

I had worked hard to meet the challenge she had entrusted me with, and for the first time in a long while, I was extremely proud of what I had accomplished.

No matter what Mr. Sulky had to say.

"A toast," Bruno declared, raising his glass at me. "To Alexandra, for her boundless devotion over the last few weeks to Chandeniers, its vineyards, its castle—and its citizens."

"To Alexandra!"

The glasses clinked, and I took a sip of the champagne to hide my crimson cheeks and my smile—equal parts happy and embarrassed.

"I just did my job," I replied modestly.

"You did much more than your job, Alexandra," Bruno replied. "And *everyone* is very grateful."

The glance he threw my way was jarring. Was he referencing the man currently pretending to ignore my existence? Had he said anything about me? Would I sound as pathetic as I thought I would if I asked?

"Speaking of my job," I piped up, changing topics before I could embarrass myself in front of my bosses, "I think it's time to unveil the name of the first Chandeniers vintage."

I walked up to the lectern, flashcards in hands, smiling widely.

"Good evening, everyone, and thank you for joining us tonight," I began as soon as I had the room's attention. "You have no idea how glad we are to have you. For those who don't know me yet, I'm Alexandra Dawson, and I'm here as a representative of Lola's Vineyards, an American wine company. Our CEO, Michael Davis, and our operations manager, Elizabeth Chadway, are here with us tonight."

I motioned to them. They both waved and signaled for me to continue; I cleared my throat.

"Nobody likes a long speech, so I promise to keep it short. Some of you may already know that there was a time when the castle of Ferté-Chandeniers was home to a vineyard. It was a small one, and after a mere thirty years of activity it disappeared during the Revolution. We are gathered here today to give the Chandeniers vineyard a chance to rise from its ashes and ascend to the glory it couldn't reach last time. For several months now, Bruno Lepic, mayor of the town, Marine Clément, representing Éric Lagnel, the owner of the land, and I have been working closely together on this project. And tonight, I have the immense honor of announcing that we are ready for the rebirth of the Chandeniers vineyard. We have signed with local craftsmen to build the storehouse, and I can promise that it will match the architecture of the castle and town. We have also been working with the INRA, and with their help we have identified a strain of Cabernet Sauvignon vine stock that is very close to what our research tells us was cultivated here. The wine brewed in Chandeniers in a few years will therefore be both modern and charged with history. With the history of this beautiful town."

This was it. In a few moments, I would present the result of several weeks of hard work, sleepless nights, rejected drawings and brainstorming sessions with Elizabeth. From the very first minute, the very first meeting, I had overseen and approved everything, from the color of the storehouse doors to the setup of the vineyard itself. I had also designed the graphic DNA of the vineyard and chosen the name of the vintage. I had all but selected the oak casks myself. This vineyard was my baby. I had poured all of my heart, my soul and my energy into it.

Excitement and dread warred inside me at the thought of submitting the fruit of my labors to the judgment of the outside world. My hands shook slightly as I moved over to the easel set up a few paces away with an enlarged brochure waiting to be revealed. Under the white sheet was a series of computerized images of the future vineyard, complete with rows of grapevines, cellar and shop, as well as the future label of our first bottles. I grabbed the sheet in one hand and tugged it off.

"Ladies and gentlemen, allow me to present the Chandeniers Vineyard and its first vintage: *La Rose de Chandeniers*."

The crowd began to applaud, and the guests nodded enthusiastically, smiling in approval. I could barely contain my emotion as I considered the brochure and its contents, hoping that wherever she was, Gabrielle was as happy as I was to see the castle come back to life after such a long slumber.

Comforted and energized by the audience's reaction, I returned to the lectern and gazed over the crowd, ready to continue with some information about the preparation of the soil, the planting of the grapevines and an estimate of when the first vintage would be ready, when my gaze fell upon him. I froze, every thought flying out of my head.

There he was, across the room, leaning against the door, azure eyes on me, his expression undecipherable.

My heart missed a beat.

I had been wrong.

He had come.

* * * *

It took me several seconds to gather my thoughts in something approaching order—instead of focusing on his powerful charisma or the fact that his deep tan made his eyes even bluer.

With immense effort, I managed to snatch my gaze away from his and glance down at my flashcards. Where was I again? I knew I was supposed to say something, something important, but for the life of me I could not recall what. I swapped the cards around. The letters, the words, the sentences all danced in front of my eyes meaninglessly. One single thought occupied my brain. He had come back. He was here.

And my heart beat stronger than ever for him.

Somehow, I managed to soldier through my presentation in spite of the whirl of emotion inside me. I felt his eyes on me all along. I tried my utmost to ignore him, to focus on the people in front of me, on my bosses, on the presentation—and I failed. My gaze returned to him every time, as though drawn by a magnet. And in my mind, a slightly—very—insane hope grew with each second.

Could he have come back...for me?

There was nothing, absolutely nothing in his face, as undecipherable as the Voynich manuscript, to indicate that he had forgiven me. But hope was a twisted, harmful thing, rushing into the smallest crack to exploit any weakness and strangle the voice of reason. Strictly speaking, there were dozens of reasons why he could be here tonight, none of which had anything to do with…us. But even as I repeated that to myself, I could not help but hope. And as I read my flashcards as coolly as possible, I hoped, waited with bated breath, dreamed of only one thing—for him to wade through the crowd, his eyes on mine, and there, in front of everyone, proclaim that he had been wrong to leave, that at last he understood that he loved me more than anything else and that he no longer wanted to live without me.

Of course, life—mine in particular—not being scripted by Nora Roberts nor by the late and lamented Nora Ephron, things did not happen *at all* the way my romantic mind and imagination would have it. Instead of passionately declaring his love, Éric vanished the minute I handed the microphone over to Bruno and Marine. And I, hurt, disappointed and apparently lacking anything resembling judgment, followed him.

Almost as though I enjoyed inflicting pain on myself.

* * * *

The December cold cut me the minute I stepped out, teeth already chattering, but I didn't pay it any mind. I glanced around for Éric, and an unpleasant sense of déjà-vu washed over me when I caught sight of him striding toward his motorbike.

Before I could think about it, I called out to him.

"Is this how it's going to be from now on?" I shouted. "You're just going to come and go like a thief, without even talking to me?"

He stopped, but barely even turned.

"What do you want, Alex?" he asked coldly.

I had never thought that I would come to regret the times when he called me "princess." "For you to have the basic decency to say hello!" I retorted, stalking up to him. "You're angry with me, fine, you don't want to answer my emails, okay, but you could at least be civilized in front of my boss and the entire town!"

"I have nothing to say to you."

The bitter cold in his voice was like a knife in my heart. Anger and disappointment welled up inside me again, as hot and strong as they had been the day he had left. The words were out of my mouth before I could swallow them back.

"Goddammit, Éric, what do you want from me?"

"What do I want?" he repeated, glaring daggers at me. "You're asking me what *I* want?"

He'd drifted closer as he spoke, so close that I had to crane my neck to meet his eyes.

"Yes! Because I don't know what else I can do for you to forgive me! To listen to me!"

We hadn't spoken in close to five months, and yet it seemed as though it had been only yesterday we were fighting on the threshold of the old stables. The long weeks apart had not healed the wounds nor soothed the pain—for either of us.

"Nothing, Alex! There's nothing you can do! It's too late!"

He turned his back before I could answer, but I seized his arm and forced him around to face me. His eyes flashed with anger. The tension between us was thick enough to cut.

"Why did you come back?" I attacked before he could say anything. "If it was just to make sure I knew that you still hadn't forgiven me and that you never would, because you're a stubborn son of a bitch and you don't *want* to try and understand, you could have saved yourself a trip. I got the message loud and clear the first time."

"I came back because I had things to sort out, and it had nothing to do with you. But don't worry, I'm leaving again next week, and for a long time. We won't see each other again."

A lead weight settled over me.

He laughed derisively.

"What did you think? That I came back to kneel at your feet begging for mercy, perhaps?"

Did he have to be so cruel?

I sighed wearily.

"I just—I just want you to listen to me, Éric. I want you to understand that I never meant to lie or hurt you. I—"

"Tough luck, princess!" he interrupted. "Too late. You had your chance, you blew it. Too bad!"

"Oh, go screw yourself!" I shouted, exasperated and out of arguments, unthinkingly stepping closer to him. "You and your goddamn temper can go to hell, I don't even give a damn anymore!"

"Fine!" he yelled back, moving one step closer too.

His face was suddenly so near it filled my entire vision, the heat of his body radiating all around me. And his smell...*God* his smell... I had forgotten how good he smelled. I was suddenly torn between the desire to claw his eyes out and the urge to kiss him silly.

For a fraction of a second, his gaze strayed down to my lips, and I saw his jaw clench. There was a funny feeling, like pins and needles, around my heart—or maybe my gut, I couldn't tell.

"Okay!" I managed to reply.

"I'm leaving."

"Yeah, go ahead. It's what you do best."

Still he did not move. He stayed there in front of me, staring at my lips. My breath came in short pants. Then he shook his head slightly and grunted as he spun on his heel. An incontrollable urge came over me and before I knew what I was doing, my hands had latched onto the lapels of his leather jacket to pull him down toward me—and without further ado, I kissed him.

Startled, Éric didn't react at first. But he didn't reject me. So I pushed my luck and hauled on his jacket, opening my mouth slightly to tease his lips with my tongue. A deep rumble rose from his chest, and just like that, his attitude switched from zero to a hundred. Suddenly his hands were all over me—on my face, tilting it back to deepen the kiss; in my hair, unraveling my bun completely; on my back, sliding down toward my ass, over it; behind my thighs, lifting one leg then the other.... Half a second later my legs were around his waist, my back against some kind of wall, and his mouth was eating me right up, greedily and passionately, swallowing my moans before they could escape my mouth even as his tongue searched for mine frantically, needily, desperately.

It wasn't a kiss mean to seduce or win me over. It was brutal, primal, intense. Uncompromising.

I had never felt so alive.

I no longer felt the cold, and I had completely forgotten where we were. My blood was afire, my skin burned and only one word rang through my mind—*more*.

I needed more, now.

I was losing my mind, and I did not want it to stop.

But it did, and abruptly at that. One moment Éric was huskily murmuring my name, and the next he wrenched his lips away from mine, setting me back down as his body released me.

Panting, he looked at me—and I hated what I saw in his burning, dark gaze. *Hated* it.

"Éric," I breathed, still dizzy, trying to keep him there.

To no avail.

He took a step back, then another, and another.

"Don't go," I begged. "Please don't go."

"Sorry, princess," he murmured. "This was a mistake. It won't happen again."

The sudden return to reality was like a slap in the face, and tears welled up in my eyes.

Éric spun around and jumped onto his bike, disappearing into the night, leaving me behind with my wild hair and swollen lips—and my broken heart.

Again.

* * * *

A week went by.

A week during which I tried—with dubious success—to forget what had happened between the two of us by throwing myself into my work. Which was easier said than done when everything about that work brought me back to him, and only him.

I kept thinking of the kiss—and of his hurtful words.

"This was a mistake. It won't happen again."

It hurt as much the hundredth time as it had the first.

After a few days of this, exhausted and running on empty, I had finally arrived at a decision, probably one of the most difficult in my life.

This situation couldn't last. For my own mental and emotional health, I had to give up on Éric. I knew he still had feelings for me. He wouldn't have kissed me so desperately if he hadn't. But it was equally clear that he didn't want to fix things between us. He didn't want to fight for me. To forgive me. I couldn't keep on hurting myself sighing after someone who didn't want me and had made it known unequivocally.

So I had typed a short message telling him that he was right, and that it was best for both of us if our paths didn't cross again. I would deal only with Marine from now on, as he had wanted from the start.

Goodbye, Éric, I'd concluded. *I hope you will be happy.*

I knew that this was a purely symbolic gesture that would only matter to me, but I had to do it. I needed to in order to turn over a new leaf.

I had wept for a long, long time after sending the message. I had felt empty, and I knew I would need time before the sensation vanished.

But it would, eventually. And then everything would be fine.

Or so I hoped.

Cheerful ringing from my cell phone brought me back to the present and into the small office Bruno had cleared for me on the fourth floor of the Chandeniers town hall until my own was built. I fished the phone out of my purse and smiled at the name flashing across the screen. Marine.

Alex, can you join me in the vineyard as soon as possible?

My fingers flew over the digital keyboard.

Is it urgent?

Kind of.

OK. Gotta finish something first, I'll be quick. I'll text you when I leave.

Fifteen minutes later, car keys in one hand, red woolen coat in the other, I hurried out of my office.

Despite the fine layer of snow on the road, the drive from the town center only took me a few minutes. I'd barely hummed the last bars to *Sex on Fire* by Kings of Leon before the turn to the future vineyard appeared in my headlights.

Still singing under my breath, I parked by the gate opening on the northern side of the grounds. Then I pulled on the adorable black felt cloche hat I'd found in a vintage shop and grabbed the flashlight I kept in the glove box.

The air outside was cold but not freezing. Wrapping my scarf loosely around my neck, I looked up. It was a cloudless, moonless night. A thousand stars glittered on high, like tiny diamonds hanging from the vault of heaven. Closing my eyes, I breathed in, letting the quiet wash over me. My thoughts drifted immediately toward Gabrielle, as they so often had over the last few months. It had been on a night like this that Thomas had asked for her hand, over one hundred years ago almost to the day. And their path had been riddled with obstacles, but their love had been stronger than any—or at least, Gabrielle had been daring and determined enough to send any roadblocks to hell, and give fate the nudge it needed.

A stroke of luck—backed, from what Flavie had told me, by hours and hours of research while I strove to defend my project in front of my bosses—had allowed her to find a letter from Gabrielle to her friend

Sophie. And so it had been from my ancestor's own hand that we had both learned how she had crossed the ocean in search of Thomas—and pulled an explanation from him.

I had sighed in giddy relief. Gabrielle and Thomas's reunion had been as epic as their first meeting, and after so much suffering, they deserved their happy ending.

It was uplifting. Gabrielle was an inspirational woman. And perhaps a part of me had hoped for an equally simple outcome when I had followed Éric after the cocktail party. But my own nudge of fate did not yield the result I had hoped. I had to face the facts. My story would not mirror my ancestor's—there was no happy ending in store for me.

Sighing, I shook my head to clear my thoughts and resolutely walked up to the gate.

"Marine? Are you there?" I called. "Why the hell did she ask me to meet her here?" I muttered to myself. "The inn would have been much more comfortable!"

The sight on the other side of the gate stopped me dead in my tracks, eyes wide open.

"Whoa! What…what is all this?"

There in front of me, dozens of small lanterns trailed a path of light through the snow, like so many miniature stars calling for me to follow.

It was gorgeous. Absolutely gorgeous. It felt like a scene from a romance, with the hero about to declare his love to his lady and—I stopped, heart suddenly racing. I didn't dare let my imagination grab hold of me for fear of a new disappointment.

I stepped into the path of light. After a few hundred meters, a familiar silhouette began to stand out in the lanterns' soft glow. My heartbeat quickened.

A few more steps and I thought my heart would burst when I realized where the path led to.

It was the old wall. Our wall. The place where Éric had kissed me for the first time. Where I had fallen for him, once and for all, without hope for redemption.

Too emotional for words, I kept walking, my eyes on the shadow of his face as he waited at the end of my path. Then, when I was only a few steps away, I halted.

"Éric."

He moved forward.

"Hey, princess."

I stared at him, unable to believe my eyes.

"You—didn't go back to Africa."

"I changed my mind."

There. Four words, four little words and hope bloomed again, waking a storm of butterflies inside my stomach.

I remained silent. Éric drew closer, his gaze on mine, hesitant.

"Alex, I—"

He broke off, glanced away, ran a nervous hand through his hair. Then his eyes returned to me, more intense and determined, and he steeled himself.

"You asked me something the other day, remember? You asked me what I wanted from you."

I nodded gently. "You said you didn't want anything," I reminded him. "That it was too late."

It had hurt.

He tilted his head in agreement.

"Ask me again, please. I want to—change my answer."

My stomach twisted wildly, but I obeyed.

"What do you want from me, Éric?" I whispered, my eyes glued to his.

His face grew serious, solemn.

"Everything, Alex. I want everything from you. I want your smile, your light, your humor. I want your heart. I want you, all of you."

Whoa...

"Are you...are you serious?"

"More than I have ever been before."

Without warning, tears rose to my eyes. I blinked, suddenly short of breath. Éric came quietly closer, cupped my face between his hands and stared into my eyes. In my chest, my heart began to swell and swell until it seemed nothing could hold it anymore.

"I wanted to hate you, Alex," he murmured, his voice heavy with emotion. "I really wanted to. But I couldn't. I had fallen in love with you, for all the reasons that had made me keep my distance at first: your light, your view of the world, as though through rose-tinted glasses, your heart as big as this planet. After the costume ball I fought not to feel anything, to forget about you. I left, because I didn't think I'd survive if I stayed in Chandeniers. I thought I had managed to forget you. I was so convinced of it that I returned here, to prove to myself that I had succeeded. But I didn't forget about you. Not for a minute, not for a second. You are carved into my heart and I can't tear you away. I—I don't *want* to. I want you to stay there. And I—I want to be in yours."

He broke off, his gaze searching mine for something.

"Alex...I know I'm horribly bad tempered and I've made you suffer, but I—I love you. And I hope it's not too late. Would you give me another chance?"

"You love me? Even now?"

"I don't love you 'even now,' Alex, I love you 'even more.'"

Oh my God.

A storm of emotion had overtaken my body. Once more, tears rose to my eyes.

"Does this—does this mean you forgive me?" I pressed anxiously.

He nodded.

"I do. Alex, I—"

I couldn't help myself. I flung my arms around his neck before he could finish and kissed him breathlessly.

Relief crashed over me, filled my heart, my body, each of my cells, pushing me toward him, searching his lips for the truth of what he had just voiced.

He loved me.

He had forgiven me.

He wanted me in his life.

Tears of joy streamed down my cheeks, and I clutched him tightly, determined to never let him leave me again.

I felt Éric's lips smile against mine and answer my kiss with equal passion and fervor. His arms closed around me, lifting me from the ground up against his chest as though he wanted to soak me in. Then he set me down again and framed my face with his hands. Our kiss turned tender, soft, as we rediscovered each other. His tongue caressed mine, sweet and heady, and I buried my hands gently into his hair.

It seemed to me the world held its breath. That the universe had paused around us, and watched as our two hearts beat as one once more.

I don't know how long we stayed like that, kissing, relearning each other. Finally Éric drew back and laid his forehead against mine, chuckling lightly.

"Sorry," I breathed. "Couldn't help myself."

"I'm not complaining, princess. On the contrary."

"I really thought I'd lost you, you know," I murmured.

"I was just stupid and stubborn. But that's over. I don't want to make myself hate you. It's too hard."

"I'm truly sorry about hurting you, Éric. I didn't want—"

"I know."

"Please tell me again that you forgive me. Please."

He pulled away and gently took hold of my face. Our eyes met.

"Alex, I love you. So yes, I forgive you."

"Promise me you'll never leave me again."

"I promise."

I knew it wouldn't be as simple as that. His job would take him away often. But I also knew what his promise meant. Even if he left for the other side of the world, he would always come back to me. The time for running was past, for both of us. We had needed several months to get there, but at last we were on the same page of our story.

"I love you," I told him, standing on tiptoe to kiss his lips again.

He smiled and held me tight. I nestled my head in the crook of his neck and sighed.

After so many false starts, so many lost chances, our story could begin at last.

Maybe Bea had been right. Maybe it had been no coincidence that I had been the one to find Gabrielle's picture. Maybe it had been my destiny to track hers and follow it to the threshold of happiness where I now stood.

Epilogue
Éric

Chandeniers-sur-Vienne

Two years later

I wake up alone in a cold bed.

I usually hate the feeling of empty sheets, the lack of her. I hate it when she isn't by my side.

But today I don't mind. I know it's for a good cause. Smiling, I get up to brew some coffee. Max doesn't even twitch as I walk by his basket.

As I wait for my coffee, I grab my cell and just stare at the image on my screen. It's a picture of Alex, taken surreptitiously last summer as she was drawing at sunrise. Out of all my pictures of her, this one is my favorite. Her hair is up in a messy bun held by a pencil stabbed through the twist, barely keeping the blond locks from falling all over the place but just enough to clear the nape of her neck, the graceful curve of which I cannot help but want to kiss in that sensitive place, just behind her ear. In the morning light, the sun casts a halo around her face. There is an absorbed, absent, dreamy look about her, and she has that half smile that always appears when she is drawing and becomes utterly oblivious to the outside world.

I love to watch her when she drifts off into her own universe. The expressions on her face are fascinating, unique. I could almost guess what she is sketching from looking at her. In this picture, I can tell from her pink cheeks that she's drawing me. I remember it vividly.

I asked for her hand in marriage that day, in the ruins of the castle. Even now, as I think back to that moment, I cannot hold back an ecstatic grin. I have never smiled as much as I have since she entered my life. And I would not change that for the world.

The coffee machine dings. I pour myself a cup, and as I down the bitter black brew, I unlock the screen and type out a message.

> *I know the groom's not supposed to see the bride before the wedding, but is he allowed to talk to her?*

I hit Send and wait, hoping she's already awake. Max rolls over, yawns, barks, looks for Alex. I explain to him that she's at Marine's, but that she'll be back tonight. He misses her, I know. So do I, even if we've only been apart for a few hours. The former stables we have been living in seem empty without her.

"*A single soul you lack, and all is bleak*," Alphonse de Lamartine wrote. My own universe will not stay bleak for long—I intend to fill it with a lot of mini-Alexes.

Several dots appear on the screen. She's writing back.

> *I think so. Hello, man of my dreams.*

Hello, love of my life.

We banter and swap a few words, and she asks me what I am doing. I send her a picture of my coffee cup and add "*you?*"

> *Drawing. Here.*

I smile, shaking my head. Only she would draw on the morning of her wedding. My phone chimes to signal the arrival of a new picture—a charcoal portrait of me. My heartbeat quickens. Have I mentioned that I love it when she draws me? When I see myself through her eyes, I feel... different. Happy. Richer. Because I hold the most precious treasure in the world—her heart.

I tap out a reply.

Nice.

I like it too. I think I'm gonna keep it.

The sketch or the model?

Three messages come in rapid-fire succession.

The sketch, of course.

*^^*

But the model too.

You better.

Two hours from now it'll be too late anyhow.

I can still run away.

Do you want to?

Nah. I'm fine here.

So am I.

*Gotta go, makeup girl's here. See you later? I'll
be the one in the long white gown, you won't be
able to miss me. <3*

Still smiling, I set the phone down and sip my coffee, thinking of her. She changed my life. Literally. She appeared one day out of nowhere with her dreams and romantic ideas and upended my every certainty, overthrew my plans and opened my eyes. I used to see life only as an endless succession of disillusions, disappointments and drab days. My everyday life was only darkness, poverty and sadness. I committed to Doctors Without Borders to change the world, but in the end, the world had been the one to change me. It had stolen my smile, my heart and everything that had pushed me down this path: compassion, empathy, the desire to do good. It felt as though the more I worked, the less things changed—and poverty kept gaining ground. I had ended up giving in. The world couldn't be changed. *I* couldn't change it.

And then she charged in like a tornado and disrupted everything. As incredible as it seems, this tiny, one-meter-fifty slip of a woman saved my father's castle and my mother's passion all by herself, and breathed new life into the town they had both loved so much and fought for to their dying breaths.

With her disarming charm and her romantic soul, she showed me that sometimes you only need a smile, a single word, to chase away the darkness. That sometimes, wearing rose-tinted glasses is the best way to see the world. That I could still be happy. That everything wasn't over for me yet.

Without even trying to, she had given me hope back. Hope and faith in humankind—two qualities that had made me into a good doctor in the first place and that I had lost along the way, somewhere on the border between Sudan and Chad.

I fell in love in a heartbeat. I just needed much longer to acknowledge and accept it. To open my eyes and understand that life without her has no meaning.

But now—now I know it.

I slam my empty mug into the sink, making Max jump, and go back upstairs to dress, light footed and eager.

The love of my life awaits.

* * * *

An hour later I am in my place, beneath an arbor covered in white roses at the end of an alley bracketed with chairs beribboned in white. Behind me, the grapevines in full bloom are the perfect touch to the romantic décor Marine has set out for us. In the distance, the castle rises proudly, its walls now bare of vegetation. Thanks to Alex, we have created a protection society and started consolidating it. It is still a long way from its former glory, but stone after stone, we will restore it. After all, we have our entire life ahead of us. A very long one, I hope.

Bruno leans on the lectern next to me, ready to officiate as soon as the time comes.

"Ready?" he asks.

I nod. More than ready.

"Nervous?"

"No."

On the contrary. I've never been so calm. My palms aren't clammy, I'm not tense, and if my heart pounds a little quicker than usual against my ribs, it is out of anticipation and impatience, not nervousness. I am where I should be. Where life has led me to.

With her.

The first bars of "Here Comes the Bride" ring out, and I glance up, searching for a face. Hers. When I see it, I gape at first; then my heart begins to race. She is even more beautiful than in my wildest dreams. An angel. *My* angel.

Our eyes meet and cling to each other as she glides up the aisle on her father's arm. I am mesmerized. Time seems to stand still yet fly at the same time. As they reach me, her father slips her hand into mine and says a few words to me. I should be listening, I know, but I can't. I hear nothing, see nothing. My whole world comes down to her in this moment, and her alone.

She will be my wife, for better and for worse, until death do us part. And beyond.

I squeeze the hand her father has entrusted me with tightly, and Alex beams at me.

She has the world's most radiant smile. It gives me wings.

"I love you," I mouth, my gaze on hers.

"I love you," she shapes silently back.

Beside us, Bruno begins to speak.

"Dearly beloved, we are gathered here today…"

Happiness spreads throughout every part of me, my heart swells in my chest and I am not ashamed to say that my throat is suddenly tight with emotion.

I am happy. Drunk with it. My mind is crystal clear.

After years of running and wandering, I have at last found what I was looking for.

A reason to stay.

In the end, I was wrong. There is such a thing as a happy ending, and Alex is mine.

My fairy tale.

My destiny.

About the Author

As a little girl, **Chloé Duval** dreamed of knights slaying terrifying dragons and damsels in distress. Today, she's still seeking, in her stories, to find again the sweetness and the enchantment of the fairy tales she absorbed as a child. A Frenchwoman by birth, Canadian by adoption, and Québecois in her heart, Chloé lives in Montreal with her prince charming and dozens of characters jostling around inside her head.